T0018600

ROBERT E. HOWARD'S

CONAN®

BLOOD OF THE SERPENT

S. M. STIRLING

Illustrated by Roberto De La Torre

TITAN BOOKS

CONAN: BLOOD OF THE SERPENT
Print edition ISBN: 9781803361987
E-book edition ISBN: 9781803361871

Published by Titan Books
A division of Titan Publishing Group Ltd
144 Southwark St, London SE1 0UP
www.titanbooks.com

This Titan edition: September 2023
10 9 8 7 6 5 4 3 2 1

Interior illustrations by Roberto De La Torre

S.M. Stirling asserts the moral right to be identified as the author of this work.

A CIP catalogue record for this title is available from the British Library.

Printed and bound by CPI Group (UK) Ltd,
Croydon CR0 4YY

To Janet Cathryn Stirling, 1950–2021,
dearest of all.

CONTENTS

THE HYBORIAN AGE

OF CONAN [CIRCA 10,000 BC]

OREA

PACHENIA

TURAN

ISLE OF IRON STATUES

VILAYE SEA

HYRKANIA

KHITAI

SULTANAPUR

Akit

Aghrapur

Ilbars River

MARA

KUSSAN

Zaporaska River

angara

KHAWARISM

KAMBULA

KOSALA

VENDHYA

CAN

MISTY ISLES

ISLES OF PEARL

SOUTHERN SEA

BLOOD
OF THE
SERPENT

S. M. STIRLING

PART ONE

SLAYERS IN SUKHMET

1

"Eyes of Set!" The soldier sitting across the stained tavern table snarled as the dice bounced to a stop on the rough splintery-worn planks. It wasn't just a curse—or from a Stygian point of view, a presumptuous prayer by an outland mercenary. Here in Stygia, "snake eyes" was the winning toss.

Here in Stygia's dung-encrusted back end, where all the garbage gets thrown, Conan thought. *Including us.*

"Double or nothing, Anjallo?" the Cimmerian said aloud, draining his mug.

Anjallo was a Zingaran, part of the core of Zarallo's Free Companions. Like Conan, an experienced fighting man, smaller but whipcord-strong and very quick, with a narrow olive hawk-face. An old scar drew one corner of his full mouth up in a perpetual sneer. Like many of the northern mercenaries here, he stubbornly stuck to the loose trousers, boots, baggy-sleeved linen shirt, and sleeveless leather jerkin that most ordinary men wore in the northern nations.

Conan was bare to the waist and wore only knee-length loose canvas breeks, seaman-style, and the naturally pale skin of his broad-shouldered, taut, heavily muscled torso was tanned the same nut-brown as his arms and legs and face, except where thin or puckered scars showed white. His hair fell to his shoulders, square-cut and as black as any Stygian's, tied back with a strip of black silk. The eyes under his brows were volcanic blue and his features bluntly, ruggedly carved, with close-shaven jowls.

Not quite a bear of a man. More like a lion, big and immensely strong but deadly fast. Lounging at ease but with senses ever spread for threats, he was covered with sweat, the sort normally shed in fighting or working hard in more pleasant climates.

In Sukhmet he sweated just sitting in the shade, and it didn't even dry off unless he was in the wind. It turned rancid until he sluiced himself down... whereupon he had a few blessed moments of coolness before being bathed in sweat *again*.

Conan didn't have the Zingaran sense of propriety and so didn't wear more than he had to in the sweltering heat, even if it meant he had to keep slapping at the buzzing flies and mosquitos that tried to use him as *their* tavern and beer-barrel.

Few threats presented themselves in the Claw and Fang Tavern, however. The innkeeper's stout sons kept human beggars out with even stouter truncheons of a local timber called ironwood, and for good reason. The swarming cats suppressed rats and feasted on the huge flying cockroaches and the ever-present termites, leaving their shells and wings and legs in drifts in the corners.

The felines were insolent beasts though, and anyone who so much as nudged one aside with a foot risked a deadly serious human mob out to gut them. Cats were sacred to

Stygians, and if one house-moggie died, the whole family from the grandparents down to the kitchen-maids shaved their heads in grief, mummified the dead beast, and buried it in their ancestral tomb as if it were a child.

They kept pythons, too, and sometimes cobras. Fortunately the big constrictors from the temples only came out at night, and weren't as gigantic as the ones in far-off Khemi or Luxor. *Those* could be big enough to swallow a man whole, and Stygians considered it an honor to feed the Great God Set's emissaries with their own flesh.

Though they prefer it when the god picks a foreigner, Conan thought with grim amusement. He'd had encounters with them himself, luckily without witnesses when he blasphemously refused to be devoured.

No witnesses except a dead snake.

Conan leaned his back against the rough mud-brick wall behind him and casually let a hand drop to his sword-hilt as the Zingaran glared with the quick surge of rage a bad toss could bring. The Cimmerian knew better than to relax in a dice-game, especially when he'd just won the round and was playing with men who earned their bread with sword and pike and face-to-face killing.

Sixes, the winning throw in the northlands, was *the demons* here. The soldier was wise enough not to invoke Mitra, even to swear. Stygians might hire his like for dirty jobs in dirty spots, but they didn't *like* them, a feeling that was more than mutual. Set was a demon of the more northerly kingdoms, while Mitra of the Aquilonians or Nemedians was a figure of hate and terror this far south.

"Curse you, yes," the other mercenary said finally, mastering himself and even giving a smile. "Double or nothing." Then his crooked grin grew broader. "I can't even blame the dice, since they're mine."

He pushed a few more thin, clipped coins into the center of the ale-stained planks and paused with his finger still on one.

Raised voices...

Then shouts, and the clash of steel on steel.

Conan and Anjallo pivoted smoothly, kicking their sword-scabbards to make sure the weapons wouldn't tangle their legs, positioning the hilts to be just where they needed them.

A young brown-haired man Conan vaguely recalled as a pikeman was facing off against a fellow-member of the Free Companions, a Zamoran sword-and-buckler fighter—one of four who served in the ranks of the Free Companions. They both had blades in their hands—the pikeman with a dagger in his left fist and the Zamoran with the little leather-and-steel shield, gripped by the single handle in the middle.

"My dice are as honest as the word of the Great God Bel," the Zamoran snarled, his words thickly accented.

"Bel, god of *thieves*!" the pikeman snarled. He was Brocas, a Corinthian, Conan remembered. "Zamora is a *country* of thieves. Thieves born to *whores*."

With that he attacked, spitting more insults. He was quick, but an occasional misstep showed he'd been punishing the sorghum beer hard, particularly considering the sun wasn't yet down. Using his buckler the Zamoran knocked aside a thrust, a sharp *bang* sounding under the growing brabble of voices. Men were yelling, demanding what was going on... or, increasingly, laying bets as the first rank shouldered the growing crowd away to give the fighters room.

"I'll be back," the Cimmerian said to Anjallo. He rose

and went forward, elbowing his way to the front. Having lived in Zamora himself for a memorable year—and in the capital, Shadizar the Wicked—it was Conan's considered opinion that Brocas' judgment was more-or-less fair.

It didn't do to underestimate Zamorans, though...

He eyed the fight warily. A little of the red wine was flowing already. Brocas had a cut on one cheek that sent blood running down his face and spattering as he shuffled and darted, while the Zamoran had a shallow gash on his upper left arm. This had gone past fighting out of sheer boredom—first blood might have satisfied honor, yet neither showed any sign of stopping. Both men were serious.

Their feet rutched on the packed dirt of the floor and the blades met again. Some of the spectators surged back, cursing as a backswing missed a man's nose only because he jerked away.

Conan's eyes narrowed. The Zamoran wasn't as drunk as Brocas, and he also wasn't fighting to kill, keeping a little more than optimum distance instead, which made him safer... but drew out the fight. He was pushing the Corinthian in a single direction, too.

Toward another Zamoran, Conan realized. He knew the four of them by sight, if not by name. The Zamoran spectator wasn't shouting like the others, or just enjoying himself. He was wire-taut and crouched as the Corinthian was pushed back by a series of showy stamping lunge-thrusts.

There was a glint of steel in the second Zamoran's hand. Not a knife, but a folding straight-razor; just right for shaving—which nearly all Zamoran men did—and ideal for cutting someone's tendon just above the heel, crippling them for a killing stroke. To the average spectator, it would seem as if the lesser and more drunken swordsman had stumbled and lost.

It was a standard tactic in the Maul district of Shadizar, and had been tried on the Cimmerian more than once.

Face to face is one thing, Conan thought. *Backstabbing is another.*

The first Zamoran distracted everyone with a shout and a flourish of high-low-middle thrusts. The second Zamoran, still crouched, moved his hand forward.

Now.

Conan's right hand snapped down, taking the crouched man's wrist in its grip. With his left hand he took hold of the collar of the man's openwork leather jerkin. Lifting him off his feet, he squeezed and wrenched sharply with his right. Bone cracked as muscle like steel cables writhed and twisted on the Cimmerian's bare arms.

The Zamoran who'd been advancing abruptly stopped, his motion stuttering as his eyes bulged in shock at the abrupt end of the scheme.

Brocas was in a fighter's trance of utter concentration, and he took instinctive, immediate advantage. His point flashed out, neatly bisected the Zamoran's throat and withdrew with a twist. Blood shot from the wound, and from the Zamoran's mouth and nose in froth and bubbles. He dropped like a puppet with its strings cut, and Brocas wheeled as he sensed *something* going on behind him.

He was in time to see the straight razor fly glittering out of the second Zamoran's hand, turning in the air and making men shout and dodge. One of them scooped it up from the floor, closed it and slipped it into his belt-pouch. Good steel was always worth something, and it had a pearl handle.

"*Quiet!*" Conan shouted, a bellow from deep in his massive chest.

Something like silence fell, enough that they could all hear the quick panting of Brocas, brought on by the sudden extreme effort of a fight to the death. Conan spoke into the silence.

"Fair combat is a man's own choice, if he wants to fight to the death, but striking at a comrade's back is another thing. I won't serve with a man who'd do that. Nor will any man of Zarallo's Free Companions." He scanned the crowd. "What say you, dog-brothers?"

There was a roar of approval, cut through with the Zamoran's scream of agony as Conan wrenched and twisted and the man's arm separated at the shoulder, broke at the wrist, and the bone of the upper arm snapped. The Cimmerian threw him down and kicked him in the ribs; it wasn't the only kick the man received as he crawled through the strings of ebony beads on sisal cords that covered the doorway. Even the cats didn't approach him.

He wouldn't live long, Conan wagered.

The din of the tavern rose to its earlier levels, and Conan got a few slaps on the back. Nobody liked the thought of interference in a duel, especially backstabbing, though if it had erupted into a brawl, things would have been different. Someone on his way back to barracks grabbed the dead Zamoran by his heels and dragged him out. Two friends of Brocas handed the dead men's swords and daggers and belts to Conan and the young Corinthian respectively, the customary victor's prize. The belt Conan received held a pouch.

Brocas scowled, then shook himself and took a deep breath.

"You saved my life from treachery," he said to Conan, his voice sullen with youth and its juices. "I owe you a debt."

Conan shrugged. "If you choose," he said. Then he grinned disarmingly. "You may save *my* life, someday, dog-brother."

"Perhaps I will." Brocas smiled, then laughed. "After I sleep this off." He nodded and turned away.

Conan half-drew the dead Zamoran's sword. It was quite fair-quality steel, and so was the dagger. The gilt-bronze buckle and fittings on the sword-belt were well-made. That made it a profitable evening, as well as one that broke the boredom of garrison duty. He went back to the table where he'd been dicing and threw the ivories again.

"Eyes of Set!" Conan said, happily echoing the other man's earlier complaint. Anjallo swore, but he paid. Everyone in Zarallo's Free Companions knew that the Cimmerian was a bad man to cross. That had been driven home by public exhibition.

"Damned if I'll dice with you again tonight," he said. "Your luck's in—especially with women, I'd wager—if the dice favor you!" Anjallo slouched off without waiting for the mug the winner traditionally bought the loser.

Conan raked in ten coppers and a small, clipped silver coin the size of the nail on his little finger, dropping them into a pouch at his sword-belt. Then he checked the dead Zamoran's pouch, which had about as much again. Adding that loot to his own, he carefully drew the strings tight. The sword, scabbard, dagger, and belt... he'd get four silver pieces at least for the whole of it.

The dicing bout had lasted all afternoon and to the beginnings of twilight. His winnings were about a week's pay for a common spearman, and half what he made in the same time as a scout in Zarallo's company... on those occasions when everyone was paid in full. Throw in what he'd gotten from the Zamoran and it made four months' wages all up, which in turn meant he had as much money as he would have if the paydays had been as regular as an Argossean clock.

To celebrate he took a long swallow of the Claw and Fang's rather sour, weak, lumpy beer. Even bad beer was better than the water from foul shallow town wells, and safer too. The greatest of heroes could still die of diarrhea.

Conan of Cimmeria had seen a great many taverns, inns, gambling dens and alehouses since he left his northern homeland more than... He counted on his fingers, then looked down at the bare toes on his sandaled feet, ticking off the years by memories and events... There were plenty of those.

More than ten years! Crom! *How the seasons fly away. The friends and maidens I played with will be raising their families now, and the men growing their beards. The ones who haven't been killed, that is.*

Taverns were a feature of civilization, back where he'd grown to manhood—or at least to the young warrior with his first downy whiskers who'd helped sack and burn the fortress-city of Venarium. Cimmerians either brewed their own ale or bartered with a neighbor for it. Bartered food they'd raised or made or hunted themselves. Coined money was a rare thing among his home hills and forests. Those who traveled relied on hospitality, which was freely given— unless there was a blood-feud.

Or the loot was taken by force, he thought. *Even sweeter then!* He smacked his lips at the pleasant memory of the casks of wine and brandy in Venarium's cellars and warehouses, of smashing in the head of one cask with the hilt of his sword then sticking his face up to the ears in the contents.

Things got blurry after that.

They could have killed us all, helpless as suckling babes while we slept it off. Good thing we'd killed all the clanless Aquilonian bastards first.

This tavern on an alleyway in the Stygian outpost city of Sukhmet was better than some he'd drunk in. Nobody was trying to rob or kill him right now, for example, and the outhouse stink from the alley beyond the door wasn't *too* bad. The day before yesterday there had been a heavy rain to sluice things away. If he hadn't spent a fair amount of time outside the walls in the countryside and wilderness, he might not have noticed the stench at all. Most didn't, after they'd been in a city for a while—though coming in from outside, the stink was obvious from miles away.

Conan grinned. The first time he'd approached a city of size, he'd been convinced everyone inside had died of the plague and he was smelling their liquified bodies.

The tavernkeeper kept a vaguely pork-based stew simmering in a great iron pot over the hob and threw vegetables and scraps and trimmings and even some spices into it as they came to hand. He could get a bowl of that for two coppers, with a lump of dense millet-bread, and an onion thrown in to munch on.

For a copper more, he could get a big slice or a long meaty rib from the pig carcass that turned on the spit there beside the stew-cauldron. That was actually fairly tasty and spiced with a good hot sauce of peppers, though the savory taste would decline to rankness before it was finished in a day or so, and another beast went on the spit. Meat didn't keep well in this clime.

Big bowls of coarse pottery around the walls held fruits exotic to him, oranges and mangoes and the like from the farms of the Stygian settlers outside the town wall. Patrons were welcome to sample, as long as they kept buying drinks, as well.

The Claw and Fang was also *worse* than some other boozing-dens he'd patronized. The wine was so terrible that even his not particularly discriminating palate preferred the beer that was the main alternative, though that was like drinking thin fermented porridge. Which wasn't surprising, really; vines wouldn't grow here. Some sort of rot got them.

Sukhmet was far south of the Styx, the great river whose valley marked the northern border of the vast Stygian empire. They made wine there, watering the vines from the river in that dry, dry land, and some of *that* wasn't bad. Better-than-fair Shemite stuff could be found there, too. Getting wine to *this* gods-forsaken outpost, however, meant weeks in riverboats and then weeks on camel-back from oasis to oasis through desert, and then over a month in ox carts over bad roads that led southeast through the greener and greener savannah toward the Darfar border marches.

It was *expensive* bad wine, too. All that transport cost silver, along with the guards who were needed... and merchants needed to hire ones they could trust not to drink up too much of the cargo, which meant higher wages too.

Stygia was a vast and varied empire, of many lands and peoples. Conan had about decided that as far as he was concerned the snake-worshippers were welcome to every blighted overheated sun-cursed inch of the place. In this part it didn't even cool down at *night*, the way the deserts did. The bugs were bad in the valley of the Styx, but here south of the desert they were beyond belief; some of the scorpions were as big as his foot, and the sting in their tails led to a long painful death.

They also distilled a yellowish-white drink from their sorghum here that had about the same effect on your head as a Vanir war axe, or at least a Pictish raider's flint hatchet. Conan waved for a small clay cup of that. The innkeeper came over with it himself, cats scattering from his path. He was a thickset middle-aged brown man in a simple linen kilt and with a shaven head.

"On house," he said, keeping his Stygian pidgin-simple for outlanders. "Dinner, too. You keep fight from too bad, smash place up."

Except for the blood soaking into the dirt floor, but dirt hid a multitude of sins.

"I thank you," Conan said, deciding to take a chance on the roast pig. Eating Zarallo's rations back at barracks, before he unrolled his pallet on the earth-bench bed, would mean beans and mush and dried meat and maybe another onion. It was part of the wage, which meant he could save toward getting away from here.

And he'd contributed some of the meat, hunting on scouting missions and setting up frameworks to dry the flesh in strips so that others could haul it back to town in bulk. The hunting here was excellent, animals familiar and half-familiar and weirdly alien swarming in astonishing numbers, sport better than anything he'd seen before.

Which was about the only compensation for being rammed up the Stygian empire's backside.

Conan spent as much time at the hunt as Zarallo would allow, arguing that it cut the mercenary chief's provisioning bills, kept his skills sharp, and let him learn the ins and outs of the wilderness. He could sell the skins and horns, but being more common, hides sold for less than a woven blanket hereabouts. There was a market for ivory, of course, but hunting elephants required special skills and trusted comrades.

So even hunting paled after a while.

We're fighting men, but we haven't had a fight *in Crom knows how long*, he mused over the wretched beer. *The moss that hangs from the trees will start sprouting on me, soon enough.*

As the innkeeper turned to go, Conan motioned for him to wait. He shoved the Zamoran's sword across the table.

"You buy?" he said. "Six silvers."

"Three," the innkeeper said quickly, then he examined the weapon and gear.

"Five," Conan countered. "Keep it, I draw on it for food, drink." That would be considerably safer than keeping it under his pallet, and less trouble than the Free Companions' treasury.

"Four and twelve coppers."

"Done," Conan said, and they slapped palms on it. "Bring pig meat and bread?"

The food arrived, with one of the innkeeper's daughters bringing it. Like most Stygian women she wore less than the men—only a loincloth. Unlike most, she had full breasts and haunches like a draft-horse, probably a dash of local blood. All those parts swayed interestingly as she bent over to serve the dishes. Then she walked away, glancing over her shoulder; perhaps his display of speed and strength had impressed her.

Or possibly his sudden accession of silver.

A voice cut through his musings, and his head came up with smooth swiftness as he eased forward on the stool, sandals beneath him and a little weight on the balls of his feet. Suddenly he was acutely aware of every dim outline in big smoky adobe-walled, dirt-floored room.

"Keep your paws off my arse, Stygian pig," the voice said, "or I'll feed you your fingers and ram your severed sword hand thumb up your bunghole with the toe of my boot."

2

Two fights in one night would be unusual, though not really rare.

It was a woman's voice… and speaking not Stygian or the pidgin-Stygian common in Sukhmet, or even one of the gobbling local tribal languages, but the slangy stripped-down seafaring argot of the seaports and sea-lanes thousands of miles to the northwest. A mongrel Argossean dialect with words from Zingaran, Shemite, and gods-knew-what mixed in. It was like the breath of a cool sea-breeze in the rank sweaty dimness.

She spoke it with a northern accent clear-cutting.

"And I'll dip it in burning candle wax first for lubrication," she added.

There was a clatter of stools falling to the hard-packed dirt, a boil of armed figures, and once again a circle of watcher's shoulders. The hubbub of delighted exclamations at yet *another* break in the monotony provided a sudden contrast to the sleepy buzz of moments before.

Valeria! he thought, with a smile of grim pleasure. Rumors had spread that Zarallo had hired her two days ago, straight off a caravan somewhere to the west.

He'd heard of her during his freebooting time on the

Western Sea, though they'd never crossed paths. She was a member of the Red Brotherhood and, judging from the songs and stories, as dangerous as any three pirates put together. Valeria's reputation said she was good-looking, too, though he'd taken that with a grain of salt. Nevertheless, he'd been looking forward to seeing her in the flesh.

Zarallo himself was a lazy businessman, or the Free Companions wouldn't have taken a contract in such a remote place as Sukhmet, away from all the serious action. Conan wouldn't have enlisted with him, either, if the Argosseans hadn't sunk his last ship. A desperate swim to shore had left him with nothing but a loinclout, a sword, and a purse containing the price of three days' food and lodging. But the Zingaran mercenary captain was also a tried-and-tested leader of fighting men, and nobody's fool, so she must have been up to his standards.

Conan stood to see better.

Stygians were a tall people, particularly the better-fed classes, but few equaled his height of a handspan over six feet. Being mostly slim, few had his weight of bone and muscle, either. Nobody looked his way, which was good— surprise could be a strong ally.

A woman's head reared across the room—dark yellow shoulder-length hair held back by a silk headband. She wore a baggy-sleeved silk shirt that had once been the same old-gold color before considerable staining and patching, now tied off in a knot below her breasts. Below that, a sash of red around her supple waist and a leather belt carrying a straight two-edged sword and a dagger. Wide silk knee-length sailor-style breeks of the same cut he was wearing, but stained with tar of the sort used on ship's rigging, and loose knee-high sea boots.

The dagger was a foot long and worn on the back of her belt, with the hilt to the left. This was significant, he knew. It marked certain styles of bladework that were common in the seaports of the west, and among the sea-rovers.

She was only four inches shorter than Conan—as towering for a woman as he was among men. And...

For once, the ballads didn't lie, he thought appreciatively. *That is a* woman, *by all the spirits, and not just a pretty toy.*

Built like a smoothly muscled she-leopard, Valeria was long-limbed, deep-bosomed, with large shapely hands. Her skin had a sailor's tan, too, though still clear with youth, with tawny hair and gray-blue eyes and a long straight-nosed, high-cheeked, broad-browed face. He'd seen plenty of male equivalents coming at him behind a Gunderman's sixteen-foot pike, but on her it looked much better.

The whole ensemble would have been striking anywhere.

In Sukhmet, it was exotic almost beyond belief.

Facing off against her was a Stygian who Conan recognized—Khafset, commander of the Setnakht Frontier Guards. The first word of the regimental title meant "Set is victorious." The grandiloquent name didn't disguise the rather shabby second-rank quality of the "official" government outfit. Normally a commander of Khafset's high birth wouldn't be found anywhere near here, and the frontier guards would be led by a promoted ranker, or at most some sprig of the minor gentry.

Rumor had it that some scandal at court in Luxor, the capital of Stygia, had forced him to choose between this humiliating exile or an execution involving very large snakes and starving hyenas. Khafset's sour-stomach attitude with his posting was well-known among the soldiers and mercenaries alike.

Apparently the man *hadn't* heard of Valeria.

"If a woman comes into a soldier's tavern, she can expect a friendly pat now and then," Khafset said, and Conan winced. "Come, wench, sit and share this wine with me. It's Argossean, and a fine vintage. My brother brought me a crate of it from Luxor, just last week."

He was using the same mixed-language way of speaking Valeria had, the argot of seamen, pirates, and the taverns of coastal cities with an Argossean accent in it plastered over his native gutturals. That supported the rumors that he came from Khemi or Luxor. For a country so large, Stygia didn't do much seaborne trade, but what there was went through the religious and royal capital cities along the Styx, which opened on the Western Sea and which even the big ships could navigate over a thousand miles east of the coast.

Northern shipping that did come from the north—to Stygia and points south—most often passed through the coastal cities of the kingdom of Argos, Zingara's enemy and rival. Conan knew that for a fact, since he'd robbed a good many Argossean merchantmen in his own time with the Red Brotherhood, sailing out of the Baracha Isles. And with the Zingaran pirates, too, though they had dressed it up with the title of *privateer*.

"I *am* a soldier, dog-dung-for-brains," Valeria said. "On the rolls of Zarallo's Free Companions and paid on the drumhead when I enlisted. I'm here to drink and dice and eat, and I get to pick who I'll screw. Someone a lot better-looking than you, pig-snout, and not with his tiny dick rotting from Ishtar's measles. Use your Argossean swill to poultice the puss-running sores dripping on your feet."

Conan rumbled laughter at that, and he wasn't the only one—some of the other mercenaries added comments of their own. Clumps rose from the tables, gathering and sorting themselves by allegiance. Zarallo's mixed bag of mercenaries scowled at the outnumbered Stygians, and got it back in full. It was amazing how fast being isolated together here had made the mercenaries into a tribe of their own. A quarrel among themselves was one thing, but no outsider could attack one of theirs.

They wouldn't shy away from a fight, either. If that had been the case, they'd have picked a different way to earn their bread. It only remained for Valeria to prove worthy of the title of Free Companion.

About a third of Zarallo's eight hundred or so were Zingarans like the commander, nearly as dark as Shemites and given to bristling waxed mustachios. Fierce as you could want if flighty, and very picky about matters of honor and respect.

The majority of the rest were from half a dozen kingdoms, foreigners to each other at home and often hereditary enemies like Kothians and Ophirites, or Aquilonians and Nemedians, but brothers within the Companions. The rest included a scattering from everywhere—one Cimmerian named Conan, for starters.

There were also some curly-bearded Shemites, crafty and fierce, four Zamorans... only two as of now... wandered far from their landlocked kingdom away off on the edge of the eastern steppes. Shifty-eyed light-fingered rogues fond of loaded dice but dangerous as weasels in a fight.

A pair of red-headed Vanir twin brothers who matched Conan's height and muscle, very good men to fight beside... when they were sober. A tattooed Pict had the expressionless stoicism and keen tracking skills expected from a man of that remote western wilderness, though he wept into his beer with blubbering homesickness and sang incomprehensible ballads when he was drunk enough, which was once a week.

There was even a scattering of blacks from the Southern Isles—what some called the *Corsair* Islands—cheerful laughing killers with patterns of scars like chevrons on their faces. And one flat-faced oddity with curious eyes and amber skin from somewhere further east than Zamora, or even Hyrkania. He didn't talk much, but was death on two feet in a hand-to-hand fight. Conan had learned some valuable wrestling tricks from him.

All sorts could be found in most mercenary bands.

What all Zarallo's bully boys had in common was being tough as rawhide, and despising their employers even more than mercenaries usually did. In turn, the Stygian soldiers of the garrison considered the very presence of the mercenaries an insult, since their empire only used foreign hirelings for duties on which its generals didn't want to waste really valuable units. The local soldiers knew it was a judgment on them and their capabilities.

As Valeria glared at the Stygian, the owner of the tavern and his wives, sons, and daughters glanced at one another and began packing up anything breakable they could reach, preparing to retreat behind a door they could shut and secure with a strong iron bar. They had experience with tavern brawls, which in a soldiers' dive like this were even more chancy than the common variety, since *all* the participants were armed and trained to kill.

The Stygian officer...

Khafset, Conan reminded himself.

The name meant "He Appears as Set," and the man did have snake-like characteristics. Of course, rumor had it that the Stygian nobility all had traces of the blood of the legendary serpent-men of ancient Valusia. At Valeria's insults, his dark-olive hawk face flushed purple-crimson beneath the folded striped-linen nobleman's headdress he wore, with two tails falling to his smooth chest and a gold cobra-head with ruby eyes fixed over his brows. It was his only garment save for belt, pleated linen kilt, and sandals. His hand drifted toward the hilt of his kopesh sword, a peculiarly Stygian weapon with a straight section that gave way to a sickle-like curve sharpened on the outside for slashing.

Conan stood and strolled forward casually, the cup of the local white-yellow lightning in his right hand. A Stygian sitting a bit behind Valeria had his eyes locked on her back in a lust that was for blood, not rut, and his right hand strayed toward the curved knife tucked into the back of the belt that held his kilt.

The Cimmerian's big left hand fell on the trooper's muscular shoulder in what looked like a friendly gesture. His fingers closed, tightening until bone creaked like wood in a vise on a carpenter's bench. He bent to murmur into the Stygian's ear.

"Let's all just watch, friend," Conan said, striving to sound genial. "Because I'd hate to have to tear your arm off and beat in your skull with it. That would interrupt the lady and spoil the show she's putting on for us."

The Stygian soldier whipped his head around and looked up at Conan, then flared in recognition. He'd witnessed the earlier duel and its spectacular conclusion. His lips were tight and pale around the edges, but he forced a snarl-smile and nodded. In turn, Conan let the hand rest lightly as he stood again and sipped at his drink. Ripping the Stygian's arm apart, the way he had the Zamoran backstabber, would start a full-scale brawl between the Free Companions and the frontier guards, and that might be less interesting than the drama he was watching.

Hissst!

Conan blinked at the brief sound of steel snapping out of a leather-and-wood scabbard greased with neatsfoot oil. He remained silent among the cheers and jeers, instead pursing his lips in thoughtful respect.

Quick, he thought. *She's death-quick.*

Valeria had drawn swiftly enough to impress him, and he'd won a good many fights because people couldn't believe someone his size could be so cat-fast. A lot of them had never had the opportunity to repeat the mistake.

Khafset had an even better point of view to judge the quality of the woman's sword wrist. Before he could react, the slim point of her double-edged blade of blue-tinted Aquilonian steel was resting on the fleshy part of his lip, just below his hawk nose. As Conan watched, a single drop of red blood showed and then trickled down the shimmering metal. One sharp push with the strength and speed and control she'd shown, and the Stygian would be dead even before he started to fall, with a foot of steel through his brain and the point buried in the back of his skull.

The *inside* of the back of his skull.

Khafset froze, and his eyes crossed for a second as they instinctively tried to focus on the point that had stung him. His hands slowly, slowly spread out and went wide, away from his own sword and dagger. He gestured for his group of hangers-on, toadies, and subordinates to sit down behind him. They bristled like the cats they loved so, but they still obeyed.

His head started to tilt back away from the point that had—just—pricked his skin, then stopped as the blade followed. It pressed with exactly the same butterfly touch, neither heavier nor lighter.

Quick, and perfect *control*, Conan thought, his eyes lighting with a wholehearted admiration that was not limited to—but certainly included—the sight of that magnificent half-bare body. *I'll bet her sweat smells good*, he thought. *And look at the way the skin of her back ripples when she moves. Ishtar and Derketa! It would be like grappling a living statue.*

As the Stygian's followers sunk back to their stools and benches, Valeria took a light shuffling fencer's half-step back. She shifted the point so it was directed precisely at Khafset's right eye, and moving in delicate circles about the same circumference as his iris, ready to dart in and out like a needle punching through cloth. Sweat that had nothing to do with the heat burst out on the Stygian's forehead.

She raised one tawny brow and her wrist tensed.

"Perhaps I was a little... less than courteous," he said.

Naked death brings out his manners, Conan thought, grinning silently again. *And he's looking at stark death right now, however nice the package.*

The soldier whose shoulder Conan held looked at him again, muttered something about pissing, then rose and sidled out the door, going along the wall to avoid attracting attention. Conan put one foot on the stool to claim it and the little round table.

"The damp heat here would try the patience of an adept of the Shining One," Khafset said. "I will leave." He bowed his head very slightly and began a slow but dignified turn toward the door.

"And I won't lift your kilt, even to spank you rosy as you go," Valeria said in the same tone of grave courtesy, with a nod that matched his.

Khafset's relief was great enough that he'd turned three-quarters of the way toward the door before grasping the sense of the words she'd used. He hesitated for half a step, then wheeled with a snarl and reached for his sword again. A man couldn't afford to lose too much face, the Cimmerian supposed, if he wanted his life to be anything but a drawn-out misery.

Thud!

The Stygian gave a high-pitched squeal and fell to the floor, clutching himself and rolling about, his mouth working as if he couldn't decide whether to puke or scream. Conan chuckled and winced at the same time. The sea boot to the crotch wasn't enough to ruin the Stygian for life, but he'd be moving very carefully for some time.

Valeria lifted her blade and kept the rest at bay for the moment with the glittering menace of its point. Stepping in, she kicked him again with nicely judged force to the face. His nose cracked audibly, but not his teeth, which meant that this had been a lesson, and not an attempt to cripple or kill.

Always kick a man when he's down, Conan thought with amusement. *It's much easier then.*

Valeria stepped sideways, sheathed her sword, without looking down, then reached out and took up the globe-bottomed bottle of wine that still sat on the Stygian's table. She knocked off the top with a quick flick of her wrist and poured a stream of deep blood-red liquid between her full red lips, tilting her head further and further back as her throat worked.

"Ahhhhhh…" Tossing the bottle through the bead curtain to crash and tinkle in the alley, she wiped her mouth with the back of her hand. "He was half-right. It is a fine vintage, and it's not gone off with travel—but it's Corinthian, not Argossean, or I'm a Pict."

The Stygian's followers had rushed forward to pick him up. Valeria jerked a thumb in the direction of the door and a pair of them grabbed him under the arms, dragging him out with his heels trailing. Bubbles of blood formed and popped on his shattered nose.

"My thanks to Captain Khafset, for inviting me to share his wine!"

There was another outbreak of laughter, which grew louder when she bowed with a dramatic flair. The rest of the Stygians backed away cautiously in their wake, swords half-drawn to keep the mercenaries from following. That wasn't likely, though—they were too busy hooting obscene suggestions and making mocking kissing sounds, rather than giving the killing snarl of the truly enraged.

"What a woman," Conan whispered to himself. "Clever, too." That performance had probably cut deeply into the problems she would face as the lone female in a gang of hard-handed stick-at-naughts like the Free Companions. Cut them by three-quarters at least. She'd only have to kill one or at most two before the rest got the message. Humiliating the Stygian had made her firmly one of the clan—someone who'd scored a public point on their common foes.

She'd kept the brawl from turning into a lethal scrimmage, as well, so Zarallo wouldn't need to hand her over to the Stygians to appease their anger. If Khafset had died, a high-ranking nobleman killed by an infidel foreigner, and a *woman* at that...

Khafset would want blood anyway.

There was no way around that.

It won't be the first time she's dealt with his kind, though, he thought. *The Red Brotherhood are a hard-handed gang of killers, so she's learned ways before this, to survive and prosper.*

The ebb and flow of the tavern returned to normal. Valeria sat, and the innkeeper's wife scurried over with some ribs cut from the pig, along with the usual side-dishes and a big pot of beer. Conan returned to his own meal and watched with a smile as the mercenaries vied to pay court. In return they got jibes, jests, buffets fit to make a man's head ring, and one half-friendly squeeze that gave the recipient a warning ghost of what Khafset had received from the toe of her boot.

The fellow sidled away, biting his lips and trying not to bend and clutch himself.

The innkeeper and his family were just replenishing the sesame-seed oil in the earthenware lamps and trimming the wicks for the second time when Valeria threw down some coins—more than the meal was worth, but not recklessly more—and pushed back her chair.

Conan rose and approached her carefully, taking an

unoccupied chair and reversing it, sitting with the wicker back in front of him, knees wide and hands resting on his thighs. She noted that, and by the narrowing of her eyes took the meaning. He was deliberately putting himself in a position where he'd be slower to reach his sword, and would have to jump backward to do it. Her gaze went over him from head to foot.

"A Cimmerian," she said, her voice very slightly slurred. "*You're* a long way from home, northman."

Holds her liquor better than most, he thought, and he smiled.

"Conan of Canach, by name," he said, in the seafarer's dialect, "and a wanderer by inclination."

"Conan of the Red Brotherhood?"

"The same, though I sailed with the Zingarans, too," he said. "That quarrel isn't mine."

The Brotherhood, pirates of the Baracha Isles, robbed and raided with a fine free unprejudiced hand from the Styx to the Pictish Wilderness. The Zingaran freebooters styled themselves privateers and in theory—since there weren't any witnesses, or none left alive—avoided attacking fellow Zingarans. The two groups didn't get along.

"I'd heard of you, but we never shipped together," he said. "Unfortunately," he added. He *didn't* add that Zingarans had sunk his last ship, leaving him penniless on the coast of Shem with only his sword, and sandals. That was when he heard Zarallo was hiring.

"Perhaps fortunately—for you," she said warily.

He shrugged and spread his hands. "I'm not Khafset," he said. "For a start, I can tell a she-wolf from a lapdog."

"Calling me a bitch, Cimmerian?" she said, but with a very slight smile.

"Only in a *good* way," he replied. "By way of respect. I heard how you made your way in the Brotherhood. You've got fangs, and you can bite hard, no dispute."

She rose. "And now I'll be off."

He raised his hands in an ostentatiously unarmed pose again, and gave her a frankly admiring look.

"Care to have me walk back to the barracks with you?" he offered. "I'm heading there soon."

"Not tonight, Cimmerian." Her gaze was coolly neutral. "Perhaps not ever."

He dropped his hands back to his thighs. "Your choice, soldier."

She staggered ever so slightly but recovered smoothly. He judged from long experience that she was just at the stage where she could still do nearly everything she could do sober... but where she was likely to try to do things she wouldn't under normal circumstances.

You can walk, but another cupful or three and you couldn't, he thought. *But you wouldn't like to hear it. Touchy as a wildcat with a sore paw, and it's no surprise.*

She paused by the bench where Brocas was sitting with his friends. They still were basking in the reflected glory of the encounter with the Zamoran.

"You," she said, pointing at a handsome young slinger next to the pikeman. "Unless you're too drunk to raise a stand?"

He bounced erect and bowed low, correcting a stagger at the end of it.

"My lady, for you a marble *statue* could raise a stand."

She considered him, blinking. "That would be uncomfortable," she said. "Come on."

Conan sighed and raised a hand to signal for another mug.

*C*rom curse it!

Conan tossed the stripped pork rib into the fierce low red embers of the hearth-fire and rose, hitching at his sword-belt as the bone crackled and popped and fat-rich marrow flared up.

Sukhmet is a bad town to wander in, drunk or not, he thought, moving toward the doorway. *She can't object to a soldier going home when he chooses, and who knows what might happen...?*

If anything was going to light a fire under Valeria's tail, a fight would do it, and a man who fought at her side might well get a pleasant surprise out of it—unlike the ones who fought against her. He nodded to the innkeeper, trying to remember what the man now owed him. Unlike many of his comrades in the Free Companions, he usually didn't keep a running tab with the owner of the Claw and Fang, or any tavern. Long experience had taught him the wisdom of paying on the nail, if you were going to pay at all.

For starters it meant the innkeeper liked him better, since he didn't have to risk having a customer die or "wander off," or finding that the company's treasury was short that month. In this case the positions were reversed; the man was holding Conan's money, and would want to keep him sweet lest it be demanded in cash.

Outside Conan felt the same disappointment as always. When stepping into the night from a room with a fire in it, he always expected it to be cooler, and hereabouts that wasn't going to happen. Stepping to the other side of the alley he unbuttoned and did what many had before him, politely aiming the stream away from the tavern, and then padded out into the gathering darkness. A full bladder might distract at the wrong moment, and the pause let his eyes adapt fully to the dark.

Only a shadow of sunset still showed in the west, down the winding street. Night fell like a hammer here, without any of the long twilight gloaming to which he'd been born. The boom of the gate-drums sounded, along with a raucous shiver from a Stygian trumpet. About a quarter of a mile away they'd be shoving the massive hardwood portals closed for the night and letting the ironwood bar drop home in the thick forged-metal brackets.

He'd had that duty himself a few times. The bar was a baulk of seasoned tropical hardwood timber as thick through as one of Valeria's splendid thighs...

Shows where my *thoughts are*, he thought with an utterly noiseless chuckle, and he padded off in the direction she'd likely taken. *Ishtar of the Shemites, what a backside that woman has.* He picked up the pace. *I'll follow far enough behind that she and her pretty toy never see me. Just in case.*

Aquilonian legend had it that a Cimmerian could come up behind you, slit your throat, and be a mile away before you even noticed you were dead—and that he'd stolen your horse and coin-purse, too. It wasn't *quite* true, but Conan often took advantage of the rumors, and had learned the hard way how to move silently.

His people hunted for nearly as much of their meat as they got from their herds, and the forests of his home held hunters that walked on four feet. The kind that weren't in the least shy of feasting on those who stood on two. If you wanted your hide whole, children uneaten, and food on your table... then in Cimmeria you had to be able to out-stalk and out-fight the wolves. City-bred men, or even ones from a tame countryside, were sheep by comparison.

Ah, Conan thought. *That's quicker than I thought it would be.*

Valeria was whistling a jaunty tune as she swaggered along with her arm around her companion's shoulders— they were about the same height. She'd probably ducked into an alley for relief, too, a bit more complicated and time-consuming for her, giving her male companion some useful guarding to do. The whistle helped as Conan ghosted close to the southern walls, where the shadows were deeper.

This district was all mudbrick, some plastered with stucco and some not, mostly three stories high with the butt-ends of the beams protruding out through the walls. There wasn't much traffic. At sundown Sukhmet's respectable folk, such as they were, went to ground and barred their doors. Those who had to move after dark carried torches and clubs and moved in groups.

The darkness was deep, broken only by the half-full moon and brilliant southern stars that could be seen through the narrow slit of sky above, and an occasional leak of lamplight. The windows on the ground floor were all narrow slits in the thick adobe walls, often barred with grillwork to boot.

Valeria and her companion halted a dozen yards ahead of him, where the narrow road opened out into a misshapen oval all of twenty feet or so at its filth-strewn widest, what might with a stretch be called a square. It was a little less cave-dark, too, since the walls didn't narrow the sky so much, though the smoke-haze was thick from the evening cooking going on all around them.

Just enough light penetrated to reveal six thugs standing across its width, and the gleam as three of them pulled long knives from sheaths under their left armpits. A fourth drew a shortsword and hefted a small buckler in the other paw, while a fifth brandished a club with a metal spike through the knob on its end. The last had a long ironwood staff of more than head height, and whirled it in a figure-eight that made a burring sound as it twisted.

"Hey, yellow-hair!" one called in the pidgin of Sukhmet's streets. "Give us your money, we let you live."

"Give us your sword and knife, we let you live," another shouted.

"Give us all your clothes and make us happy, *maybe* we let you live," the last said, with an illustrative hip-movement and one-handed clutch at his loincloth. "Or you die very good!"

"Your friend he can kneel and make us happy."

Conan could hear shutters slamming shut and being barred in buildings close-by.

Valeria chuckled and gave a happy sigh, pulling her companion along without stopping her forward stroll, but

Conan could see the taut readiness in it. The mercenary slinger frowned until the situation penetrated his ale-fuddled mind; then he drew a dagger with one hand and pulled his sling from his belt, whirling it like a whip.

The thugs looked at each other in surprise, then shrugged and began to close in, the ends of their line curling inward in a way that showed they'd worked together before. Valeria hadn't drawn a weapon, and they probably thought of the odds as six-to-one instead of six-to-two.

That was still bad enough...

Conan regarded this type of street-rat the way a wolf did their four-footed namesakes. He'd been a thief by trade in his first exposure to cities, but he'd robbed rich merchants and others even more dangerous, including a magician and a fallen *god*. And usually in the victim's own well-guarded mansion, tower, or fort. He hadn't stooped to preying on passers-by.

Invisible in the darkness, he squatted on his hams to watch the show. If the toughs had taken their work seriously, they *might* have had a good chance. As an old Cimmerian saying went, even Lugh Longspear couldn't fight two if one of them was behind his back. But as it was...

Hisssst!

This time the blond woman didn't stop after the quick draw. Whoever her teachers had been—probably her Gunderman father, the professional guardsman—they'd taught her how to do a good stepping lunge, and she'd learned the lesson well. Keeping the flat of the blade horizontal to the ground and less likely to jam in bone.

The point went through the throat of the bravo with the shortsword, cutting off his shout with a brief agonized gurgle of astonishment as his windpipe instantly filled with the jets of blood from the arteries in his neck.

She didn't stop then, either, moving past him fast and wrenching the sword sideways like someone jointing a goose, sending blood out in a huge fan that cast gouts in the faces of the men to either side. It looked black in the dimness.

The slinger whipped his weapon around the neck of a man distracted by the woman's bewildering speed and yanked him forward. He came in a running stagger, nearly jerked off his feet and windmilling his arms... including his knife-hand, which left him exposed to a stab up under the breastbone. The victor had just long enough to start to grin before the spiked club smacked into his left shoulder with a sound like a butcher's cleaver. His expression turned into a rictus of snarling agony, but he rammed his knife into the club-man's crotch, which brought a shriek of pain.

His advantage was short-lived as a knife buried itself in his chest.

Valeria was past the man she'd spitted and wheeling before his body hit the ground with a limp flaccid *thump*, and her dagger flashed into her left hand. The thugs halted in shock for a crucial instant. They probably hadn't seen the details—even in the light of day she'd have been a blur—but it was clear that the one she'd spitted had a neck was open to the air all the way to the spine.

In the darkness it looked like sorcery.

The mercenary slinger lay dead, too, but two Stygians were down beside him. That meant half their number, shocking casualties even for experienced fighters, and these were street-toughs.

"Good choice, Valeria!" Conan murmured to himself.

"He was the only one with real gear, and he *might* have known how to use it." In his experience, even full-time pirates could be careless hack-and-smashers, fishermen or merchant sailors with delusions of warriorhood. Most didn't live long. Despite being a woman, Valeria had lasted several years, enough to win some fame.

"You run now," she said helpfully, in very basic Stygian. "Run away, little boy-boys, run away."

The living three looked at each other, then rushed her, the two knife-men in the lead. Conan was astonished for a second as Valeria turned and began to flee. Until she suddenly dropped flat on her back, curled into a ball, and rolled against the ankles of the leading thug, her steel-bearing arms still stretched out to either side.

It would have been difficult to dodge even in daylight. At night and close range, and working up to full-tilt pursuit, the knife-man barely had time to squawk as his shins thumped into her and he went over full-tilt, planting his face in the hard-packed dirt. Instantly he went limp, probably breaking nose and jaw and any number of teeth, possibly his neck as well, from the way the body convulsed.

The other thug with a knife showed rare good sense in not trying to do anything but turn around, take her advice, and run as fast as he could while she bounced back to her feet with lithe ease. Eyes bulging, he went past Conan's hiding place in a heedless dash.

The man with the staff who'd laughed as he clutched his loincloth came forward, sweeping his long weapon around his head and howling. Valeria skipped aside, ducked under a swing, and thrust with clinical precision into the back of his knee-joint, twisting the sword as she withdrew it. The man went over, and the very weight of his ironwood staff and the strength of his swing spun him around in mid-fall. His berserk howl of rage turned to a squawk of dismay and then a shriek of pain.

Valeria waited only long enough to check that her companion was well and truly dead, then turned and ran in earnest. With all the thugs down or gone, it was probably reflex learned in civilized cities where the night-watch showing up would pose a potential problem.

Unlike Sukhmet, he thought.

Conan could hear the husky, reckless chuckle of her mirth as she ran full-tilt at the wall and sheathed her weapons as she ran. Springing to a barrel-top with her foot barely touching it as she leapt upward again, she clamped her hands on the railing of a balcony, swung up nimble as an acrobat—or a sailor—ran up a drain-pipe like a squirrel, and disappeared onto the flat roof.

The light patter of her feet was interrupted by a yell from a family sleeping there under the stars, as many did in this hot box. Then a carol of laughter fading toward the next street over.

Conan rose and strolled forward. The man with the quarterstaff was just coming to one knee, clutching a damaged shoulder and moaning. His other leg dragged limp and twitched as it bled.

"Not your night, rat," the Cimmerian said cheerfully, grabbing him by the back of the neck. The thug wasn't a small man, but the iron grip lifted him most of the way off his feet, and there wasn't much fight left in him either. He squealed as fingers like steel rods threatened to separate the base of his skull from the rest of him.

"Who paid you?"

When there was no answer but a thrashing gurgle, Conan walked three steps to the wall Valeria had climbed and thumped the man's face into it. Not hard enough to stun or kill, but enough to get his attention, even with his wounds.

Conan leaned closer.

"Who paid you?" he repeated, his face much closer to the street-rat's.

The man's eyes rolled toward him, probably seeing only a glint of blue eyes and a hulking shadow, and feeling a grip like the grapnels used to lift cargo out of a ship's hold in a well-found port. Perhaps he thought he was in the hands of some night-spirit or monster from local legend.

"Don't know!" he gasped. Another *thump* against the wall and he said more hurriedly, "Truth, by Set! Wore a hood! Paid us—said the woman was coming—take her. Sounded... Sounded like a toff, like a noble. From the north! Set and Derketa be my witnesses!"

"Thanks for the truth, friend," Conan said. Drawing his arm back, he rammed the man's face into the iron-hard mud brick three more times, full-strength.

The body didn't move when he dropped it. Rifling through the club-man's belt pouch produced a handful of coppers, one silver piece... and a gold Stygian crown, with the coiled python on one side and a pyramid with an eye in the center on the other. It looked fresh from the mint—there was one here, in the governor's compound, which used the output of the local mines before it was shipped north.

Conan whistled softly. If it was genuine...

He bit, and the gold was greasy-soft between his back teeth, pure with only a little silver in it. It *was* genuine, and that meant six months' wages for a skilled scout like himself. Ordinary folk didn't handle gold coins more than once or twice in their lives, and only if they were lucky. Gold was for princes, nobles, rich merchants, and bankers, and the temples of powerful priesthoods.

And for the military, where thousands of men had to be housed and fed and armed, and paid wages better than ordinary laborers ever saw. Now and then for pirates, or mercenaries after the sack of a city—if they were *very* lucky.

Quick examination showed that each of the other dead thugs had one of the coins, along with a coil of rope, a cloth bag with a drawstring just right for popping over someone's head, and a folded blanket in which to wrap the victim. Those might be just the tools of intended theft, but he didn't think so, not with the gold coins and the man's story.

Someone… almost certainly Khafset or one of his cronies… had paid the men to do a snatch, intended to have Valeria carried off to where he could take a suitably prolonged revenge for his humiliation, not to mention his pricked lip, broken nose and bruised testicles. Nobody would be much upset at the disappearance of a newly signed outland mercenary, much less prepared to accuse the highest-born noble in the district. Not even the governor would do that.

The Cimmerian grunted, thinking hard as he dragged the bodies by an ankle or wrist into a small laneway that opened off the oval. It was a dead-end, with a pile of fly-buzzing, maggot-swarming debris including a dead dog or two piled against the cross-wall at its end. Many small red-glinting eyes stared at him from it and then vanished.

With a full-armed swing each time, he threw the bodies onto the mid-slope of the garbage, and some of the contents slid down over them. The stench was bad enough that he took a step back for a moment and spat aside to clear his mouth. The dead thug's club proved a useful tool to rake more down. After a moment's work no obvious human parts showed, and the odds were the bodies wouldn't be discovered for a week or more.

Nobody would care when they were.

Sukhmet was that sort of town.

He had a moment's mild regret that he had to include the slinger, who wouldn't get the cremation the worshippers of Mitra used, but if he was found, the uproar would be distracting.

Returning to the street, Conan flipped aside the club to clatter to the hard dirt. Best not to leave that near the bodies. Someone would steal it before dawn, if only for the copper or two the iron in the spike would fetch. Speaking of which…

I can't spend *the gold*, he realized. *Six pieces! Not for everyday.*

He'd have to go to a moneylender to change them for silver, and pay through the nose not to have the authorities informed that an outland mercenary was flaunting wealth he couldn't possibly have come by honestly. Even so, he was ahead by a handful of gold.

I could get passage back to the coast in a good caravan, he thought, *and for nothing if I sign on as a guardsman. That would leave me with a year and a half of scout's pay to get me back to the Isles, or wherever else I want.*

It was tempting. He was thoroughly sick of Sukhmet.

But the thought of Valeria's eyes as she held the Stygian with her sword on his lip... The vision wouldn't leave him. Then he brightened.

In a little while, she will be as sick of this place as I am.

4

Conan woke on his pallet in the barracks, to the long quick rattling roll of the sunrise snare-drum and the brass blatting of the trumpets. Stretching, he rose to seek the jakes, then the bathhouse to sluice himself down. He dressed and proceeded to stand in the loose line in the barracks square as the drum ended and the roll was called. The rule in the Free Companions was that you were ticked off first, before assignments for the day, and it seemed to work well enough.

The clerk began to call names.

"Conan, scout, attached to company headquarters!"

"Present and fit for duty," Conan responded in a voice both bored and loud.

Standing on the stretch of dirt between the quadrangle of two-story barrack-halls, armories, and storerooms in peeling stucco over more adobe, most were yawning and scratching under the bright hot dawn sun. They answered to their names as they were read off from the parchment roll. A few reported themselves ill and were told to go see the surgeon. Conan suspected that was mostly hangovers looking for a dose of willow-bark or the like, though the usual fevers and gripping bellies were always a problem.

They all had their personal side-arms—they didn't turn out with armor and pike or helm and crossbow except to drill with them or to fight—and they didn't even smell too badly.

Except for one Zingaran, who staggered out halfway through, fell to his knees and puked up a remarkable quantity of the local brew, much the worse for wear and smell for its hours-long stay in his gut. The clerk's lips compressed at the sight and stench. He was a northerner himself and might have been anything from a Kothian to a Nemedian by his looks and, contrary to the usual stories about the men skilled with pen and counting-tray, he was built like a muscular hitching-post and had one eye covered by a patch, with grizzled gray in his close-cropped hair.

"Arparos, pikeman file-closer," he said in a voice like iron given a throat, "drunk on duty, fine one week's pay and two weeks on barracks work detail." The luckless Arparos looked even seedier than before, if that was possible.

"Valeria, skirmisher." The big woman's voice rang out in her clear contralto, though Conan thought she looked slightly more worse for wear. He nodded inwardly, unsurprised at the role she'd been assigned. Zarallo was nobody's fool.

How she'd fare in a push of pike was an open question, but he'd seen what she could do in the sort of open scrambling encounter expected by a skirmisher—or a pirate in a boarding action or longshore raid. A different set of skills was needed than for straightforward head-butting between formed-up masses.

She wore the same sea-breeks and boots as yesterday, but a long linen shirt with sleeves and a floppy canvas hat with one side tucked up and ornamented with a peacock feather.

CONAN: BLOOD OF THE SERPENT 57

For all her sailor's tan, the sun here was hard on a northerner who didn't take precautions.

Next came the day's duty assignments. Starting the day after tomorrow, the once-a-month route-march of twenty miles, followed by pitching a fortified camp, battle drill out in the countryside, and then a march back.

Today had nothing posted on the chalkboard outside the captain's quarters. As long as nothing specific came up, Conan intended to grab a bowl of porridge and some bread, and then spend a couple of hours using a double-weighted practice sword and shield against the pells, strong wooden posts driven into the ground at the other end of the drill-field. That would be mixed with throwing spears and drawing the bow.

Then he'd see if he could get someone to match him for a few bouts of sword-sparring and wrestling and all-in, and after the afternoon sleep—a sensible custom in many of the hot lands he'd visited—he would run the circuit of the town's walls a few times carrying his fighting gear. It was the best remedy for the stale feeling after a day on leave, spent dicing and drinking.

"Conan, scout, and Valeria, skirmisher, report to the commander's office after morning parade," the clerk bellowed.

Conan's brows went up. Whatever it was it would be less boring than another day in garrison.

The commandant's house was set catercorner to the main encampment, bordering on the space kept open around the inside of the city wall. From the outside it looked like yet another two-story adobe block, with only narrow slit windows on the upper level.

Two men in mail shirts stood guard before the dark copper-studded polished wood of the doors, sweating stolidly and holding their seven-foot spears to one side with the butt braced against their right boot, round shields on shoulders, and plain bowl helmets. The helms were wrapped in cloth—in this climate or the deserts to the north the steel got hot enough to produce blisters.

Their mail shirts were likewise covered in light cotton surcoats. Cotton was an expensive exotic luxury back in the northern realms, and Conan had never even seen any until well after he left Cimmeria, but it was cheaper than linen here. The sigil of the Companions was on their breasts, an ornate gold letter "Z" on a black circle.

They crossed their spears as the pair approached.

"Who goes?" one growled.

"Conan the scout, summoned by the commander."

He didn't show his impatience with this ritual, when the man knew full-well who he was. Every place and folk had their customs, and it was rarely worth offending those among whom you lived. Zarallo had learned his practices in the royal army of his homeland, but they didn't differ much from the other northern kingdoms, and those all had a family resemblance born of centuries of regular warfare.

"Valeria, skirmisher, summoned by the commander."

The spears were withdrawn. "Pass, comrades," the sentry said. Conan groaned inwardly but kept his silence.

Inside the structure had the layout that a Stygian gentleman expected—that was the sort of man who'd occupied it when this was a purely Stygian garrison. Two courtyards, one just inside the front doors and one further back, with an open gate between the two and arched colonnades all around. The front would be public rooms and the rear family quarters.

Through the gate to the flower-rich inner court, Conan caught a glimpse of Zarallo's stout wife, at breakfast with her children and surrounded by maids. Then an aide—one of Zarallo's young cousins, he remembered—gestured them through to a big chamber Zarallo used as his office.

It had a floor of blue tile interspersed with cream-white, and smoothly plastered walls painted in Stygian style with up-and-down panels portraying colorful scenes of court ceremony, religious procession, and sacrifice. Some of the latter could be a bit unnerving, and those were the ones that had easels with large maps standing in front of them, blocking much of the imagery. It would be offensive to deface them—blasphemous to Stygian ways of thought.

This was a sensible compromise.

For maps Stygians used strips of a reed paper glued together at the edges, but Zarallo stuck with the northern habit of making field maps on soft-tanned leather with hot needles to burn in the lines. There were baskets full of scrolls, and two clerks—this pair more of the weedy, rabbity type Conan expected—clicking abacuses and scratching away at tables on the other side. An open strongbox had the interesting glint of silver, and coins clinked as they were weighed on a jeweler's scale, counted, and wrapped in parchment.

The whole place smelled of hot plaster, water, and

huge vivid tropical flowers from the gardens, with a faint underlying tang of greased steel and sweat-soaked leather that was inseparable from a war-camp, even this part of it.

"Conan! Valeria!" Zarallo said, beckoning them.

He sat behind a large table with an embroidered linen cloth over it. An empty bowl and platter had been pushed to one side, holding fried fish and rounds of flatbread. They reminded Conan that he hadn't eaten.

Zarallo was a Zingaran of more or less gentlemanly but originally impoverished background; tanned olive skin, a scar kinking his long nose, of medium height, broad-shouldered but getting a bit paunchy in his fortieth year. His chin-beard was trimmed to a point, his mustaches were waxed to stand up like a plains-buffalo's horns, and his long raven-black hair was dressed in curls that fell to his shoulders, mixed with the first gray threads.

The polished breastplate and high-combed morion helmet he'd wear outside were on the table, too, with his use-battered rapier and dagger lying across them. There were also scrolls pinned open by gauntlets and ink bottles, and piles of Stygian reed-paper.

His black eyes went to Valeria.

"Can you ride, skirmisher?" he said. "How well?" he said, not waiting for an answer. "And can you use a blade from the saddle? At all, or barely?"

She blinked in surprise. "Yes, I can do both," she said, adding, "sir, and well enough. My family had a farm, and my father trained me when I made it plain I wanted it. He had no son and wished to pass on the skills. I can fight in the saddle. That is, I won't cut off my mount's ears or fall off, but I wouldn't call myself a cavalry trooper. Most of my warring has been done at sea, or on raids where we came ashore in longboats."

"Good." He grunted and shuffled among the documents. "Good enough, at least. Because this is a formal complaint—" He brandished a piece of reed-paper embellished with the glyph-like signs of the Stygian script.

"—from the provincial governor, saying that you set upon one of his officers unprovoked, broke his nose, and inflicted... 'other injuries.'"

"Drew blade, pricked his lip, kicked him in the balls, then dosed his nose with the toe of my boot to correct his humors," Valeria specified, and Zarallo fought down a smile.

"As for provocation?"

She shrugged broad shapely shoulders; even then Conan found the gesture riveting, and he thought he heard one of the clerks across the room miss in the steady rhythm of quill pen on paper, then curse when he blotted a line.

"Well, he grabbed my arse, and tried to stick two fingers where they shouldn't go," she replied. "Seemed to think I'd like it, and he was very, very wrong."

Conan fought down a snort of laughter, and Zarallo didn't try.

"I was there, Captain Zarallo," Conan offered. "It's as she said, and she handled it cleverly—there would have been men dead, starting with the Stygian, if she hadn't, and a pitched battle between our dog-brothers and the snake-lovers. Instead it ended in a drubbing and laughs, not guts and brains on the floor. Some of the Stygian's own men wanted to laugh at him, you could see it in their eyes."

Valeria gave him a quick look with narrowed eyes, then

nodded, acknowledging his account of the wit she'd used to manage the incident, he thought. This made it plain he wasn't just flattering her to gain favor.

She was no fool, either.

"I thought that might be the case," the Zingaran said, the hissing accent of his native tongue stronger as he tried not to grin. They were using the mixed dialect of the mercenary bands of the western world, not all that different from the seafaring argot.

Zarallo went on to Valeria. "If I were going to get upset when you hard-schooled an over-eager swain, I wouldn't have hired you. Anyone could guess it would happen a time or two, with a woman in a man's trade—and a hard man's trade at that. Still, Khafset's a noble and he has influence here in this pisspot, however much trouble he might have encountered at court."

He tapped another paper. "There's a convoy heading for the Wedi Shebelli gold mine tomorrow morning."

Conan nodded and said—mostly to Valeria, "That's the reason the Stygians bother to hold this district, the mines. It all covers about a hundred and fifty leagues south and east." There was trade in slaves, ivory, emeralds, ostrich-plumes, rare ornamental woods, and the like, but gold was the thing that undergirded the others. Conan had never sought to be a merchant, but to be a predator he had to know his prey.

Zarallo flicked the document. "The Stygians claim a big chunk hereabouts, and do have a grip around Sukhmet and points north, but past a long day's march south of here they only hold the mine compounds and a few outposts on the Darfar border. There are still plenty of locals in the hills and forests who hate them for their slave-raiding and the taxes, and who'll jump them any time it looks possible. The convoys are an obvious target.

"They're adamant, even though the rains have started. Idiots. Who gives a shit if a few mercenaries die along the way?" He tapped the paper again. "We're contributing an escort, mounted scouts, and skirmishers who'll guard the convoy along with the Stygian reinforcements headed for the mine garrison. The ones stationed there now will be coming back with the convoy, but apparently they've had losses and will need help."

He did grin now. "Help with the gold ingots, too… to be sure, to be sure."

Then he gave an almost imperceptible sigh. Valeria's eyes narrowed thoughtfully, and Conan's thumb touched the hilt of his sword. If harvesting gold with steel hadn't appealed, none of them would have followed the mercenary drum, or been pirates with the Red Brotherhood.

Zarallo continued with brisk practicality.

"You'll both be going along. You, Conan, because you're my best scout and you know the countryside here. You, Valeria, because you'll be useful, and because I don't want anyone in Sukhmet seeing your face *or* that yellow hair for the next month. Out of sight, out of mind. Let the fuss fade with the bruises."

"By then, Khafset's face will be less sore, but still lumpy," Conan said, grinning. "And his balls will be swollen like pomegranates. Maybe he'll just keep putting his hands *there*."

He was rewarded by Valeria's chuckle.

With obvious effort Zarallo made himself scowl, and the listening clerks gargled as they choked down mirth.

"Take warning, woman," the commander said, "if you *had* killed Khafset, I would have had to throw you to the wolves—or here, to the hyenas—however much the snake-worshipping swine had it coming. So keep your head down and do your work. Dismissed!"

They saluted and left.

Once they were outside, Valeria turned to Conan.

"You've been there before?"

"Not to this mine, no, but to a couple of the others."

"What extra gear will I need?"

He grunted in appreciation. That was the right question, and if she hurried she had just enough time to do some quick buying.

"Well, the horses come from the company's herd, but I'd slip the stablemaster a little something to get the best, if I were you. You'll need some mail—light stuff, for this. The Companions has some you can get on credit. And…"

Conan learned much of his horse-craft after he left home; in Cimmeria, chiefs kept a few ponies, but the bulk of the land was too hilly and too thickly forested for ordinary folk to bother. His father had been a blacksmith when he wasn't farming or hunting or fighting.

Part of his learning had been done in Zamora and points east, where the endless steppes meant nobody walked if they could find a nag, and he was a quick learner. The tall rawboned mount he took from the company's herd was well-enough trained, big enough to carry his weight without collapsing, and after a little settling of who knew what and who was master, it was satisfactory. He made sure that everyone in the skirmisher detachment had at least one reasonable remount along, too, as the convoy mustered in the dust of the beaten area outside Sukhmet's south gate.

They were supposed to depart at dawn, so naturally it took about two hours more for everyone to muster, especially the town contractors who were renting the governor their carts and draught-beasts for the convoy.

Valeria picked a smaller beast, about thirteen hands, with more of the desert-Shemite strain that was present in all Stygian mounts, and he could see solid competence if not brilliance in the way she handled it. The ex-pirate had a light steel helm slung to her saddlebow, a rolled-up sleeveless vest of meshmail lashed behind the crupper of her saddle, and a crossbow over her shoulder with a quiver of bolts at her belt.

She gave him the same quick professional once-over, noting the heavier rolled mail shirt behind his saddle, and the bowl helmet with a riveted nose guard and a leather neck flap covered in a fan of steel splints. He had a four-foot recurve bow of horn and sinew at his left knee as he sat, with a quiver of bright-fletched arrows on the other side.

"You can use that from horseback?" she said. It wasn't a common skill in the western kingdoms.

"A bit, though I'm no Turanian," he said. "I rode with the Kazakhi near the Sea of Vilayet for a while, though, and they all use them. The fighting's all on horseback there, except when you storm a town or fort or the like. Without a bow, you just wave your sword and yell insults."

She whistled. Turan and the Vilayet Sea were the eastern fringe of the known world, though while he was there,

Conan had heard tales of kingdoms and tribes and empires further east. Of treasures and wonders, and he recalled them wistfully now and then.

Perhaps, someday...

"There are pirates on the Sea of Vilayet, too," he added. "No horses at sea, but they use these bows before it comes to hand-strokes."

Valeria snorted. "If there's enough water and something to steal, there are pirates."

The rest of the company's contribution to the escort was thirty mounted skirmishers and scouts, including a dozen Shemite archers with bows much like Conan's.

The Stygian contingent that would stay at the mines was much larger. A hundred Stygian footmen carried broad-bladed spears and wore bronze helmets shaped much like the linen headdress upper-crust wore, with breastplates and coffin-shaped shields of boiled and lacquered elephant-hide.

A hundred more were archers from some black tribe called the Nubakans that carried laminated bamboo bows even taller than their wielders' long-limbed height, and knives and hatchets for close work. They were naked save for goatskin mantles and headdresses made from the manes of lions, and their muscles were impressive even by Cimmerian standards.

Besides that there were forty lancers in scale-mail shirts and half a dozen chariots, light wicker two-wheeled vehicles carrying driver and armored warrior-archer, pulled by horses much like the ones the lancers and Conan rode. For the most part the mounts were better-looking, with plumed headdresses not unlike those on the helmets of the warriors they carried.

Conan cocked an eye at them. "Old-fashioned," he said. Nobody else had used war-chariots for a very long time.

"Stygians," Valeria replied, and she shrugged.

Which was true enough. Stygia kept up customs that had been ancient when its northern cousin Acheron fell before the swords of the barbarian founders of the northern kingdoms, deep in the misty past.

The rest of the convoy was a long column of mule-drawn or ox-drawn wagons with canvas tilts and long coffles of slaves, each of about forty with the riveted metal collars on their necks linked together by iron chains. The men also had their hands clamped in ironwood manacles, and each coffle had a trio of drivers and overseers with short swords, clubs and whips.

Sukhmet was a collecting center for the slave trade, captives from Stygian raids and purchases from Darfar and the other southern kingdoms. The commerce was split about equally between exports to the north, to Stygia and Shem and even Koth and Argos, and the mines close by. Gold mines ate men, though there were a fair number of women in the coffles too. Valeria studied the stretch of stinking misery out of the corner of her eye, her expression grim.

"Plenty of slaves in the northern realms," he observed mildly, though mines there tended to use convicts instead.

"Not where I was raised," she said darkly. "Except a few rich men's servants."

She glanced at him. "No slaves in Cimmeria, either, from what I've heard."

Conan smiled grimly. "No. We kill our enemies in our blood feuds and nail their heads over the door or put them on a rack before a shrine. Or we sell them out of the country and let some ignorant foreigner get their throat slit in their sleep or their house burned down around their ears. There was a chief north of my clan's land who liked to keep his enemies around in chains. Not for work—for show. He blinded and gelded them first, and cut out their tongues."

She chuckled at that. "Safe enough then, I should think."

"No, when he came out to gloat, one of them tripped him and ripped his throat out with their teeth before the chief's men could drag him away. Heads are safer."

"I wouldn't buy you to hoe my turnips," she said, then murmured, "Other things, perhaps, but not that."

He gave no indication that he'd heard, then stood in the stirrups and shouted.

"Zarallo's—"

He stopped himself before he said *Zarallo's men*.

"—Free Companions!"

They all looked at him as whips cracked, oxen bellowed, mules brayed, and wheels began their eternal creaking. Though they wouldn't start to squeal like tortured pigs until the morning's dollop of grease dried away.

Conan chopped a hand forward and used the old mercenary's trail-call.

"To Hell or plunder, dog-brothers—march!"

5

They were still within the ring of settled country around Sukhmet at dawn the next day. Ox-wagons just weren't very fast, slower even than the trudging pace of the slaves. Each of whom carried a heavy basket on their backs or on their heads. The women were chained neck-and-neck but not manacled. All were loaded with the bags of meal that would feed them.

The weather was holding, with only a hint of ominous clouds on the western horizon. Valeria walked over from where her bedroll had been spread, with her saddle for a pillow and her horses hobbled nearby. Conan had donned his mail shirt and a cotton surcoat, she noted. Unlike the sentries outside Zarallo's headquarters, his was just a plain brown-green.

"It's time for that?"

"Aye," he said, making a sweeping gesture: "Take a look at the houses."

She did so as she returned to her own supplies and untied the leather thongs that held her rolled-up mesh vest. Outside Sukhmet there had been few villages, just a thick scattering of adobe cottages and the occasional courtyard-centered manor of a merchant or retired officer who'd decided to stay in the south and be a big fish in a small colonial pond.

Between them had been strips of plowland sprouting yams and millet, cotton and sorghum, vegetable patches with red, green, and yellow plants she couldn't name. There were weedy fallow and cropped grass pastures for goats, cattle, pigs, and the odd horse. Orchards of citrus, palm, and mango, and shea-butter trees and vines grew here and there where a stream could be damned to water them, or a shadoof lift stood beside a shallow well.

The further out they went, the more the peasant huts were gathered into clumps that presented a blank-walled outside to the world, with heavy wooden gates and room enough inside to corral the stock in an emergency. The manors didn't just *look* fortified; they were, and most had watchtowers rising thirty or forty feet high. All the Stygians in sight, even the peasants, carried bows or spears and had longer blades at their belts. This was unlike what she'd experienced in the valley of the Styx, up in Stygia proper, where common folk stopped and fell on their faces whenever soldiers went by.

"The native tribes raid the Stygian settlers here, sometimes," Conan said.

Valeria nodded, putting the information away. "Why do they settle here in the first place, then?"

"They're mostly paid-off soldiers or their children or grandchildren. A lot of them marry women from the local tribes, or buy slave girls and free them and marry them. Often they get a grant of land if they stay, with no tax for their lifetime and only half for their children. It's not the rich black dirt you see in the valley of the Styx and the crops are different, but they don't have to pay half their harvest to a landowner, either. Plenty think it's worth the risk."

"Would the natives go after a convoy with a strong escort?" she asked while settling her sword-belt back about her waist now that her mail was on.

He watched with clear interest the wiggling process necessary to don the armor. Conan had never seen a woman as unselfconsciously at home in her body as she was, she suspected. Or one as given to ignoring male glances. She had grown used to such behavior, though it still was irritating.

"I don't know," he said, "and when I don't know, I'll wear the mail and sweat. What I *do* know is that they may shoot arrows from ambush and run… which is another reason I'll wear the mail."

"An arrow through the brisket from behind a tree can ruin your whole day," Valeria agreed gravely.

In the early morning light they strode off toward the mercenary campfires where chickens bought from the locals were roasting. Each took a healthy portion, juggling them from hand to hand until they were cool enough to rip apart and get their teeth into. The appetizing smell made Conan ready for the day—that and the scent of horses and sweat, the rattle of gear and clang of iron and the bright stretch before them, laden with possibility.

He relied on his unit to take their example from him—skirmishers needed to be able to think for themselves. A genial cuff to the back of the head knocked down one man who'd decided he didn't yet need to gear up.

"Wear it and sweat in it and like it, Darcarus," Conan said cheerfully. "Crom knows you're not much use alive, but dead you'd just stink even worse."

The man shook his head as he rose, grinned, and obeyed. The armor wasn't heavy; skirmishers needed to be mobile, and not to overburden their horses when mounted. They checked their gear and that their canteens were full of the good spring-water from this campsite. Then Conan ordered them to fall in, and led them to the front of the column. He hadn't yet put his helmet on, but that was for practicality, to be able to see and hear better.

The Stygian commander was in his chariot and talking to a priest—shaven-headed and without the strip of chin-beard Stygian nobles cultivated, dressed in a black-dyed linen robe with a python-skin over one shoulder like a bandolier and carrying a long ebony staff with an alarmingly realistic bronze-and-gold cobra-head rearing at its top. The cleric was about Conan's age, gaunt in the manner of a man whose inner fires ate for and at him, his face like a starved vulture.

He glared with open hostility.

That turned to hatred, complete with a sneer, as his eyes lit on Valeria. Then he turned on his heel and walked away toward the open-topped two-wheel wagon he and his servant occupied. It had a staff standing up next to the seat. What flew from it wasn't a flag like those the Stygian military carried, triangular sections of cloth dangling point-down from a horizontal crosspiece. Instead it was a silk tube in the form of a serpent, mounted in a bronze ring atop the wood and sewn with a pattern of thin gold and silver scales.

A gust of hot wind coming from the south caught it and it hissed with alarming realism as it filled and writhed.

"What the demons was that about?" Valeria said with a growl. "I've never met the man before, but he looks like he'd be happy to see me flayed and salted."

"I don't know, but you'd best watch your back," Conan answered, "lest you wake to find a dagger in it."

The Stygian officer in his chariot, with his plumed bronze helm under one arm, finished off a chicken-leg. He tossed it aside for the big black ants that swarmed there. Then he licked his fingers and turned an unfriendly but not overtly hostile eye on Conan. Apart from a quick glance, he ignored Valeria completely.

"Yes, outlander?" His name was Akhenset, which meant "Strong for Set."

Conan saluted with right fist to chest. He needed the man's cooperation to perform the task Zarallo had entrusted to him, and Zarallo was his chosen war-chief, to whom he owed loyal service as long as he was with the Free Companions. As long as its captain kept up *his* end of the bargain. The Cimmerian had a craftsman's approach to war. This created an aversion to sloppiness or wasted effort.

"Sir," he said in Stygian, "we are scouts. To let us go ahead, please? Danger here, we find. Get shot at first."

The officer opened his mouth to speak, and Conan half expected him to say, *"No, go eat our dust in the rear, accursed demon-worshipping foreigner."* Then he paused, and visibly reconsidered when he thought of what it would look like if he was ambushed while his scouts trailed behind at his order. Then he nodded.

Good choice, Conan mused.

"Keep in touch," the commander said, amplifying the simple Stygian phrase with gestures. "Understand?"

"Yes, sir," Conan replied. "Must can tell you what we find, eh?"

"Good. Be off and get about it, devil worshipper."

When they were out of earshot, Valeria spoke in a low voice.

"Are all Stygian officers that arrogant?"

"No. Most are worse," Conan said. "Crom alone knows why." Then he added, "You'll work under my eye. Today and tomorrow, at least."

"Why?" she asked bluntly.

"Because I'm in charge of this detachment," he said with equal straightforwardness, "and I know the others but I haven't seen you work before. I know you can *fight*, woman—that I saw with my own eyes."

And I saw more of it than you know, he added to himself before he went on, remembering how she'd demolished the street-toughs and then skipped away over the rooftop. "I need to see how you work as part of a band. Whether you can take orders and do what's needful fast, and how good you are at using ground and spotting things on land, not sea. I don't want to find out when our lives are at stake."

Her lips firmed, but she nodded briskly. It was an honest answer, and he could see she appreciated that, rather than honeyed words or flattery.

The villages grew fewer, then ceased, and so did their plowed fields. There were cattle under the guard of armed herdsmen now, and one last small fort. Then only endless rolling grass, stirrup-high or higher, green with the recent start of the rains rather than its usual straw color.

Wherever they looked was a steady scatter of flat-topped thorny trees usually not more than twenty or thirty feet high, singly or in clumps or short lines where some underground feature watered their roots. Sometimes the termite-mounds were almost as tall, miniature steep cliffs twice the height of a man, made of red dirt packed together with their sticky extrusions.

Trees and brush grew thicker on the occasional rocky hill, often growing in cracks in cliffs of reddish stone. Troops of baboons swarmed in many of those, leaping and screeching as the humans passed, sending skyward flights of long-tailed, vividly colored birds.

"See those?" Conan said to Valeria.

"The baboons? Like big mean dogs, only smarter and with hands," she said. "Saw plenty on my way to Sukhmet, but I never saw one I liked much."

"They hate men, because farmers kill them whenever they can," Conan said. "But around here... about a day's journey further south, really... there's a flat-country type that's bigger."

"How much bigger?"

"Four feet at the shoulder," Conan said, and she made a small involuntary sound like *yeee*. "Heavier than I am, the weight of a small lioness, fast, and just as smart and mean. They hunt, and they do it in packs. Scarce, but bad news when you see them."

"Sounds interesting," she said stoutly.

The dirt road turned into a track, with only the occasional patch of wheel-rut to show that caravans came this way. Distant herds of game replaced the livestock, antelope of a dozen kinds from shin-high shy darters with miniature spike-horns, through bouncing-ball types that swarmed past like manic dancers, to calm-eyed eland bigger than cattle, towering giraffes in small groups or alone, and once the hulking menace of a rhinoceros. Word went back not to stare at it or make too much noise, since they charged at any provocation—or none—and could be as fast as a galloping horse for short distances.

Several times lions stood on hilltops or the edge of a belt of bush, watching as the caravan went by.

That one licked its chops, by Crom!

They approached a river, flanked by a wide belt of taller trees and thick brush. Conan sent a messenger back instructing the convoy to halt. He dismounted half his skirmishers and led the way, sword in hand, into the riverside brush while the others kept guard. Valeria accompanied him and blinked at how fast visibility closed in. The undergrowth was denser than in the forests of the Tauran hills where she would have hunted deer and wild boar. Conan ghosted through thickets that caught at her with thorns like barbed fishhooks, and could move in armor without the rustling, clinking sound that others would find inescapable.

"How do you do that?" she asked. "Be so quiet in war-harness?"

Conan shrugged. He'd been pleasantly surprised at how well she did in the thickets, and reminded himself that she hadn't grown to womanhood in a seaside town or fishing-village like so many sailors. Or stuck to the home-hearth all the time, weaving and kneading bread and keeping toddlers from falling into the fire.

"Practice," he said, "and wearing soft leather under it. My mail is wired to the backing every inch, up and down, and I keep it well-oiled." He added, "There'd be fewer dead men on the Cimmerian frontier and the Pictish marches if you folk weren't so loud. You're better than some of your breed, woman, but it still needs work."

Before she could respond, his head jerked up at a faint sound, and Valeria's an instant later. The tattooed Pict slid down a dangling liana from a branch not far ahead of them, agile and landing lightly.

"Cimmerians move like buffalo," he said, grinning through sweat and the devil-mask of his tattoos and making heavy stomping motions with his feet. "Aquilonians like a *herd* of buffalo, if buffalo are drunk." He added a stagger to the mime. "People further away even worse."

Conan scowled; the feud between his folk and the Picts was older than any recorded history and vanished into the mists of time and legend. He'd journeyed to the western marches of Cimmeria to fight in it, as had many youths in his homeland. By custom clans at generations-long blood feuds with each other still welcomed such volunteers. When compared to the fight with the Picts, the bitterest feud was just a falling-out among family.

Nevertheless, the man was useful, and thousands of miles of distance gave Conan a new perspective.

"Anything, Gahonre?" he asked the Pict.

"Man-sign, but old. Days." He held up his right hand—his black bow was in his left—with four fingers spread and the thumb folded down. "Little more, little less," he said, waggling the thumb to indicate a small difference. "Small fires, bare feet, few cooked bones, fish heads."

"Good," Conan grunted. "Go back and tell the Stygian commander we can march to the river and cross."

"Feathers-on-helmet in the little horse wagon?" Gahonre replied. "I go."

He trotted off, running in a tireless springy trot toward where his pony was tethered, wearing only a loincloth and a quiver of arrows and a belt bearing knives and a long-handled hatchet. Two colored feathers were stuck in his own braided black hair. As he did, more of the Free Companions caught up with them.

"This would be a good place for an ambush, wouldn't it?" Valeria said, looking around.

"Not bad," Conan agreed. "Best if you could catch the convoy halfway across the ford, but there's not much room near the trail in this riverside brush—it's too narrow. If you had too many men it would be easy to spot. From the way the birds and beasts fled or went quiet, if nothing else."

"Right. The point of an ambush is to swarm the ones you're attacking, fast, before they get their feet back under them."

He nodded and turned to the leader of the squad of Shemite horse-archers who'd halted at the edge of the brush.

"Zarkabaal, fan your men out on the other side."

"How far?" the Shemite asked, stroking his carefully curled beard.

"Long bowshot."

Then to his skirmishers. "Fan out on the other side, too, but close to the edge of the brush—ten yard intervals either side of the path. Yell out if you see anything, and if it looks like it walks on two legs, shoot fast. There aren't any friendlies hereabouts, don't worry about that."

Not that they would anyway, he thought as one tapped his crossbow and snorted quietly. Being hired men, they didn't much care about things like the Stygian government's standing with the locals. *We won't be back here, at least not until the return trip.*

The ford was a space about twenty yards wide where the banks were naturally low, and decades of passing convoys had broken them down further. They'd also thrown gravel and small rocks into the water, and the hundred yards between the banks sparkled with sun-bright blinks where the current broke over them. Since the rains were only starting, it wasn't very deep at this time of year, but every year the floods carved new channels or scoured out deep spots that could swallow a man whole.

The Shemites took the water at a fast walk, standing in the stirrups and holding their bows and quivers and their sheathed curved shamshir swords high as the water crested and broke on their horses' chests. Occasionally one would hit a deep spot and the horse would vanish save for its head and neck. Even then they kept their weapons dry.

Then one reached a hole and went off his horse with a shout of alarm. He might not have made it to shore if two of the others hadn't tossed him one of the ropes they kept coiled at their saddlebows. Reaching the edge of the river he sat aside and dried off his gear—cursing all the while and glowering at his comrades' gibes, even though they'd saved his life.

When the rest surged out of the river on the other side they broke into a canter, opening out until there was a hundred yards between each and four times that between them and the river. That put them along the crest of a low rise, and Zarkabaal turned in the saddle to carefully survey the area. After a long look and a bit of shouted consultation among his men, he gave an exaggerated wave.

"Here, give me a hand with this," Conan said to Valeria.

He took a long bundle of wrist-thick rope slung across the back of his remount and began knotting it around a tree at the water's edge on the downstream side of the ford. It was a straight tree as thick through as his waist and with huge roots buried deep in fractured rock.

Valeria responded without wasted words, taking the other end of the rope, heeling her horse across the water. For a brief moment he lost sight of her at the deepest point, but she came back into sight, climbed out of the water and halted beside a similar tree on the other bank.

"This?" she shouted with a broad gesture.

"Aye!" he bellowed back.

She ran a running loop around the tree and a one-way slipknot that let her hitch one end to the horn of her saddle. The beast backed up while she took in the slack with quick jerks of her other hand. The thick rope rose out of the water, little jets squeezing out of it as it came taut, and then when it could be tightened no further she did a quick clinching-knot.

Well, she's a sailor, Conan thought, with a slight nod to himself. She had to know rope in that trade, merchant *or* pirate, and how to work with someone else to manipulate it. Even a galley had a lot of rigging, and the deep-sea three-masters the Barachans used had miles of the stuff.

Sending his own horse across the stream, he saw for himself how deep it got—concerning but manageable as long as they were wary. That was one reason convoys went out before the rains began; some idiot must have blundered. Joining her on the other bank he looked over her work from the saddle and gave a few testing tugs while she sat on a rock and poured the water out of her sea-boots.

"Solid," he said approvingly, and he ignored the glare she shot him. "That'll help keep the carts from getting lost if they start to float downstream. They can bump against it while they're hauled to the south shore. Plenty of men, plenty of beasts to do the pulling."

"Float?" she said. "As laden as they are?"

He shook his head. "They'd bog down if we took them over laden, or tip over if they hit a hole or a boulder and spill everything. The Stygians will have the slaves cart most of it over and pile it up, or put it across the mules' backs, then reload on the other side. They'll only use the strong ones, since they need to hold whatever they're carrying over their heads."

"Moving like greased lightning, aren't we?" she snorted, obviously thinking of how long that would all take.

"Oh, this is the easy part of the journey."

Conan kept the skirmishers fanned out for the whole of the crossing. This meant that the Stygians had to do all the heavy lifting, a fact that gave him a warm satisfaction. This wasn't going to make their employers love the mercenaries any more than they had before, something that left Conan profoundly unmoved.

He napped beneath a tree with a hat over his face, but rose when the slaves were unshackled to carry the barrels and bales and bundles and sacks across the ford. He had ordered the deep spots marked with poles, but the way was still treacherous.

The Stygian commander must have been thinking along

the same lines. His hundred-odd infantry spearmen were tallying on lines, ready to help drag the wagons over, and his lancers were on picket duty along a wide-thrown perimeter, but the Nubakan archers he had standing by with arrows on their strings, in two equal parties on each side.

The archers answered to their own commander and two lesser officers who were marked by bursts of ostrich feathers tucked into their matts of frizzy hair. Every few minutes they plucked up handfuls of grass and tossed them into the air, a practical way of keeping them all conscious of what the air was doing.

Despite the risk, one of the slaves made a break for it as soon as the chain was pulled through the loop on his iron collar and the shackles on his wrists removed, springing forward and buffeting aside an overseer. The man was tall, long-legged, and well-muscled, and he jinked agilely from side to side as he sprinted for the bush. The others in the coffle began to move uneasily, darting glances to either side.

That was a problem with sending men to a certain, prolonged, and agonizing death in the mines, Conan thought silently, watching the drama unfold. They really didn't have much reason *not* to try any desperate ploy, no matter how futile.

One of the plumed officers shouted.

Two archers rose and stepped forward from their squatting ranks.

They moved without any particular haste, and the first drew his long shaft past the angle of his jaw, muscles knotting in his arms and writhing beneath the ebony skin of his broad shoulders. The arrow flew the thirty yards in a flat blurred streak and lanced through the fleeing slave's calf.

Valeria's face registered surprise. "I'd think they were better shots than that," she said. "Rumor has it they hunt elephants with those bows."

"They do," Conan said, keeping disgust out of his voice. They had to kill the man, if only to keep the others under control, but there was no reason to toy with him. "Watch for a bit."

The slave struggled to his feet and went on in a hobbling parody of his original swift speed. Then the second archer's bow snapped, and the arrow skewered the slave's *other* calf. He went over with a shriek.

"Oh," she said with a grimace.

"That's it," Conan said.

"Making an example?"

"That and having some fun. They're bored, too."

The slave managed to get to his feet again, though with loud whimpers of pain and biting his lip until blood flowed to mix with the sweat and drool on his chin. This time the Nubakan archers drew and shot with smooth speed, so that four arrows were in the air at the same time. Conan heard the wet thumping *thack* of the impacts, one after another, sound treading on sound. Two plunged into the fugitive's hipbones and two more went through his shoulders, making him flex like a branch in a high wind before he pitched forward and lay jerking and moaning on the riverbank.

Tall plants with flowers of red and blue waved over his prostrate form, cruelly bright.

Two of the Stygian overseers ran forward and dragged him back by his wrists, his eyes white and rolled upward in his contorted face. The archers strolled over, wrenched their shafts free, and watched with idle interest as the slave drivers sank wooden hooks into his armpits, threw ropes over a branch, and hoisted him up to swing there, bleeding and moaning.

There was the flap of large wings as curious vultures gathered, along with a flock of something like carrion crows with raven beaks and white markings from shoulders to breast interrupting the black. When the humans stepped back they closed in, squabbling among themselves.

A long shriek split the air.

Crows always go for the eyes first, Conan thought. *Juicy, I suppose.*

The work proceeded. Cargos were piled up on the dry ground on the south side of the river, the ox and mule-teams brought over, and then the hundred spearmen hauled each wagon across, before the whole caravan was reassembled and the convoy set out once more.

"Well, this is more fun than watching mud dry," Valeria muttered.

"Or watching the horizon for a ship that never appears," Conan said, speaking from piratical experience.

"No, that's better," Valeria said. "You may not get a fight and a rich prize, but you can always *expect* one. If not that day, then the next. Or a warship, and some danger to spice up the season."

"Don't worry," he said. "There's danger here and a dozen different kinds of it. You just haven't met them yet." He looked up at the sun. There was little variation between the seasons in the time of sunset here. It was something he'd found disconcerting at first.

It was well into winter back home. The sun would appear late, make a brief arc across the southern horizon, and then sink out of sight… and that was assuming the day hadn't been occupied by a black blizzard.

"Just the right time to hunt deer, back in the Tauran," Valeria said. "We'd have the wheat threshed and in the bins by now. The deer aren't skinny yet, and they gang up in places where they've trampled the snow down. Any venison we got, we could pull it back on sleds and put in the cold-pantry, and it kept fine till spring. Or wild pig, nice and fat with the fall acorns. My mother used to mince both, mix the meat with spices and salt and chopped onions and bake it into lots of little pies about the size of your fist—"

She gave a glance at his hand where it rested on the pommel of his saddle.

"—well, of *my* fist, and we'd put them in the cold pantry, too. Just take one out when you wanted it and put it on a plate in the kitchen hearth near the embers, and come back when hot gravy's bubbling out of the holes in the top of the crust. Just the thing to sit down to with a pot of mulled ale, when it's snowing outside."

Despite the heat of the day. Conan almost groaned at the thought—though for him it included a naked blond woman sitting on his lap as he tilted a mug of the hot drink and the shutters rattled with the storm.

Still…

"We may have some sport today, if we're lucky. I got the idea from how the Kozaki hunt wild aurochs near the south shore of the Vilayet Sea. Meat goes off fast here, but there are plenty of mouths."

Conan saluted and wheeled his horse about.

6

"Aye, hunt if you will," Akhenset said. "Once we've reached our campsite for the day."

Conan followed his thoughts. The noisy passage of the convoy moved most of the game frustratingly out of reach. Yet the Stygian didn't dare let his Nubakan archers disperse to forage for fear of guerilla attack or slave escapes or even an uprising while his forces were scattered.

Moving more than five hundred mouths across this much distance was a pain in the fundament, much like carrying a chunk of ice in hot weather, but it was the food stocks that melted. Only the abundant grazing made it possible at all.

Thus, if Conan's troop brought in meat, all the better. If they didn't, the blame and shame would be on them. In either case they took all the risks, and if something went very wrong… well, dead mercenaries didn't draw pay.

Conan saluted and wheeled his horse about, moved a ways off, and then gathered his skirmishers.

"We've got Akhen's permission—"

There was a wave of snickers as Valeria made a vulgar pun on the man's name.

"—to hunt." Several started to move, and he shouted, "Hold!"

Half the troop were ready to explode in a dozen directions, with game visible all round and men driven to distraction by the monotony.

"You fools, if we scatter, *so do our kills.*"

Gahonre the Pict muttered something in his own language. Probably something on the order of, "*you buffalo will spook the game—better I go on my own.*"

Conan gave them all a hard look.

"This isn't like hunting in a forest, *especially* by yourself." He singled out the Pict. "This is grassland, and your prey will be large. If you go by ones and twos, even if you make a kill you'll spend most of the time before dark getting each carcass back, most likely fighting off lions, leopards, hyenas, and baboons. Or native skulkers pleased to catch us unawares. Remember, it isn't our home range."

Gahonre was looking thoughtful.

Pict or no, he was nobody's fool.

"If we go in force," one of the men said, "won't that many horses and men together spook 'em, too?"

"Not if we do it right," Conan replied. "I've hunted on horseback before this in big open grassland. First we ride in column southeastward. Looks like there's plenty of game in that direction, and it's where we're going." The Shemites, who came from dry grassland country themselves, nodded as he went on.

"The game will just move aside to let us pass—they see men go by every month or so, always on this track. Then, on my signal—"

An hour later, a mob of grass-eaters fled in front of Conan's party, sending up a choking cloud of dust that dropped and thickened to a coat of thin mud when mixed with the hunters' sweat, and made their horses look like earth statues. Then the creatures stopped. Zarallo's skirmishers had moved as a column, then spread out into a sickle-shaped line and turned north again toward the Stygian convoy, whooping and bellowing and pushing ahead of them any animals caught unawares.

Now the mass of beasts—by this time numbering in the hundreds—saw and scented the Stygian camp. The alarming smell of woodsmoke, coupled with as many humans as would populate a small town, brought the beasts up short. All they could do was mill about in confusion.

The first in sight were the line of Stygian lancers on picket duty, but there were clumps of Nubakan archers among them, and the whole camp would be buzzing with the word.

"Go! Go! Go!" Conan shouted.

Fresh whoops rose and, from the Shemites, loud invocations to Ishtar the huntress, one of the many faces of that versatile deity. She had plenty of worshippers in Stygia, too. The lancers heeled their mounts into a loping hand-gallop, and Conan let his knotted reins fall on the horse's neck, giving it the heel again when it took that for a signal to halt.

Caught between two fears, the mass of animals, mostly leaf-eaters, whipped themselves into a panic. Conan leaned to one side and pressed a knee to loop his mount around a knot of savannah buffalo—enormous black creatures with horns that started thick in a great cob of wrinkled bone over their foreheads and then curved up into wicked points. Sometimes that breed attacked lions on impulse, and would wait around for a day or more, bent on trampling and goring. Anyone who wanted to tackle *those* was welcome to them.

One of the skirmishers didn't know the stories, or hadn't believed them. He ventured too close. Suddenly a head went down and a tail up, and the beast charged.

"Get out of the way you—"

He'd been going to say "fool." The man proved that he was one by halting to aim his crossbow, realizing at the last moment that it was far too late. The bolt from the crossbow banged off the boss of bone across the beast's forehead even as it made impact.

The horse went over with a scream. The man hit the ground rolling and tried to run. He might as well have been standing still when the ton-weight of enraged animal struck, tossing him high and then goring him with a curve-tipped horn that went under his ribs like a pike point.

Another toss and the man's body struck the ground like a broken doll.

Nobody else dared to come close to the buffalo after that.

The meat of the grown ones was shoe-sole tough anyway.

Conan headed for a knot of eland, big handsome beasts with long spiral horns, dewlaps, and huge meaty bodies fawn-colored above and white below. Some would yield as much as a third of a ton of meat, and he'd hunted them several times since he arrived in Sukhmet. They tasted very much like beef—very good beef. Just then they were making good speed, eyes bulging in panic, their horns laid to the rear along their backs.

At twenty yards he stood in the stirrups, using the flexing of his knees to even out the movements of the horse beneath him. Lifting his bow he drew to the ear and loosed.

The powerful war-bow had a draw of more than a hundred pounds, much more than was needed for ordinary hunting. Most of the arrows in his quiver were broad-heads, razor-edged triangles more deadly against unarmored foes than the narrow bodkins designed to punch through mail and—by a fortunate non-coincidence—just right for hunting. Men or beasts, bodies were bodies and blood was blood.

The arrow flashed out in a blurred flat arc. It hit the big eland bull behind the shoulder with a flat wet *thwack* sound and blood shot out in a fan from both its gasping nostrils, once and twice and again before it collapsed.

His next shot wasn't as good—as he'd told Valeria, he was no Turanian, no horse-archer born to saddle and bow. Every tribe of steppe nomads did this sort of hunt three or four times per summer, as training for war as well as for meat and horn and hides. But the arrow did take another eland through the paunch, and crippling was as good as killing just then, even if it offended his sense of workmanship.

True to his word, mass hunting in open country like this was different from stalking game one by one in the woods. They could double back and finish off the wounded at leisure, or the men from the camp could do it.

Reminded of the pirate woman, he glanced around. She wasn't far away; on the other side of the clump of eland, in fact. He couldn't hear her over the sound of many hundreds of hooves and the excited screams of a mob that included wild horses—odd-looking ones with black-and-white stripes and bristly manes like a Pictish haircut. Her mouth was stretched wide in an exultant shout as she rode close enough to shoot one-handed with her crossbow. An eland went down with the bolt in its left foreleg, and that was another heavy load of meat. Then she slung the weapon; it was too awkward to reload on horseback, much less at a gallop.

Instead she drew her sword, plunging it through another animal's spine and leaving it crippled. Someone had been listening to his little talk on the workings of a mass hunt. The Shemites were killing with a will, emptying their quivers and the extras they'd slung over the saddle. They had been *born* to the saddle and the bow, being recruited on the edges between the desert and the sown up north of Stygia.

The northern riders were mostly emulating Valeria's hocking draw-cuts and stabs with their swords.

Conan finished the last of the forty arrows in his quiver and started to draw his own longsword, when suddenly there was nothing in front of him but a spray of mounted Stygians, work details, and carts from the camp. The lancers were stabbing everything they could reach, and the Nubakans were loosing arrows fast, and with a fine disregard for Zarallo's skirmishers.

"*Hold up!*" Conan bellowed. "Hold up, Crom curse you, don't ride into bowshot of those Nubakan bastards!" Nevertheless, one of them already shot an incautious Stygian's mount in the rump. It threw the rider to the hard ground, where he lay groaning as it bucked and jumped. The Nubakans grinned and nudged one another as they watched.

Conan turned in the saddle and looked back. Scores of dead animals were scattered in their wake, and more were limping about, helpless as the hunters returned to finish them off. Even the slaves would have meat with their swill tonight, albeit it would be tripe and brains cooked into the porridge.

He thought about joining in killing the wounded beasts, but the rest seemed to have it well in hand. Instead he made sure that his hunters got the choice cuts to carry back to their fires, not something he could count on in a large mixed band like this. By custom in every nation it was the right of the ones who corralled and took the game. Even the most boastful Stygians knew to respect those who would stand at their backs in a fight. These were his followers—Zarallo had placed him in charge, and that made him responsible for their rights.

Valeria led two mules straining against the dead weight of big bucks slung over their backs. Conan had stripped to his loincloth, was liberally bedaubed with blood, and tossed a nicely plump eland liver onto a stretch of rawhide just stripped off the same beast. Certain she must be appreciating his long, muscled form, he hid his smile and nodded toward the pile of organ-meat.

"The best part."

"If it's fresh and roasted on a fire before it can go bad," she replied. "Mind you, chops and roasts and steaks are fine, too—almost anything is, when compared to biscuit and jerky."

"That they are," he agreed, silently considering other things that made life worth living. His task completed, he headed over to a spring just outside camp to sluice down. This was a regular stop for any convoys destined for the mines, and the stream had been blocked by a crude earth-and-rock dam to make a pond where buckets could be filled. The spot for washing was downstream of that, and the stock watered further along.

The camp that night was more festive than most, with the scent of roasting meat and the hissing and spitting of drops of fat falling on the embers of dozens of cookfires. Everyone was able to gorge their fill. The Stygian commander had the sense to break out more beer than usual, and in return Conan sent him a gift of prime livers.

A collection of bones grew around him as he leaned against his saddle and ate, a pot of the beer standing beside him. Across from him Valeria was doing the same, though she was working on a long skewer with chunks of liver, mixed with bits of onion and fat. Cimmerian game meat was very lean, and the beasts here weren't any different.

He threw the bone into the fire and leaned back on one elbow.

"Good sport I promised, eh?" he said casually.

She swallowed and wiped her lips on a twist of grass before she threw it into the fire.

"Good sport indeed," she replied. "Not like anything I've had before, though hunting boar is most like it."

Boar hunting was done in groups, with nets and dogs, because wild pig traveled in groups. It could be suicide to face a half-dozen black bristly masses of gristle and hide bigger and heavier than the hunter, with tusks like curved knives.

"Hunting from a galloping horse..." she continued. "That's new."

"Sport's good, in its place," he said. Then he caught her eye and with a flick of his eyes looked out toward the darkness.

She laughed.

Conan felt a moment's surprise, and he fought down a scowl. For a single instant he felt for Khafset, before his mind revolted at it.

"I'm among the few free women in this camp," she said in a not unkindly tone, "and the only unattached one if you consider the camp followers and some of the Stygian soldiers' wives." She kept the words quiet enough that they were drowned by the laughter, the mercenaries' hideous attempts at song, and the remarkably good singing and stamping dance of the Nubakans.

She was right. The only other women in camp were in the slave coffles, and the slave overseers sold time with them for a few coppers. Conan had never considered that; he didn't find imprisoned, unwilling women arousing.

"D'you take me for a fool, Cimmerian?" she continued. "To have every man in camp deciding he deserves seconds?"

Now he did scowl. He rose and strode away, though he didn't seek the slave women. Instead he borrowed an axe and spent an hour reducing tough thornwood to kindling.

7

"Where's that priest?"

Conan leaned forward with his hands on the pommel of his saddle. It had been five days since the hunt. Several hours out from Wedi Shebelli, they'd been met by the mine garrison's own scouts, riding on horseback, then escorted back along a path that almost might be considered a dirt road. Several large boulders had been visibly rolled out of the way.

Valeria pulled her horse over to ride beside him. She leaned close so that they could speak without being overheard.

"I don't know," she said, "but I found something where his wagon was camped last night, with a dead beast beside it. It was like an oversized rat with a squashed-in face."

He grunted as she showed him something in her palm. It was a charm, made in the Stygian fashion. A miniature woven woman's form, with one of Valeria's distinctive blond hairs wound around its head, and the hands and feet bound. A long thorn had been driven through its body, too.

"That's a death fetish," he said. "Illness, foul luck too... making you slow when you need speed."

"Thought so," she said, "though I wasn't sure." She

plucked the hair free, cut the bonds on the little figurine and then shredded it.

"Why would the priest have anything against you?" he said.

"I'm not Stygian, and I'm a woman," she said, and Conan shook his head in bewilderment.

"Maybe Khafset put him up to it," the Cimmerian said after a moment. "He has reason to hate you, and these priests of Set are mostly nobles, too. They might even be related."

"Pity if something happened to him," she said grimly.

"Be careful about that," he warned. "If they find out you tried to hurt a priest of Set, they'll flay you and salt you and then try to think up something *really* nasty. Fall in—and let me know if you see him again."

The path stuck to the ridges in this bit of rolling savannah, winding to avoid going down into the more densely wooded bottoms. He turned in the saddle and called to the other scouts.

"Anyone seen the priest?"

"Priest?" several voices replied.

"That priest of Set who started out with us," he said. "I can't recall seeing him lately, or his wagon. The one stationed here should come out and greet the new one, part of the handover ceremonies for the garrison."

The skirmishers looked at each other and shrugged. Valeria frowned and nodded. The priest's absence was a mystery, and Conan didn't like mysteries. They had a way of coming back and biting him on the arse when he least expected it.

When they arrived, more of the garrison turned out, lining the entranceway. The troops who'd be departing in two days' time looked as notably cheerful as the new arrivals were glum, many of them smiling and nudging each other when their underofficers weren't looking. With a regular *thump* of feet in hobnail sandals, the relief troops from the north marched behind Akhenset. The Stygian commander rode like a statue in the polished splendor of his chariot, to the rhythm of the drums and the occasional bray of a tall trumpet.

Conan caught several of his men looking the place over, catching one another's eyes and snorting quietly, as if to say they'd be just as displeased if they were going to be stuck here. Compared to a place like this, Sukhmet started to look like Tarantia or Shadizar.

The community lay at the base of a range of rocky hills—ones that had been forested before the woodcutters set to harvesting them for fuel. They were increasingly covered in low thorn-bush. Here and there lines of white glinted where the underlying quartz showed through the gray-brown-green covering. Those streaks sparkled like jewels where water tumbled down the bare white rock and the sun struck wet crystal.

It was pretty, in an eerie alien way.

The settlement at foot of the hills was not. While it had a depressing similarity to Sukhmet, unlike the mud-built or rammed-earth construction of that town the mine's buildings were mostly of mortared stone or rubble. There were a couple of inns that made the Claw and Fang Tavern look like a palace.

"This place looks like it was built... and kept up... by idiots who didn't give a damn," Valeria muttered.

"Built by slaves, and the people overseeing them are the

chamber-pot scrapings of the Stygians," Conan said. "Even those are counting the days until they leave."

There was a wall all around, about twice man-height tall, formed from stones of irregular size and shape rough-mortared with clay, and a wooden fighting platform behind that. Laughable in comparison with fortifications in the cities of the civilized world. Once they were through the gates—wooden and clumsy yet very strong—there was a large ring of trampled bare dirt and a set of compounds.

One group of buildings might have been a mirror-image in half scale of the much-loathed home base of Zarallo's mercenaries in Sukhmet. That would be where the garrison was to be quartered. A mansion of sorts, for the governor of the settlement; several smaller houses for supervisors and bureaucrats, rows of huts for the overseers, skilled workers, and those who served at their beck and call.

Just visible, the mine-entrance was at the furthest point uphill, a dark arched hole in the side of the incline, glinting white in the afternoon sun because it had been cut into a formation rich in gold-bearing quartz. Right below it were a dozen long, low barracks buildings for the slaves, half-sunk into the ground and thick-walled with wooden watchtowers over the single entrance. Even at a distance, the smell of human squalor could be detected.

Everything was drab, smut-marked by the charcoal fumes that poured from a low-slung smelter with its tall chimney. There were huge wickerwork baskets of charred wood fuel stacked near it, covered by a thatch roof on a tall network of poles.

The only splash of color was the temple of Set. It wasn't very large, a square stone box covered in painted stucco, but it had a row of the typical bottom-to-top tapering square pillars at its front, and a tall black-basalt statue stood on a platform before the columns, showing the slimly muscular figure of a kilted man. He was taking one stiff step with a sandaled left foot, hands raised, holding a crook-headed staff and a severed human head hanging by its hair. Almost certainly it was meant to represent a northerner's head.

An altar of the same inky stone stood in front, blocky and carved in low-relief, with statues of squid-headed humanoid figures stationed at the corners. Censers smoldered at each end; trails of rotting black blood traced a path from a central depression to gutters that ran into the mouths of the squid-men. The blood swarmed with huge black flies.

The walls beneath the flat roof showed blazingly colored patterns telling stories in a mixture of stylized murals and the odd-looking pictographic Stygian script. Many of the stories focused on snakes, or things that were part snake, or things that were just *things*, more often than not eating human being or doing things less identifiable but just as unpleasant.

Tree-tall flagpoles at the corners of the temple lofted giant serpent shapes, inflating and hissing in the hot breeze.

Instead of a man's visage, the rearing head of a cobra, its hood spread, rose between the statue's shoulders. Gold-and-ruby eyes glaring down on the entire settlement, the sculpted stone showing the linen headdress of a Stygian aristocrat on its narrow skull, and the twin tails on its breast.

The smell of incense and old blood, and a somehow metallic-organic impression from the temple were strong even amid the hard stink of the nearby slave barracks.

"Crom smite me dead," Conan said to himself. Beside

the altar, surrounded by lesser clerics and flunkies, stood none other than the starved-looking priest he'd seen talking to Akhenset at the beginning of their journey.

"He must have somehow gone on ahead… but why?" He turned to Valeria. "From the look he gave you, he near broke out in hives at just being close."

"Maybe he doesn't like Mitra-worshipping northerners?" she suggested, tossing her head. With her helm across the saddlebow, her tawny mane whipped from side to side.

"Stygians don't like outsiders, true," Conan agreed, "but it's been three thousand years since your ancestors threw down Acheron and sacked the temple of Set in Python. Besides, there's a dozen others from those countries in this detachment."

"Maybe he doesn't like northern *women*?"

"He'll be an unusual Stygian, then."

That brought chuckles. The slave-trade ran in both directions, and blond females fetched high prices in Shem and Stygia both. "Anyway, a week's travel alone through hostile country in a mule-cart, just to avoid seeing one head of tawny hair…?"

"It's probably not as risky for him," Valeria said. "He's a high priest of Set… which means he's a magician."

Conan swore and made a gesture with his hand—not one begging help of Crom, for that bleak deity gave no aid. It was a prayer for the strength to fight a threat on his own. *Sometimes* Crom gave that. Several of the other skirmishers looked uneasy too. Set was hated in the northlands, but to his followers he gave riches—and great power.

Power that could kill you, and worse.

Everyone knew that.

The outgoing commander of the mine garrison waited in *his* chariot for Akhenset to approach. He was very similar in looks and attire, except that he was a decade or so older and looked as if eating and drinking had been his defenses against the boredom and misery of this posting. His hawk nose was lost in a pudgy mass, with dark circles under his bloodshot eyes. Akhenset drew up alongside and the two Stygian leaders clasped forearms. The fat officer ceremoniously presented his replacement with a bronze-handled mace carved in serpent-scale patterns.

All the troops cheered dutifully as Akhenset turned his chariot and flourished the weapon above his head, a symbol of the power of life and death he would wield at the mine-compound and its surroundings. As he did, his troops chanted.

"Hail to the most noble, O Akhenset, favored of emperor and god."

"May this mace smite the enemies of Set!" he responded.

Conan suppressed a laugh as his own followers joined in the cheers, brandishing their blades aloft and speaking in their native languages. He understood some, and heard their "supplications."

"Up yours, least noble, O Akhen-snake-screwer!"

Valeria chimed in with enthusiasm, and gave scatological advice with a broad grin as she waved her sword.

"May your mace bugger you well!"

Conan thrust his own heavier blade skyward. "Crom give you what you deserve!" he bellowed. It was nicely ambiguous, and very unlikely that anyone within a thousand miles could speak Cimmerian.

The departing officer looked noticeably happier as his

driver turned the chariot back to his own forces. Those were carrying their field-gear on their backs, while their baggage-carts, families, and camp-followers were all waiting on the south side of the open space—it would be an exaggeration to call it a square. Some of them started to leave the instant the hand-over was official, sidling slowly along the wall to avoid attracting attention, then hurrying through the gate and out of sight.

The priest of Set stood by the altar and gestured imperiously, both hands in the air.

Overseers prodded a coffle of slaves forward toward him, ones brought from the half-cave kennels where they were kept. Conan blinked slightly at the sight of them, simply because he wouldn't have thought wretches that thin could walk. They were caked in filth, with weeping sores around their shackles and elsewhere, some with fever-bright eyes and others with consumptive coughs. This was the reason they'd come south with hundreds of replacements.

These wretches were about to serve one last purpose.

Sounds came from behind, and Conan looked over his left shoulder. The incoming coffles had been herded up to the northwestern part of the open space, close to the mouth of the mine. They were squatting there.

Under minimal guard.

That's asking for trouble, Conan thought. *I wouldn't have them here at all, especially if the priest is going to do what I think he's going to do.*

The chain that linked the sacrifices by the collar was unlocked and withdrawn. The slave drivers' whips cracked on backs thick with off-white scars. As they saw their destination, the doomed men and women flinched back, some staggering and gripping each other, but the high priest stepped forward himself and locked eyes with the foremost.

He began chanting.

Murmurs rose from the Free Companions and some of the newly arrived slaves. Conan was too far distant to entirely make out the priest's words, but somehow it didn't sound like ordinary Stygian, or like any language he'd ever heard—and he'd run into scores of them. He strained his wilderness-bred ears to catch something.

"… y'mg shggath, ur-coei, *teliki*…"

The lead slave's face went blank and he stood erect, stepping forward almost briskly. The priest of Set smiled. Conan snarled at the sight, and several of his men began murmuring prayers as they looked aside. Valeria watched gravely and her face was white, especially around the lips. Some of this magic had been directed at her, through the little image crowned with a hair from her head.

Four muscular acolytes in black kilts seized the slave by wrists and ankles and spread-eagled him across the altar. Lesser priests shook the frames of their sistrums, and metal clattered on metal with a discordant hint of harmonies that normal men didn't want to hear.

"Io, Setesh! Setesh! *Setesh!*" the high priest shouted.

"*Io, Setesh!*" the Stygian crowd shouted back, wiggling their heads back and forth.

Like snakes, Conan thought. For a moment he could have sworn that he saw something behind the altar—a burning plain, a moon set in a lake of liquid obsidian before the cyclopean towers of a city…

He shook his head violently and the image vanished like the shadow of a dream-memory. He focused again as the high priest drew a curved dagger and struck, swiftly and with skill. The slave shrieked, returned to himself for an instant, then the sound ended in a gurgle. Two more strokes, then the priest's free hand shot into the gaping hole the knife had opened. When he withdrew it, he was holding up a heart, hand stretched up toward the statue.

Still it beat, once, twice, three times.

The priest flung his arms wide and screamed another clotted set of syllables. Conan's vision blurred again, and for an instant he could have sworn that the squid-faced stone monstrosities at the corners of the altar turned their heads.

"*Lir and Manannán mac Lir!*" Conan swore.

Two deities of rivers and streams, more given to helping humans directly than mighty, distant Crom. The Cimmerian shivered. He didn't consider himself a reckless man, and there were few men or beasts he feared. Things of the otherworld were a different matter.

The body was tumbled off the altar and down the steps. Conan had heard that in parts of Stygia the hierophants feasted on the bodies of the sacrifices. He didn't know if that was true, or the sort of lurid story people loved to whisper in corners. What he *did* know was that even if he had favored cannibalism, he wouldn't have wanted to eat that particular body.

The acolytes seized another slave and the ritual began again. As the sacrifice screeched, Conan thought he heard other screams, coming from behind. He tore his eyes from the grisly spectacle.

PART TWO

REBELLION AT
WEDI SHEBELLI

8

 One of the overseers had turned his back on the replacement slaves, staring with flushed face and open mouth at the grim drama of blood and sacrifice taking place beneath the towering statue. Two large slaves had crept closer to him, waiting for their moment—and then they leapt, looping the chain that linked their iron collars around the man's neck.

A look of astonishment gave way to bulging-eyed horror. All he could do was gurgle wordlessly, then he died in a matter of seconds.

Conan's eyes narrowed at what happened next. The other slaves in the coffles clawed at the overseers closest to them, and the two who'd killed the first snatched a hatchet and shortsword from the dead man. They laid the chain stretched over a rock, drawing it taut. A man from the next coffle over seized the weapons and struck a succession of hard blows. The soft wrought iron bent, spread, and snapped. Then the man cast down his own chain and the first two repeated the process.

A single break in the chain freed a whole coffle of forty men—a weakness in the design, Conan realized. Within seconds both coffles had thrown themselves on the nearest

Stygians, and the process went rippling through the entire mass of five hundred men and women.

The shrieks of the dying Stygians were lost in the killing roar of the rebels.

More of the freed slaves went running upslope, away from the temple, carrying weapons in their hands. Not to flee, he thought, but heading for the slave barracks where two thousand others were held.

They had a plan, Conan thought. *Every Set-damned Stygian fighting man is here in the square, in front of the temple, with their packs on their backs and their gear and womenfolk back in the carts.*

"Dog-brothers!" he shouted, sweeping out his sword and using it to point. Still mounted, most of Zarallo's detachment had been staring in revolted fascination at the sacrifices. Some had been deliberately looking down at the ground instead. Now they jumped, as if he'd thrown cold water in their faces. Several blanched.

Conan thought swiftly.

"Zarkabaal, there's no room to fight here," he said. "Get your men down to the gate."

The Shemite understood instantly, nodded curtly, and called to his troop. They turned their mounts and moved off as quickly as they could, shouting. Their commander spoke fair Stygian, Conan knew, and most of his men could manage simple sentences. They whacked at cart-drivers and their teams, using bowstaves and riding-crops

A stream of carts—civilians, and some of the garrison—began bolting through the open gate.

Hundreds of slave rebels swarmed the temple of Set. The statue looked down in reptilian indifference as the acolytes were slaughtered. Conan spared a fractional instant to hope that the high priest had been, as well.

The same massed charge hit the two Stygian commanders in their chariots. Akhenset had sense enough to try to wheel his war-car back toward the ranks of his troops, but the wave of slaves was preceded by a cloud of flung rocks, picked up from the arid ground. Just as the two-horse team moved from a walk to a trot and began to wheel, one stone smacked into the Stygian's face in a splash of red and flipped him backward to the ground.

The horses stopped and screamed, rearing and lashing out with their hooves, but many hands clutched at their harness. The slaves tore the half-naked driver from the car in a clutching frenzy that ripped out hanks of his hair even before he disappeared into the chaos of sweat-soaked limbs.

Where Akhenset had landed there was only a circle of naked bodies, feet stamping and rocks pounding down. The fat Stygian in the other chariot had time for two or three full-armed slashes with his *kopesh* sword before he and his driver met the same fate.

"Follow me!" Conan shouted, heeling his horse sharply. The overrunning of the temple had given the mercenary skirmishers a crucial few seconds to set themselves. Conan cut downward at a wild-eyed figure grabbing for his rein. To his left Valeria's sword swung with scalpel precision.

Then they were past the front of the Stygian lancers. Overhead flights of arrows whistled past and landed among the slaves, making them recoil—the Nubakans had been taken by surprise, but with each cry from their officers, they responded like warriors, fanning out in front of the gate and shooting in volleys. A few of their number ran for the supply wagons, grabbing armfuls of bundled arrows.

The Stygian horsemen ignored the mercenaries. The young man who commanded them was a relation of Akhenset, Conan remembered. He drew his sword and cried out.

"Follow me!"

With that the young soldier booted his horse into motion. The forty lancers behind him did likewise, bringing their round shields around on their left arms and lowering the steel-tipped spears.

"Don't!" Conan shouted, but it was too late.

The Nubakan archers stopped shooting as the Stygians blocked their field of fire. The lancers had barely enough time to get up to a trot; big horses carrying men in scale armor could be fast, but they needed at least a clear hundred yards or so to get up to speed. Here they didn't have it.

In the first instant, the lancers still killed a fair number of slaves—naked bodies were terribly vulnerable to mounted men who knew what they were doing. Most of the lances were left in the bodies they struck, so the riders drew swords and lashed out as they drove forward. But the speed of the attack slowed... slowed... and then stopped. Though each armored man was vastly superior to a naked slave, soon their horses were bucking as knives and rocks and teeth and fists gouged into flesh.

The first riders went down soon after that.

There was a heaving as bodies buried them.

At least this gives us a little more time, Conan thought as the rest of the frenzied mob converged on the fight. Then he heard the sound of splintering wood.

Looking up, he watched as one of the skeletal guard towers

toppled. Soon thousands of desperate rebels would be here, and once they were out they'd stop to smash open the huts that held their working tools. This would give them shovels and picks and rock-breaking hammers. Conan knew the inevitable when he saw it.

"Too many!" he shouted in Stygian to the leader of the archers. "Too close!"

The Nubakan leader had patterned scars on his forehead and gray in his tuft of a beard. The black eyes framed by the headdress made from the mane of a lion were cold and unafraid as he looked up to the Cimmerian's mounted figure.

"Get out, stop, shoot in the gate!" Conan said, making gestures that he hoped would direct the archers to the entry, where they could form up to counter any massed rush.

The Nubakan gave him a crisp nod and shouted orders in his own tongue. The archers turned and sprinted out of the gate in good order. Reaching the carts filled with panicked, screaming civilians, they thinned down to single file to pass through the crowded portal.

It's a miracle they're not jamming the gate, Conan thought. *A horse and a sheep to you for that, Lir and Manannán mac Lir.* The two blocks of Stygian spearmen were still in shock, and some of them were visibly wavering. If they bolted, the gate *would* be blocked, and the slaves would swarm them all, tearing them to pieces.

A rock went by Conan's head. He whipped around and spotted Valeria trotting back, blood running from her sword and a slave slumped to the ground, sprattling as he bled out from a neat downward stab over the collarbone.

"Thanks!" he called.

"Put on your buggering helmet, you Cimmerian maniac!"

she shouted, clapping her own in place, yellow hair billowing past the steel cap. Conan followed her example as he rode up to the Stygian ranks. He used his sword to point toward the gate.

"We fight. Step back when I shout!" Then he swung out of his saddle, dropped to the ground, and slid his round shield onto his arm. He stood before the serpent banner. "Remember the women and children!"

The ranks stiffened. They might be peasant conscripts, but they'd all been in the southern borderlands long enough to know what to expect if they were taken by the rebel slaves. Many of them would have wives—or women, at least—and children among the crush pushing its way through the gate.

That fact would strengthen the spine of even the weakest.

"Valeria!" Conan called. She came up and took the reins of his horse. "Get the skirmishers on our flanks and clear any abandoned carts. I'm not going to be able to look behind me much to see where I'm stepping."

The Stygian infantry rallied and their drummer beat a complex rhythm. They formed in ranks three-deep, their big coffin-shaped shields under their eyes. The first rank held their spears low for the gutting stroke. The next two held them overarm to stab past the shoulders of those in front, and would be ready to step forward if someone fell. That bristling rank spanned more than the width of the gate. Conan looked over his shoulder and judged how long it would take for the mob to get out.

"Hold!" he shouted again in his limited Stygian. He knew a fair number of military commands, as well as essential phrases like *give me drink* and *how much for the night?* The spearmen braced themselves, muttering prayers or snarling or licking pale lips.

Their first impetus spent, the freed men and women lost momentum. More and more joined their ranks, however, pushing ahead and stooping for rocks. One woman ran forward to power a throw, and from behind Conan Valeria's crossbow went *twang*. The slave pitched onto her back with a short bolt standing in her breastbone.

That raised new fury in the slaves, who unleashed a flurry of rocks. Most rattled off shields and helmets, and with a stroke of his shield he batted one aside. The hard quartz rang on the layers of laminated hide stretched across a stout wood frame.

The shadows lengthened as night approached.

The sounds of chaos increased.

Voices shouted in half a dozen languages, and the slaves poured forward again, but they hit as a spray, not a solid baulk in formation. It was individuals against a machine—naked, poorly armed individuals. Spears stabbed, voices screamed and wailed, steel struck flesh and brought that special raw shriek. When the attackers finally recoiled, a dozen slaves lay dead before the line of leather and metal. More were moaning and dragging themselves off, bleeding and crippled.

The Stygian formation shifted to replace its own casualties. Over his shoulder Conan watched Valeria and several others drag the wounded to an abandoned cart that someone had left with its two mules still harnessed. With a farm-girl's efficiency she quieted the spooked beasts.

"Two step back!" Conan shouted in rough Stygian. "Two step, and hold. Hold!" The formation obeyed, and not too raggedly.

As they did the roar rose again. Another rush. Snarling brabbles of close-quarter savagery, without a thought of mercy or quarter on either side. Sometimes slaves would throw themselves on the spearpoints and hug the shaft that was killing them so those behind could grapple with the soldiers. Men cut, shoved, smashed, heaved a step forward or back, bled, and died.

More steps backward, and Conan's sword ran red from the trail of bodies he was leaving as he retreated—that heartened the Stygian spearmen, too. Another glance revealed that the gate was empty except for a few unconscious bodies and mounted skirmishers shooting over the infantry's heads.

"Left side, right side, fall in behind!"

He only had to say it twice. The formation changed, becoming six deep and just wide enough to back out the gate, along the path cleared by the skirmishers. The slaves were forming up again and this time their front rank was armed. Spears, swords, shields and helmets, daggers and hatchets taken from the dead soldiers.

There was a growing knot of thinner, wilder-looking attackers armed with miner's tools, the first of the overwhelming mass that would be pouring from the slave barracks. There were plenty who'd fought in wars of their own between the tribes and kingdoms south of Stygia; battle-captives were a prime source for the slavers. These pushed and shoved, sometimes slapping faces and kicking buttocks and screeching commands.

When the slaves started forward again they had some semblance of order, more even than in some Vanir war-bands Conan had seen. On either side some of the rebels clambered up the ladders to the fighting platform that stood behind the wall's parapet. There were heavy stones stored all along the wall. If they got over the gate, they could hurl these over the edge and break the infantry phalanx.

"Back into gate!" he shouted, and everyone sidled to the rear, stepping cautiously and keeping their points up. Another flurry of flung rocks, and then the crash of impact. He cut at a man carrying a Stygian kopesh, and the blades sparked. An instant later the metal edge of Conan's shield took the man under the jaw, shattering bone. Spearheads drove past him on both sides...

"*Step back!*"

They stepped.

Conan followed suit and felt an ugly wind as a block of stone fell past his face, close enough to take a tiny fleck of skin off his nose. The sting made him swear mildly. Then there was screaming from above, frustration and rage clear where meaning wasn't. As more stones fell the slaves surged again, so most of the projectiles struck them, rather than the Stygians.

He had to seize the moment...

"*Retreat!*" he bellowed.

When he'd told them to, the Stygian spearmen had stood. Now he told them to run, and they did that, too. Out through the gate and into the curve of Nubakan archers waiting with arrows on their strings. The spearmen broke to either side, screaming curses at the sudden glitter of arrowheads. Conan had been expecting—or hoping, at least—for just this. He fell flat and swiveled on his belly to watch the results, grinning like a happy wolf.

The rebel slaves packed the gate worse than the Stygian refugees had, gripped in a killing rage that could be more powerful than fear. The Nubakan chief barked an order and dozens of bows were drawn to the ear...

At the sight, howls of hate-filled bloodlust turned to screams of well-founded panic. The leading spray of rebels turned and tried to push their way back through the throng. Those who hadn't seen what was waiting, however, kept trying to push *forward*. An inextricable mass of heaving human flesh.

The long Nubakan bows were as powerful as any Conan had seen, even those of the Bossonian archers who had guarded Aquilonia's borders so long and so well. At barely thirty feet, shafts made to hunt elephant drove through human bodies, sometimes through two at a time. Three volleys flashed out, and then half the bowmen shifted to raking the parapets instead.

Conan came erect with a lithe movement and ran at a crouch. Once he was through the Nubakans he reached Valeria, took his reins, and vaulted into the saddle, wiping and sheathing his sword. A swift glance revealed that the Stygian refugees, their carts and baggage animals were— mostly—heading northwest along the trail, shepherded by Zarkabaal's mounted archers.

A few ran witlessly in various directions, and he mentally dismissed them to the deaths their stupidity would surely bring. It would be night soon, and even with the full moon, they wouldn't survive alone.

"Valeria, take the rest of the skirmishers—"

Instantly the warrior woman gave him her full attention. Conan wasn't surprised. She was sharp-witted, could fight, and had commanded ships and men in her time with the Red Brotherhood. Blood ran down her sword, and there was a long scratch on her steel cap where something had hit, hard.

The mercenaries would follow her.

"—and find us a defensible campsite. Within one hour's travel. The distance this witless rabble we've been saddled with can make in an hour. Go!"

She did.

Conan turned to see that the archers had advanced a little, mostly collecting arrows from the ground and the bodies of the fallen, while some kept the mob of slave rebels at bay on the parapet. As he watched the archers retreated, and their commander formed them up.

Gelete, that's his name.

They started after the Stygian spearmen, who were trotting to catch up to the refugee convoy. Conan cantered over to the archers and leaned down to offer his hand. Gelete was puzzled for an instant, then recognized the northern custom and shook.

"Good work," Conan said. "Brave men, they fight well— fight *smart*."

Gelete nodded with somber pride. He said something in his native tongue, then stopped and translated. "We sons of lion. Fight elephant, fight rhino, fight lion, fight men." Then he smiled, teeth white except for a few gaps. "You too. Smart! Not like—"

He made a wiggling gesture, like a snake, obviously meant for the late and unlamented Akhenset.

"He fool, fool, fool," the Nubakan archer continued. "You command now?"

Conan shrugged. "Need command, bad, we do."

"That is—what word—*necessary*, yes. All die if no..." He

extended a hand with fingers spread and then clenched it into a fist. It was frustrating to talk in a language neither man spoke well, but the thoughts Conan had to express were simple.

"March north, make camp, guard," the Cimmerian said. He hesitated, then pulled out the Stygian word he knew that fit at all. "Guard *tight*. In case—" He pointed to the fortified mining camp, and then made a gesture with his hand palm-down and fingers wiggling to mimic many legs running.

Pillars of smoke were rising over the camp. He would bet that the slaves were burning down their barracks, and a good deal more. Understandable, but short-sighted. They'd be starving in a few days, and fighting among themselves in a week, he judged. Most would strike out in doomed efforts to return to their scattered homes. But for the moment they were still dangerous, and their blood would still be up from the thrill of revenge.

I'd have done the same thing in their place.

"Yes," Gelete said. "Good plan."

9

The convoy made camp. It was only a few miles from the mine compound, but marching after dark would be too risky. Unencumbered, the rebel slaves could have sent a part of their number to run down the Stygians and mercenaries, and darkness would take away too much of the advantage. While on the move, discipline and gear would fail against numbers and ferocity.

Conan didn't much fear an attempt to overrun their camp, though he kept all the Nubakans, his skirmishers, and half the spearman on sentry-go while it was pitched and secured.

Gelete showed them a trick his people used to protect their traveling camps; cut thornbush and small acacias—formidably fanged with iron-hard thorns—and drag them into a circle around the encampment, laced together and secured by stakes driven into the ground. The wagons were placed just inside. He called it a *zariba*, and with many hands it hadn't taken long to erect.

Looking at it from the outside, Conan had decided that even for men in armor it would be painful to break through, and delay an attack long enough for the camp to be roused. For the nearly naked rebels it would be a much more serious obstacle.

It was no obstacle to arrows, however, and the Nubakans could shoot from the cover of the wagons. No scratch force like the slaves—

Former slaves, he corrected.

—would pose any threat.

Once camp was set up and reasonably safe, they prepared a scratch meal of mush and bits of a couple of floundered oxen, charred on the outside and raw within. Then they began to examine the contents of all the wagons, carts, and packs.

"*Aaaaaah*," Valeria said softly as the chest-lid swung back with a creak. "Oh, that is *so* pretty. Ohhhhh, yes, yes!"

She's never looked on me *with such favor*, Conan thought—but with an inward chuckle, for the sight restored his good spirits, too. Tired and irritated, he'd begun to feel the effects of hours spent bullydamning and shoving at terrified refugees to keep them from getting everyone killed or slowing them down, which would accomplish the same thing.

Of course, I'm not a chest filled with gold.

Excess baggage would slow them down too, especially in the oppressive heat, but the Stygians clung to it like leeches. Hence this rough sorting, with an emphasis on the *rough*. He had to use his fist or the flat of his sword occasionally as they went from wagon to wagon. By the time they were halfway done, by silent mutual agreement they just evicted the owners and made them stand fifty yards off.

Now and then he'd been tempted to just leave everyone, take his skirmishers, and head for the ocean...

Never more than now, he thought, looking down at the latest open containers, lit by the reflected light of the fires off the canvas tilt and by the flicker of a clay lamp Zarkabaal held in one hand.

It also lit the Shemite's slow, delighted grin. His dark eyes caressed the contents the way they might have a lover stripping down for bedchamber sport. Most of the gear in this wagon was goods from the household of the dead commander, the fat man the equally dead Akhenset had come to replace. In the scramble to get through the gates, two chests—each about big enough to hold a newborn babe—had been thrown in among them, under piles of robes and bedding and brass candlesticks shaped like snakes and scorpions, and packets of kitchen spices.

The spices were light in weight and high in value, and would be dumped into the mercenaries' stew.

But these chests were another matter entirely. Made from thick short planks of some hard glossy black wood, with arched lids carved from a section of log, edged and strapped with hammered steel. The hinges were internal, the mark of a container designed to hold valuables.

What they held…

The gold came in rough-shaped disks, each about the size of his palm, as thick through as his middle finger, and heaped high. He picked one up, hefted the dense weight, marked the soft metal with his thumbnail, and dropped it back in the chest with a dull *clunk* of gold on gold. Judging from the weight and the rumors they'd heard, this was the full six-months output of the Wedi Shebelli mine—or at least of as much of it as the fat Stygian commandant had intended to put on the official books.

Presumably his *unofficial* share would have been hidden somewhere else. Gold and its mining were a royal monopoly in Stygia. That meant that a little stuck to every official's hand it passed through on its way to the treasury in Luxor.

"We can't just take it and run," he said with a sigh as Valeria joined them.

"Why *not*?" Zarkabaal demanded. He slammed the pommel of his sword into the lock holding the other chest, and murmured again as he opened it and lifted the lamp high to reveal a duplicate heaping of raw wealth.

"Why *not*, by Chemosh of the Plunder?" the Shemite repeated. "We could all be rich men!" He stroked his curled black beard. "There's this villa outside my city of Dan-Marcah… with a good spring, a vineyard, olive groves, fruit-trees, honest pomegranates and apricots and almonds—none of this southern dung. That and a townhouse, shares in ships… Lying on my couch sipping wine and looking out to sea from the tower, with pretty women fanning me with ostrich-plumes on ebony staffs…"

Gelete shot him a look. "My men get share! Many cattle, much land; bride-price for wives! Why we fight for—" The term he used in his native tongue contained the word "Stygian" and, from the gesture that accompanied it, highly uncomplimentary opinions of their romantic lives.

"Shut up, both of you," Conan snarled. He slammed both the lids closed, turned, and peered around. Some of his skirmishers and Gelete's Nubakans were nearby, but not within earshot. Except for the ones on guard, most were asleep. It had been a trying day.

There was a full file of the Stygian spearmen who'd taken to following him with embarrassing doglike devotion since he'd gotten them out of the rat-screw at the mine, fought at their head, and even saved their women and gear. There weren't any Stygian noblemen left, and the soldiers were used to being told what to do.

"Think, Zarkabaal," he said as he turned back, his voice low and urgent. "Do you think you could cross the length of Stygia, north to the Styx, down it all the way to Khemi, and over the border into Shem, then across most of Shem—Dan-Marcah's on the coast near the Argossean border, isn't it? All with your share of *this* in your baggage? None of your men would boast in a tavern?"

The swarthy hook-nosed man opened his mouth, then closed it again.

"We could go west from here…" he suggested.

Conan clenched a fist and slammed it sideways into one of the wooden hoops that bore the wagon's tilt. It cracked under the force of the blow, which had his own frustration behind it. What he had suggested was exactly what he *wanted* to do—and planned to do, someday soon. Not yet, however, not until there was a chance of success.

"Think, man! We're not far west of the bend of the Styx." He jerked his thumb to the north, where the great river did a sharp turn and headed for the Western Sea. "Two thousand *miles* and more through the savannah kingdoms to the Black Coast, Darfar, Meroe, Kush, Bornu, the others… and they all know the value of gold."

The Shemite nodded reluctantly. The coastal cities of Shem were in that trade too.

"Then if you make the coast, yes," Conan continued, "there are traders who ply those waters, and they'd all cut your throat for it unless you take ship with a cousin who just *happens* to be there… and he might cut your throat, too. Maybe not if you promise him half—and that's the merchant skippers who *aren't* pirates."

"My people's homeland is south of the Styx, east of here,"

Gelete said, eking out the words with gestures. "Maybe we go there? You welcome. Strong men, brave. I… how do you say… I speak for you with the elders. Get cattle, wives, fields. Neighbors help build huts for you. Beer, beef, screwing, good fighting, good hunting, many sons."

Conan sighed. To him, that was tempting—but he knew the Shemites and northern mercenaries in his new following. They would consider it exile among savages. It mattered less to him because by their lights he was a savage, too. Even if he agreed to it, he'd grow as bored there as he'd been at home in his father's hut.

Valeria gave a blue-eyed glance sidelong at the Nubakan chief and then rolled her eyes upward for an instant as if to say that went double for her. A land where men traded cattle for wives, and daughters weren't even worth mentioning, didn't seem to hold much charm for her.

"Nubaka is south of Taia, isn't it?" Conan asked.

"Yes. From here… cross Darfar, cross Punt, cross Keshan, cross Zembabwei, then Land of Lion-Men, we say—in our tongue, Nubakaara. Green hills, sweet grass!"

"Do they love you Nubakans in Darfar, Punt, Keshan, and Zembabwei?"

"Ummmm… no. Raiding, both ways."

"How do you get to Stygia to take service… to fight for them?"

"We go north along Styx, boats, paddle, many weeks." He was getting visibly more thoughtful about a fifteen-hundred-mile overland trek through hostile realms, all while bearing a treasure.

"You want to give it all back to the Stygians, Conan?" Zarkabaal burst out. "Ishtar! I thought better of you!"

"No, no," Conan said, making a patting gesture at the air. "Just *some* of it. No risk, no gain, but not stupid-greedy, either. The Stygians will think we're heroes for rescuing *any* of the gold—and their people, to be sure. They may even give us a reward.

"Here is my plan…"

An hour later, Conan sought his bedroll.

The skirmishers had two campfires, and they'd liberated a four-mule wagon, stuffing it with enough jerky, sorghum meal, and beans to get them home—

Or at least to Sukhmet, Conan reflected. He wasn't sure if anywhere in the world was truly "home" to him now.

—if they were careful. It also held a selection of easily carried valuables they'd accumulated one way or another. Not far away was a picket-line with their horses and remounts, the latter including all the spare mounts from the now-dead Stygian lancers and Akhenset's other team. Mercenaries tended to be sticky-fingered when anything useful came to hand. Or just caught the eye.

The fire was bright with the flammable part of the goods that his troop and the Nubakans had ruthlessly purged from the convoy's baggage. By burning the excess, they made sure none of the Stygian civilians would try to smuggle back any non-essentials, and slow them down. They'd be eating the oxen, driving them along for food rather than letting them set the pace with yokes on their necks.

Zarallo's detachment had only lost two men. One dead outright, one with a gut-wound that would infallibly be fatal, and an assortment of other injuries that would probably heal and wouldn't slow the men down too much in the interim. That was a minor miracle, considering the fix they'd been in at Wedi Shebelli.

Best they think that without me they'd be dead, or being tortured to death by the rebels, Conan thought, gravely returning respectful nods and waves. *As it is, they're getting away with a tidy packet of loot. Though by next sundown half will have convinced themselves it was their own wonderful sword-work and heroism.*

Valeria gathered up her saddle and bedroll from where she'd dumped it by her horse.

"How long do you expect to keep this all secret, once we're back in Sukhmet and you hand out the shares of the gold?" she asked, *sotto voce*. He turned his head and smiled thinly at her.

"Long enough for me to get out of Sukhmet," he said. "Do you love the place?"

She coughed back a laugh and shook her head.

"No, but I enlisted with Zarallo to let the flames die down on the Western Sea. Quarrels in the Brotherhood."

"Sukhmet has flames of its own, now," he pointed out. "And you are the torch."

"Men!" She snorted and shouldered her saddle. Then she walked off, bending to the right, and found a spot under the wagon.

Conan did a last tour of the perimeter. He was very tired, but didn't want to wake up amid screams, flames, and a horde of rebel slaves swarming over the *zariba*, throwing things before closing with spear, sword, knife, fists, and teeth.

Not far off he found a wagon, not well concealed but

unobtrusive enough that his eyes almost slid past. He was startled to recognize it. Not many of the wagons had a closed wooden body, but this did, decorated with the wiggling line sigil of Set. It was the priest's wagon, and the priest himself sat beside it, his face unreadable.

He turned away as Conan glanced at it.

Crom! he thought. *Of all the people to survive, why did it have to be him?*

I suppose I could...

No, I've no reason to kill him or cast him out, not if I'm going back to Sukhmet.

10

By the dawn of the third day Conan decided that the slave rebels weren't dogging their tracks. It made the morning bowl of dull gritty mush and undercooked dried beans taste a little less of worry. He put it aside—a Stygian darted it to take it away for cleaning—rose from his squat and stretched, settling his sword-belt.

The day was dawning clear, hot, and damp, which wasn't a surprise, since the season of rains was only just starting. They'd made slow progress yesterday and when a spate of thunderstorms doused them, they had been forced to stop for the afternoon. From what he'd heard, even when the rains were at their peak it was mostly a matter of an hour or two of heavy thunderstorms every day or two, like the gods dumping a huge bucket of water out of the sky. Not the endless dark, dank chill and drizzle Cimmerians endured for weeks on end, sometimes in late summer right when the grain was coming ripe.

The track shouldn't become *too* muddy.

The joys of leading a war-band, he thought. *All dash and fire and plunder and glory and bards chanting your name.*

It wasn't the first time he'd been a leader of men, but this was about the most mixed multitude he'd ever had at his tail, and its traveling village was by far the biggest. The camp-followers in particular thought they could come to him for everything up to and including marital advice and how to keep their toddlers from wandering off.

It'll be lost pets next. At least I can see to feeding them. Good experience, too.

Conan had ambitions of his own—a little vague and formless right now, but they didn't involve returning to his clan with nothing to show but scars and a sword, a few trinkets and some stories to tell the young around the fire on winter evenings.

Long cold dark winter evenings.

Cimmeria never lacked for those. Everything else, yes; chill and gloom, no.

Leading a charge was something he knew he could do well, and even managing an emergency retreat like the one they'd just endured. Men would follow him when the blades were out and Crom's red wine flowed. They wouldn't follow for long, however, if he bungled the other parts of a chief's work, though. Starving men knew who to blame.

Now, the hunt.

There were ways to accomplish it that didn't mean slowing the main convoy from its necessary pace, which reminded him of a glacier on a mountain near his birthplace, anyway. He walked over to where Gelete was finishing his bowl of mush and beans and jerky, conferring with his underlings. Along the way he collected Zarkabaal, with the Shemite still brushing crumbs out of his beard.

"We'll do another drive hunt today," he said, "but different." At least he *thought* that was what he said. His Stygian was pretty bad, and Gelete's only a bit better. As it was, Zarkabaal helped out, and Conan did his best to memorize the translations, learning how to speak Stygian with a thick accent from the northern coast of Shem. Cursing internally, he reminded himself that he was a fighting-man, not a scholar, and "understandable" would have to do.

With luck, he wouldn't start a war.

"We'll pick our next campsite while some are off scouting the game and your men are on rear guard," he said. "When you reach it, leave the Stygians to put up the *zariba*."

A few slashed bushes would do to make the trail unmistakable—the Nubakans were good trackers, as he'd expect from men who hunted for a big part of their living, and herded cattle in the savannah for much of the rest.

"I leave two-three men to boss that at campsite," the Nubakan leader said. "Otherwise the Stygians—" He uttered a phrase in his native tongue. There were confused glances, but a little back-and-forth established that he meant "*screw it up*." Although it seemed to more literally involve getting a goat pregnant.

Conan nodded.

"When you make the spot we've picked for the camp, take the rest of your men and fan out about half a mile past the camp; that far away the fire-scent won't be close enough to spook the game we drive. This rabble is certain to kindle some as soon as they stop, unless we waste men to stand over them."

They cast back and forth for the words that got the meaning across, and Gelete nodded. He wet his thumb and held it up, looked up at the brilliant blue sky and its scattering of white cloud, then consulted his subordinates again.

"Good plan," he said. "Also, wind blow from northeast today." He added a waggle of his hand to indicate *probably*.

"Even better," Conan said. "You hide your men half a mile past the camp, then we drive the game in, and you shoot. Carefully!" he added, and Gelete grinned whitely.

"Good plan," the Nubakan repeated—it seemed to be his favorite phrase. "Easier drive game with horses, we Nubakans got more bows. Work together, get more meat. No accidents with bad shot. Because you not Stygians." Another smile, and a wagging finger. "Try not drive anything too big. No elephant, no rhino, no lions. Ivory too heavy now, anyway."

He wore two necklaces of lion teeth and claws around his neck, and had interesting scars on his chest and elsewhere that looked like they'd been caused by claws, as well as blades. Conan looked at the decorations.

"You have enough of those?"

Gelete's face went grave. "This one—" He touched one of the necklaces, and then the lion-mane headdress that framed his face. "—from my manhood hunt. All Nubakan warriors must take lion when young, become warrior."

Conan gestured agreement. There were many rites that turned youth to man, among many different folk, but that was a common one. Among Cimmerians it was less formal, but bringing home the skin of a panther would do. The head of a clan enemy was even better. Then when a serious fight came, you could be confident the man next to you wasn't some fainting flower who'd leave your sword-side unguarded at the wrong moment.

"This one…" The archer-chief's finger moved to the second necklace and he spoke with somber pride. "This one eat my brother. I hunt, just me, take his skin, put skull by fire, wear teeth and claws."

Conan nodded again, acknowledging a deed worth doing.

What were the bonds of kinship for, if not to have someone to stand by you in life and take vengeance if you fell?

I like these Nubakans, by Crom. They are indeed the sons of lions, he thought. Then he said, "Good. We drive, you shoot, everybody eats."

He left the Nubakans discussing their role in the hunt and went back to his own fire, calling the skirmishers in and giving them his plan, with Zarkabaal translating into Shemitish this time instead of Stygian, since some of his men had nothing but their native tongue. Everyone seemed fairly pleased.

Valeria was scrubbing out her bowl with handfuls of sand and some water. They'd picked the campsite for a clear stream, and long experience had them keeping their eating gear clean. War-camps bred disease, and their movements spread it far and wide. Why and how, not even sorcerers knew, but there it was.

"I'm as fond of fresh meat as anyone," Valeria said, "but is this worth the effort, if we want to get back to Sukhmet as fast as we can? If the local tribes get wind of the way the mine was overrun—"

"And they will," Zarkabaal cut in.

She nodded. "They're more likely to try and attack us. They don't love the Stygians, I hear."

"Nobody loves Stygians," Conan said.

"Stygians must, or there wouldn't be any little Stygians," Zarkabaal said with a grin. "But apart from that, no. Nobody in Shem, certainly—not even the ones they've bought and paid for in the southern parts."

Valeria's bland glance told Conan that she knew he meant *"whores and collaborators, if there's a difference."* Yet

Zarkabaal and his riders were working for Stygian gold, nonetheless.

"Yes, it's worth it," Conan asserted, "especially since it doesn't slow down the convoy—at least not much. It's not just about eating fresh meat because it tastes better than this cowdung mush. If we get enough that we can dry some, we can feed more of the grain and beans to the mules and horses. That cuts down on how long we have to let them graze, and it means they can work harder without foundering. They'll have less to carry and pull."

That got plenty of nods. Everyone was familiar with working-stock, most of them from childhoods spent in farming villages. A few looked surprised before they agreed, since the trade-off hadn't occurred to all of them.

They stood and moved to saddle their horses.

"I've been too long at sea," Valeria said to him, "and forgotten how important horses and mules are to everything ashore." She cocked an eyebrow at him. "You're not just big and fast, eh?"

"And you're not just lithe and quick," he said, giving her a glance.

"You're better with a sword than flattery."

That left him fuming a bit, but then he noticed an odd-scented smoke coming from the Stygian priest's little closed cart as he rode past to the head of the long column. A pair of spearmen walked in front of it. They saluted him by banging the spears in their right hands against their long coffin-shaped shields, akin to the fist-to-chest gesture so many armies used.

"He's making hunt-magic, captain," one of them said to Conan, and he smacked his lips. "He had us collecting hair and scat to bespell them. Good eating! Not like back home in the north by the river, where you can be strung up by the gentry just for taking a duck from a marsh."

Hunt-magic was familiar too—every shaman, chief and hedge-witch in Cimmeria did the like, and the individual hunters had their small private rites and gestures. He'd seen similar things everywhere he traveled. Still, Conan felt the back of his neck prickle a little at the thought and the smell, as he remembered the sacrifices committed under the reptilian gaze of Set.

Priests of Set still like fresh meat, akin to other men, he told himself. *Even if they don't cut out its heart on the altar.*

"This is a good place for the camp," he said the next afternoon. "I'll check it over, then we leave the Stygians here and go on ahead."

They were in an area of rolling hills, though the one ahead of them was cut off as if broken. Its eastern edge rose at a gentle slope to a triangle of land, but on the northwestern side there was an abrupt, rubble-strewn drop-off almost like a cliff, particularly right at the top. It was the perfect location, and as an added bonus, three-quarters of the way down the steep side was a pool fed by a fast-flowing spring. That had probably been what undermined the rock in the first place, eating away at it until it collapsed.

The overflow from the pool splashed down the rocks amid flowering bushes and butterflies and bright swooping birds with implausibly long tails. Some of them built bulbous communal nests dangling from the branches of trees. Those were like nothing he'd seen anywhere else, astonishing constructions of woven grass and twigs with multiple entrances and birds coming and going like the dwellers in one of the big buildings that filled some of the crowded cities in Shem.

Conan looked at them and grinned, shaking his head. If he spoke of them back in Cimmeria, listeners over the age of six would just snort and walk away. He'd have done the same himself.

It's good to travel far and see strange sights.

As he dismounted at the base of the west-facing incline he looped his reins around the limb of a bush. Then he clambered up the loose crumbled rock of the slope with the casual ease of someone who'd played cliff-climbing games all his youth, when he'd collected eggs from some birds that nested on sheer rock-faces for his family.

Sniffing, he scooped up a handful of the water that ran out and down the steep rock, tasted cautiously, then stuck his head in and gulped. It was good, cold from the depths of the rock, and crisp... and he was thirsty. The spring area smelled clean, too, of wet greenery and coolness and damp rock. That meant nothing had crawled into the water and died, at least not lately, though he could see the clean white skull of something with fangs lying on the sand at the bottom of the pool.

He came up blowing and shook his head like a wolf. When traveling with hundreds of companions, good water was about the first thing to locate at a night's bivouac.

No wonder I'm thirsty, when I sweat so much, he thought, throwing handfuls over his bare torso. *It makes you crave salt, too.*

"Go around the hill and bring my horse to the top," he called back over his shoulder. "I'm going to check the approaches on this side!"

Slipping his sword around until it hung down from the small of his back, he traced a path with his eyes and jumped. The first part of the climb was only a bit more difficult than the lower slope, but the last three man-lengths were nearly straight up and down. Once, a bit of the coarse pale stone studded with what looked like seashells broke beneath his fingers. With most of his weight on that hand he had to drop half his height and grab quickly, hanging for a moment over empty space before he swung back into motion.

"Good climbing," Valeria said after he hoisted himself up to the top. She was already there, and handed him the reins of his horse. He looked back over his shoulder at the long snake of the caravan.

"That's nothing!" Conan said, flush with exhilaration. "Try doing it with a deer-carcass lashed to your back."

"In midwinter, with a snowstorm blowing, ten Picts waiting at the top and a pack of hungry wolves down below, and…" she said, trailing off. "I thought Cimmerians were men of few words."

"Only when we don't have anything to say."

The sun behind his back, Conan scanned the area ahead. The ground was on an upward slope, but not steep enough to be difficult on this east-facing side. It was mostly covered in thigh-high grass that was a mixture of old straw-color and fresh green, with the occasional blushing-red termite mound. There were enough trees and scrub for the *zariba* and for firewood. Up here sentries could keep everything in sight for miles, and a few pacing along the edge of the steeper western side would be ample security.

"This is *almost* good enough for a game-jump," he said. She shot him an enquiring look and Zarkabaal mirrored it. "Where you drive the herd of game off a cliff. Then there's nothing but skinning and butchering."

Zarkabaal's eyes took in the slope. "Too wide at the base for that," he said, "and too steep. They'd see and recoil, or break to left and right."

"*Almost*, I said." He looked at the sun. "It's getting on. Let's leave the marker for Gelete and get out there to round up some meat. The Stygians can begin setting up camp while we're off—the Nubakans will be here shortly."

11

What did that Aquilonian grandee call it? Conan thought an hour later. *An embarrassment of riches?*

He wiped his hand across his brows; dust smeared in sweat to a consistency like thin drippy mud, but the stinging in his eyes was better... for a little while.

At the time he'd thought the Aquilonian an irritating fop. For a youth from Cimmeria there was no such thing as *enough*, especially when he saw the riches of the southlands and compared them to the iron austerity in which he'd grown up, where the wolf that tried to eat you provided meat that was a treat to boast of, after you'd boiled some of the rankness out of it.

What was ahead of him, though...

"Even in this country, that's more game than I've ever seen," he muttered under his breath. "More than we can use!"

Meat didn't keep more than two or three days here, unless they paused to dry or smoke it. Worse, wasting the fruits of the hunt repelled him on a visceral level. They couldn't even salt it down in barrels, since that worked best in cool weather—one of the reasons late fall was slaughtering-time in the northern countries.

A great herd of the striped wild horses grazed right in front of him. Nearby more of those bouncing-ball antelope things leapt three times their own height and more. Weird bearded creatures with forequarters higher than their rumps boasted upturned horns amid tufts of hair that made them look as if they were wearing odd hats, and this time there *was* a group of giraffes, like living siege ladders.

All of them were just trudging along ahead of the sickle-shape of mounted skirmishers, vanishing into a haze of dust and dimly glimpsed thorn-trees and grass. As Gelete had predicted, the wind was in their faces. That meant the dust the beasts kicked up was, too, tasting vaguely salty and mealy, and the smell of the massed animals and their waste was rank.

"Ishtar of the Huntsmen!" Zarkabaal said. "It's a *dull* hunt. I didn't think that was possible, except when there's *no* game."

"Better dull than—" Conan began.

His horse screamed in bulge-eyed panic.

The lion came up out of the dust as if it had been tricked into existence by a magician, but the way the animals scattered ahead of it argued for an all-too-physical reality. It was in full charge, twenty-foot bounds with its tail held stiff and its eyes locked on Conan. A big male with a huge mane that ranged from black to a tawny yellow and matched its coat or Valeria's hair. Easily twice, perhaps three times his own weight, full-grown but young, growling like a water-powered saw cutting through stone.

Throwing himself off the horse was easy, since his mount had time for one frantic leaping twist before the lion struck. Plummeting to the ground, Conan heard the *thud* of impact before he landed, loosely curled and hoping his sword-hilt wouldn't hit him anywhere essential.

It didn't, and he whirled to his feet, using the impact of his rolling fall to land in a crouch. The sword flashed into his hands; he carried what they called a bastard longsword and drew with the double-handed grip. It had a long hilt, a blade suitable for use single-handed if you were strong enough, yet still long enough to take advantage of a double-handed cut.

The lion—amazingly—didn't bother with the horse it had knocked down. It pivoted in a smooth doubling motion. Some of the Free Companions shouted. Arrows and crossbow bolts flew past the beast.

One more jump and it was in the air again, heading straight for him, plate-sized forepaws spread wide to knock down and pin, huge red-and-white mouth gaping for the killing bite. He couldn't out-quick a lion, any more than he could any other variety of cat, and running away from one was certain death.

Once a big cat had committed itself, however, its weight made sure the leap would continue. So Conan leapt, as well, *toward* the lion, sword held low with the point down and toward the left. The beast saw him come, hunched in midair, and one huge paw edged with curved knife-sized claws came slamming toward his face, ready to tear it off his skull, and half the bone beneath.

Conan had gambled on that. Before the lion could launch its strike he turned his rush into a stepping cut, pivoting to his right, bringing the heavy blade around in a sweeping stroke from low left to high right, pushing shoulders and torso and gut-muscle into it as his feet landed. He could almost feel power flowing up from the earth and through his hands.

The sweep of the lion's limb, combined with his own huge effort, made it seem as if he'd rammed into a falling wall. The impact sent him tumbling again. The wind went out of him as he slammed down on his back, and he whooped air back into his lungs with a savage effort of will. His right hand went numb, so he drew his dagger left-handed.

The lion went tumbling too, the liquid grace of its leap wrecked by the impact of the keen blade. For a moment it squalled and writhed, biting at its own half-severed forelimb with a blind savagery aimed at whatever had hurt it. In that instant the cursing Shemites controlled their horses and managed a second volley. Four shafts missed, but the rest struck; in eye, throat, belly, and five more in parts of the chest.

One of the shafts brushed Conan's leg as it sank a double handspan into the hard earth, whereupon Zarkabaal began beating that archer over the shoulders with his bowstave. It was mostly symbolic through a mail shirt, but sincere enough, judging from the sound of the blows and the sputtering guttural Shemite curses.

The lion gave a long low moaning grunt and rolled onto its side. Then it came back upright, fixed Conan with that disturbing yellow stare and began to drag itself toward him. Halfway across the short distance between them it gouted up blood from its mouth and nose, swayed, collapsed, bit savagely at the ground and died.

Conan sheathed his dagger, rolled to his feet and worked his right arm, swinging it and flexing the fingers until the numbness left. Then he picked up his sword, and cursed mildly. There was a nick in the cutting edge where it had hit the dense bones of the lion's forelimb.

"I'll have to file that out," he said, before wiping and sheathing the blade. Then to Zarkabaal, "Thanks… but you and your men ruined the pelt." Looking for his horse, he found it writhing on the ground with two broken legs. *Damn*.

Leaning down in the saddle, Valeria looked over the lion. "You nearly cut its paw off!" she said flatly, shocked into matter-of-fact amazement. "And a foot of the forelimb! That's the first time I've seen a man strike swifter than a cat."

Conan paused in the messy business of cutting his horse's throat. It was the last favor he could do the beast.

"I didn't," he said. "I out-thought it."

At her raised brows, he went on. "Beasts are more predictable than men. If you do one thing, they have one reply—and they use it. When you know what they're going to do, you're one step ahead of them, and it makes up for their speed. Big cats use that paw-strike if you come at them, so you can start your cut before they do."

The tawny, sun-faded brows went higher against her smooth tanned skin.

"You have lions in Cimmeria?"

Conan's mouth crooked in a smile. "No, but we have panthers in plenty, and cats are cats." He bent to work the saddle and tack off the dead horse. "Someone bring my remount," he added. "We have a herd to drive, or Gelete will be very disappointed in us."

"Stop shooting!" Zarkabaal shouted as Conan and the rest of the skirmishers came riding up. "Don't waste arrows!"

The Shemite peered out into the dusty plain below the hill; the sun was low in the western sky behind them, casting long shadows. Gelete and a few of his men came trotting up, grinning, their long bows pumping in their left hands as they ran with a springy, tireless gait despite the day's ending in sultry heat. The herd was dispersing now that they weren't being driven, the scent of blood sending them on their way.

"Never see such targets!" he exulted in his bad Stygian. "You drive them good, Conan."

"It too easy," the Cimmerian replied. "Now we drag the best carcasses up to the *zariba*, and—"

Shouts rose. Something different was happening out there in the dust-cloud. What it was became clear all of a sudden.

Valeria appeared, her horse doing its bulge-eyed best to fly, with the rider bent over its neck and urging it on. Right behind…

Rhino! Conan thought.

He hadn't noticed the big dim-witted pugnacious beast— it must have been in the center of the herd, hidden by dust and hundreds of other bodies. He'd never hunted them— not worth the effort and risk, for the most part—but he knew enough about them to see that this was a big one, with a club-shaped, scalloped head and square mouth. It was huge even for its type, four tons at least, with a nose-horn the size and shape of a scimitar. The horn was lowered to gore and toss, and it could probably toss a horse twice head high, much less a human.

The beast was gaining on Valeria's mount, its thick stubby legs a blur.

"*Out of the way!*" she cried, waving her arms. "*Out of the sheep-buggering way!*"

One look at the oncoming horn produced instant obedience. Conan's new horse was ready to mount, but it reared. He leapt, grabbed the bridle, slugged it back to all fours and swung into the saddle. Zarkabaal's Shemites had scattered, allowing the rhino to pass, and now they were following along behind, shooting enthusiastically.

Normally it was the right reflex, that instinctive desire to join the action and do the enemy any harm you could, the mark of a real fighting-man. This time it was catastrophically *bad*. Zarkabaal bellowed for them to stop, but it was too late.

The rhino had already been as fast as a galloping horse, but the beasts were as densely stupid as they were belligerent. Normally it might have just stopped when it didn't hit its target, and mooched off to eat grass.

Now a half-dozen arrows decorated its massive haunches, and it reacted as if stung to utter fury. Worse yet, the *zariba* was coming up fast. Stygian soldiers and their camp-followers were coming down to skin and butcher. They scattered screaming out of the way.

The long curved horn was almost touching the rump of Valeria's horse when—using hand, thigh, and voice—she gathered the mount for a leap. It responded nobly, soaring higher than a tall man's height and clearing the stretch of thornbrush. Conan drew a breath to relax... and then used it to curse as the massive rhino simply lowered its head and tore through the barrier as if it were made out of cleaning-rags and straw.

A half-grown thorn-tree went pinwheeling into the sky as

the huffing engine of destruction carried on into the camp, leaving more screaming in its wake. Valeria's horse had gained about three lengths, but that wasn't going to help much.

Conan's spurred his horse into motion and took what was left of the *zariba* with a skipping leap and two bounds, and then settled into a pounding gallop, swerving occasionally to dodge a cart or a cowering human as Valeria and her bellows-panting pursuit tore up through the center of the half-made camp.

The cliff! he thought. *It's too late for her to dodge!*

The rhino slowed for an instant as half a tent wrapped around its head and blinded it. Tossing it free the animal churned its stumpy, powerful legs once more. Conan was close enough behind it that he was tempted to draw his sword, but decided not to. Chances were, all he could do was anger it.

The end came swiftly.

A final toss of the rhino's horn gored into the left haunch of Valeria's horse. In the same moment she pulled her feet out of the stirrups and leapt to the right. The push of her long legs and the convulsive bound of the horse tossed her to one side, and she vanished from Conan's sight. The horse shrieked like a hundred women in childbed as it went over the edge and saw what awaited it.

The bigger an animal was, the worse the results if it fell. A mouse falling over that cliff would walk away, a cat might get a bruise, a human would break bones... and a horse would go *splat* as it turned into a bag of bones, viscera, and blood.

Something that weighed four tons had a worse fate in store.

The rhino's slow brain kept it going until a frantic last-instant attempt to slow down, but the edge of the precipice broke under its weight and it went over in a hoarse grunting bellow of amazing volume. That cut off an instant later with an earthshaking crunch of impact.

Conan swung out of the saddle with his mouth in a grim line as he walked to the *new* edge of the cliff. It would have been a quick death for Valeria, at least. With trepidation he looked down. The rhino had landed on top of the horse, and both were giving their last twitches, lying in a spreading swath of blood fifty feet away and a little below the spring-fed pool of water. He couldn't see much of the horse, and the rhino had burst on impact.

If she was under that, she would have, too.

"How about a hand?" a contralto voice called.

A yard down and several to the side, just beyond the edge of the fresh break, Valeria hung by both hands from a dwarfed tree growing out of a crack in the rock. With a laugh, Conan knelt and extended a hand. She swung one-handed and grabbed his wrist. He clamped his hand on hers and stood, heaving; it wasn't much of an effort for him, but she wasn't exactly a sylph of a girl.

Valeria was covered in sweat, dirt, and blood from free-flowing scratches, and showed a fresh red bruise on her face from when she'd tumbled free. She also looked magnificent, in his opinion.

"Thanks," she said when she stood on the solid rock, looking down. Two of Gelete's archers had already reached the dead beasts. They were using their belt axes to hack at the base of the rhino's horn.

"Mitra of the Sun damn all rhinos to eternal midnight," Valeria spat. "That was a good horse!"

"Lucky it didn't land in our water," Conan said. "I wonder what rhino liver tastes like?"

"We'll find out," she said, brushing back strands of hair, then she shot him a look. "Remind me not to hunt with you again. My odds are better in a melee on a bloody deck!"

"Speaking of luck, don't throw the dice anytime soon," Conan said. "Not with your pay riding on it. You've just used up a year's supply."

"Luck?" she snorted. She was visibly controlling her breathing, and one cheek twitched, which showed admirable self-command.

"Not luck!" she went on. "Nothing but skill—and all the agility of a cat!"

"Four or five of its lives, too," he said, twisting a Stygian saying.

Valeria reached for her canteen and found it missing. Conan handed over his, and she poured a handful into her cupped palm, scrubbed it over her face, then drank deeply.

"Ahhh! Though if someone was casting hunt-charms for us, they worked too damned well."

Conan's eyes narrowed, and he grunted thoughtfully.

12

Two days later, Conan was still thoughtful as he looked at the Stygian priest's wagon in passing. The expressionless driver was, as usual, all that could be seen, but the trickle of incense-smoke and the sound of chanting showed the presence of the bald-headed, skull-faced terror.

The more he considered the game-drive, the less natural it seemed.

His spells are of weight... but I'll warrant that my sword is quicker, the Cimmerian mused. *He'll summon few demons with his head resting six feet from his corpse.*

For some reason the priest-magician seemed to have a hatred of Valeria—and now Conan—that went far beyond the generalized dislike many Stygians harbored toward foreigners. At the thought of decapitating the man, he let his hand fall from the pommel of his blade and brought his horse back up to a canter as he paced along the length of the convoy.

Killing a hierophant of the Serpent would mean he had to kill every Stygian man, woman, and child in the expedition. Even then, *someone* would talk. Sukhmet might be the arse-end of Stygia, but that would sting them in the arse, like

Zarkabaal's archers with the rhino. News would reach all the way to Luxor and Khemi, probably by no natural means and very quickly.

Even if he ran from here to the Vilayet Sea and hid in a cave when he got there, the Stygians—and their sorcerers—would hunt him down. His death, when it finally came, would not be pleasant.

No matter what his treachery, there's no evidence that would save my skin, or Valeria's, he thought. *Perhaps a slaying by stealth, at night, with nobody the wiser. I've done it before—Yara in his tower—but he never knew I was coming until it was too late.*

Shaking his head, he put the thought aside.

They had a river to ford, and even with no slaves to watch and fewer wagons heavy-laden with tools and supplies, it was going to be tricky. They'd seen massed thunderclouds to the east, in the higher ground where the nameless waterway had its birth, and the water had risen. The flow was deeper and more powerful, flexing beneath the smooth surface like a wrestler's great muscles.

The air was thicker, as well, so the waterside with its breath of coolness was a bit of a relief under the blaze of the noonday sun. So was the odd gust of wind-born spray. Gelete came up to him as Valeria and another rider breasted the water to the other side, with a heavy rope held between them. The south-bank end was already secured to a large boulder.

The Nubakan commander was frowning.

"See?" he said, pointing upstream and down.

Conan looked, knowing better than to ignore the concerns of someone who knew the locality better than he did, and

Gelete was neither a fool nor a faintheart. This wasn't the Nubakan's homeland by a long shot, but it was similar enough to it.

"See what?"

"Sand, mud, banks," Gelete replied.

Conan looked again. The river spread out from the higher ground eastward, and the banks weren't quite as well-defined. There were sand and mudbanks to either side of a stretch of water a hundred yards across—say half bowshot—and here and there downstream he saw patches of reeds and swamp.

"Tracks say much game through here," the Nubakan said, and Conan reminded himself not to confuse fluency with intelligence. He felt stumble-tongued often enough himself in the twisting gutturals.

"Move twice year—wet season, dry season, south-north, north-south."

Conan's Stygian had improved a bit on this trip, and it took him only a few seconds to grasp what Gelete was telling him. This was a corridor for game migrations, a squeeze-point where movements over a front that encompassed miles narrowed to cross the water. He'd heard about those massive treks, though they weren't a feature of the northlands.

The Vanir and Aesir say that there are migrations of those oversized deer—caribou, they call them—north of their border.

This far south, the migrations could be enormous, teeming masses of animals more numerous than the inhabitants of a great city. Being caught in such a movement would be yet another pain in the arse.

"Not now?" he said.

"No, just over," Gelete said, pointing out places where the banks had been trampled down. "But…"

"But what?" Conan said.

"Where game cross river, wait is... wait are—" This time it took a while to get his meaning across, and eventually he had to call over one of his men who had a crocodile-hide quiver to hold his arrows. "Beast this skin," Gelete said as the leader of the horse archers joined them.

"Crocodiles," Conan said. Zarkabaal filled in the Stygian word.

Damn, Conan thought. He'd seen the animals now and then, once in the Styx. Nasty skulking beasts sometimes bigger than a man, and there was a pair of crocodile skulls outside the south gate of Sukhmet...

Crom, those skulls were half my height long or more, he remembered. *And that was just the head.*

"Just how big do crocodiles *get* here?" he asked.

The Nubakans talked among themselves, adding in broad gestures. Gelete turned back to Conan and shrugged.

"When from egg, this long."

He held his hands a few inches apart.

"Get older, get big. Get big, big, big—"

His hands showed increments of size.

"—until crocodile dies. Big I see at home... my height, half again." He marked the dirt with the heel of his sandal and then paced out a stretch ten or eleven feet long. "Heavy like one bull. But Nubaka land of hills. River bigger, crocodile bigger. Styx biggest. Eastern edge."

"The Styx?" Conan said. "In Khemi, in the moat, not that big."

"Stygian hunt big ones where they many peoples, for make safe cattle, children. In Styx by Nubaka, far south, very big. I show."

He called a name, and one of his men loped over. He had a thong around his neck, and on it was strung a tooth. Slightly curved, sharply pointed, and about the same length as the span of Conan's index and little fingers, if he splayed them apart. If the rest of the animal was in proportion, that was a *very big* crocodile, and no mistake.

"Crom," he swore.

Conan looked at the river. If they attacked herds of game during a migration, there was scant hope they'd be scared away by human voices and splashing! Turning back, he asked, "How did he kill *that*? And why?"

The man talked to his chief. Gelete turned to Conan.

"Take strong wood, wood like bow, spear-point on each end. Bend in half. Put in meat. Throw to crocodile. He eat, meat go away in stomach, steel go—" He made a sharp gesture, as of a bent spring snapping open. "Crocodile take no more cattle, children, women who fetch water."

Conan grunted. That seemed like an appropriate way to deal with the treacherous beasts, who could lunge out of the water to drag you in and drown you.

"This isn't a very big river," Conan said. "Not small, but—"

Gelete pointed westward. "Big there. Crocodile come for game go past." Then he grinned. "Tail meat of crocodile good in stew," he added. "Hide very…"

A moment's consultation.

"… good. Good, strong? Yes. Use for this, for that."

Conan thought for a long moment.

"Gelete, half your men on the north bank, half here—watching for crocodiles."

The Nubakan nodded and gave his orders. Half his

archers trotted into the water, holding their bows and quivers overhead—which was all they needed to do, given their scanty garb. The other half waited with shafts on string, covering them until they splashed up on the other bank. There they strung themselves out along the bank, bows ready, looking back the way they had come.

Conan ordered the Stygian spearmen to take to the water, standing in clumps on the shallower parts of the crossing. By then the heavy rope was stretched as tight as it would go, and the wagons were ready. Strapping his gear to his mount, he stripped down to his breeks and the belt that carried his dagger—the sword wouldn't be much good if he was swimming. He accompanied the first wagon, with a party of strong men tallied onto ropes tied to the upstream side, holding tight to keep it from tilting.

The water tugged at his legs as he rode and his horse made heavy going, sinking breast-deep and swimming in a few spots. He turned on the north shore and headed back to an improvised raft carrying a good deal of what was left of their supplies, less important now that they were only two days' march from the outermost Stygian settlements. There food could be bought—or commandeered, for those on the kingdom's business.

With the crossing fully underway, wagon after wagon followed, as did files of camp followers with their baggage bundled on their heads, some carrying squealing children.

The screams started just as the raft reached the north bank.

It grounded, with the waiting men coming out knee-deep to unload it. Suddenly there were shouts and a volley of arrows from the Nubakans on the north bank. Their powerful bows sent the long arrows sleeting into the water, and long scale-armored forms erupted, limbs thrashing and sending up geysers.

Conan whipped his head around. His horse turned, too, but he had to keep it tight-reined as it showed its teeth in a snort, rolled its eyes, and laid back its ears. A knot of Stygian spearmen were in the water, plunging their weapons into the chaos, heedless of arrows landing near them. There was another shriek as one of them vanished beneath the surface with blurring suddenness.

In the same instant something lunged half-out of the stream in a frothing wave of spray, great jaws longer than a man's arms closing on a whole upper torso and sinking back with a twist that flipped the victim's thrashing legs vertically into the air for a second. Then the froth was mixed with red.

That created a gap and more of the reptilian killers pushed past the spearmen, despite their frantic thrusting. The creatures were visible only as nostrils and eyes, and the wakes they left in the shallow water.

Valeria's horse reared, with a great crocodile clamped to its belly. She went into the water as the beast began whipping its head back and forth to tear loose a chunk of its victim. Flesh ripped and bone snapped and the mount's guts spilled into water that was rapidly going from silt-pale to bright red. Whipped further into a frenzy, more of the predators drove toward it.

A wagon capsized as half a dozen of the great reptiles attacked the mules pulling it. The chorus of terrified shrieks grew louder and more frantic.

Not a dozen paces away a Stygian soldier ran back and forth along the north bank, shouting at someone in the water and visibly nerving himself to plunge in. He hesitated a little too long, or his legs flashing along the water's edge were too tempting. A crocodile lunged half its considerable length onto the bank, clamped its jaws on one leg and dragged him back into the water, heedless as he stabbed at its bone-armored skull and a dozen arrows punching into its head and forequarters at point-blank range.

There must be scores of the beasts attacking, Conan realized. "Crom, give my arm strength!" he bellowed aloud. Nothing happened, of course—Crom didn't respond to prayers—but his eyes locked on a rock that split the current downstream of the ford.

He'd wondered where the priest of Set had gotten to. Now he knew.

The man was on that rock.

Not clinging like a drenched cat crawling away from reptilian death, either. He was kneeling on the rock's surface, somehow in full ceremonial fig as he'd been for the sacrifices at the mine. And there was a body before him as he raised the curved knife, chanting. It was a naked Stygian child, bound and squealing as the steel punched into the torso.

Another figure had been pushed to one side, gutted.

Two more struggled uselessly against their bonds.

Crom! This time Conan's bellow was wordless, but beneath it ran a thought. *He's summoning them!*

The Cimmerian hammered his heels into the horse's flanks and flogged at its haunches with the loose end of the reins. The beast shied, tried to turn against the pressure of the bit— naturally enough, since it had no dog in this fight and knew perfectly well what crocodiles were and what they wanted. Then with a despairing whinny it plunged into the water.

Conan headed straight for the rope stretched downstream

of the ford, which was now festooned with men and women clinging there desperately. One man vanished abruptly as he watched, wrenched free of his desperate two-armed grip on the rope. Another tried to climb *up* onto the rope, and even managed it after a fashion... until the armored snout of a crocodile rammed her free and back into the waiting fangs.

Closer, and Conan could see the long forms under the water, their armored tails sculling as they slipped effortlessly though their natural hunting-ground. Two headed for his horse's churning legs.

Better you than me, nag, Conan thought.

He kicked his bare feet clear of the stirrups and brought them up, crouching in the saddle. As the reptile's swift approach turned to a lunge, he unleashed all the power of his long legs in a desperate leap toward the rock where his enemy wrought magic. He soared over the rope, and his outstretched hands knifed into the water.

A shock of coolness, and he was eeling through it toward the dimly seen base of the rock. He resisted the impulse to look around wildly as he stroked, but a moving shadow on the sand of the river-bottom gave an instant's warning. He whipped aside just as the crocodile arrowed in from the direction of the south bank and slammed its jaws shut.

Action happened without thought, in a whirling knot of motion. His left hand clamped on the beast's foreleg, even as his right whipped the foot-long dagger from his belt and drove it home. He aimed in the pale, soft skin at the base of the throat. Most of a crocodile was armored in plates and scutes, but only fine scales covered the softer skin of their undersides.

Both arms were nearly wrenched from their sockets as the beast convulsed, and the dagger didn't strike the throat.

Instead the point drove home in the reptile's belly, just below the breastbone.

Conan let go of the foreleg and clamped both hands on the hilt of the embedded dagger. His feet hit the sandy mud of the river-bottom. Bracing himself, turning the point against the direction the reptile moved, he pulled with all his might as the crocodile's own lashing tail drove it past. The keen foot-long blade dragged down, opening a four-foot slit from breastbone to the midpoint of the belly, jerking at him savagely as it cut through tough muscle and organs.

Then it was past, whipping the surface into a sparkling sheet above him and sending out a cloud of blood that hid the light.

The Cimmerian flexed his knees and shot upward, whooping in a long breath as his head broke the surface. He'd retained a death-grip on the hilt of his dagger, and now he clamped it between his teeth as he stroked out for the rock that was the sorcerer's perch.

Fingers and toes gripped stone, and he pulled himself upward with desperate speed. He had to strike before the priest of Set knew he was there... and getting himself out of a river full of teeth provided an added spur.

The riven side of the little crag gave him good handholds and he went up it agile as an ape, keeping his breathing under control. When he came over the edge of the rock to the sloping surface of the top, he saw that chance had put him behind the Stygian. Even better, the priest-sorcerer was oblivious, swaying, chanting, and focused entirely on his ritual.

The last sacrifice saw him though, and the boy's eyes were wide as Conan swarmed over the edge and drove across the four feet separating him from his enemy.

"Ry'lla, aie Setesh, aie Cthu—"

With one big hand he clamped around the Stygian's neck, choking off the meaningless words. The other caught the hilt of the dagger as he dropped it from his teeth and drove it home, over and over again, with all the strength of his right arm. The sorcerer collapsed beneath him but wriggled—snake-like—long past the point where he should have been dead.

They rolled over the rock, face-to-face now, and the priest's lips moved again, spewing sound as well as droplets of blood.

"Set... curse... you!"

Conan drove the blade home again, this time up under the chin of the starved hawk-face, up and into the brain. The unnatural glitter of the dark eyes died at last.

The Cimmerian came to one knee, panting.

"You curse me? I *kill* you, Stygian pig," he gritted. Then a thought came to him, and he glanced around, snatched up a linen bag from the priest's sacrificial gear. A moment's cutting and twisting, and the priest's head was in it.

The body went over the edge with a kick, and there was a final turmoil of crocodiles as they fought over the bloody titbit. Conan stood, controlling the frenzy of battle and looking out over the ford.

Nearly all the remaining people and gear were over on the north bank now. The massed attack had stopped, the beasts returning to their natural behavior—which did not involve pack-like assaults pushed past the point of filling their bellies.

The frenzy stopped the instant the priest died, he thought grimly, and he scooped up the last, the living child as he leapt. They splashed into the water, and Conan waded ashore on the north bank.

A pike point drove toward him—

—and into the mouth of a crocodile behind him. He whirled with a curse, snatching for his sword. The beast's jaws clamped shut, severing the tough seasoned wood of the sixteen-foot shaft just below the long pyramid-shaped point, but the same shearing power drove the pike's head into something sensitive. The animal let loose a bellow and retreated, turning and diving into water red with blood and littered with the floating bodies of men and beasts.

Brocas of Corinthia threw down the useless pole that the crocodile's bite had made of his pike. His brown hair was plastered to a face pale with effort and spattered with someone's blood, but he grinned as he offered his hand.

The toddler clung to Conan with arms and legs as he came to dry land, bawling at an earsplitting volume. Though no louder than his mother wailed as she came running up. She took a moment to drop to her knees and hail him in the Stygian fashion, throwing up her arms, then clutched the child to her breast.

He ruffled the boy's hair, then grasped Brocas' hand.

"Shrewdly struck, dog-brother," he said. "Your debt is paid. Those jaws would have closed on my arse if you hadn't given him that thrust."

"Now *you* owe *me* a mug of beer," Brocas said.

"That I will pay, and down another with you."

Then he saw that the eyes of the crowd were on him, and he scowled as they broke into a chorus of shouts and hails.

"Get to work!" he bellowed. "Take a count of the gear and who's missing!"

They leapt to obey.

13

After camp was made that night, Conan took stock with the other leaders—Zarkabaal and Gelete—and with Valeria, who wore a mysterious smile and had a canvas sack at her feet. Conan had his own, smaller sack; it was the one containing the priest's head, and they'd all gotten a glimpse.

He intended to throw it out to see whether even the hyenas and ants could stomach it. Sometime soon, since in this climate the stench would be noticeable quickly, but that had to be done where it wouldn't be noticed. This meeting was about as private as the encampment itself could be, the fire being thirty feet away from anyone else. They were in plain sight of scores of eyes, but nobody could follow their conversation.

Some of the Stygian spearmen were making sure nobody got too close, and doing it with enthusiasm. The crocodile frenzy at the ford had increased Conan's standing in their eyes. Wading out of the deadly waters carrying a Stygian soldier's child hadn't hurt, either, and the glamor on the priest's sacrificial perch had held until he was dead.

Everyone just assumed the reptiles had gotten him.

"You all saw," Conan said, his voice low and serious, "how the crocodiles stopped when he was gone. Three dead, and another child to follow." He spat into the fire, sending up sparks.

"Why didn't anyone else see the priest?" Zarkabaal asked, his eyes going distant for a moment as he remembered the lay of land and water. "That rock stood out like a thumb, and it was only a little way downstream from the ford—maybe a quarter bowshot—but I didn't see a thing until you jumped into the water with the boy."

"High Priests of Set are sorcerers. All of them a little, some of them a lot," Conan said. "I called on Crom just before I noticed him... Crom, the god of my people. Crom doesn't help you, but he gives you the strength to fight for yourself."

"How very Cimmerian," Valeria murmured under her breath.

Conan went on. "So he gave me the strength to see through the illusion." At his words the circle around his fire made signs—hidden from outsiders' views—and murmured protective prayers.

"Why? Why *ye'ibabi liji inati* priest do what he do?" Gelete said. "Most those the crocodiles eat, they Stygians, too."

Valeria shrugged. "Sons of... rulers like that usually don't care much about common people at the best of times," she said. "In *Stygia*? The commons are lucky the nobles and priests don't choose to eat their children like suckling pigs, because if they wanted to, they would."

The Nubakan chief nodded with a grimace. He seemed to recognize the truth of what she'd said, but found it revolting. In the abstract, so did Conan. A Cimmerian chief didn't have any power his clansmen-warriors didn't give him. Without their loyalty and sword arms, the chief was nothing. That was true among most barbarians, and from Gelete's reaction it was so in the home of the Sons of the Lion, too.

Conan had been in civilized lands long enough to be used to their behavior, though that didn't mean he had to like it.

"He hated Valeria, for some reason," Conan said. "I don't know why—maybe that she's a northerner, and looks like someone from the ancient tales."

The people of the northern kingdoms that had risen out of Acheron's ashes were thoroughly mixed with the folk their tribal ancestors had overrun in the migrations and wars back then, if only because descendants of slaves gradually won their freedom and merged into the general population over scores of generations. Men from Poitain, in southern Aquilonia, mostly looked a lot like Zingarans. Kothites had a heavy dose of Shemite blood and some of them could have been Zarkabaal's cousin once removed, as far as appearance went, if not in speech and dress and custom.

"So he—" Conan used his foot to nudge the bag. "—likely did it to kill her, and perhaps me, as well. Anyone else… they were the price of his success. What he paid to hire the crocodiles as mercenaries, so to speak. His sorcery could make them attack, but they couldn't tell one human from another."

Or maybe Khafset asked him to do it, Conan thought. *Nobles and priests hang together in Stygia—often from the same families.*

"On top of that, we lost the gold," Zarkabaal said dismally, prodding at the fire with a stick until sparks flew upward, like more stars in the darkness of a moonlit night.

"I saw that wagon go over myself, and half a dozen of the beasts smashed it to splinters while I shot at them. The only good thing to come out of this cursed trip, and it's wasted in some crocodile's droppings or scattered down miles of river bottom haunted by the ugly brutes."

"No, it isn't." Valeria laughed, a soft husky chuckle. "No thanks to *you*, though, you fierce bearded heroes." She nudged the bigger canvas bag at her feet. "My horse got eaten, I *almost* got eaten... but I dived in and got these out of the wagon. Both of them. Good thing we tied them shut after we broke the locks, eh?"

There was a moment of echoing silence.

"That took nerve," Conan observed.

All of them looked at her with admiration, and she basked it in like a great golden cat—the human sister of the lion that had almost ripped Conan's throat out. That made him think of the Stygian priest again, which helped to damp down the reaction looking at Valeria produced in him.

"I was a pirate." She shrugged and gave him a sidelong glance that was full of mocking knowledge. "It's not the first time I've gone into dangerous waters for gold. A tiger-shark off the Baracha Isles will kill you just as dead as a crocodile, and the salt sea stings worse in your wounds."

Conan reached over and with a grunt lifted the sack. It was an unexpected effort for him, and probably weighed nearly as much as Valeria did.

"How in the name of Manannán Mac Lir did you get these up? They're *heavy* and that water must have been... eight, nine feet deep?"

Valeria's grin grew wider. "I tied them together with a rope, and then used a horse to haul them up from the north bank," she said. "Nobody was paying much attention while they ran around screaming… and I'm a sailor. Rope I understand, Mitra knows."

There were murmurs of admiration once more. That took not only nerve, but skill and coolness of mind.

"And lots of people saw the wagon go over," Zarkabaal gloated, raising his bottle in a toast, and looking as if he'd like to rub his hands at the same time. "Now we can keep it all!" He said that with hope, but without much conviction.

Conan and Gelete both shook their heads.

"No, if we said it was all lost, the minute any of us shows a glint of gold they'd think we stole it all," Conan said. Then he brightened. "It means we can keep *more* of it, though. Say, half. The rest we have to return."

It took a moment to thrash out the meaning, then Gelete agreed.

Valeria was silent.

"We can just say that the other half of it was lost in the crossing," Conan continued. "Plenty of wagons and gear were lost, and everyone in the convoy will swear to it. If we're careful, nobody but the four of us should know, and we can share it out with our followers later as we planned." This was very much the way the Red Brotherhood divided a prize between captain, quartermaster, and crew.

Then Valeria bristled.

"I should get a bigger share," she growled. "I saved it *all*." She put on an appearance of pious virtue, and Conan suppressed a laugh. "And it's all there. You can count it. So— four shares for me, that would be fair."

He snorted. "You *are* a pirate."

They all chuckled, and Valeria shifted to mock umbrage.

"No, I *was* a pirate," she protested. "Now I'm a mercenary. There's a difference!"

"Yes," Zarkabaal said dryly. "Dry feet, sometimes, and less throwing up." There was more laughter at that.

They had cheered up substantially.

"We should all agree to give her a double share," Conan said, "like we've earned as the leaders, taking a bit from everyone." He peered at them, one at a time. "That's fair." When he'd gotten assent, and without much grumbling, he continued thoughtfully, tugging at his square chin:

"We should hide it before we get past the border of the settled land—but not too far from Sukhmet. When we want it, a man on horseback could get out and back in a day, calling it a 'hunting trip' perhaps."

There were more nods, but also suspicious glances. What was hidden could be retrieved…

Zarkabaal gritted his teeth and sighed.

"I think Conan should be the one to bury it, and only he knows where," the Shemite said. "If all four of us here know where it is… well, my people have a saying." He uttered a string of throaty gutturals, and translated. "'Two men can keep a secret, but only if one of them is dead.' The Cimmerian is a man of honor… for a pirate and a mercenary."

"I am," Conan said, serious as death but conscious of Valeria's smile. "I won't cheat my own crew, or my comrades in arms."

Gelete nodded. "We have same saying about secrets," he agreed. "Conan hide it, but just Conan!" He glanced at Valeria. "You brave, good fighter, woman. Smart, too, but not know you like I know Conan. Plenty smart brave fighter steal, if he can. If *she* can, too."

She nodded, tight-lipped.

Before she could reply, a Stygian woman—perhaps a half-Stygian, being blunter-featured and darker than their usual aquiline-faced light brown—came over, carrying a pot of hot stew.

"Antelope, beans, and some of our last onions and wild greens," she said, bowing low and smiling broadly at Conan's gesture of thanks. They ladled it into their bowls. The late Stygian commandant's packets of spice had been put to good use by his cook, who'd also survived.

"This good," Gelete said, smacking his lips after a taste. "Good as my first wife made, Gods keep her." The Nubakan sighed. "Would be even better with crocodile-tail meat."

Conan shook his head. "Not those crocodiles."

"Why not?"

The Cimmerian looked around the camp; they'd lost forty or fifty at the ford.

"You wouldn't know who that crocodile had known, if you know what I mean."

Gelete roared laughter, along with Zarkabaal and Valeria. Conan reflected that his command of Stygian was improving if he could joke in it.

14

Next morning Conan rode out alongside his skirmishers. He made a hand sign to Zarkabaal, and led them as they all fanned out ahead... including Valeria, who cast a meaningful look over her shoulder at him as she legged her horse up to a trot.

He smiled wryly to himself.

Would that look was for me, and not the gold!

Conan turned his horse east, away from the rest. There was higher ground that way, and riding into the sun meant it would be harder for anyone else to see where he was going. Now and then he'd take shelter, usually behind a big thick-trunked baobab tree with its puffy writhing branches that always made him think the plant had caught leprosy. A swift climb and a long look assured him he wasn't being followed.

By anything human, at least, he thought.

That thought gained meaning when several lions got to their feet and watched him pass. As he looked over his shoulder, one of them licked its chops with a large red tongue. It stared at him and his horse, sighed, and slumped down in the shade of a termite mound where it rolled on its back for a nap, great paws in the air. More often they hunted in the dusk and dawn. Vultures squabbling over bones not far away were probably cleaning up the remains of the morning's repast.

It seems unnatural, big cats hunting in packs like wolves, he thought. *Well, this isn't Cimmeria.*

As he rode further, his horse snorted a warning—not frightened but alert. He came over a rise and saw a stretch of marsh where run-off from the hills to the east left a big pond edged by reeds. Two elephants were wading through the wetland, using trunks to gather up water-growth and stuff it into their mouths, flapping their huge fan-shaped ears against the clouds of biting insects they stirred up.

A hippo floated in the pond, eyes and swiveling ears showing on its massive square head like those of a gigantic frog. It snorted a spray of breath from its nostrils. Along the shore various antelope bent their heads to the water; they moved aside as he rode down through the thickening belt of trees and brush.

Conan hefted his bow, kept an arrow on the string, and his eyes roving as his mount bent its head and slurped up the muddy liquid. He didn't stay longer than he had to. Nor did any of the game animals, except the ones like the elephant and hippo and some of the massive black buffalo standing contentedly up to their bellies in the marsh.

They don't have to worry about lurking predators—the reverse, if anything.

It would be scant consolation that a beast wasn't going to eat you after it gored you full of holes, bit you in half, or squashed you to a pulp underfoot.

"Sets us in our place, eh, Caithaona?" he said, using the Cimmerian name he'd bestowed on his mount. It meant "Steed of Battle," and he slapped its neck.

Right, he thought.

A half hour had passed and he was considerably higher—high enough that the air had gone from *very* hot to simply hot. Large bare rocks blocked his view at times, and below him the rolling tawny-green, tree-speckled plain stretched to the limit of sight, with an occasional glint of water or a trailing dust-cloud from a moving herd.

No human settlements were in sight. War had passed over these territories long ago, when the Stygians came south of the deserts to found Sukhmet. Ever since, their hand had lain heavily on the land, with a general policy of reducing the population back down to helpless harmlessness whenever it showed signs of growing. They maintained control by enslaving and exporting, or slaughtering in the name of Set, or some combination of the two.

Sometimes very convenient plagues broke out, too, which mysteriously bypassed the Stygians. They hadn't done that recently, though, because after the first few times counter-plagues had launched right back at them. Proof that the magicians and deities of the surrounding black kingdoms were not to be ignored, either.

Sometimes hillocks of bare rocks balanced on each other in unearthly looking columns of weathered granite, or heaped up like a pile of monstrous gravel. Whenever there was any soil a dense tree cover grew, laced together with vines. Conan's target was a trident of stone that had been visible for miles, and whose rocks were a distinctive blushing pink.

Reaching the formation, he tied his horse to a convenient bush close to a trickle of water, but not too tightly lest some lion or leopard happen by. Then he slung bow and quiver over his shoulder by their belts, with the arrows and the bow pointing to the right, and threw the saddlebags over his left shoulder. Then he began to climb.

He grinned as he felt the weight in the bags, sixty or seventy pounds and enough to make him grunt a little. Gold wasn't bulky, but it was heavy, heavier than lead. It was probably imagination that made this weight feel fraught with possibilities, rather than just burdensome. Sweat was… different, somehow, when he shed it carrying a treasure won at the sword's edge, to a hiding-place only he would know.

Conan took the slope carefully—he wasn't trying to reach the top, just to find a good spot while memorizing the way he came. That part wasn't difficult. He'd always had a good eye for ground. The footing beneath him was harder; he'd rarely met this sort of bare rock-on-rock country before, even in Cimmeria's stony hills. He tested each footfall before transferring his weight. At last he came to a ledge with a sheer eight-foot inner edge, and another narrow shelf above that.

Further up…

"Lir and Manannán mac Lir!" he swore in delight.

Above him two titanic slabs rested against each other. Where they met was a lopsided triangle of blackness, twenty paces wide at the base and half that tall. It looked to go back some distance into the hillside, which was perfect.

Backing off to the outer edge of the ledge, Conan cautiously tossed the saddlebags up onto the next surface. The bags were tough, thick leather of some sort, which treated differently would have made a good shield. They landed up above with a dull thud, well to one side. That way he wouldn't unintentionally grab for a handhold, and get the bags instead.

There was only room for four paces between him and the near-vertical eight-foot rise, and he considered the rock carefully—he was familiar with this sort of terrain. Taking two quick strides, he sank down into a crouch and *leapt*. His foot landed on a faint ridge four feet up, and his hands slapped down on the sloping edge, where the rock was granite-slick but rippled by wear. He didn't push much on the foot, but it steadied him while he clamped his fingers on the rock and did a quick heave.

That left him crouching before the entrance to the...

Cave! he thought exultantly. That was perfect. *It* is *a cave*.

The saddlebags weren't entirely full of gold. He pulled a torch out of one, a length of ironwood with a splintered end bound in cord soaked in the black liquid that seeped out of the ground around here—he'd seen it in the east, too, around the Sea of Vilayet. Sometimes seepages like that caught fire, and burned eternally.

Checking the saddlebag, he confirmed that he had a second torch, as well. Pulling flint, steel, and a pinch of dried moss from the little pouch at his belt, he used them and blew cautiously. The moss caught, and he moved the first torch closer, moving the tarred, frayed edges of the cord into the small flame. It wavered as he breathed on it and caught, blue flames spreading over the surface of the soaked rope, and then adding yellow and red as it caught in earnest.

With a grunt of satisfaction he slipped the flint and steel

back into their pouch and pulled his belt around so that his sword hung in its usual place. Lighting a fire this way was a skill his father the blacksmith had taught him. More often than not, Conan's mother had to come and get a coal from the forge and carry it to the hearth. Valeria was the same. She couldn't light a campfire even with a bucket of charcoal already blazing.

That was less of a disadvantage on shipboard.

I can't seem to stop thinking about her, Conan mused. *Damned inconvenient.* He shook his head to clear it. *Now to work.* Taking the blazing torch in his left hand, he drew his sword with his right. It wasn't impossible that men might use this cave, and was fairly likely that something *else*—perhaps even more dangerous—was lairing-up in there.

The ruddy light cast flickering shadows above and around him as he warily followed the downward-sloping tunnel. There was soot on the rock overhead, but it was faded and ancient. The air was dry and there was no water seepage that he could see. That meant an age and more. Humans—or something that needed fire for light—had come this way, but not for a very long time.

Better and better, he thought. *Not hard to reach, but long odds that anyone will stumble across it.*

Sunlight faded away behind him, particularly after he went through a narrow spot that bent sharply rightward. Then the floor sloped up again, into the rocky mass of the hill, and for a stretch of yards he had to bend nearly double before things opened out again.

After a while he noticed something on the walls, and halted with a grunt of interest, raising the torch.

There were paintings, ones that skillfully used the colors

and natural ridges and bulges of the stone, yet in no style or manner that he'd seen in all his travels. Scenes of the hunt: tiny stick-figures with bows and javelins hunting antelope, or lions, or once an elephant with upreared trunk in a swamp. Various animals, including black-and-white spotted cattle shown with loving care.

There were depictions of war and ceremony; battles where short red-colored bowmen fought taller, darker figures with almond-shaped hide shields and broad-bladed spears and axes. Or the bowmen and spearmen together battling monsters—chimeras of man and beast, or men with the heads of cobras. Those might be symbolic representations of Stygians, or they might be the actual serpent-men told of in the oldest tales, from the nightmare times before the oceans drank Atlantis and the dreaming cities.

These gave way to scenes of dance, or of sacrifice, offerings to the gods of cattle and goats and sheep, or massed ranks raising spears in tribute to a larger, more elaborately decorated figure standing above them on a rock. That might be a general, or some great king... or a god, or a combination of those.

All of it looked very old, even older than the last of the torch-soot.

The tunnel didn't branch, though he could see no signs of tool-marks on the walls. At last it opened out into a cavern, smoothly floored in sand. Conan lifted the torch high— it was still burning well, though he'd light the second for the return journey. He realized that for once since landing on the coast of Shem, he was decently cool. There was a springlike temperature that spoke of the bones of Earth, far from the blazing sun above.

Metal glinted ahead, across the cavern. He stiffened and his grip tightened on the hilt of his sword, but the glint was unmoving. Conan moved closer in a wary crouch, sword ready; then he straightened as the circle of torchlight brought what backed against that wall clearer and clearer.

This wasn't just a cave: it was a tomb.

A king's tomb, at that, he thought.

The throne was a massive affair of carved ivory and ebony, backed by two crossed tusks larger than any he'd ever seen before. The figure seated there was desiccated, but naturally so, not the elaborate mummification the Stygians practiced. It was near-naked, so the great wound in the torso that had killed him still showed. The body must have been near-empty of blood even before it was brought here to its final resting-place.

Across the dead king's thighs rested a spear with an ironwood haft that even Conan would have found as heavy as he could handle. The bowed head bore something that was not quite a crown such as he'd seen northern kings wear. More of a golden diadem, studded with polished, uncut gems in barbaric abundance, and the remains of tall bird plumes. Before his feet were scattered treasures—rusted weapons, tattered shields, more ivory, jewels, a heaped dusty store combined with things that might have been cloth or ordinary wood before they decayed to dust.

Nothing had been attacked by animals or birds or insects.

That is not natural, he thought with a prickle along his spine.

The tall surface behind the throne bore more of the vivid ancient tales of battle and wild faring, and at their center

The throne was a massive affair of carved ivory and ebony.

a massive picture of what he was certain was the dead king himself, spear and shield held aloft over his head. The air bore no scent of decay, only a quiet scent of...

Ancientness, he thought.

As he drew nearer, Conan felt a pressure—not a hostile one, but an alien and uncompromising soul-voice.

Leave, it said. *Touch nothing, and* leave.

The Cimmerian drew himself up, and raised his sword in salute.

"Great King, sovereign and warrior, I will touch nothing of yours. I hail you, for I too am a warrior, and I offer this tribute, for your leave and protection." He went to one knee and laid down the saddlebags. From within he pulled one of the palm-sized gold ingots and placed it among the other treasures.

There was a moment of echoing quiet.

Then the feeling returned, redoubled—that he should go—but this time it was a warning, like a battle-comrade's shout.

Behind you!

There were things it was folly to ignore.

He inclined his head again and turned to retrace his steps, dropping the saddlebags just outside the entranceway to the cavern chamber. From this side he could see something over the natural arch he hadn't noted before: a huge painted hand, raised palm-out.

Conan paused only to pull out and light the second torch, and then retraced his steps, this time faster than he'd come.

Thank you for the warning, ancient King!

15

Conan's horse was still where he'd tethered it, but it was tossing its head and rolling its eyes, sweat on its body that couldn't have resulted from standing by water under the shade of bushes. He slung his bowcase and its quiver back to the saddle, tightened the girth.

The horse was too nervous to bother with its usual trick of swelling out its belly to leave the girth loose. Conan swung into the saddle.

"All right, Caithaona, let's get back to our friends."

The narrow winding path hid them from observers below, but Conan didn't like the way it *felt* this time. The high steep vine-and-bush grown sides were quiet, far too quiet—few birds, no dart of the tiny rabbit-sized antelope that frequented steep spots here, no scream of a rock-hyrax before its burrow. Every detail was different from the lands where he'd been born, but the overall effect was all too familiar. Something dangerous was stalking through these rocky defiles, and everything that could do so, had gone to ground.

He glanced overhead.

Wide black wings showed against the blue afternoon sky. Vultures and kites, on patrol for the killings that were a constant of life here, as in most places. But what died would likely be bigger and more meaty than in lands less abundant with beasts.

The gulley opened out, turning rocky rather than sandy, and steeper for an instant as it went down to the belt of trees and brush at the foot of the steeps, where the rolling savannah and its thigh-high grass began. What wind there was came from behind, hot with the sun-heated surface of the rocky hills, and still it was deathly quiet save for the buzzing of insects.

There was a *click* of rock on rock.

His horse happened to have its haunches bunched as they went down the sloping ground, and it leaped off them, soaring down the slope and then landing in a scramble, making its rider clamp his legs hard of the barrel. Conan caught a movement out of the corner of his eye, more of a flicker of shadow than anything else. He drew and struck back behind himself to his right and upward with a quick reflex.

The heavy blade clove air with a hiss, and then there was the thunking *chunk* of impact in muscle and bone. The angle was awkward, but the salt smell of fresh blood told him he'd struck home, and there was an earsplitting shriek that was halfway between a man's and that of a big cat.

The horse didn't stop, bounding through the rocky scree and brush as fast as it could go, but he could feel it was still under control. The Stygian lancer who'd trained it was dead at the Wedi Shebelli mine, but he'd done a good job of getting it over the natural equine trait of being uneasy around spilled blood.

Conan had enough time to hunch over in the saddle

and twist his head to look back. It was an animal, as he'd thought—a bull baboon, but of the giant southern savannah breed he'd heard of but not seen. It was bigger than he was, and heavier, with a huge mane around its face, wolf-like down to the amber-yellow eyes, except for the higher forehead. Its left hand-like paw must have been stretched out to grab at its prey, and now it was split to the wrist between the two middle fingers.

Blood fountained, and the animal thrashed and rolled in a cloud of dust and twigs and pebbles, shaking the limb and screaming over and over from between gaping jaws that parted wide, laden with teeth that would have done a lion credit. Then it slumped, whimpering, and the flow of blood dwindled. The sword must have severed the big veins when it cut into the wrist.

They hunt in packs, the stories say.

Conan and his mount plowed through thick brush now, where the hills met the savannah and the runoff from the slopes provided more water than further out. Flickers of movement showed to either side, khaki-brown fur almost the color of the soil half-glimpsed through leaves and blossoms and thorns and shaggy vines. He made a rough count; at least a dozen of them, and if the horse went over they'd swarm him like vultures over a corpse.

I'd be a corpse by then, *too*, he thought, shouting with laughter, calling out a Cimmerian battle-cry and taunt.

He bent over his mount's neck, urging it on. The brush thinned and he saw the baboons more clearly. They ran at a rocking pace on all fours, their hand-like forepaws slapping down and their haunches—lower than their shoulders—driving them forward in bounds that made them about as fast as the horse, at least for a little way. The Cimmerian wiped his sword and slid it back into the sheath, no easy feat when a horse was galloping over rough country.

Foam began to fleck the roan gelding's neck, spattering on his thighs and body. Caithaona couldn't keep this up forever, either. As they came out onto the rolling grassland he pulled his Shemite bow out of the case, then an arrow, and let the knotted reins fall on the horse's neck at the horn of the saddle. The mount checked very slightly as he leaned back, remaining obedient even with a dozen great predators after it, their breath carrying the rotten-meat stink of carnivores.

Creak of leather, hard muffled pounding of shod hooves on turf, the flatter slap of the baboons' passage and yipping, shrieking hunting-cries from their throats.

He could see them better now; they were spread out in a semicircle with the ends of it nearly level with him. Most of the pursuit was the females of the troop, and probably a few more were somewhere behind him, looking after their young, but these were formidable hunters in their own right. Mostly of his own weight and probably stronger, one for one. A trio behind him in the middle of the formation were males, with the manes shaggy around their vulpine muzzles, but not as thick as the first Conan had struck down—that had probably been their sire, if other pack-hunters were any guide.

All had red tongues lolling over their fangs, and those amber eyes, far far too intelligent...

Conan looked ahead and swore. There was a ridge, a steep one, and they were herding him toward it.

His knees guided the horse to the left. It obeyed, but

the baboons there pressed harder to cut him off. He had to cover more ground, slanting away from a straight flight. The beasts were far more keen-witted than wolves or dogs, but they'd have little experience with horse-archers.

The outermost of the left wing of the pack's formation was a big rangy female who must be two hundred pounds if she was an ounce. Her build recalled legends of man-wolves, or the ghouls said to haunt the frontiers of Argos and Zingara. Her panting jaws were open wide, tongue lolling, strings of slaver blown away by the passage of her galloping pace. Conan stood a little in the saddle and let his knees work like springs. When a Shemite or Hyrkanian did this, their upper bodies hardly seemed to move.

But they're born to it, Conan thought. *It's where the arrow goes that matters at seventh and last.*

The shaft went past the angle of his jaw, and a flat snap followed as he let the string roll off his fingers. Raw strength wasn't enough to draw a heavy bow like this—he needed to know the trick of putting his gut and lower back into it, not just his arms and shoulders. And...

Snap.

The shaft came close enough to the she-baboon's nose to give her a startling whap on the sensitive spot. She leapt six feet into the air, squalling and slapping at the injured organ, tumbled half a dozen paces with the momentum and the bad landing... and then was on her feet and galloping twice as hard. Perhaps it was a personal matter for her now.

Conan wasted less than a second in unkind thoughts about horse archery, and put another shaft to the string.

"Let them get closer," he muttered.

The ground rose, and his horse was laboring now. The

baboons weren't carrying riders, it was, and he was a big man with a fair weight of gear along. The steep drop toward which the pack had been herding him was off to the right, but the hill was still bad enough. A little further left, toward where it was just a low swell...

The two baboons on that side curved in toward him, close enough that he could hear their panting over the drum of hooves and creak of leather and the slapping of their own paws on the ground. They ignored the bow as he raised it—it hadn't really hurt their packmate the last time, after all.

Snap.

The lead baboon jumped again, but this time there was a hard wet slapping sound as the arrow punched into her torso. She went over in a squalling tumble of dust and bits of savannah grass, and then in a horribly human gesture wrenched the arrow free and collapsed, coughing up gouts of blood and lung with a racking sound. The animal behind her tried to halt in a skidding plume. That froze her while Conan pulled another shaft to the angle of his jaw and shot.

Snap.

This one went right through the beast's throat and out in a double flash of red. Conan put his head down and clapped his heels into his mount's flanks. Up the rise and over it, and he was into the rolling savannah proper, with only a few high hills on the northwestern horizon to make him certain of his course.

He looked behind and swore.

The baboons were further back, but they were spreading out in the same sickle-shaped formation and keeping up the chase. Albeit a little slower, which was fortunate since he had to let his horse cut its pace, too, or it was going to drop dead on him.

He bared his teeth at the sight. This was not natural, because the baboons were acting as if this was an *assault*. Predators didn't *fight* their prey, not in the human sense. They killed for food, or for fun if it was easy. If the prey was too dangerous or if it moved off their territory, they just went away and killed something else. Wolves and lion-prides only fought their own kind over pack-boundaries and mating.

Set... curse... you. The last words of the Stygian priest-magician echoed through his mind; and with them came the memory of the lion charging him.

And that rhino going after Valeria, he thought.

Then he remembered the lion just looking at him this morning, and slowly grinned. There might be a curse, but it couldn't have been mighty enough to turn *all* the animals in this land against him. He'd have been torn to bits, smashed to paste, devoured, or all three if that was so. Those lions would have attacked him, instead of just licking their chops.

In that case, perhaps two could play at the game.

Conan looked ahead, scanning the land and his own memories. All these flat-topped thorn trees looked alike, but there were four over by that rock, and there were the vultures... He booted the horse up from a canter to a shambling gallop—all it could do after the mad dash from the hills of the cave. The wind was from the west, and the horse began to whinny and toss its head as it scented predator, but it knew what was chasing them, too.

The lions were napping, scattered in the shade of the trees.

At the drum of hooves, one of them leapt to her feet, and a cub squalled and ran for the shelter of a nearby boulder. *That* cry of fear and distress had them all up, and more cubs following the first. Ten pairs of yellow eyes—eight females and two big maned males, probably brothers—locked on him, and lips drew back over teeth he could see clearly, probably amid growls he couldn't hear.

Conan shrieked out a Cimmerian war-cry, the type used in a charge. He'd screamed the same challenge when he went up the scaling-ladder to Velitrium's wall, when he was still a youth of fifteen years.

The lions milled about, angry and confused…

Then they got a sight and scent of the great plains baboons that were following him. That was something they understood; an enemy, like a pack of hyenas, out to take their food and kill their young.

Conan put his head down over the horse's neck and flogged backward with the loose ends of the reins, left-right-left. The mount barely needed it, with another set of meat-eaters within sight and hearing and smell. A roar went up from the two male brothers, shatteringly loud at only a few dozen feet away, a sound that made the hair bristle along his spine—because it said, at a level far below thought, *this beast eats men.*

The stance in the saddle let him look backward as the giant baboons realized what they were galloping into. A lioness and a baboon went over, rolling in a cloud of dust, until the great cat managed to get its hind legs up and rip downward in a shower of blood and bright pink intestines. All three of the male baboons leapt for a maned lion, and they went over in a tangle of paws and jaws as the brother danced around the tangle, striking with both paws in blurring-fast slaps—slaps tipped with long, sharp claws.

Conan turned his face westward and grinned wider as the chorus of growls and shrieks, roars of anger, and screams of pain fell behind him. After a while he let the horse shamble to a walk, and later swung down out of the saddle to lead it for a while. It would need a few days in the remount herd before it could be ridden again.

If it didn't die before he got back to the rendezvous.

He bellowed laughter at the sky, sending a flight of birds up from a nearby thicket.

"The curse has missed again!"

16

Conan kept his face blank as he lifted the chest of gold ingots, let it thump down on the governor's desk with a *thud* and muffled dull *clank*, and threw back the lid.

That blankness made him much less conspicuous than the elaborate expressions of virtuous ignorance that Valeria, Zarkabaal, and Gelete had pasted on their faces. Zarallo and the portly governor of Sukhmet and its surrounding lands—

Wenamun, that's his name, Conan thought, dredging it out of his memory. *And isn't it just like a pudgy parasite to only show up when the gold is laid on the table?*

—both glared at them with squint-eyed suspicion. Any man who was a leader would have done the same, since they had instinctively adopted expressions used to disguise guilt.

The governor was a thick-set Stygian in his late middle years, his dark eyes shrewd in a face rendered grotesque to the Cimmerian's eyes by the kohl that ringed the source of that suspicious glare. Wenamun trailed his fingers down each side of a wrapped linen headdress, the tails of which dangled on his chest.

"This amount is insufficient," he said. "You should have had the spearmen search the bottom of the ford after the attack by the crocodiles!"

Zarallo's clerk translated what the Stygian bureaucrat and minor nobleman said, into the northern-based language the mercenaries used. By his scars, the clerk once had been a soldier, and he struggled to keep the scornful contempt out of his voice as he rendered the Stygian's words. There was plenty of both in Wenamun's gravelly voice, too, but Conan was quite confident they were directed at a different target.

Conan spread his large, battered hands.

"How... Sir?" he said. "They weren't going to go back into the bloody water that consumed their comrades and so many camp followers, certainly on my say-so. I wasn't in their chain of command—I commanded the company scouts, not the Stygian troops, acting as leader only because theirs were dead. They might have obeyed a Stygian leader who told them to do that. They wouldn't obey me, and I had no way to compel them." He gestured behind. "Scout Valeria here rescued the one chest on her own initiative—I didn't tell her to do it." He added, "Sir."

"I agree with my scout commander," Zarallo said smoothly. "He could not command the Stygian troops."

Wenamun swelled, looking as if he'd burst at the end of the process. The cream of the jest was that he couldn't disagree with what they said—Luxor would condemn any such disloyalty, and denigration of the divine superiority of Stygians.

The governor's ire was in contrast to the smooth quiet opulence of their surroundings. The second-story chamber looked out on a courtyard of pools and lotus-flowers and bougainvillea trained over arched trellises. They could be seen clearly between slender stone pillars carved and painted to resemble bundles of papyrus reeds.

The rest of the big room was scattered low-lying furniture of carved and inlaid wood on a marble floor, with taller-than human figures carved and painted in the stylized Stygian fashion on the walls—the shoulders always faced outward, for starters, and the face was always in profile. Mostly they were engaged in hunting or ritual. On one wall there was a bronze serpent rearing its head, with water coming out of its fanged mouth and falling into a carved stone basin.

Being governor here isn't a high-rank job, Conan thought, *but it's well paid. Not surprising, when gold's the reason for this outpost.*

Wenamun took one of the ingots out of the chest and pushed it across the table in front of him.

"Captain Zarallo," he said. "It is my opinion that your men saved what could be saved. Take this as reward for them, and for you."

He spoke as if the words hurt his mouth. Three shaven-headed Stygian clerks in kilts and sandals sat cross-legged on mats to one side of the governor's chair. One used a reed pen to make a mark on the roll of papyrus he held, while the other two stood, emptied the chest, counted and weighed the ingots, re-packed them and tied the chest up with cords and wax seals bearing the governor's stamp. Since it was being done in public, Wenamun would have to send it all to Luxor without the usual under-the-table deduction.

Behind him, three girls clad only in feathered headdresses, each with a string of beads around the waist, waved fans of snowy ostrich-plumes set in gold-and-turquoise triangles mounted on ebony shafts to cast a cooling breeze on Wenamun's sweating corpulence. Conan's eyes strayed to them. Two were local girls, jet-black and statuesque with more colored feathers in their hair, and the third was a blond northerner, passable in looks but an exotic rarity here, and probably very expensive.

Valeria saw him looking and raised a brow.

Conan shrugged very slightly.

Well, if you're *not interested…*

She snorted slightly as they exited the governor's mansion with his kohl-shadowed glare belying his flattering words. Zarallo preempted any banter as he walked a score of steps away and turned to confront them, his goatee and mustachios bristling as he glared into the blank bland innocence of their faces. The few locals in the vicinity formed a bubble of space around the dangerous-looking armed foreigners.

"How much?" he said.

They glanced at each other.

"Don't try to diddle me on this," he growled, keeping his voice low. "I'm not a Stygian who can't make a fuss because he can't afford to have his king's inspectors arrive from Luxor to look at the books. How much did you hide?"

Gelete shrugged and took a step back, as if to say, *my share is my share.* Zarallo gave him a look of grudging respect along with a nod, and then turned back to his own employees. He crossed his arms on his breastplate.

"Well?"

Conan shared a glance with Valeria and Zarkabaal, and breathed deeply. Captain Zarallo was shrewd and wouldn't be baffled by any story he could create. Making up things on the spot wasn't one of his strengths, and he didn't think Valeria would be any better. Zarkabaal *would* be better at it, but Zarallo knew that and would discount anything he said.

"We kept half," Conan said. "There were two chests.

We discovered them after we got out of the Wedi Shebelli mine, in the mine commandant's wagon. The plan was to divide them between us and the Nubakans, and then divide our half according to Red Brotherhood rules."

"Except for me," Valeria said, setting her fists on her hips. "I'm the one who dived into the river at the ford of the crocodiles and got them back, while Conan was hauling Stygian brats—"

Wisely, she didn't mention the priest of Set.

Not while they were in Stygia.

"—so I get a captain's share!"

"That's fair," Zarallo said, pursing his lips judiciously.

She brightened. Then he went on. "A double share of half what you kept, after Gelete gets his. The rest goes to the Free Companions, into the common pot."

None of them spoke, and none were happy—certainly Conan wasn't. But that was the rule for plunder. Once you got beyond the level of stealing the shoes and belt-purses off the dead and grabbing a bottle of wine.

Zarallo's voice turned genial, in fact almost apologetic.

"The Stygians are cursed slow with the money they promised for our services—and they're always short after Wenamun finishes skimming."

Conan grunted, and the others offered equivalents. Late pay or clipped coin was a depressingly universal feature of a mercenary's life. That was one reason most preferred service in time of war. Employers tended to come closer to paying on time, then, to avoid riots, desertion, and switching to the other side. In war there was more prospect of wholesale plunder, too. Zarallo might like a quiet life, by mercenary standards, but he was conscientious in looking after his men's interests. That wasn't something a soldier could count on with every captain.

A tenth of the company's official ranks were "ghost warriors"—names on the rolls without bodies attached, and their pay went to the captain. That was long-standing custom, accepted by all. Zarallo didn't try stretching it, much, which made him a paragon.

"Now, where is it?" Zarallo said.

Another long pause and the commander tapped the fingers of his gauntleted hand on the steel armor.

"Be sensible," he said. "You can't turn ingots into coin—that needs moneylenders, bankers, and any you found who'd deal with you, they'd skin you alive. *If* you could get it out of Stygia in the first place, which isn't likely."

Conan and Valeria developed identical sour expressions. They'd both been pirates, and privateers lost half or more of the value of loot when they fenced it with merchants willing to engage in under-the-table deals.

"One of my cousins is a banker," Zarkabaal said. "He'd deal honestly, for family's sake, and take no more than a fair commission. He'd ask two-tenths, and settle for say, half or three-quarters of that."

Given the ruthless ferocity of Zarkabaal's expression and the hard muscular body beneath it, Conan found that hard to believe that one of his close kin spent his time behind a counting-board, but it might be true. The Shemite cities were famous hives of trade and manufacture, and the cunning of their merchants was legendary.

"Your banker is three months' travel away," Zarallo said. "I can cut the gold into smaller pieces, unrecognizable, and mix it with *other* gold and silver in a bag with a fair amount already there. Move it through suppliers and moneylenders so it can't be traced. You'll get your share… now, and without awkward questions from the Stygians. If you could manage it at all."

His clerk nodded thoughtfully, with his fingers making involuntary twitching movements as if he was writing.

Conan shrugged agreement—albeit unwillingly. He didn't like tricks with counting-boards and seals and stamps. Striking his opponent over the head and grabbing the spoils was more to his taste.

Not that long ago, he wouldn't have grasped any of what the mercenary officer was talking about. More likely, he would have thought it a scheme to cheat him—the sort of thing men in civilized lands did as often as they drew breath. Being a wandering man, however, he had picked things up.

A lot of southerners had learned a painful lesson—that he wasn't a brainless brute from the backwoods. Some had survived the education. Others had not.

"You fix our share for us?" Gelete said.

"Half and half," Zarallo said, and spat on his palm. The head of the Free Companions and the leader of the Nubakan archers slapped their palms together and shook.

"You honest man," Gelete said, and then grinned whitely. "Besides, I know how much gold… and where you live."

And I have scores of archers who can hit a bird on the wing at a hundred paces, Conan added in. The Cimmerian could appreciate the cleverness of that. Trying to learn precisely where the gold was would look suspicious—what reason could he have, except a plan to go get the whole of it himself? He *did* know, however, the amount he was due.

The Nubakan turned and walked off.

Zarallo turned to the rest of them. Conan bent his head and gave a quick, accurate description of where it was. He also told them of the dead king and his tomb. Zarallo pursed his lips at the description.

"Uncanny," he said, "but what isn't, in Stygia?" He went silent for a moment. "We'll be putting out patrols south of here, to make sure that the neighbors don't take advantage of the uprising at Wedi Shebelli. The rest... the rest will take time."

The commander and his clerk strode off.

Conan stretched. "I'm for a drink and a game of dice," he said. "Care to join me?" he said to Valeria.

"No," she said bluntly. She turned and followed Zarallo.

Conan ground his jaw. Zarkabaal grinned, his teeth snaggle-shaped but white in his curled black beard.

"I could use some wine and a few throws, Cimmerian," he said, making a dice-casting motion with his cupped right hand.

"You're not nearly as pretty," Conan said sourly. Then he gave a grin. "And not if we're using your dice."

"Ah, but I know a place run by a Shemite woman where the wine's actually not bad," the Shemite said. "And there are girls; clean, and not too expensive."

"Lead on," Conan said, but his eyes were on the diminishing sight of Valeria's shapely figure. It seemed to taunt him with every motion.

17

Conan opened his eyes, and swallowed against a rush of nausea.

The next pallet blurred in his vision as he blinked crusted lids, and the morning drum throbbed as if it were located directly between his abused ears. A trumpet squealed like red-hot needles thrust into his head. Waking naked, as usual, he heaved himself upright and staggered to the jakes to empty his painfully distended bladder.

As he went, the queasiness in his stomach emphasized how badly the long dim barracks room—a narrow rectangle of mud-brick walls and rammed-earth platforms with straw matting pallets—smelled. Not least because the rations were heavy on beans and lentils.

The jakes were worse, and he emptied his stomach into the trench as well. That made him feel marginally better after, and he was a little steadier still when he walked... carefully... into the ablutions room with its rough stone pavement.

Zarallo had seen that it had plenty of water, and there was enough to douse himself down thoroughly and then rinse, spit, and drink four dippers from a bucket specially brought from a spring outside the walls. For some reason that made men less likely to come down with belly-fevers, always a menace to troops garrisoned in a city.

He'd once squatted on his heels and listened to a philosopher in a city in Ophir talk learnedly about spirits that infested human waste and escaped into drinking water. That had left him shaking his head at the madness that afflicted civilized men. Everyone knew that the spirits concerned were little men with hobnailed boots and red caps—at least everyone back in his clan's village knew. They put out bowls of blood to appease them, every time they killed a pig or steer.

Cities were unhealthy because they were unnatural, a perversion.

Washing made him feel well enough to walk back to his pallet, tie on a new loincloth, and don a spare pair of short breeks. It was still painful to walk outside into the bright hot sunlight as he buckled on his sword-belt and answered to the morning roll call. Then he walked over to the pells, picked up a double-weighted shield and double-weighted practice sword of some hard local wood, set himself, and found an opponent.

He felt not the slightest impulse to go for his bowl of porridge.

"Yaaaaah!" he shouted—and winced as the cry seemed to lift off the top of his head. *Now I know what it will feel like to be seventy years old*, he groaned inwardly. Not that there was a chance in a thousand he'd make it to old age like that. *More likely I'll become king of Aquilonia*, he thought with a rueful grin.

An hour's vigorous practice sweated most of the misery out of him. He was just stopping for another long drink of water—from the same source—when shouts and the clatter of hooves brought his head up with a jerk, sending his sweat-wet black hair flying. Through it he saw a horse galloping for the barracks-gate.

Valeria of the Red Brotherhood was bent over its neck, flogging behind her with the ends of her reins, and her face fixed in a fighter's grin. She whipped past him with her long hair like a golden banner, then out through the portal and onto the streets.

Conan calmly finished the dipper of water and wiped his face on his forearm. This was going to take some thought.

He wasn't the best man in the world to come up with a plot or a scheme or a tale on the spur of the moment. But a hunt… a hunt, now, that was a different matter.

Zarallo looked harassed when Conan walked into the room the commander used for meetings related to the Free Companions. A Stygian officer was standing before his desk, a man who looked vaguely familiar.

"I demand that you produce the unnatural bitch immediately, outlander!" the man said loudly. "We know for a fact that she has returned from Wedi Shebelli."

"Lord Nebset," Zarallo said, "I simply can't. Despite my commands that she be confined to barracks awaiting charges for her crime, she fled. My men report she rode her horse out of the south city gate not long ago."

"Then find her," Nebset said. "Find her and bring her to me for gutting!"

"I assure you," Zarallo said in what was probably intended to be a soothing tone, "every effort will be made to apprehend the criminal."

"If you can't, I will do it—I and my blood kin," the Stygian officer said, his voice low and menacing. "Even the dead will take up vengeance."

What does that *mean*?

He stormed out past Conan, snarling guttural curses, so angry that white showed all around the pupils of his dark eyes. Conan strolled up, left hand on the hilt of his broadsword, and thumped his right fist to his breast in salute.

"Ishtar in the Underworld," Zarallo snarled, shuffling through his papers. "What do you want now? Get out of here... No, stay, I'm going to need the scouts. That bloody pirate bitch born from Hell's arsehole has done it now! The turd's in the soup."

"What's she done?" Conan said, hiding his smile. *Whatever it is, it won't be dull*, he thought.

"You know that Stygian officer she kicked in the balls?" the mercenary commander said. "Named Khafset?" He spat out the word.

Conan laughed, and it didn't even hurt much.

"I was there," he said. "What a woman!"

"What a *she-devil*," Zarallo ground out. "For reasons known only to the venom-addled brain of a Stygian noble, Khafset decided to have a second go at our Valeria."

Conan laughed again. "Some men don't learn what *no* means, even with a boot to the balls and a swordpoint to the nose," he said. "How badly did she beat him this time?"

"She didn't," Zarallo ground out. "He waited until she was... what's the sailor's expression for having a skinful?"

"Until she was three sheets to the wind," Conan said, frowning in concern, and then he remembered Valeria's expression as she thundered past. That hadn't been the look of someone running from defeat—not at all.

"Until she was three sheets to the wind and went out into an alley to find a spot to water the gutter. Caught her while her breeks were still around her ankles, came up behind her and tried to stick it in." He had to suppress a smile. "Instead *she* stuck it in."

Conan frowned again, and then his brow cleared, and his teeth showed in a grin of snarling approval, like a happy wolf's.

"By Crom. You mean she knifed him this time?"

"Twice, with that foot-long duelist's dagger she carries. Stabbed behind herself once, and got him in the inside of the thigh, probably aiming for his balls." Conan nodded, picturing in his mind where the hilt of the dagger would have been when her breeks were down.

As close to her left hand as it is when they're up—and the inside of the thigh... that's a vulnerable spot, full of essential things and on the way to the crotch.

"Then when he let her go and bent over to grab at the wound, she turned and slashed him across the eyes. He bled like a stuck pig."

They were both silent for a moment, playing the scene out in their minds with the long experience of veteran fighting-men... and veteran brawlers in taverns and back-alleys. Zarallo's irritation held a grudging respect. That move would work… *if* she was quick as a snake, and if she didn't hesitate at all but struck like a cobra herself.

"Then what?"

"Then she hoisted her breeks, went back to the tavern and finished getting drunk!" Zarallo's big battered black-haired hands clamped on the desk-table in front of him. "She turned up for morning parade yawning and scratching, just about when the city watch found his bled-out corpse in the alley."

Conan made a noncommittal grunt. "He fell on his own deeds," he said. "Back in Cimmeria, any woman who did that would have a song sung in her honor. Though it might start a blood-feud," he admitted. "Or maybe not. Forcing a free Cimmerian woman is a nithing deed, so you can't complain if she cuts you. It doesn't bind your kin to vengeance, either, especially if they don't like the man to begin with."

Zarallo went purple.

"Wenamun doesn't think so!" he bellowed. "Khafset's donkey-diddling brother *Nebset* doesn't think so!"

Ah, that's *why he looked familiar,* Conan thought, raising a brow and jerking a thumb over his shoulder in the direction the Stygian officer had gone.

"The very same," Zarallo growled, "and he's *not* in disgrace in Luxor—he was just visiting. Khafset was his brother, and there may be another sibling here. I'm not sure. These Stygian lords breed like rabbits. Between wives and concubines, twenty offspring are nothing to them. Nebset told me, in so many words, that if it doesn't look like we're doing what we can to find Valeria, his masters in Luxor may dismiss us. It would be 'unfortunate,' he said, if we met a bloody end as we departed Sukhmet."

Conan grunted thoughtfully.

"You want me to take the scouts out?"

"For a start," Zarallo said. "I'm going to have to send a dozen patrols to beat the bushes." Then he paused for a moment, and one eyelid drooped very slightly. Conan was puzzled for an instant, then inclined his head, also very slightly indeed.

Zarallo went on in a blustering tone.

"You don't have a problem with that?" he questioned loudly. "I thought you wanted to put her on her back yourself? Me, I'd rather bed a rabid fox-bitch, but no accounting for tastes."

"I wouldn't have minded," Conan said, keeping his voice casual. "She's stuck-up, though, and you're right, the company's in danger."

"Well, get to it, then!" Zarallo said, then he turned: "Gavrillo!" he shouted. "Get me that roster!" Conan saluted again—Zarallo ignored it—and turned to go, strolling out while he tapped one thick thumb on his chin.

If there's one thing that would get me where I want to be, it's rescuing her from this, he thought, and his grin grew wider. *Besides, I'm bored to tears with this running pustule on Stygia's stinking unwashed buttocks, anyway.*

For all his bluster, Zarallo hadn't tried to put Valeria in the guardhouse before she made a break for it.

He doesn't want to catch her, he mused. *Zarallo just wants to make the Stygians think he wants to catch her. Have everyone running around looking busy and beating the bushes and making a lot of noise.*

Speaking of that...

He walked out into the courtyard of the barracks-square,

roaring for the scouts and Zarkabaal. The Shemite turned up a few minutes later, looking about as seedy as Conan had felt when *he* woke up. Nevertheless, his grin was sincere.

"You Cimmerians are men of iron," he said admiringly. "Half the girls at Madam Jetzabaal's will sing your praises—"

"The wicked woman Valeria has treacherously knifed and slain the great Stygian noble Khafset," Conan said loudly. "Because he deigned to take notice of her, the bitch!"

Zarkabaal gazed at him blankly for a moment, and began to say something. Conan winked obviously. The Shemite threw off the wine-fumes and his usual shrewdness returned.

"*Abomination*," he proclaimed with an ostentatious look of horrified outrage, clapping a hand to his forehead and wincing at the impact. "She should be flogged with scorpions!"

Conan winced, as well.

"We must prepare the scouts to pursue her," he said. "Prepare them *thoroughly*."

"Yes, yes, this is a task of great importance," Zarkabaal agreed. "We must avenge the noble Khafset. No effort will be too great"

For Zarkabaal, Conan knew, preparing thoroughly would involve a bath, breakfast, and a trip to have his hair and beard trimmed and curled with hot irons in best Shemite style.

Conan spent the morning seeing to the horses—he selected three for himself—and getting the pack saddles stuffed with supplies, all charged to the company's account. It was just short of noon when Zarkabaal rejoined him, gnawing at the leg of a roast chicken.

"Is all in order?" Conan said—again loudly. Zarkabaal belched—also loudly—tossed the stripped chicken-leg aside, and as if in thought stroked his newly curled beard with its light coating of scented oil. Then his eyes went wide.

"Aha! By the great god Chusor, patron of metalsmiths, we have neglected to have the horses reshod. Bless Chusor's wisdom. It would be ill to have them cast shoes while we pursue the criminal Valeria, a true child of Lamashtu's wickedness."

The Shemite intoned it piously and bent to touch the earth and mark his forehead.

"To the blacksmith!"

Now that is clever, Conan thought. *Just enough truth in it to look good on a report. All well-wishing spirits, remind me never to try to win a contest in sneaky with my good friend Zarkabaal.*

As in most places, the smithy nearest the barracks was where the locals gathered to exchange gossip and tall tales. The hearth was in the open courtyard of a building, surrounded by thatched galleries, and folk stood back from the charcoal.

The smith was delighted to have two dozen new horses to shoe, and he and his apprentices set to with a will. They were naked save for leather aprons and sweating as they worked the bellows and hammered blanks amid an odor of scorched metal and sizzling oil, a hiss from the quenching bath, and a *tink-tink-tink* and *clang* as nails were driven home and crimped.

After an hour, the blacksmith stood straight. "That's all the ones that need doing," he said. "Most of the others are nearly new-done."

Conan shook his head and wore a grave face.

"We have an important mission," he said. "We can't take chances. Do them all."

The blacksmith shot him a look, but he had done what honesty required. Gathering his workers he set to with a will on the other beasts. A vendor brought beer, and Conan paid him to hand a mug to all the scouts.

Zarkabaal did the same for his horse-archers.

The sun was heading west as they rode out the southern gate, and a haze of dust hung over the dirt of the rutted road that led south to the savannah and the mines.

One less mine now, of course, Conan thought.

He had no doubt whatsoever a Stygian expeditionary force would arrive in a year or two. They would retake the mine, execute any rebels they could catch, in suitably drawn-out fashion, and round up enough new slaves to put it back into production. Stygians weren't always swift; in their rigidity; the organs of their state were like moss overgrowing a statue, product of a history that stretched back beyond the time of legends.

However, they were always very, very patient.

All mounted and leading at least one spare horse per rider, the column of two dozen scouts made ten miles before they camped for the night. That was good time, especially since they left enough margin of time to buy two sheep from a Stygian farmer, along with vegetables and goat-cheese and unwieldy loaves of bread.

Roasting the sheep then was a pleasant change from

rations in Sukhmet, and made Conan grin at how like a nice, leisurely hunting trip this was—especially without buffalo or rhinoceros. He inhaled the savory smell.

Zarkabaal came over and sat, using his snaggle teeth to strip meat off a rib.

"I notice you brought three remounts with you, and enough supplies to keep a man for a month," he said quietly. The men at the next campfire were making the night hideous with attempts at song.

"You're a smart one, when you're not drunk or hungover," Conan replied in a similar quiet tone. "If for some reason I weren't to return to Sukhmet, would you be willing to see that my scouts get their share of the gold? Even," he added grudgingly, "that damned Pict."

Zarkabaal leaned over and extended his hand. Conan took it, a hard quick pump.

"I will," the Shemite said earnestly. "By Ishtar who loves faithfulness and Melquart Lord of Battles, who prizes a warrior's honor I swear it—may they turn their faces from me if I do not."

18

"**Y**es, I saw her," the farmer's wife said.

The roadside farmstead enabled them to water the horses from the well with its shadoof—a tall, pivoted pole next to the low wall that made it easier to draw up the wooden bucket when it had filled. Conan's eyes flicked over to make sure his horses were getting their share, and then back to the fat farmwife.

There was something odd in her tone.

They were getting close to the border of Stygian control, and the mud-brick huts had pitched thatch roofs that protected them from the heavy seasonal rains. Already a couple of heavy showers had slowed their progress. The air was thick with moisture and at times the roads were so muddy as to be nearly impassable. Conan didn't regret the delays, though, and in this region rains dried off quickly.

The dwellings were surrounded by a yard-high earth berm overgrown with straggly grass and weeds. On top of that were arm-thick poles ten feet long driven into the dirt and woven together with the branches of dried thorn-trees, iron-hard and studded with hooked needle-sharp thorns as long as a big man's fingers.

Through it he could see villagers going about their tasks,

a round dozen dealing with a swarm of chickens who spent the night in woven coops hung from the branches of a big baobab tree. Others using pots with many small holes to water rows of plants in a kitchen-garden, pounding something in mortars—probably grain, and keeping a swarm of toddlers from committing suicide in the many ways to which children that age were given.

Under the white sun of midmorning it all smelled of hot dust and acrid cooking-smoke, and powerfully of cow-dung; there were other thorn enclosures nearby to hold livestock, and it looked as if the farmer spent as much time with his animals as he did on the fields of millet, sorghum, cassava, and cotton. Men and some women were hoeing as the weeds took heart with the rains and tried to outrace the crops for the sun's light.

"A tall, white-skinned woman with yellow hair?" Conan asked again, and she nodded fervently. Then, astonishingly, she burst into tears that rained down on the basket she was carrying, her broad dark face contorting in grief. She had a fair amount of local blood, as well as Stygian.

"The poor, poor woman," she said, wiping her eyes. "I wouldn't take her money for the eggs I gave her, though I put the basket down and skipped back." Conan reflected that given her heft she probably skipped like a hippo, and she jiggled a little as she unconsciously matched action to words.

"What was wrong with her?" Conan asked, a little worried.

She gave him a dubious glance, seeming to find his blue-eyed gaze unpleasant.

"Leprosy, of course!" she said. "What else could make a human being so pale? The poor thing, she'll be dead soon, rotting alive. So ugly—and those strange eyes, blind-looking as if they were covered in cataracts… though she could see at least a little."

Zarkabaal, olive-skinned to start with and sun-darkened, chortled. Conan silenced him with a look. The Shemite pinched the bridge of his hooked nose hard, to keep the chuckle from growing into a full-throated guffaw.

The peasant had mistaken a northern complexion for a lethal skin disease. Conan supposed she'd have thought the same of him, if it weren't for the way he'd bronzed under these southern suns. She probably thought his eye color meant *he* was half-blind, too, or suffering from cataracts.

While Zarkabaal fought laughter, Conan frowned in thought.

"Has anyone else of note passed through recently?" he said, handing her a coin. "That for a shoat." The woman looked at the copper piece, and her expression turned to delight. It was a good price for a young pig, this far from town.

"Of course, noble sir—we have one just ready for the knife, a fine plump little pigboy." Then she concentrated. "Anyone else… anyone else passing through…" She frowned.

Zarkabaal took the hint and passed her another copper coin for the basket of peanuts, which was gross overpayment. He put the basket across his saddlebow and began shelling them, then popping them into his mouth. Conan reached over for a handful and followed suit, enjoying the oily richness that crunched between his strong white teeth. Foods like this were one of the good things about being a wandering man.

They'd be just the thing for sitting around the hearth on a winter's day back home, he thought, *with mead mulling and the snow coming down.*

Mind, I miss walnuts.

The farmwife hesitated a moment longer, then spoke with obvious care.

"A nobleman came through, not long after the poor, poor leper. We loyal subjects gave him all he wanted and did not presume to question him, of course. None can doubt our loyalty to the Anointed of Set!" She drew a sinuous line through the air and hissed. It didn't seem terribly sincere.

Other deities—such as Derketa, the local avatar of Ishtar, goddess of passion and fertility—often attracted more fervent devotees among commoners in Stygia than did the remote and terrible serpent god of the clergy, nobles, and generals and the far-off divine king in Luxor.

"He didn't stay?"

"No sir," she replied. "Rode through quickly, with two horses on a leading string, just picked up a chicken and some mangoes."

Conan nodded thanks as two of the scouts brought out the protesting, doomed piglet, prodding its ribs and grinning as they tied its limbs and slung it over a packhorse.

The column was much further south by nightfall. Conan was pushing them, and there was some grumbling at the sudden turn from holiday jaunt to serious business. He got sidelong glances, from the Pict for example, because they'd understood out that their *search* for Valeria was for form's sake.

They were wondering why he'd changed his mind.

Before I knew Nebset was on her track, it didn't matter

where I came up with Valeria, as long as she was in a good mood when I did. Now it's a matter of getting to her before he does, because he's out to avenge his brother's blood.

They got three more confirmations of the yellow-haired woman moving south during the day, and fast, though nobody else wept for her leprosy. Most just thought she looked strange and ugly, though a few of the men were enthusiastic for her strangeness. None of them thought an armed woman was anything of note.

Warrior women were vanishingly rare among Stygians, even rarer than among the northern kingdoms and *much* rarer than for Cimmerians or Picts, but the customs of some of the black kingdoms around here were different. In one of them, Abomey, the king's elite bodyguard regiment were all women, theoretically his wives and in truth a corps of celibate amazons.

Only two of the peasants were willing to say anything about Nebset. Smart commoners didn't dwell on the habits or doings of their betters—certainly not with strangers, though locally it would be gossip to be spread for months. Their caution was even more common here than up in the valley of the Styx, where the Serpent-born were much thicker on the ground. Most likely that scarcity was one of the reasons ordinary Stygians settled here, and the aristocracy shunned places like this whenever they could.

On the morning of the third day they were still moving directly south from Sukhmet, and the road petered out into a game-trail. There were no sign of humans, except a slew of cow-pats and an abandoned thornbrush enclosure where someone had corralled cattle for the night. The game was thickening, though—there were a couple of hundred of the lyre-horned antelope with white blazons on their foreheads, grouped around a seasonal pond. They raised their muzzles from the green new grass to gaze warily at the humans, and other herds scattered into the distance.

"Scouts!" Conan rose in his stirrups. "You're under file-leader Zarkabaal for now. I'm doing a one-man swing myself, to cover more ground."

He waved his saddlebow and grinned. They grinned back, assuming he wanted to do some hunting unencumbered by company, and were willing enough to eat the results.

Zarkabaal cantered over.

"We will see you at sundown, Conan," he said loudly. Then he leaned closer and spoke quietly. "Or in the afterlife. Or in Dan-Marcah, where you will be welcome in my family's house, if you come visiting. I will keep your share of the gold for you."

Conan laughed, feeling a great weight lifting from his shoulders at the thought of being on his own again.

"Don't bother," he replied. "Keep it for yourself—I probably won't be by that way. After I find Valeria I'll be heading for the coast, and then it's a ship and the Red Brotherhood for me, or the Zingaran privateers. And more gold."

Zarkabaal shrugged. "I'll keep it anyway. I can use it as security for loans, so the money won't be idle, or I'll have my cousin the banker put it out at interest. It will be ready for you if you come or send for it." A flash of a grin. "Though I *will* keep the interest, my friend. There are limits to what I can do, even for a comrade. But the drinks will be on me, if you come!"

Conan sat his mount with his three horses on a leading

rein, waving while Zarkabaal took what were *his* men now off to the northwestward. They dwindled and vanished, and he was alone.

PART THREE

DEATH
BEYOND
STYGIA

19

"Alone," Conan said aloud. "Finally free!"

The Cimmerian roared gusty mirth, alone under blue sky piled with white clouds. Then he turned his horse's head southward, bow in his left fist, eyes and ears drinking in the manless silence, broken only by the clop of hooves, the creak of leather, and the wind soughing through tall grass and brush and trees.

As he rode cries emerged of long-tailed weaver birds building their fantastic tenements, and a crunching sound as a giraffe bent its head to the top of a tree and wound its long prehensile tongue to draw leaves and twigs into its mouth before rising to give him a glance from the height of a siege tower. The thunder of a herd of gnu as they fled, the pig-grunts of a sounder of wart-hogs in the thickets by a little seasonal stream, the darting heads and maniacal laughter of a pack of hyenas loping along at twice bowshot before they turned away.

The hot air was clear, too, of the stink of civilization. It wasn't Cimmeria, though, and being alone in any wilderness was risky—the slightest injury might kill him, and he had to sleep *sometime*.

And that damned curse.

"I never want to see or smell a city again," he declared to no one. "This is how to live. Plenty of land, no politicians, lots of animals, clean air." His exultation lasted far longer than he would have expected.

Then it was back to the business at hand.

The game trail turned toward a creek, more than the usual trickle now that the season had started. Conan dismounted, looped the reins around a branch, and let the horses drink. Holding his sword and going down on one knee he examined the tracks in the bare moist soil leading down to the water.

"That's it," he muttered.

His finger traced a hoofmark. It had a nick in the shoe—an imperfection he'd seen before along the search. It was one of Valeria's. From the state of it, she was still about three days ahead, heading straight and fast while he had deliberately dawdled.

What brought a frown to his brow was the overlay of *other* shod hooves. He was reasonably sure those were Nebset's, hot on the trail of his brother's killer. They weren't all that much older than Valeria's, which dismayed him. Nebset was much closer to her than he was, and Conan would have to work hard to make up the difference.

It surprised him, too. He hadn't expected the man to follow a trail this well.

Stygian nobles hunt, but they usually have trackers to do the hard work, he thought. *He's doing a better job of chasing her than I like, curse it… and curse him.*

Valeria wouldn't expect pursuit, not out into the wilderness like this. Certainly not pursuit by a lone man, who could make better speed than a unit of scouts. Then again, she wouldn't be as helpless in the wilderness as most sailors would, since she'd been a countrywoman and one who as a girl hunted the forests of the Tauran. She'd learned a bit more since, as well, on the long trek to Sukhmet and the return.

Yet that was like being able kill a cow in a stall as opposed to hunting lions, when it came to being wilds-wise.

Conan grunted. *Nebset is a civilized man, too, from the most ancient of lands. How's he pushing this fast?*

It was time to cross the ford and take up the trail on the other side. He started to rise to his feet... and then turned that into a frantic leap backward, unleashing all the power of his long legs.

The Cimmerian's bare back skidded across the grass when he landed, but there was no time to pause and catch his breath as the crocodile lunged out of the water in a burst of spray, a breath of carrion stink puffing over him as the great jaws slammed shut a scant few inches from his face.

Conan rolled frantically to the side as the half-ton weight of carnivorous reptile punched down where he'd been lying an instant before. In the same motion he shoulder-rolled to his feet, then turned that into a jump half his height straight up as the armored, saw-edged tail smashed sideways in a strike that would have shattered his legbones if it had connected.

Then it was hack and wiggle and dodge. The crocodile looked ungainly, but it was snake-swift, could charge faster than he could run, and it weighed about the same as a fair-sized bull. The lunge out of the water was just what he'd heard they liked to do, grab their prey and drag it in, but the dogged pursuit wasn't.

He felt an eerie chill at its persistence.

Not natural.

The action pushed him away from the water, back toward a low rocky hill. In a flash he knew what he must do if he wanted to live. He turned and went up the slope at a bounding run. The reptilian killer was faster than he on the flat, but its splayed stumpy legs weren't built for climbing. Conan turned, and dropped his sword. It clanged on the rocks, and he bent and snatched up a boulder the size of his own torso, wrenching it free of the soil with an effort that made his sinews crackle. It was heavier than he was, too.

The reptile came up the slope after him, nearly close enough to lunge by the time he had the rock poised overhead. The predator was pushed along by the muscular tail that made up a third of its fourteen-foot length. The four-foot jaws gaped once more, like a gateway into a world of rotting flesh, red and pustulant white. It bellowed as it lunged toward him, and he shouted back, a wordless grunting sound that seemed to push power into his back and thick-muscled arms.

Thud!

The boulder struck right at the rear of the crocodile's mouth, where its jaws merged, and they tried to snap home by reflex. Then it was thrashing its head back and forth, its bellows turning to a strangling gargle as rock filled its throat.

Conan snatched up his sword two-handed and struck at the shoulder-joint of the monster's left forelimb with a twisting slash that combined the power of shoulders and back and gut and legs into a cleaving blow. The impact cut through the scales and then made the familiar *crack* of steel hammering home in parting bone.

An instant later the beast's tail swept his feet out from under him and he landed on his shoulders, rolling down the slope in painful contact with rocks that tore at his mostly bare flesh. At that, he knew he was lucky it had hit across his calves, and from the rear. If it had been from the front it would have snapped bone because legs didn't naturally bend that way.

He landed at the base of the hill, winded and battered and bleeding, but hale enough to stand quickly. A glance showed that the killer beast was dying, and that its thrashing death-throes were dangerous in themselves.

The diamond concentration of a life-or-death struggle hadn't allowed attention for everything else. Abruptly he became conscious the fact that one of his pack horses had torn itself free from the leading-rein, and was bucking in circles as it kicked itself free of the pack-saddle across its back. It spewed sacks of trail-biscuit and jerky in showers of edibles, and when he approached it ran off, rending the air with the horse version of panicked screams.

The other three horses were rearing and snorting and shaking their heads, shifting their hindquarters with the reflex of animals whose main weapon was a backward kick. He swore, then advanced with his hands spread.

Calming them took a quarter-hour of soothing with his voice, then stroking their sweat-wet necks and feeding them handfuls of the biscuit, which they found reassuring. Their eyes were still rolling when he'd finished, but they weren't as likely to try to follow their brother-gelding in his headlong dash across the countryside.

"Which will end in a lion's belly," he snarled, "and serves the cowardly beast right." He kept his tone low, however, so as not to spook the other mounts. Then he looked at the ford, and up and down the tree-lined river, and sighed.

"A man lives as long as he lives," he said to himself. "Not a day more, not a day less."

The horses weren't enthusiastic about getting their hooves wet, not after seeing and smelling what had come out of this stretch of water.

"Sooo, boys, sooo," he crooned, as he led them forward. "The vicious beast is dead."

A glance over at the hillside showed that was true, save for a few slight jerks of its tail as it lay on its back with its pale belly to the sky. Its jaws were still agape, with flowing blood slowing to a trickle that matched the spot where its foreleg had been cut off near what would have been a shoulder on something less primeval. That hung by a scrap of tough hide.

"I cut off its leg and jammed a two-hundred-pound boulder down its throat, and it's still twitching," Conan said, with a grin that belied his bloody, mud-covered, battered self. "This country is interesting, but when I settle down, it won't be in a place that has crocodiles in the rivers."

The cool water felt good on the raw parts of his body as he walked into the purling flow with his hand firmly on the lead horse's bridle. Halfway across he ducked under and came up blowing, though he was uneasily conscious that he was sending the scent and taste of blood downstream. From what he'd heard, crocodiles were solitary hunters, with the bigger bulls staking out the best hunting ground, digging nests into the banks of rivers and patrolling up and down. Not least against rivals of their own kind encroaching, except during their mating season.

Given the dead wizard's curse, though, the animals might not be following their natural behaviors. That monumental pile of catastrophes back when they were shepherding the Stygian refugees certainly argued for it.

Cutting the wizard's head off solved the immediate problem, he observed, *but it doesn't seem to have stopped him in the long run*.

On the other side of the swollen creek he checked the tracks again. As before, Valeria heading straight south, and Nebset following swiftly behind.

When they were back in the savannah and safely away from the water, he rummaged for a moment in one of the saddlepacks and came up with a stone jar of ointment that he then slathered over his wounds. That stung badly, but the men who'd been with Zarallo longest swore by it. Unfortunately for the Argossean healer who mixed it up, it hadn't helped him when he was close-coupled with a harlot in a Sukhmet alley, then knifed by the woman's pimp.

Ironically, they said it was also good against the pox you caught from women of the night.

He transferred his saddle to one of the spare horses. Conan was a bigger load than the pack saddles, and the animals would last longer with the weight shared between them. Cimmerians kept horses, but not many—their land was too bleak, too densely forested, and too hilly for them to be of much use. Oxen pulled plows and carts and sledges and timber, and the shaggy local ponies were mostly for chiefs or messengers in a hurry.

Men could run down horses anyway, over a course longer than a few days.

Since leaving his clan, Conan had acquired considerable horse-craft, and he knew how fragile the big beasts could be. He had sixty pounds on Valeria, who was a big woman, say fifty on Nebset, who was three inches taller than her but slender in the way Stygian nobles usually were. That extra weight on the horse's back was going to slow him, and losing that third horse would make it worse because he couldn't switch off as often.

Pacing himself and his beasts was going to be tricky.

"A stern chase is a long chase," he said. That was a maxim he'd picked up while pirating on the Western Sea.

After an hour Conan stopped under a wide-spreading acacia to let noon and its greater heat pass. Hobbling the horses to graze and feeding them more biscuits, he gnawed on hardtack, jerky and dried fruits that tasted like mildly sweet leather, washing them down with lukewarm draughts from a waterskin. Then he took a nap.

When he woke the sun was further to the west. He looked at it longingly; the sea was that way, and the sea-road led wherever you wanted.

Valeria had better *be more friendly when I catch up to her. After I've killed Nebset.*

Conan led the horses out, but this time he didn't swing into the saddle. Instead he hung his sword from the saddlebow and traveled beside the horse on his own two feet, first walking quickly, then trotting, then a slow run, then the same thing in reverse. Over and over again, the long coarse grass brushing against his thighs. This was the hunter's pace, the pace that could run any animal to death if kept up long enough. It would spare the horses, making up for the loss of the remount to crocodile-inspired panic.

It was a relief to really stretch his legs this way, and his deep chest swelled and sank in rhythm with the pumping of his right fist. His left hand rested on the saddle, helping to steady his run. His eyes were on the ground up ahead, reading the signs—a campfire under a tree that left a burn-scar, horse-droppings, hoofmarks, brush cut for firewood.

He grunted laughter in time with the panther-light fall of his feet and springy stride. There was one good thing about being last in the line of pursuit. Valeria probably didn't realize she was being chased, and neither did Nebset.

Nebset wants to kill Valeria; I want to kill Nebset—each person in this chain wants to kill the one in front of him.

It's a race of killers

His grin grew sharklike. He'd seen a mosaic once in—it was that city-state between Zamora and Corinthia, where he'd been hired to break into the mansion of Nabondius, the Red Priest. So long ago that he'd forgotten the city's name, though some memories were vivid still. There had been rogues enough, but it was some of the art that had struck him, young and heedless though he'd been.

One painting had shown an undersea scene—though he'd never yet seen the ocean. It showed a line of fish, each bigger than the last, and each chasing the one ahead of it with gaping mouth and curved rows of teeth.

That was Nabondius, Conan thought. *For all he claimed to be but a student of the natural arts, he was a treacherous snake—but he had an eye for a joke.*

He made camp hours after sunset. It was two days later, when the three-quarter moon set and it was too dark even for his night-keen eyes to be sure he hadn't wandered from the trail.

"I'm catching up," he said to himself. "Two miles to Nebset's one, and he's still three days behind Valeria, I'd bet on it. I'll get to him first, and then the reunion."

The country had altered over the course of his travel. Things had grown steadily greener as he went south; the grass was taller than his belly button now, and a brighter color, starred here and there with flowering bushes that had huge crimson blossoms the size of his hand. They swarmed with the vicious southern bees but gave off a soft, languorous scent that made him recoil despite its sweetness.

The game was thicker and included more elephants—there were herds with scores or hundreds of the hulking gray-brown beasts, like hills that walked, and he gave those a wide berth. He hoped those hadn't been caught up in the sorcery, and might have prayed to Crom, but as usual that would have done him no good.

The patches of forest were bigger and taller, fewer of the flat-topped thorny acacias and bulbous baobabs and more towering giants. Their edges were thick with brush and vines starred with flowers, their interiors gloomy but open where the high canopy shadowed out lesser plants.

Rain became more frequent but no great hardship; he was

used to traveling in the wet, and the coolness was pleasant when the thick drops fell.

The campsite he chose was an obvious one, in the side of a hill and under a clifflike overhang that would provide a little shelter if needful, which the towering clouds in the west said it might be. More hills stretched to the east. A small spring leaked from a crack just above head-height, and the red-black rock was mostly hidden by a thick wall of vines.

It was so obvious a campsite that it had been used, repeatedly... from the tracks and the fresh ash, and from the bush that had been their improvised latrine, it had been used by both of the people he was following.

Good enough for them, good enough for me.

He watered the bush himself, grinning at the thought of how some peoples he'd met considered the number three sacred. Retying his loincloth, he went back to squat by his campfire—there was a semicircular pile of rocks to keep the light from showing to anyone further out, needful in the extreme since this was a little above the level of the rolling countryside.

Around noon, near as he could estimate, he pulled out a small cooking pot and shaved handfuls of jerked game-meat into it, and then filled it with water and added some salt. The board-hard sun-dried meat turned to mush by now, and he added hardtack biscuit that he broke up with the hilt of his dagger.

It was fuel rather than food, but it stopped his belly clamoring after a hard day of running and riding. He scrubbed out the pot, drank deeply from the spring, and lay down on his blanket roll. There was no need to cover himself in this climate, only to close his eyes...

20

They snapped open in what nose and eyes said was the gray just before dawn. The eastern horizon was behind the cliff and the range of hills beyond it, but there was a little light leaking from that direction into what was otherwise absolute blackness, since clouds had covered the stars.

There was a scent of cooling ash from the banked embers of his fire. The horses looked up from their drowsing on the picket line he'd rigged, snorting and shifting.

For long instants that noise covered the sound that had woken him. Then he heard it again, the unmistakable slap of feet on dirt, someone running... and running toward him, the harsh rasping breath of exhaustion. An odd high chirring *woow-woow-meeroo* sound came behind it, the thud of paws. Behind that, two horses just breaking into a gallop.

Conan slid his broadsword out of its sheath and ghosted forward. Just then the first fingers of real light came over the summit of the rocky heights behind him and he could see a human figure running toward him. Black—a local— tall and long-limbed, running like someone who knew how but was nearly at the end of their tether.

A woman, or I'm a Pict! he thought.

From behind her came two animals moving very fast; cats, leopard-sized and spotted but longer-legged and with smaller heads.

Cheetahs! Conan thought.

Those were curious hunting cats of the savannahs, faster than any game, and unlike any other species of feline—they had odd doglike paws with dull claws that could not be retracted. Stygian nobles used them for sport, trained from kittenhood and carrying them on pads behind their saddles like ground-running hawks that they loosed at antelope. Probably the upper classes of other kingdoms did, too, since the beasts were native here but not in the valley of the Styx to the northward.

The woman was heading straight for the cliff, perhaps to get a place where her back would be covered. She wasn't going to make it, not quite. Evidently she thought so, too, for she turned and crouched, snatching up a fallen bough to use as a club.

Perhaps it was that which tipped Conan into action; or perhaps the glint of metal on several horsemen following along behind the hunting-cats. Cheetahs didn't grip their prey with claws and jaws like other big cats. Instead they ran into them at speed, knocking them over and stunning them, and only then went for the throat. It wasn't a subtle strategy, but from what he'd heard they were stupid to a degree that made a household moggie look like a Corinthian philosopher by comparison.

The cheetahs ignored him as he dashed forward, pinpoint-focused on the woman they'd been chasing. As she turned they went from very fast to blurred streaks traveling at twice the best pace of a fast horse, faster than anything that didn't have wings. They couldn't keep that up for long, but they didn't need to.

The woman threw herself aside at the last possible instant, swinging her improvised club. There was a thud of impact, and then both cheetahs were past her as she rolled over and over on the grassy slope.

Then they noticed him. They must have been specially trained to hunt human game because they didn't try to slow down and go back for a kill. They came right at *him* in their turn.

Conan decided to strike earlier than the woman had. To anticipate an enemy's actions made you effectively half again as quick as you normally were, and these beasts seemed to have only one tactic—a headlong rush, a leap, strike, and run on past.

He stood erect as the cheetahs came on. Then when they were committed to their attack sprint, he dropped abruptly to one knee even as his sword sang in a hiss of cloven air.

Crack!

The heavy blade of the broadsword met the lead cheetah's forelimbs just below where they joined its greyhound-like body. Hitting a lion had been like carving into living hardwood; this was much lighter, as of a body more fragile than a man's because it was built for extreme speed.

He would have sworn there was a look of imbecile astonishment on the cheetah's face as it flipped head-over-arse in midair with both its front legs sliced through. It landed five paces behind him, gave a squall and a final *squeal* as it thrashed in a puddle of its own blood, and died.

The other cat hit him.

Like a sixty-pound furry boulder flung from a catapult.

Conan went over backward with a grunt, then another as his back hit the ground. He didn't let the near-winding stop him from twisting frantically and bringing the sword up, with the point presented in the direction the cheetah had gone. As he'd expected it came at him out of the dying gloom, lunging for his throat where it should be waiting on the ground after the stunning impact.

The point of the sword went in under the base of its skull and its own impetus and the rock-hard brace of the Cimmerian's bent legs drove the steel home all the way to the hilt. The cheetah bit savagely at the cross-guard of the weapon, and then it, too, died.

Conan turned in a three-quarter circle and flung it off his steel with a motion like the hammer-throw at the harvest-fair games back home. Like the hammer, the cheetah flew off his sword to thump down a dozen paces away with a smoothness lubricated by its own blood.

Then the two mounted handlers were on him.

Or on *them*, for the woman was back on her feet. They were using light pad saddles, with a blanket strapped behind for the cheetahs, and were lightly equipped themselves with steel-strapped leather helmets, hide vests, and short leather breeks. They were mounted on rangy, rawboned beasts that looked fast though not fancy, But they had swords as well, point-heavy slashers. They drew them and bored in; perhaps they were enraged by the death of their charges.

Conan rolled to his feet and pivoted to face the first, sword held two-handed and point-down to his right, his panting breath slowing. The rider was as rangy as his mount, his dark skin sheening with sweat barely visible in the early light. His mouth contorted in a snarl as he held his blade ready for a slashing chop with the weight of man and mount behind it.

Balanced on the balls of his feet, the Cimmerian was still as a statue for an instant as his would-be killer clapped bare heels into his horse's ribs and charged with a shriek of rage. Conan waited until the blade's swing began.

Then he ducked and let his right knee go slack at the same time. The steel whisked over his head with a malignant hiss. His knee touched the ground, but his weight was still on the ball of that foot, and the power of his calf and thigh drove behind the cut he delivered to the hock of the horse. Its own weight and speed added to the force of the cut that slammed through hands and wrists and arms to shove his body around.

Which was fine, since that was the way he wanted to face. The horse went over with an earsplitting scream of pain, and then its ribs slammed into the rocky dirt. Under them was the rider's right leg, and he screamed himself. Then again with his face contorted in terror as Conan leapt and pounced, driving the point of his own heavy blade completely through his target's torso from left to right and into the ground below, then wrenching it free in a shower-gout of blood. He wheeled with frantic haste to face where the other horseman would be.

Needn't have bothered, he thought.

That move was just in time to see the other man go back over the crupper of his saddle as a fist-sized rock smashed into his face. The woman who'd thrown it followed with another in her hands, a bigger one. She landed knees-first on his chest with a force that by itself would have broken bones, and her hands pounded up and down like someone grinding grain with a mortar and pestle, slamming the bigger rock into his face half a dozen times.

The man sprattled and died as his skull cracked and his face turned into a gruesome mush with two detached eyeballs hanging out of it. Then she rose, tossed aside the rock, and looked at Conan. Her eyes were blazing, but her voice was level and calm as she spoke through the heaving breath of life-and-death action.

"More come," she said, pointing westward. "Darfari lancers—a dozen. More footmen. Here soon." She spoke Stygian, which was the common tongue around here, with about the same elementary command as he had.

"Can't run," she continued. "More cheetahs, faster than horse. Hide-hide. This way!"

She dashed off toward the cliff, and he followed. He'd killed the man, the *Darfari* man, more-or-less from reflex. That wouldn't mean anything at all to the man's comrades, of course. For all Conan knew the woman could be some sort of vile criminal, a poisoner or kidnapper, but he was on her side now, like it or not.

Evidently she knew something he didn't.

She snatched the sword, dagger, and belt from the huntsman she'd killed, and she slashed out to cut the picket-line holding Conan's horses. It was the right move; the pursuers would think that they'd ridden off on them, and waste time running them down while they hid. *If* there was a place to hide.

There was.

With swift care, the woman nudged aside a curtain of flowering vines that hid the rock in a riot of purple and pale yellow. Then she dropped to her belly and, pushing her weapons in front of her, wiggled through an opening that looked like a lopsided triangle below. Conan bent sideways to snatch up his groundsheet and breeks, then dove into the narrow entryway.

He followed, but not without some uncomplimentary references to the bowels, nether regions, and love-lives of various deities. His shoulders made passage a lot less comfortable, and in passing he had to leave some skin on the coarse sandstone rock. It helped that it was wet with seepage, and hence slimy slick.

The light quickly disappeared. He could see the slightly paler soles of his chance-met comrade's feet ahead of him. Then there was nothing but the sound of her breath, the passage of their bodies over the bottom of the tunnel, and the slightly musky scent of her sweat and his. Abruptly there was sand beneath him—he judged they'd come a dozen times the length of his body, and felt more than saw the space opening out around them.

She laid a hand on his arm and spoke in a low hiss.

"Turn. Listen. Kill, if any come after."

He turned, conscious of her beside him. Then he felt at the rock, and strained his eyes to catch the ghost-dim light that he could see, now that his eyes were accustomed. The tunnel they'd come through was ahead of them, just barely wide enough for a man to crawl, but not for his arms to move much. An intruder might be able to use a spear a little, but they'd have to bring a lantern, too. From here they could strike at men as helpless as a fish in a barrel.

Conan let his breathing slow at last and had time to start feeling his scrapes and the itches where his sweat was drying. There also were the welcome coolness and the smell of damp rock and sand. That reminded him to redon his breeks, which would be essential if he didn't want to leave valued pieces of himself abraded away on the rock. That required some contortions, but he kept it silent.

There was a very slight rustle from beside him. Right on its heels came the sounds from outside, oddly muffled and distorted as they traveled down the narrow twisting cleft in the rock. The beat of hooves, and high-pitched chirruping and what sounded for all the world like a cat's enquiring *meow-row-meow*, but magnified ten or twenty times. Voices, in a liquid gurgling language of which he understood not a word, but he did hear the universal disgust of men who'd hoped to come up with a foe, and found him gone.

Or her *gone*, Conan thought.

There was a shrill protest from a cheetah, which he guessed was prompted by the toe of a boot, and then a very human snarled order. The massed clatter of hooves, and silence fell again.

He grinned in darkness.

On the one hand, he'd lost three horses and his supplies. On the other, he hadn't been stabbed by half a dozen hallooing lancers, or knocked out of the saddle and fanged by a pursuing cheetah that could do twice the speed of a horse. More than twice the speed of any horse Conan was riding, given what his weight did to a mount.

The woman tapped him on the arm again, then touched a finger to his lips and ears. He took the meaning. The smart thing for the Darfari pursuers was to ostentatiously ride off, and leave some warriors to ambush whoever emerged, helpless as a half-born babe while they wiggled out of the rock.

After a while they turned again, and Conan followed his chance-met companion. She tapped him with a signal when it was safe to stand and walk—though when they did he stooped and kept a hand in front of and above his head.

The woman was tall, but not a giant. She seemed to know where she was going, never hesitating when they came to a branching. He felt around the turns they took and nodded—unseen—to himself when he found a pattern of three horizontal chips taken out of the rock on the side to which they turned. These caves were marked.

"Your name?" he said after a while, in his basic Stygian. "Where from?"

"Name Irawagbon," she said. There was a grin in her voice when she added, "Means… 'Enemy Tried to Kill Her and Failed.'"

He laughed outright, and the sound echoed. That was a good name for someone with the spirit and skills he'd seen in the brief savage fight.

"I from *Ahasu*, means King… Osakwe—which name is 'the Lord Agrees.'"

Ah, Abomey, he thought. That was a neighbor to Darfar's southeast, smaller but by repute fierce and unafraid of a fight.

"King Osakwe wife, me," she added. "King's spear wife." This puzzled him until he remembered the Abomean king's amazon guard regiment and its legal fiction of marriage to their overlord.

"Is this Abomey?" he asked, slapping his foot on a patch of rock to show what he meant. This time *she* laughed.

"Thing which many wise men crack their heads for," she said, "and warriors crack each other's heads for." That took a moment to get across. Talking in a language foreign to both was a problem he was familiar with.

"This Abomey, this Punt, this Darfar, this Stygia," she said. "All say, my-land, my-land, but no men here, no farms—only beasts. Maybe kingdom of lion, of hyena, of elephant."

He nodded, then grunted agreement because she couldn't see him. From what he heard, many of the black kingdoms south of Stygia were big—in area and folk both—but their populations were islands in a vast sea of wilderness, separated by great stretches where only nomads, hunters, and raiders went.

"Who you? Where from?"

"Conan," he said, "a Cimmerian." Then had to explain that Cimmeria lay far north of the great western kingdoms, which amazed her—Argos and Koth and the rest were realms of myth to her.

"A friend of mine was in the same warband as I," he said, "but a Stygian tried to take her by force."

Irawagbon snorted with the air of someone unsurprised.

"She killed him and fled, with his brother chasing her, heading south."

"Run south, past here?" This time he could hear surprise in her voice.

"Yes. Is that strange?"

"Much south here, forest… jungle, we say. Bad to travel. Then lands cursed. Go there, get eaten by—" They had to hunt back and forth before he understood she meant something reptilian and enormous, or *"taller than four men, heavy as elephant, eat people,"* as she put it. After his encounters with crocodiles Conan wasn't eager to meet such a dragon-beast. On the other hand, it might just be a myth, and was certainly hearsay. The jungle-forest he believed, however, since he'd seen the land grow bigger and more plentiful trees steadily as his pursuit ate the miles.

Conan shrugged. Whatever was to the south, he'd follow.

"I am sick of Stygia," he offered.

She chuckled. "Hyenas of gods puke up stinky snake-meat Stygian souls." He wasn't surprised. Nobody much liked Stygians, except other Stygians—and that not always.

"I followed them to kill the Stygian," he continued, "and travel with her back to our lands. Why are you here? Were you caught on a raid?"

"No," she said. "On a—"

The curse of limited vocabulary struck again. Eventually he grasped that she and some others of her regiment had come to visit a long-forsaken shrine of Derketa—who was a queen of battle and the underworld, as well as a goddess of love and fertility—where the Darfari had come upon them while they slept the sleep of the Black Lotus, seeking visions. Attacking pilgrims was as frowned-upon here as anywhere, but they hadn't been able to resist finding the hated spear-wives helpless.

"Derketa tell me to wake, but I slow with juice, get caught," she said. "Then later, knife one... knife get stuck..." That brought a mutter of what were probably curses in her native tongue. "... then I run-run. Old talk tell of these caves—lead to shrine."

They came into a larger cavern, one with a crack high up that opened to the outside. The light it let in was dim, overshadowed by thick brush and trees, and long tendrils of vine that hung through into the cave, growing more bleached as they descended almost to the sandy, rock-studded floor. After nearly an hour in pitch-darkness, even meager light seemed like a blaze.

The Cimmerian and his new companion took a long look at each other, the first time they'd had the leisure to do so.

"Big men, in Cimmeria," she said, giving him a frank once-over.

"Fierce women, in Abomey," he replied.

She looked it, too—as much a big she-leopard as Valeria and with a similar build, allowing for the difference between pale blond and midnight-black. Her wiry hair was cropped close into a sable cap, her features high-cheeked, full-lipped, and with a slight arch to her broad nose and a chevron of scars on each cheek.

That face had a look he knew as well; someone who recently had been beaten with fists, and the rest of her was comparably battered, though bruises didn't show as well against her complexion as they would have on a Northerner. She was utterly unconcerned with her complete nakedness.

Well, people in these lands go naked a fair bit, or with only a loincloth, he thought. *With their weather, I'm not surprised, and their skins are better guards against the sun than a Cimmerian's.* He had learned that through harsh experience.

"Where now?" he asked. "What?"

"Rescue my sisters of the spear," she said. "Then we help you with you chasing Stygian—horse, gear, help along way until we must turn for home."

Conan hesitated. He hated the thought of giving up any of the time he'd gained by pushing so hard, but he couldn't just go back the way he'd come, carefully though he'd memorized the turns in the darkness. And even if he did, he had no horses.

The Darfari were far too likely to slice him as he came out, unless he waited a long time... a long time without food, because there was nothing edible in these caves. Even if they didn't, heading straight south would be far too likely to be heading straight into their arms. Which would mean straight onto the points of their lances.

"By Crom, why not?" he said. "They were blasphemers to attack pilgrims to a shrine, anyway—the Gods will hate them."

He held out his hand. That required explaining, then she shook, and he went through her people's version of the gesture.

"So, where?" he asked.

Irawagbon pointed up. "Follow." Then she tied her captured sword and dagger to the end of a carefully chosen vine and leapt to grab one of the thicker ones, swinging up hand-over-hand, which was an impressive feat of athletic strength.

I don't think I'll tell Valeria about this when I catch up, he thought. He spat on his hands and went up in his turn.

21

They were both panting again when they reached the ceiling of the cave. Irawagbon went first, back against one side of the crack in the rock and feet braced against the other. Conan winced slightly at the thought of more abrasion on his back and shoulders, already scabbed over from the rough fight with the crocodile and the tumble he'd taken when the second cheetah hit him that morning. But there was nothing to be done about it, and back in Cimmeria he'd climbed cracks and crevasses in plenty using this technique.

Hauling himself into the crevasse, he braced his feet and waited until his companion was ten feet along. The brighter light closer to the surface made him squint. There was a breath of hot air, too, and he groaned inwardly at the thought of leaving the pleasant coolness of the caves for the swelter outside.

Then he followed; he was slower than she, because it was more cramped for him. The last ten feet were narrow enough that he changed his posture, going head-up and lifting himself with feet and hands, and occasionally other parts of his body.

Just before his head went out he waited for a moment,

letting his eyes adjust to daylight again after so long in darkness. Then he thrust up, slowly so as not to draw any hostile eyes. Irawagbon was lying prone, giving her surroundings a careful scan. Conan heaved himself out and did likewise.

She hauled up the vine with her weapons and belted them on.

To the east the hills faded into the distance, expanding from the one on which they lay like the surface of a wedge. Like this one, they were flat-topped, but divided by steep rocky slopes and narrow ribbons of riverside lowland as if it had been a tableland, a level plain, that was then cut into separate chunks by rivers. The process was incomplete, and many of the hills were joined by narrow bridges of un-eroded rock.

The flat tops had shortish tawny-green knee-length grass, mostly, with brush around boulders and the odd thorn-tree, also flat-topped and much like the savannah further north.

The slopes between the hills were varied—bare rock, thin grass, thicker scrub, and here and there a patch of taller forest. The riverside swales were forested, and densely so, with tall straight-trunked trees woven together by vines, all thick enough that only a glint now and then told of moving water. The hot wind was exceptionally damp, and piled clouds to the east told of a passing thunderstorm.

The grass felt a little wet beneath his feet, and he could see a broad shallow pond nearby with more of the small trees around it, probably a seasonal slough.

There was an intensely green scent to the air, a little dusty, and also a faint spark-and-sulfur scent that was another tell-tale of lightning strikes not long ago. He bent an eye on the rubble that was piled along the edge of the flat summit, and his father's blacksmith lore told him that it was ironstone, probably rich enough to smelt if anyone wanted to do so in this huge unpeopled stretch.

He had two knives on him; an all-purpose camp knife about five inches in the blade, and a ten-inch dagger. With a pointing thumb Irawagbon indicated she wanted the tool rather than the weapon and he offered it hilt-first, resting across one palm. Her face lit in a grin as she took it, tested the edge, and nodded to him.

After a few minutes of silent scrutiny the Abomean came to one knee and used the knife to cut handfuls of grass and lianas, her fingers working skillfully as she wove them into a belt and pouch and slung it over one shoulder, stooping to pick up smooth rocks of the right size for throwing, and some smaller ones. He offered his groundsheet, and she cut herself a loincloth from it, twisting it deftly about her hips, taking the time to poke a new hole in the dead Darfari's sword-belt so it would fit snugly about her waist.

That let her sheath her weapons and carry them more easily. Then she looked at him critically as she handed the camp-knife back.

"Give me this much leather," she said, pointing at his breeks and then indicated something the length of her arm. "Make weapon—" She mimed whirling something around her head and following through with an outstretched arm. He *did* know the Stygian for that.

"Sling," he said.

"Sling," she said, nodding and looking as if she was memorizing the term.

He dropped his breeks and tossed them over. Irawagbon

expertly cut spiral strips from the lower edge of the leg-coverings, knotted them, and then used a bit of the coarse heavy cotton cloth of the groundsheet to make the pocket. She dropped a rock into it, whirled it once around her head and let fly.

It smacked off the edge of a boulder fifty yards away with a sharp *crack* and a shower of sparks and rubble that confirmed his guess about the composition of the stone around here. She wore a satisfied smile, and he nodded soberly as she knotted the sling around her forehead like a headband, tying it off with a slipknot he recognized would let her whip it into action with a single motion of her hand.

Her improvised pouch could hold as many suitable rocks as an archer's quiver could hold shafts. That would be very useful indeed. Slingers weren't very common in Cimmeria or the northwestern realms, but he'd seen them in action elsewhere, and the projectiles were deadly weapons in the hands of the skillful... and she obviously was.

It would be useful for hunting, too.

Then she tossed the breeks back to him. When he redonned them, they were a bit above the knee on both legs, but functional enough. While he was doing that, the Abomey woman laughed. He looked up enquiringly as he buckled his sword-belt once again.

"Nice—" She said a word in her own language and slapped one hand on her own muscular but shapely right buttock.

"Arse," he filled in helpfully.

"Nice arse you," she said, and winked. "Except pale like belly of dead fish. Maybe arse you get killed, you no know because can't see?"

He snorted. She had a warrior's sense of humor, too.

"Where now?" he said.

"Shrine that way," she said. "Darfari blasphemers not gone yet, likely. Few to guard so many spear-wives, must stop to… fetter? Chain? And get food for trip. We go hilltop, there, there, there."

He looked up. It was about noon.

"How many suns?"

"Two," she said, helpfully holding up that many fingers. "Kerchaki country in between," she added, then shrugged with a can't-be-helped expression.

"Kerchaki?"

"Beast. Like man, but hairy, big. Big *teeth*…"

They talked around it for a while as they went. She seemed to be describing some sort of great ape.

"Ah, gorillas," he said.

She knew the word in Stygian. Conan only did because Governor Wenamun had one in his menagerie, and allowed the citizens of Sukhmet in to see it occasionally. But she shook her head.

"Gorilla further south, in deep woods. Big, but not fierce, only kill if you attack. Kerchaki look same-not-same. Different. Clever. Eat more meat. Dangerous. Cunning enough, make no noise when strike."

Conan grunted thoughtfully. He'd had experience with dangerous apes more than once, in the hills around the southern end of the Vilayet Sea far to the northeast, and elsewhere… not least in the house of Nabondius the Red Priest, who'd kept one as bodyguard-pet. It had turned on its master at the last.

And there's that curse, he thought uneasily, but he didn't let it show on his face.

They trotted on in silence—using the hunter's pace, walking and speeding up gradually to a slow run and then slowing again, stopping for a few minutes every hour or so. At the third pause, Irawagbon snatched the sling from around her brow, loaded an egg-sized pebble, whirled it once around her head and loosed. A hundred yards ahead of them a bird that looked somewhat like a quail leapt up and fell limp with its head nearly torn free.

A covey of the same burst free from a stretch of bushes with red-and-blue berries, and the sling whirred three more times, taking them all down at nearly a hundred yards.

They gutted both quickly, plucked them as they walked, then tucked the feet of a pair each into their belts. The birds drained as they walk-trot-ran-trot-walked. It was messy, but she wasn't squeamish at all. A few times she stopped and pulled up some herb or root. He silently thanked his luck that he'd fallen in with someone who knew the local vegetation.

They ran on into the swift dusk of these southern lands, then through the night as long as the moon was up. It was waxing and offering more light. Conan had been looking for a good spot. He'd already started to point when Irawagbon spoke.

"There right place."

They smiled and headed over to the little declivity he'd seen. A dead thorn-tree provided tinder-dry wood; Conan ripped off branches with casual strength, conscious of the woman's admiring looks. By the time he had the fire built—the light wouldn't show beyond the rim of the little hilltop hollow, and nothing nearby was higher—she had the butterflied birds pinned with twigs to green branches.

The smoke didn't matter in the dense dark, since it couldn't be seen.

When the flames had died down to coals, the Abomean rigged the birds on makeshift supports and set them to grill, tucking the roots she'd dug in around the edges.

As soon as the food was done, they buried the fire under clods dug with their knives, and then demolished the meal. He savored the smoky-rich taste of the roasted birds and the filling quality of the roots. A good stamping ensured that the fire was well and truly out.

After they'd licked their fingers clean, Irawagbon grinned at him from where she'd laid her half of the groundsheet.

"Hei-eh, Conan," she said. "Ask?"

"Ask what?"

"I see pretty arse again?" He could just make out the double-handed clutching gesture she made, along with a broad wink. Then she added, "Feel, too?"

No, I definitely *won't tell Valeria about this part of the journey*, he thought as he walked over.

Some time later he yawned, then stopped as a thought struck him.

"You not afraid—"

His hand shaped the air over her belly.

Irawagbon groaned softly, rolled her eyes and slapped his arm.

"*Now* man asks?"

He shrugged.

"Spear-wife has marriage—" she began. Another pause

to find words. Eventually they settled on "rite." He wasn't sure that was correct, but he didn't know the Stygian for "ceremony."

"Priest puts on spell—that word?"

Conan nodded, and she continued.

"Have baby only with husband. King, eh? King have plenty bed-wives. No touch spear-wives." She sighed. "Us four thousand spear-sisters, no baby."

Conan grinned, a lazy expression. "You no—" He altered his smile to a comic mask of sadness and longing. "—for King?"

Again Irawagbon rolled her eyes. "King has—" She opened her hands six times, for sixty years. "And—"

She repeated his gesture of a massive belly and pulled her head down to mimic jowls.

"—like hippo... and smell. Some spear-wives, all good with women, that not against law. Me I like—"

With one arm she made a graphic thrusting gesture.

"—better. Not get much. What Stygian word, woman go—"

She made the thrusting gesture again.

"—with man, married?"

"Adultery," Conan supplied, after a moment's thought.

"Adultery," she agreed, "get buried alive. So be careful." Then she looked at him, cocking a brow he could barely see in the dimness. "You not like bee-man," she said.

"What?" he asked.

"Bee sting once and die," she said with a strategic clutch. "Not you! No snore now."

Irawagbon took the first watch.

Something brought Conan out of deep slumber, snapping into full alertness as he always did—hangovers aside, when it took an effort of will.

It was the noise.

In fact, he realized, there was suspiciously *little* noise, given how loud the night should be here with the buzz and chitter of insects, the calls of birds, and the cries of beasts from lion-roars and the mad screeching laughter of hyenas.

It wasn't entirely quiet, but it was much quieter than it should have been, and it was very dark. Half the stars were obscured by clouds and the moon was down. He hissed softly, expecting Irawagbon to ghost up at once. She'd already shown that she was about as good in moving in the dark as he.

Nothing.

Alarm shot through him like a bucket of cold water poured on the stomach. He rolled up into a crouch, sword in one hand and dagger in the other. The dense darkness at least had the advantage that he wouldn't be given away by a glitter off the honed edges. He sniffed at the still, warm night air, then softly padded forward.

Irawagbon had showed him the spots from which she intended to observe, four of them. Pacing around a perimeter was a useless type of sentry-go, only practiced by idiots and civilized men—if there was a difference.

Then the silence was broken again. By a long hooting screech, bellowing, loud, but about a quarter mile off to the north. It wasn't human, not quite, but not entirely the scream of a hunting beast either.

Kerchaki, he thought, and he felt the hair bristling on the back of his neck as he remembered what she'd said. *Cunning enough to be quiet when they strike.* He ran his hands over the ground around the rock Irawagbon had chosen as one of her listening-posts. His hand brushed leather.

It was her sling.

He wound it up quickly and stuffed it in his belt-pouch. Then a spot of dampness. He brought it to his nose; blood, though he tasted it to check. Conan felt around carefully. There were a few more spatters, but none of the pools he'd expect with a mortal wound. The most plausible explanation was that whatever it was had crept up, given Irawagbon a clout hard enough to leave her unconscious or at least in no condition to resist, and then carried her off.

The Cimmerian went back to the embers of their fire and kindled a small branch. Then he walked carefully back to the rock and held it low, looking about for a few moments. That showed him Irawagbon's footprints in a few places, and then other impressions. Manlike, but bigger than Conan's own, broader, and driven deeper than his own footprint would be... which meant weight at least half again his. And with the big toe splayed out a bit to one side and the others longer than they should be.

He smothered the torch—at this elevation, it was like waving a banner. He'd seen feet like that before, mostly on things trying to kill him and coming far too close to success. It was very rare for him to fight anyone stronger than he was, or with keener senses. When he expanded the possibilities from anyone to any*thing*, however, that no longer held.

"Kerchaki right enough," he muttered to himself under his breath.

The broken weapons-belt she'd been wearing confirmed his guess. The only question now was what to do about it. He could wait another couple of hours until sunrise—but that would probably leave Irawagbon unpleasantly dead, if she wasn't already. Or he could pursue now, with only that screech to go on for direction, with enemies who'd be stronger than he was and more importantly much keener of hearing and scenting. Possibly better able to see in darkness.

On their own ground, at that.

He took a deep breath and shrugged as he wrapped up the sword-belt and slung it over one shoulder. Irawagbon was a comrade, and he'd agreed to help her. That meant there was really nothing to do but follow, and without waiting.

Drinking his fill of water, he hitched his sword-belt around so that it would be less likely to catch on something, and rigged a makeshift cup from a fold of his ground sheet, filled with dirt to hold a few embers so that he could carry fire without the light showing.

Then he turned until an inner sense told him he was facing the direction from which he'd heard the long savage cry, and walked into the night with sword in his right hand and fire in his left.

Steel and fire…

22

An hour later, Conan halted.

For once it wasn't because some unseen thorn-thick branch had nearly taken out his eye. As far as he could tell, he had reached where the shriek had come from—from his best estimate, he was within a hundred paces of it, more or less, and had no way whatsoever of telling which way the source had gone.

He snarled silently at the thought, but crouched a little lower and made his breathing slow, deep... and quiet. He was down in the thick forest at the bottom of the steep valley, and there were rustles and clicks and hoots aplenty. Down here, past the edge of the canopy the undergrowth wasn't as dense.

Thud.

Thud.

Thud-thud-thud...

Drum? It was faint, but not faint enough to be the echo of the blood in his ears.

No, not quite, he thought. *Something* like *a drum, though. Curse these cliffs! The echoes make it harder...*

This way, yes.

He moved as quickly as he dared, then halted again as a

The Abomean warriors.

sharp scent revealed a vine bleeding pitch-like sap. A few cuts, and he fashioned a trio of torches with heads made of vine wrapped around long branches. They went over his back in an improvised sling.

As he made his way through the nighted forest there was a little more light filtering down. The clouds had parted, showing a nearly full moon still climbing in the sky. It was about an hour to its peak. Even with the canopy, it made easier his progress.

The throb of the not-quite-drum grew louder, though echoes still blurred it—louder, and more insistent. The beat was quickening, gradually but certainly. He bared his teeth again, this time in frustration at how little he knew. Did it have something to do with the moon? Picts killed their enemies at set phases of the moon, sometimes. Or was it happenstance?

Louder still, and the time between beat and echo he could tell he was close. Dropping flat and continuing on his belly he crept forward, bush to bush, along behind a fallen, rotting log—which turned out to house a lot of stinging insects with bites like little lances of fire. It didn't alter his steady careful approach, and the moonlight in the circular clearing ahead was brighter and brighter.

Thump.

Thump-thump-thump-thump…

Carefully he used one finger to part the tall grass—or possibly some sort of forest reed—in front of him.

Apes, he thought. *Kerchaki*, she'd called them.

Killer apes.

They didn't look precisely like the Vilayet monsters he'd seen before. About the same size, which meant big, taller than him even when upright on short, thick bowed legs. And like them with arms that hung down to their knees, densely furred, though with black hair rather than silver-gray. Shelf-like ridges of bone over pronounced jaws with nostril-slits above, thin lips drawn back to show that those jaws were full of fangs that would do a panther credit.

From what he could see, a dozen females and their cubs were located in a clump, huddled in what looked like a big nest made of piled-up grass and boughs.

Ah, he thought. *Like a giant heap of kindling.*

A plan began to form in his mind.

The five adult males were dancing in a circle, whirling, leaping, screeching, waving crude clubs or banging together big rocks held in their fists resulting in showers of sparks. Slaver ran down their jaws, and their faces were framed in hair—great clumps on their cheeks that hung down to their collarbones, and stiff roaches on top of their long, loaf-shaped heads almost like a lion's mane.

Their scent carried over the warm humid air, rank with musk and dirt.

The dance wasn't quite the animal riot it seemed. It moved around a center, and Irawagbon was there, bound with a clumsy welter of vines to a fallen tree-trunk. He could see her eyes glitter in the moonlight, and her face was stark but the fear carefully controlled. The long lean muscles in her arm tensed and relaxed as she worked to try to move the coil up over her shoulders.

It couldn't succeed, but it did his heart good to see it, proof that she was a real warrior and never gave up. The scatter of bones nearby, chewed and often broken open, showed the fate that faced her. Some of them were human, others animals, with big cats in the majority. The skulls were lined up in rows, long-since picked to gleaming cleanness by insects, and some starting to crumble into the dirt.

This had been a place of ritual for a long, long time.

There was one male who wasn't dancing. He was the largest, and from the silver shot through his black hair and fur, the oldest. The twin plumes that fell from his cheeks were solid white. He crouched near Irawagbon and beat at the earth with two heavy sticks.

Not just earth, Conan thought as he carefully set aside the cup of stiff leather lined with dirt and holding the still-hot embers. *That must be hollow... maybe buried hollow logs?*

The sound boomed and thuttered through the hot, insect-shrilling night. A bat went overhead, intent on its own concerns, like any such creature back home... except that this one had a wingspan as long as his outstretched arm. It struck something, and parts rained down around Conan as it flapped on.

The dance altered. Instead of circling, the males started to run inward and prance back, their screams interspersed with growls and their fur bristling, arms reaching high overhead. Conan glanced up. Yes, the moon was nearly at its zenith, which the ape-men could probably tell by the way shadows fell in this place they visited each month by night. They'd keep their dance going, then a final rush, tearing the sacrificial victim into gobbets and devouring them raw.

Not now...

Not now...

Now! he thought.

He gripped one of the torches from the sling over his back and thrust it into the cup of embers.

Whoosh!

It caught instantly, flaring up. He carefully didn't look, to keep as much of his night-vision as he could. In the same instant he cleared the bush ahead of him in a single raking stride, charging for the other side of the clearing.

Lost in their dance of blood-frenzy, the kerchaki took crucial seconds to react. By then he'd lit another torch, thrown them into the piled brush of the females' nest, and lit another to keep in his hand as he wheeled frantically around to face them.

The dry grass and wood caught with a roar. The females snatched up their young and fled in every direction, shrieking. One of them was burning, too, and she went into the darkness under the trees like a screaming comet with a tail of flames.

The dancing males turned and saw him.

They reacted in near unison with a charge, aborted by the fire with heat he felt more and more on his back. Conan snarled satisfaction. He'd wagered that the kerchaki had an animal's reflexive fear of fire, and it looked as if he was right. They circled at the edge of the firelight, snarling and mouthing and making little four-step advances and then recoiling again. He turned smoothly to face each, flourishing the torch, firelight ruddy on the steel of the sword in his right fist.

The *thud-thud* beat stopped. That brought a slight mental stutter, for it had woven itself into his very heartbeat during the brief spell of frenzied action. Conan gave what had been the center of the sacrifice-dance a flicker of a look.

The senior male there—probably the chief of this band— had roused from his trance-like focus. Now every hair on his body and head stood erect as he drummed again—but this time with his fists on his own chest. The bristling made him tower even more massive against the backdrop of the night. The firelight turned his eyes and fangs and the silver tips of his fur blood-red as he charged, slapping a palm down every third step or so.

The others scattered out of his way.

This one is not going to stop because he's afraid of flames, Conan thought as he set himself. The charge ended with a leap, arms spread wide with head-sized hands ready to grip and tear, great jaws gaping.

Conan dove into it, flickering forward when some corner of his mind knew the big bowed legs were tensing as they landed. His warrior's mind drew the curve of the leap so that he knew where the beast-man would be. His left hand rammed forward like Valeria's as she used her slim blade, but his didn't bear steel. It had a yard of hardwood with a ball of burning sap on the end, and it went home in the gaping fanged mouth.

The kerchaki patriarch's scream was loud, even with that gag, and he wasted a crucial second snatching the tormenting thing out of his mouth, clawing with both those enormous hands.

Conan used that moment to attack with whirling speed, his right hand matching the strike he'd made with his left. The broadsword flashed forward—there was no time to be precise about the target—just through the torso below the massive ribcage. A soft heavy resistance he knew of old slowed his wrist for a moment, and then a grip with the strength of a god clamped on him with bruising, wrenching force.

He released the hilt and had just time enough to brace

knees and arms against the beast-man's massive body as the arms closed around him. For a moment he felt like a child, or a rat in the jaws of a dog. A grunting strain, and muscle crackling along his arms and shoulders and arched back, a sensation like the strain just before he would break.

Then the kerchaki threw him aside.

Conan flew through the air like a tossed doll, but managed to gather himself and hit rolling, and not to have all the wind knocked out of him. The man-ape grabbed at the broadsword and wrenched it out. It looked like a mere dagger in the giant paw, though it was heavy enough that most men could only have used it two-handed, and long enough that the top of the hilt was above his navel when the point was on the ground. The creature started to roar out another challenge, but this one was accompanied by a fan-shape of blood droplets stretching out half the distance to Conan.

Then the little red-shot eyes under the shelf of bone rolled up, and it collapsed forward like a falling tree. He could feel the massive thudding impact through the ground beneath his body, and the outstretched arm came nearly to his feet.

Levering himself erect, he fought breath back into his chest and snatched up his sword once again, ignoring the kerchaki chieftain's dying twitches and the cloud of the death-stench. He nodded once, respectfully. This had been a worthy foe, and he noted the details—one day his women would sing of this fight, and of the foeman he'd slain as an enemy chief, not just a beast.

Broad strides took him to where Irawagbon was struggling more vehemently against the vines wrapped around her, her teeth and eyes showing white in the fire-shot dark. She nearly had her left arm free by the time he came within reach.

"Hold still!" he barked, and he swung the heavy sword with a surgeon's precise movement. Long strands of the vines fell back, lopped free with the tip of the blade. She shook the rest free and he tossed her the bundled sword-belt. She caught it.

"I'm always giving you weapons," he said.

"I need much-much," she replied, flashing him a smile, and then taking a long breath and letting it out slowly as she buckled it back on. "Old saying," she went on in her basic Stygian. "Brave die once, coward many time."

He nodded, familiar with it. Versions of that were present in every language and land he'd ever encountered.

"Is stinky lie," she said. "I brave as dung, and I die big-big many time tonight!"

He answered her grin, and she looked up at the stars.

"Shrine that way," she went on, pointing south and a little west. "Go!" With that she sprinted easily in the moonlit night, and Conan followed. Pulling alongside her, he held out his water bag.

She sucked at it greedily, without slowing her pace.

23

They were *almost* arguing when they approached the site of the shrine to Derketa in the gloaming of dawn. The religious structure—

Ruin, he thought, from what he could see of it.

—occupied the head of a south-facing valley. The hills had subsided, and they watched from atop an oddly-shaped pile of rocks that the centuries had weathered out of the ground and left piled atop each other.

There was a massive platform behind a retaining wall. Others could be seen as they ghosted forward up the valley, though not as large as this. They were all made of dry-laid granite blocks, fitted with amazing skill and with gaps that would barely allow a knife-blade to be inserted. The style was strange to his eyes, with rounded corners and sometimes semicircles of steps built into a gap, or a big soapstone carving of some sort of bird—perhaps an eagle.

It was fine stonework, but utterly unlike the styles with which he was familiar in the northern kingdoms, or for that matter in Shem or Stygia. The terraces were overgrown with brush, and occasional tall trees that might once have been cultivated… or their remote ancestors might have been. Towers of the same style stood here and there, some nearly intact, others looking bitten-off or tumbled into mounds. Several of them flanked the roadway that led up the center of the valley.

They avoided that, of course.

Once they dodged a Darfari cavalry patrol, a small one of four men, by the simple expedient of lying stock-still and letting them yawn their way past, talking in their own liquid-sounding speech. He was conscious of how Irawagbon's lips peeled back from her teeth at the sound, and the effort of will it took her not to launch against them.

Closer, and they sank down behind a low tumbled heap of stone that originally could have been anything. They could see the threads of smoke from campfires. Irawagbon counted them and exhaled in relief.

"They have not left, or not many. As many fires as when I escaped."

Conan sniffed. He could smell a little cooking, mostly meat, and there was a light brabble of voices, the neigh of a horse.

"No sounds of pain," he said neutrally.

Meaning that normally in his situation they might expect the captors to be abusing the captives as the mood took them. The Abomean woman gave a snarling grin.

"Teeth," she said, pointing to her own.

"Teeth?" he asked.

"Darfari be bastards. Too, all-all-all be just *ignorant bastards.*"

It was light enough to see her make an expression of drooling idiocy and scratch her head and her backside at the same time.

"Think magic makes spear-wives have teeth—"

She pointed to her crotch.

"Bite off man-part."

Conan managed not to wince. He'd heard of that in folk tales all over the world, a thing of witches and demonesses. Evidently they took it *very* seriously around here. Or at least they did in Darfar... and who knew but that sometimes it was true? He'd seen things far more unnatural than that, among sorcerers.

I saw a man sink into a jewel, and his tiny form crushed by a fallen god, Conan thought. *Compared to that, what's a set of teeth in the wrong—very wrong—place?* Even so, the thought was grotesque.

"Darfari men, little-little-little" she said, and she held up thumb and forefinger about three inches apart. "Can't spare much."

He hid a snort of laughter at that.

Evidently, they and the Abomeans had about the same sort of mutual loathing common to Cimmerians and Picts. It was almost homelike, even if it might kill him. There were the bonds of kin and clan, and there were the enemies of your blood, and there were the bonds of oath, spoken and unspoken.

"We're not just going to run in," he said.

"You run in against kerchaki," she pointed out.

"Kerchaki are more beasts than men," he said. "I could frighten them with a fire."

"We get spear-sisters free, all good," she said. "Only twenty Darfari. Rip apart."

He grunted. That was true enough—if they could magically make fetters drop away. The Abomeans could swarm armed and armored men with numbers and hate; the slaves at the Wedi Shebelli gold mine had demonstrated as much. It cost, however. Cost heavily, and to work well at all it required surprise. Conan had managed to pull the Stygians there together before they were buried, and gotten most of them out.

Here it would be a score of armed men against four-score of captives, and the captives all tried fighters, not peasants who'd been unlucky when slave raiders passed by.

Still...

"Quiet now," he said.

They moved forward by slow stages. The Darfari were only twenty men—subtracting the party who'd been chasing Irawagbon, and who upon meeting Conan of Cimmeria had come down with a bad case of death.

The soldiers were probably becoming anxious about that.

They also might be wondering if Irawagbon had reached her people and set a rescue party in motion. This territory was on the border between Abomey and Darfar. The inhabited center of each realm was surrounded by a large area where people faded out into wilderness. With borders undefined—which meant disputed and fought over.

The ancient shrine of Derketa was neutral ground.

In theory.

Conan and Irawagbon came to a tall baobab tree with an absurdly swollen trunk, the spray of branches fifty feet up looking as if it had been transplanted from a smaller, if still substantial, growth. If the bark had been smooth they'd have had to cut holds in the soft pulpy wood, but there were enough natural overgrown wounds in the bark.

"I'll go first," Conan said quietly, hitching his swordbelt so the long blade hung down behind. "Wait for my signal."

Kicking off his boots, he leapt up and grabbed for holds. Using both fingers and toes, Conan was smiling a little as he climbed. The leap had been more energetic than he'd intended—it wasn't often that someone pinched his buttocks from behind, and Irawagbon grinned unrepentantly as he looked down.

"*Nice* arse," she murmured.

He swarmed upward, grimness tempered for a moment. The thick trunk hid him well. The best way for the Darfari to guard their position would be lone sentries or pairs flung out in a wide net, but even with the captives in chains, that would thin their ranks dangerously.

Instead…

He peered cautiously through the leaves, his head beneath one of the lower branches that shot out in all directions from the top of the bulbous trunk. A hundred yards away, over the last of the stone terracing walls—this one shaped like a horseshoe—lay a complex of open-topped rooms, bare to the morning sky where roofs that had probably been of wood and thatch had decayed to nothingness long ago. That would be more rapid in this land of savage heat and rainfall.

Most of the chambers remained tumbled and empty. A few looked as if the Darfari were using them to stable their horses and store their gear. The scent of animals and horse-dung came plain to him on the hot wind, along with the smell of men, green vegetation, rocks, and wetness. There was less than he might have expected. This group of lancers had been traveling light, without many of the grooms and servants men of such rank would usually demand.

The high platform that bore the image of Derketa, shown as a woman with a strange flower in one hand and a spear in the other, was strictly separate. It would be blasphemy to folk of both kingdoms for a man to go there, and Conan didn't look at it too closely.

Offending strange deities was never a good idea.

The main hall that stretched south from the platform was thick with people. Irawagbon had said that eighty of her fellow warriors of the bodyguard regiment had been captured, and that looked to be about how many were crouched or lying or standing at one end, between walls of granite blocks twenty feet high. The end wall cut off a view of them all, but he could rough-count the total by assuming the hidden space was as densely packed as what he could see.

Conan's nose also told him how their captors were handling the problem of human waste. They weren't.

His companion had said the captives were chained. Conan turned and beckoned her, and she went up the trunk as easily as he had, though faster. She sat in a crook of the branches to his side and a little higher and gave a snarl as she looked at the ruined temple.

"Not much changed," she said. "But see?"

She pointed, and outside the hall were racks made of lashed poles. He nodded. They were familiar, racks for drying game-meat until it had the texture of old wood and would keep forever if you didn't let it get wet. Low fires cast smoke upward, and a man with his left arm in a sling was waving a branch now and then to discourage flies not daunted by the smoke and smell. There was no sign of butchering, but a leather thong and a hook hung from a tripod of poles about Conan's height and a handspan more.

"When they have enough, they will leave, march north," Irawagbon said.

She spoke quietly. The air around them was full of the rustling leaves. As their shimmer hid shapes behind them, their flutter drowned sound. No voices would carry far in a valley where wind boomed around rocks, tossed the limbs of thorn trees, and made the thigh-high grass ripple on the flatter spots. Still, it was good practice not to take chances.

"The women are not chained," he said. "They are in those things like catch-poles." The sentence required a lot of back-and-forth, the usual irritation of both speaking in a language foreign to them, and not very well. At last she grasped that he thought she had meant metal chains.

"Who would go to that expense?" she said, or that was what it amounted to. "Ironwood is plentiful."

Ironwood was a common tree here, especially near water, and indeed very hard, though not literally as hard as iron. It could be cut with a good axe, though not without a lot of strenuous work and constant re-sharpening, but it *lasted* like iron, and that was a great virtue in lands where rot came quickly, and insects abounded much like the shipworm that burrowed into hulls on the Outer Sea.

She didn't know what a catch-pole was, and he realized he'd dropped an Aquilonian word into the rough Stygian; it was a fork on the end of a long pole that city watches sometimes used in civilized lands, with a spring-loaded bar that clicked home when you thrust it around a fleeing miscreant's throat. Conan had snapped apart one that a Nemedian dog had tried to use on him, and then beat the man to death with it, early in his wandering days and before he'd fully grown.

That was how the prisoners were tethered. In pairs with poles that had a Y-fork at either end. One fork went around each neck, secured in place with a stick of the same wood, lashed across the open end and held with notching and lashings of wet rawhide drawn tight and let dry to an almost metallic strength. Their hands were secured behind their backs with a smaller version of the same thing, like a wooden version of the hand shackles he'd seen used from Stygia to Hyrkania.

"Iron costly," Irawagbon said. "Keep for tools, weapons."

Conan nodded. Metal was scarce among his folk too, and among the Aesir and Vanir to their north. Though not that scarce. The Picts, those misbegotten savages—

Sorry, Gelete.

—who really didn't even deserve the name of barbarian, didn't make it at all. They used flint or copper, when they couldn't buy or steal from more cultured folk.

The kingdoms south of Stygia knew the art of smelting metal, but their methods were more primitive than those in civilized lands, and the results scarcer. Stygia got much of its iron from the north, Shem or Argos. They knew the way of building a furnace well enough, but trees for charcoal were scarce in the long-cultivated valley of the Styx, where only stark desert lay beyond the black earth watered by the annual floods.

Conan grinned.

"This makes things easier. I'm a blacksmith's son and learned some of his art." She cast him a puzzled look, but he waved it off. They didn't have the time. "For the life of me I couldn't figure a way to quickly free so many from fetters, even if I had the tools, which I don't. But wood... even very hard wood... that's another matter."

Irawagbon's face cleared. "*Told* you," she said. "Didn't

know word 'chained' meant iron. Was thinking, nice arse, but thinking with it, too. Know you not—"

She mimed terror.

"—so thought, stupid."

Just then there was a commotion among the Darfari. They both fell silent and watched keenly. Two of the armored men went into the section with the captives, kicking some aside, and cursing what was getting on their strapwork boots. They grabbed one woman, dragging her out by her bound wrists and hair, and her yoke-mate followed, stumbling to her knees and then doggedly getting up again. The one that had a hand locked in her wiry mop stooped and picked up something else to take, as well.

They threw her down in front of another armored Darfari, one whose mail had every second link gilded. Conan could see the prisoner was thick-set, and thought there was gray in her hair, though it was difficult to be sure with distance and the filth that caked her.

Irawagbon spat.

"That one name Nawi." She relapsed into her own language for a sentence, then said, "Ruler of One Hundred Spears."

Commander of a company, Conan thought. The Abomean officer's captor showed something to his commander, then held it to the lashings that secured the wooden hand bindings.

"Ah," Conan said. "She was using a piece of rock to try and saw open the lashings. Brave, and stubborn. Very hard to do that, behind your back the way she is tied."

The Darfari threw the rock aside and looked as if he intended to draw his sword and cut at her. He settled for a couple of full-force swings of his booted foot instead, probably moved by thoughts of what she'd fetch on the slave market if she was still alive when this cavalry troop returned in booty-laden glory.

Irawagbon hissed with every kick.

When the Darfari commander was finished, he made an angry gesture and one of his men stooped. He appeared to tie on fresh strips of wet rawhide to replace those which had been abraded by the rock. Then Nawi and her crouching yoke-mate got more kicks as they were dragged back to the stinking mass of misery.

The day crawled past. Conan lay patiently in his perch, eyes always moving to note any variation in the routine. A little past noon the Darfari threw sticks of the dried meat to their captives and what looked like reeds.

The women didn't scramble for the food—their discipline was still holding, and they shared it out instead, wasting nothing, then peeled the reed-like stalks and ate the interiors. Buckets of water followed, and it was even more impressive that the first went to the injured, including the commander, who was just regaining consciousness.

Despite the abuse he witnessed, Conan grinned to himself. The Darfari had four-score prisoners intended for the slave markets of their capital, and they were reduced to doing servant's work to keep them watered and fed. That they didn't try to make the captives do the grunt labor indicated a begrudging respect—or fear.

He said as much to Irawagbon. Her smile was sour.

"Send to mines," she said. "Never see sun again. Or fight lion, big baboon, for Darfari annual custom." Getting that across required more translation, which at least passed some of the time. "Darfari dog-dung say, custom for their gods. But watch, yell, make bets."

The Cimmerian reflected that he was getting a very one-sided view of the Darfari empire. If a Gunderman was asked about Cimmerians, or a Nemedian about Aquilonians, the impression would be that they were depraved, worthless Set-worshippers, too.

After their post-midday sleep, a custom Conan had seen all the way from Poitain in southern Aquilonia to... well, here... the Darfari warriors fell to serious work.

The dried meat they'd accumulated was packed into rawhide containers made by stretching the hides over stick frames until they hardened like board, some sized for pack-saddles on horses and others of what looked to be sixty to eighty pounds, in shapeless bundles probably intended to be carried on the captives' heads. That was the standard way women bore loads in these lands. The rest of the preparations were things like going over harness, sharpening weapons, and making minor repairs on armor and man-tack and clothing.

"They leave tomorrow dawn," Irawagbon said. "Two weeks' march to Darfari border fort, with coffles. We follow and ambush? Or attack tonight?" It was clear which she favored, but she was canny enough to know that they had to agree.

Decision firmed in Conan's mind.

"Tonight. Moonset," he said. "Let's get some rest."

Irawagbon grunted her approval.

24

When the moon finally dipped below the horizon, all that was needed was to take up their gear and move, with no more than a few murmured words. It was densely dark, with only a few fires in the Darfari encampment throwing flickering light on the upper reaches of the ruins.

Derketa, Conan thought. *We come to free your worshippers and punish those who blasphemed against your sanctuary. Help us now—or be damned for an idle bitch!* It wasn't exactly pious, but he hoped it might bring results.

They ghosted through the clicking, buzzing, odorous night toward the base of the final terrace wall. Just over the edge of it he could see a flicker of muted red light from a fire. The Darfari sentry hadn't moved; very sensibly he kept to near the hole where the gate had been, squatting with his backside on a protruding rock that let him look just over the crest without exposing more than his head and part of his neck.

Irawagbon moved in utter silence, back a little from the base of the wall, with the loaded sling in her right hand. Conan climbed the rock face with a skill that was much aided by the fact that the stones didn't even try to fit as neatly as the style of masonry he was used to facing. Despite its age, however, it was solid beneath his fingers, like an irregular cliff—and the Cimmerian had climbed many a cliff. As a boy before his voice broke, he had done it with a woven basket clenched in his teeth, collecting bird eggs for his family.

He came directly beneath the parapet and brought his feet up to secure toe-holds that left him crouched with his head only a few feet short of the top. Then he drew his dagger and waved it in a broad arc that his comrade could see despite the darkness.

Silence, and he waited patiently despite the tension on his muscles. Irawagbon acted as they'd agreed, throwing a rock to fall, tapping and thudding. Conan heard the *rutch* of sandals on dirt, and the sentry padded over to the wall, peering out into the darkness to see if it was some random animal's scratching or something he needed to address. He yawned and scratched as he ambled over.

"*Hisssst.*"

The man started violently and leaned out over the wall to look downward. This close Conan could just see his eyes widen, white against the dark face and below the white cotton headcloth. He opened his mouth to shout and the Cimmerian poised to stab.

Thwack!

A rock the size and shape of a hen's egg smacked into the man's face, right over his nose, and there was a splash that looked black in the gloom. Something spattered on Conan's face, the familiar salt-and-metal taste of blood. The Cimmerian went over the parapet in a single vaulting motion as the man pitched back. There was a thudding and rattle, not too loud, and he landed beside the man. Beside the body, rather, for there was no need for the precautionary hand he clamped on the sentry's throat. Even so, he could feel the windpipe crumple under his grip.

Scant instants later there was a light sound as Irawagbon vaulted over the parapet. He'd already stripped the weapons belt off the dead man, with its sword and knife. She took up the spear the guard had leaned against the rock where he'd been sitting, a seven-foot thing with a broad blade. A moment of studying the jagged outlines of the ruins to the north, silhouetted against the stars, and then they were moving forward again.

Nineteen, he thought.

That many Darfari left who were any sort of fighting-men, not counting the man with the left arm in a sling. They slid forward again. Beyond this point the plan was fairly simple, and he was relieved at that. Complex plans had more ways to fail.

There was another sentry on top of the ruined wall of the large rectangle that had been some sort of great hall or assembly area. This was the greatest danger. If he spotted them, things would go very bad, very quickly.

The good part was that he—like his predecessors they'd watched all day—thought the thing he should watch most closely was the prisoners within, not some unforeseen attacker from the vast wilderness without. Conan stopped and waited while Irawagbon crept closer and closer, then they both froze as a twinkle from the man's spear showed that he'd turned around.

Conan counted his breaths; thirty-two until the guard turned back to look down at the carpet of spear-wives within.

Irawagbon didn't waste any time.

Her sling whirred again, and again there was a *thwack*

of impact—harder this time, because it struck the back of his head.

Eighteen.

The man and the spear both pitched forward, and there was a chorus of cries from the women below as the body landed on them. There came a cry of startled pain as some sleeper found a spear cleaving her flesh. They tended to fall point-down.

A snarled order followed in the Abomean tongue, and even then Conan smiled at the contrast of a leader's unmistakable tone, an order on the lines of *shut up* combined with some obscenity and the fact that it was a deep-throated growl but still unmistakably female.

His amazon companion hit the wall running and scampered up it at a speed that produced a heart-stopping moment when she was fourteen feet up over the tumbled blocks at the base of the wall and missed a handhold. She recovered, reached the top, reversed, and went down the other side. Probably even faster than she'd climbed, because there was a very brief exchange in her native tongue and then one Stygian word.

"Come."

The Cimmerian climbed swiftly, pivoted over on his belly and climbed downward. When he was still ten feet up he spoke quietly but firmly.

"Out of the way."

He dropped, and landed in a crouch, with breathing—and a powerful stench—close about him. There were already sounds, of blades hammering on hard wood. Irawagbon hadn't been idle, and every woman freed would help with the others. There were her sword and dagger, the dead cliffside sentry's sword and knife, and the ones the man atop this wall had held. A snarling murmur ran through the seventy-odd prisoners as their limbs and necks were cut free, and quiet swearing as sheer willpower forced cramped muscle back into action.

Wood snapped as others broke the yokes by main force as soon as their hands were loose. With every sound, however, he expected the soldiers to be roused.

"Let me through," Conan hissed and he ran forward. That required some shouldering and shoving, but he could tell that the Abomeans knew he was coming—enough not to try to hit him, at least. Then he was past the last of the soon-to-be-freed prisoners.

And barely in time. Two Darfari in full kit of hauberk, helmet, and shield careened into the big room, glints and glimpses in the dark until one of them lifted a lit torch in his left hand and shouted in dismay as he saw the boil of action. Then a snarl as he saw the Cimmerian. His comrade stood in slack-jawed shock, but the man with the torch was keener of wit.

He threw the blazing thing in to a pile of brush and firewood that flared up with a whooshing, cracking rush, slapped his comrade on the back with the flat of his sword, and charged. The other was on his heels, not timid but simply slower.

Both of them gave ululating war-cries and charged, the long horseman's swords naked in their hands. Two alert armored men against one who was naked save for leather breeks provided bad odds, but odds had never bothered the Cimmerian overmuch.

Conan didn't let the darkness or the uncertain footing

beneath slow him, either. Broken stone was scattered over the interior, some of it covered in human waste, and it turned beneath his feet several times, nearly throwing him aside. A twisted ankle would mean quick death. The light from the pile of brushwood was waxing brighter quickly.

A Darfari sword slashed at him, and his blade met it in an upward sweep, a clang of steel and shower of sparks and shock to the wrist.

It was worse for the other man, who grunted and took a half-step back as the force of Conan's blow nearly tore the crude weapon from his grip. The Darfari's shield came up, as Conan slapped his left hand onto the hilt of his broadsword and delivered an arching cut with all the strength of his massive shoulders and arms.

There was a thudding, crunching *crack* as the Aquilonian steel slammed into laminated rhino-hide and tough wood. The blade sank in nearly to the fuller ridge in its middle, and the ironwood frame cracked across… So did the bone of the arm beneath it, and the Darfari wailed.

Conan wrenched at his weapon, shattering the broken shield-arm at the shoulder-joint, at which the man fainted. Then he pivoted with desperate speed. Even a god couldn't fight two, as the saying went. The weight of the shield and the man attached to it dragged at his arm, but it turned out to be moot, because rocks thrown by hand hit the second Darfari in the head, making his helmet clang.

He staggered back, coming up again to a fighting crouch and raising his shield against more flung stones.

It did him little good as five screaming she-devils struck. Three had broken yoke-poles held like spears. Another was Irawagbon, with a real Darfari spear, and the fifth was the stocky company commander who they'd seen kicked into submission that morning, wielding another. There was nothing submissive about her now, and the point of her spear went past the edge of his shield and into his bare throat just as Irawagbon's went through the slit below the waist and into his thigh.

He gave a single gurgling shriek and fell.

Seventeen, Conan thought, stepping back and finally freeing his sword with a foot planted on the corpse.

Eager hands stripped the enemy warriors' gear from their belts and backs, even as the last of the captives were cut and smashed loose from their bonds. Shrill shrieking battle-screams began, then echoed from the high stone walls. The man whose arm Conan had shattered recovered just in time to feel a spear-wife's hand close on his scrotum and see a knife flash. His bulging eyes swiveled up with a last shriek. From the amount of blood, he wouldn't be waking up from *that*.

Sixteen.

Another brace of Darfari tried to hold the broad empty doorway at the north end of the ruined hall. Six of the spear-wives bent, heaved up a broken building-stone and ran at them, casting it with malignant perfection at the men trying to control the gap. A dozen more poured into the breech, stabbing and hacking. The rest swarmed after and Conan stood, slowing his breathing and wiping his sword, hearing the clash of weapons elsewhere in the ruins. He had lost count.

One final burst of steel on steel, and a man's hoarse scream of agony that seemed to go on for a very long time.

"Not one left," he said when it finally ended.

25

The first thing the liberated Abomean troops did was break out their captured weapons. Then they took turns scrubbing themselves free of caked filth, each group standing guard over the others. Then they donned their kit.

Which turned out to be leather breechclouts, light tunics of tough cotton that came to just above the knee, all dyed green with red chevrons in patterns that denoted rank, sandals that strapped up the calves, and belts carrying dagger and shortsword as well as pouches for small items. All wore tight leather helmets over their close-shorn heads, strapped with brass and steel, and similar guards on their forearms.

About half carried spears. Those added elephant-hide breastplates and tall narrow shields of the same—Irawagbon explained that they had a legend that their founders back in the mists of time had been women who hunted elephant, and who'd turned up to rescue an equally legendary king and become his bodyguards.

The other half were slingers and carried small circular buckler-like shields slung over their backs, as well. The slings themselves knotted around their helmets. After that, and while their healers treated wounds, they ate. Their captors had starved them, to cut the risks of guarding them.

Conan noted with approval their priorities, and joined in the meal, wolfing down stew and roast meat and baked wild roots and greens and flat cakes of unleavened meal. The Darfari had been well-supplied. Irawagbon translated for her commander as they made their hasty dinner.

"Chief of a Hundred Spears Nawi, she say, you give us chance, so honor commands we help you, too."

Conan nodded and brought right fist to chest in salute to the hard-faced woman across the campfire outside the ruins, in the open space south of the perimeter wall. Nawi smiled thinly.

"Also, she say, you go same way we do toward home, part way at least."

He'd expected that would be their reaction, but took nothing for granted—he supposed there were as many faithless rogues here among folk black of skin as there were anywhere else, and as many among women as men, come to that. It was good to find otherwise with the Abomean warriors.

"First however, Gagooli bless you. She... walks with spirits."

Gagooli was an older woman, but lean and wiry enough to keep up with the youngsters who made up most of the unit. In charge of the brace who doctored injuries, she'd donned her kit, too, but it was of a different sort; body-paint, including a white daub across the eyes and forehead, a blanket of soft red-dyed goatskin studded with gold ornaments, a headdress that included large feathers, and a gourd rattle on the end of a stick. She tapped that in the air around his head before sitting cross-legged beside Nawi.

There she spoke, first in her language and then in Stygian

considerably better than Conan's. What she said caused rustles and stares and invoking signs.

"Derketa speaks to me of you. She says you are Her avenger!"

Well, that will help, he thought.

They moved to the rear of the ruined temple, where he bowed his head and touched his brow in the direction of the cult statue. She wasn't a goddess he worshipped, but he didn't hate her the way anyone not raised Stygian detested Set. From what he'd heard, Derketa was a deity of love and pleasure and fertility—but also of war and the underworld of the dead, like Ishtar.

"I thank her for her favor," he said. In this time among the civilized lands, he'd learned that it never hurt to be polite, and there was nothing people resented more than a slight to their gods.

For that matter, gods can be touchy, too.

"And She says you are under a curse. A curse from a follower of—"

She spat into the dirt.

"—the Serpent of Hell."

That meant Set, but they were probably reluctant to say the name, lest the deity be summoned. Behind him there were more gestures and murmured invocations—all the Abomeans save the posted sentries were gathered to watch and listen. It was the first time Conan had been in a gathering of warriors where he was the only man, and it felt a little strange.

Or quite strange, he thought further.

He'd enjoyed Irawagbon's company, occasionally very much indeed, and it had been a good little set-to. Yet on the whole, he'd be glad to be back alone on Valeria's trail as soon as possible. Or on the trail of the late unlamented Khafset's brother Nebset, and *then* on Valeria's trail, and hopefully more.

Conan scowled and spoke. "I kill a priest of... of the Serpent God," he said.

There were gasps.

"He tried to kill me, set crocodiles on me and my comrades as we crossed a river. Sacrificing children—children of his own people—to gather power. So I fought my way through the crocodiles and cut off his head. I think he was kin to another Stygian, an officer who tried to force himself on a friend of mine, who is a warrior woman like you. She killed him, but had to flee from the Stygian lands, and she is pursued by his brother. The curse still seems to follow me, but I will not let it turn me from my duty to save a comrade. I follow to—"

He decided not to say *rescue*.

"—warn her lest he kill her from ambush."

And earn her... gratitude, he added, but to himself rather than aloud. *Women can be odd about such things.*

His words brought more murmurs, and some leaned forward to slap him on the arms and back. One tousled his hair, and he had to stop himself from glaring blue-eyed murder. He'd never liked that, even as a boy, though his father had been ready to turn it to a clout across the ear if he objected.

"Can you break the curse?" he asked Gagooli.

She answered with discouraging quickness, a sharp shake of the head.

"No," she said. "It was laid by a powerful magician who invoked... his god. But it is strange. The curse of a dead man is... dead. It may work, but it is not a thing that emanates from a living mind. This one is halfway between that and the work of a living man. It is anchored in the land of common day, somehow. What I *can* do is shield you from the eyes of the spell, for a while. Shall I?"

Conan nodded emphatically. "I would be most grateful."

Nawi spoke, and Irawagbon translated.

"Commander say yes, do this thing, we owe you much."

The Abomeans proved as good as their word.

With Conan they left the next morning, trotting as tirelessly as Irawagbon had shown she could, off southward with the rising sun on their left. The horses of the dead Darfari were reserved for the wounded, but Conan found it not much of a hardship. The spear-wives were mostly lighter than he, but he had longer legs than any of them, and was in as hard condition.

They could still run into the dirt many armies with which he'd marched. To their advantage, they had no baggage train, no camp followers and no supply train. With forty skilled slingers, they didn't even have to stop to hunt; birds and small animals, gazelle and the like fell to them all through the day, so at sunset they simply had to cook what they'd killed or plucked up from the ground and off bushes and trees as they passed.

The third day was lost to a downpour so powerful they couldn't see to proceed. It passed by evening, and they made camp.

On the fourth day he rose, washed, ate, and filled his

lungs with the warm clear air. Nawi and Irawagbon came as he strapped up his bedroll, and Gagooli. She looked a bit worn, as if she hadn't been sleeping, and she offered him a bracelet. He accepted it, a band of leather with designs in beadwork stitched on the outer surface.

"This is Derketa's Arm," the walker-with-spirits said. "Shield you. Makes clear the footprints of your enemies." He took it gratefully, wrapped it around his thick left wrist, and tied the thong. It probably couldn't hurt, and might well help.

Nawi led a saddled horse, and Irawagbon led two more with loaded pack saddles. The younger woman looked a little woebegone, and he thought he knew why. She was going back to a life of involuntary celibacy, which was enough to depress the cheeriest soul. He grinned at her, and when Nawi turned her head to consult with the spirit-walker, she stuck out her tongue and gave him a quick kick in the ankle.

He suppressed a yelp.

The spear-wife commander turned back to him, and they clasped wrists, her grip firm and dry and hard.

"Now we go there," she said through the younger spear-wife, pointing southeast. "Spirit-walker says, you go there." Her arm shifted directly south, to where the savannah rose in green waves, speckled with beasts by ones or twos or in clumps, trees growing more common and larger in the distance.

Anticipating his question, Gagooli shrugged. "No, I do not see your friend," the shaman said. "She is not of this land. Neither is your enemy... but he is linked to the curse laid on you. Linked by blood, perhaps; and perhaps he is part of the spell, part of what keeps it bound to this world. Or he may have something of the magician, an amulet or icon. Or all of those. He follows your friend, you say, so to see him is to see her." She added, "That way. See the tall, forked mountain?"

He did when he followed her pointing arm, though only just. He wouldn't have thought someone her age could match his keenness of vision. Then he shivered.

She probably wasn't seeing it that way.

Gagooli smiled at him wolfishly, showing strong yellow teeth, and likely guessing his thought.

"Go there, you will find his tracks on the western edge."

He nodded.

The spear-wives packed up with their usual speed. Irawagbon turned and shouted, and all of them lifted their arms and cried:

"Conan! Conan! *Conan!*"

He waved, swung into the saddle, and put his mount up to a loping trot, two pack-animals following behind. When he looked over his shoulder a few moments later, only the fact that they were trotting over a rise let him see the ant-tiny figures of the Abomeans. Their green tunics faded into the rainy-season grass. Sunlight glinted on spearheads.

He turned back to the southward track.

There *was* a track, heading more or less toward the mountain Gagooli had indicated. The way was probably carved by paw and hoof, not human feet, but it was there nonetheless, winding to keep to higher ground.

Suddenly he threw back his head and laughed, a booming carefree sound that startled a flight of bright blue-and-green long-tailed birds out of some trees ahead. He had a good horse and an open road, an enemy to catch and...

And Valeria, he thought.

26

"Crom!" Conan swore.

He was in the foothills of the forked mountain, skirting it to the west—where Gagooli had said he'd find the tracks of those he pursued.

Not if I'm pounded to mush first, he thought.

The rocky foothills were like brush-covered pimples on the savannah, with the mountain behind them in dense forest. The trees grew tallest right at the base of the hills, as well as along a river that ran away southwestward, which he could see running away for miles.

What he could also see was a disturbance in the brush just a hundred yards south, and the long, crooked nose-horn of a big rhino—the square-mouthed variety—poking out of it. It trotted out and stopped, raising its huge head and snuffling, flicking its long oval ears. The wind was directly north-south at that moment, carrying its scent to the animal. The horn went down. The beast walked... and then trotted...

...and then broke into a run.

Apparently there were limits to Derketa's Arm. He'd come to recognize the signs of the Stygian priest's curse. This rhinoceros wasn't just losing its temper because he was too close, and it wouldn't stop when its tiny mind lost interest or it got a little tired.

He pulled his horse's head around and clapped his heels to its flank. It was a tall beast, fifteen hands, since the Darfari cavalry ran to big men, too. Jolted into a run with a long-legged speed, the two pack-horses followed with their heads and necks extended, laying back their ears and rolling their eyes in terror at the thud of feet behind them.

The rhino was three times a big horse's weight, pushing four tons, and nearly Conan's height at the hump. It could move fast when it wanted to—faster than a horse for a little while... and what it sought to do would only take a little while.

A high equine scream made him whip his head around. The long tip of the rhino's horn had scored the rump of the last horse. It swiveled, trying to twist out of the big beast's path, but the leading rein slowed it and it half-fell. Then the horn went into its belly with all the momentum of a four-ton weight of enchanted rhino behind it.

Conan had some idea of the strength of those massive shoulders and necks, but his eyes still went wide as the horse was thrown up and behind the rhino, bits and pieces flying from the pack saddle as it turned and then crashed down. There was a reason horses were terrified of falling; an animal that large smashed if it fell any distance, which this one now did, its panic-stricken cries cut abruptly short in a splash of blood and loud snap-crackle of breaking bone and neck.

Bad country for horses.

He drew his knife and slashed through the leading-rein. The first packhorse got away with nothing but a wound from a side-slash of the rhino's horn. That also burst the girth of its saddle, which spilled off as the animal ran away into the savannah, occasionally bucking and kicking its heels in the air in hysteria.

"Good luck with the lions!" Conan snarled over his shoulder. He was starting to think that Set must *really* not like him, specifically. The feeling was mutual.

"But *I'm* not a god."

The game-trail he was following dove into the riverside brush, rearing up on either side of him as his horse galloped, increasingly interspersed with real trees that grew taller. Branches threatened to sweep him out of the saddle, and he leaned forward over his mount. Its breathing was starting to sound labored, like a tired bellows in a foundry, and foam spattered at his face.

The trail wound downward toward the water. The breathing of the rhino, far too close behind, sounded labored too, but the unnatural purpose in its little piggy eyes kept it coming. Before long he would reach the river—a stream far too wide for his horse to jump, he decided. The beast was panicked and would plow into the current, and then its heavier pursuer would plow into *it*.

And him.

If I throw myself off on the downstream, I may be able to swim fast enough. There wasn't anything else he could do. He bared his teeth in a fighting grin.

Further south, the sound of the horse's hooves and the massive thudding impacts of the rhino's three-toed feet changed their timber, growing softer despite the lung-straining effort both were putting forth. The water was getting near, and his surroundings grew darker and a trifle cooler as the trees closed their canopy overhead, dangling vines that slapped at him. The forest was loud with monkeys and birds fleeing in chattering, squawking terror at the onrush of the beasts.

The trail levelled out—

—and there was a near-naked, short brown man in the trail ahead of him, waving his arms and shouting.

In Stygian, though with a thick accent:

"Death! Death ahead! Pit, pit, pit!"

Then a wordless scream of terror as the fellow saw what was following the mounted man.

Conan only had seconds to react. He swerved the horse to the left, as much as he could given the narrow trail and the thick vegetation beside it. He leaned far down in the opposite direction, rightward, his weight coming onto that leg in the stirrup. The reins in his left hand, he extended his right arm like a sickle, and snatched up the person who'd warned him.

Thud.

The impact wasn't quite as bad as he'd feared, though this technique often was used by the Turanians to pick up people running *away* from them—women, usually, on raids—and the Kossaki had copied it. Conan had learned it among them; those rogues of the steppe included broken men and wanderers from every land in their ranks. Anyone who wanted loot and to fight Turanians and wasn't bothered by hardship or danger.

As it was, the effort very nearly tore him out of the saddle. His left foot came free, and he saved himself only by catching the horn of his saddle with his left heel, another Kossaki trick. The horse staggered as it ran along the left side of the track, the ground slipping out from under its right-side hooves.

It recovered with a wrenching effort that enabled Conan's desperate lunge to come back upright. The trail that had looked as solid as earth was revealed to be a great hole covered only in a framework of woven branches and twigs, topped with a few inches of dirt.

That he saw in a flash as he dashed by. Behind him there was a crackling, a huge squeal of terror, and then a thud combined with a wet, meaty smacking sound. The squeal ended in a gurgling blubber and Conan reined in his mount.

The man he'd snatched up dropped back to the earth as Conan slugged his horse back on its haunches. It reared, flailing the air with its hooves, and then stopped after half a dozen more paces. The Cimmerian slid out of the saddle himself, holding it for a moment with his large hand on the bridle while it danced sideways around him, as if he were a hitching post.

Then something close to sanity returned to its eyes, which still rolled as Conan tied the animal off to a path-side tree. It stood with wide-spread feet, panting like a bellows, its head drooping and foam and slaver dropping from its champing jaws, the rank scent all around him of the sweat that soaked its hide.

He turned with quick wariness. The man—or boy?—had saved his life, but experience had taught him to trust no one until given good reason.

The figure rose and dusted himself off, or at least scraped the damp dirt off his torso. He walked back and picked up his gear. There wasn't much of that. He was short—barely coming to a handspan over Conan's belly, which accounted for the ninety pounds or so of weight the Cimmerian had hefted. His dress was a loinclout of leather, a flap falling before and behind, tucked through a belt of twisted leather thongs. That and a string of blue trade-beads around his neck were all his clothing.

His gear consisted of a pouch and one of the cheap trade knives that were currency around here, worn at his belt, and a short bow and quiver with a cap that he picked up from where he'd tossed them aside.

He grinned at Conan, an engaging expression showing very white teeth. His skin was brown, lighter than most folk in this region, but his short cap of hair was even more tightly-kinked, his cheekbones very high and his eyes slanted like those of a Hyrkanian out of the lands east beyond the Vilayet Sea. A little gray at the temples made Conan revise his age upward from the one his slightness and size had suggested. Despite his five feet of height, he looked strong in a wiry-muscular way that suggested endless endurance, with not an ounce of spare flesh on his body, and he was proportioned like an athlete.

Either he's a dwarf, or his people are just short, Conan thought.

"You save me," the man said.

"You save *me*," Conan replied.

They both laughed the easy laugh of men to whom peril of life and limb was a regular thing.

"You no Stygian."

"No, by gods." Conan spat, then slapped a fist on his chest. "Conan, a Cimmerian." As usual, he might as well have claimed to be from across the unknown reaches of the ocean. Instead of trying to explain, he jerked his chin at the slight man.

"Ich'keomon," the local said in turn, pointing a thumb toward himself. "Sākhoen," he added, which was probably the name of his people, since he did the thumb motion again toward himself, and then waved around. "Sākhoen," he repeated, as if to say *"we are here."*

The tribal name contained an odd clicking sound not like anything Conan had heard before, and which he was certain he couldn't duplicate if he practiced for months. The same sort of sounds had been in the long call he gave. That made it a stroke of luck—

For a change, good *luck.*

—that the man spoke some Stygian, since it was the trade-language in these lands.

Conan walked over to the edge of the pit; it was about twelve feet long, which was why the rhino's rump still was half-protruding at its northern end. Something else projected; a great sharp stake of ironwood which had run into the animal's chest, a blood-wet foot of which came out its body just at the base of its neck. He thought there was another in its belly.

As he watched the gigantic beast gave a final twitch and died, its blood seeping out to make mud of the damp bottom of the hole in the ground.

Without warning or sound, more folk came out of either side of the trail. Six men like Ich'keomon, and eight or so women with a family likeness—yet unlike the slimly muscular men, with backsides of spectacular proportions. All of the females except one wrinkled white-haired crone carried or led at least one child whose ages ranged from babes in arms to a boy nearly old enough to be a warrior.

They all moved with casual ease through the brush, even the toddlers, and in near-perfect silence, as good as Cimmerians and Picts back home. That seconded Conan's guess: these people hunted and gathered for their living, and were no farmers—not even farmers who hunted a good deal, like his own people.

The women wore broader loincloths and carried woven baskets over their backs, many of them full of greens and wild fruits. They also carried digging sticks of skillfully shaped hardwood, and had stuck in their belts what were probably throwing sticks for small game. Every adult had a knife; eight of the same trade-staple iron type that Ich'keomon bore, the rest of worked flint or volcanic glass.

All of them looked warily at him, until Ich'keomon gave a short speech, full of arm-waving and much of it with a finger pointed toward Conan.

That brought friendly smiles.

Then they stripped off their scanty clothing, swarmed down into the pit, and began butchering the huge animal. Long swaths of the thick hide were stripped off and laid on the dirt of the trail, and then the meat and organs on that. Children waved to keep off the flies. Men and women popped morsels into their mouths as they worked, particularly of special treats like the liver or tongue.

Conan didn't join in the butchery—not from squeamishness, since from the time he could walk he'd attended at the funeral disassembly of everything from chickens to elk—but simply because there wasn't room for someone his size among the little folk in the tight confines of the pit.

At the last, Ich'keomon emerged, bearing the horn of the beast, itself two-thirds his height. He was a glistening statue of blood but stood proudly as he presented the horn across his palms.

"You for, save me," he said. "Stygian trader want—pay knives, beads."

Rhino horns were in great demand. In Shem and Stygia they were used by magicians to help men harden themselves, and polished to an amber glow with colorful striations they made valuable ornaments—things like knife-handles and fancy cups. Weight for weight, it was worth much more than ivory.

He couldn't lug it around, of course... Then again, if there was a way he could use it to ram up some Stygian officer's arse...

"How much merchant give for horn?"

The little man frowned, and listed various things his people wanted from the northerners. He noted how much rhino horn they'd need. As Conan had assumed, they were being royally screwed, even given the dangers and costs of getting merchandise from here back to Sukhmet or one of the other border outposts.

He gave the Sākhoen chief a rundown on exactly what rhino horn would fetch when the Stygian or Darfari merchant sold it on in Sukhmet. He didn't mention what it cost in Stygia proper, or Shem, much less Tarantia or Zingara. From Sukhmet to the northern markets, the mark-ups were ordinary enough. The big profit lay in getting the stuff from these children of the forest and bush.

Ich'keomon's face grew grimmer as Conan spoke, and he turned and translated for his band. They all stamped and did what was probably cursing in their clicking tongue. He turned back to the Cimmerian.

"What they get for—?" he began, and what followed took a little time, during which the butchering went on. Fires were lit and the women started smoking the meat, as well as grilling choice bits. He accepted a skewer of liver, enjoying the strong-tasting juices as they ran into his mouth, nearly burning his lips.

It turned out that the Sākhoen sold ivory, too—they had no other use for it, except for tools—and the feathers of exotic birds, plus herbs like the dried petals and pollen of the black lotus. Conan didn't know precisely what some of them would fetch, but he had more of an idea than his new friends did.

"Stygian dogs!" Ich'keomon cursed. "Lickers of dung!"

Conan nodded agreement. Many ordinary Stygians weren't that bad, but he thought it was a fair description of their nobles, priests, and merchants. Of course, those categories were loathsome enough in most civilized lands, but Stygia's upper castes took the cake as far as he knew—and his experience was wide and varied.

Ich'keomon's face fell a little when Conan turned down the horn, but he struggled to explain what he was about. The Sākhoen all nodded in sympathy as their leader translated. Pursuing an enemy was perfectly understandable to them, and curses, and rescuing a woman.

"I come, help you track. For days—"

He opened one hand, conveying five.

"—or until strike trail."

27

In the morning they set out; Conan had eaten as much rhino as he could, but he couldn't take more than one day's fresh meat in this climate. Instead his saddlebags bulged with roots and nuts—some of them surprisingly good—and dried fruits. That was one benefit of gaining the help of people who really knew the country.

Ich'keomon—whose name turned out to mean something like "quick and fierce"—was another. He had only the vaguest idea of the world beyond a week's travel on foot. Stygia was north, other lands north of that, Darfar was over there and Abomey southeast of that, and so forth. Yet every rock, tree, hill, and swale, animals and weather and water, were there to him in the way Conan's father had known the peculiarities of his forge and tool-racks and the colors of heated metal. Ich'keomon explained as he went.

"Nobody go there," he said, pointing directly south. "Too high, too steep, no way through. Go south, go *around*, that way."

He made a curving gesture, as if bearing east of south and then south again.

"See tracks there, because only few good places cross rivers, get water, so?"

"It is so," Conan said, and he was extremely glad he'd snatched Ich'keomon up when he nearly went into the pit.

He'd have followed roughly the same path, but without the local man's knowledge it would have taken a *lot* longer. Either Nebset had shown great skill at tracking, or something more uncanny. That meant the Cimmerian didn't have an unlimited amount of time to catch him before the Stygian caught Valeria. What would happen then was up to luck and the spirits, but Conan's nights were filled by the thought of the blond warrior-woman.

Day followed day, with Conan riding or trotting beside his horse, and impressed by the diminutive man's endurance, which tried even the Cimmerian's iron thews. The mountain loomed to their left, and the trees grew thicker. Ahead a blue line of hills showed, first as a mere hint when the ground rose and he had a clear sight in that direction, then as a definite line on the southern horizon.

"Trees," Ich'keomon said, pointing to them. "On hill, over hill—big-big trees, many-many."

Conan knew he meant forest… or jungle, and a big one, stretching further than the Sākhoen hunter's knowledge. The detailed information on plants and animals gave way to tales of monsters and demons. Which might very well be true, too.

At midmorning on the fourth day, Ich'keomon stopped. He looked around, at the sky, and then sniffed.

"Someone camp, that way," he said, pointing to a clump

of trees below the side of a hill. "Maybe two day, maybe four day." He trotted forward.

Conan followed with a slower but longer stride, ignoring the streams of sweat that ran down his torso. At least as long as he kept to the open and moved, it did dry… eventually. He had dismounted to spare his horse, but it was still tired— men could run horses to death, given enough time, and the coarse grass here wasn't the best fodder in the world. Fortunately it was fresh and green, at least.

I'm tired too, he thought. *Valeria, you had better appreciate what I'm doing for you! I've fought rhinos, giant ape-men, and Darfari lancers to rescue your backside.*

The location was shady and there was a pool of good water nearby, though Conan noted that the campfire and other signs were quite a distance from the pool. That was sensible—otherwise some beast might come for a drink in the small hours of the night, and stay for a quick meal, if there wasn't someone to keep watch. Someone like the Sākhoen hunter.

Doubly so, given the curse, he thought darkly.

Catching the Stygian was going to be a pleasure.

There was a spot that had been dug out slightly, where the coals of a fire rested. Conan knelt beside it and held his palm out over it. That gave him less than it would in the north, since the contrast between embers and the air was less in these hot lands. He looked and tasted, too.

"Two or four days since the last fire," he agreed, as he spat aside. Ich'keomon grunted assent and started quartering around the fire pit. Twice he stopped, examined the ground, and sniffed deeply.

"Use twice." He peered at his companion. "Maybe one woman, then one man next day, two day," he said. "Like those you hunt." Conan gave him a questioning look, and the hunter went on: "Man-piss, woman-piss, smell different, little bit. Woman-piss older, little bit, too."

The Cimmerian was impressed, though he'd noticed often enough that the Sākhoen's senses were very acute, even by his standards. They'd probably seem like sorcery to a city-man.

"Stygian good tracker," Ich'keomon added. "Follow fast."

Good tracker or guided by a dead magician, Conan thought.

By unspoken mutual agreement, Ich'keomon let Conan sleep the night through, which would be the last time he could do that safely for some time. He awoke naturally at dawn, and nodded thanks to the Sākhoen, who had the courtesy common to what civilized folk called barbarians.

Then he did a double-take. Draped over a nearby log was a snake… one about twelve feet long, its scales green on the top with chevrons of red on its head and upper neck. It was dead, the back was broken in two places.

"Heads for you!" Ich'keomon said.

"Poison?" he said, nodding at the snake and miming choking and collapsing.

"Much-much," the little hunter said cheerfully. "Bite big

animal, blood come out everywhere." He indicated eyes, ears, nose, mouth and anus. "Die bad-bad, quick-quick. Poison make soft, easy to eat."

The curse, Conan thought and cursed himself—in his mother-tongue.

"We are even," he said.

Ich'keomon shrugged. "We friends." Then he gripped both Conan's hands in his people's gesture of farewell. "Spirits walk by you, give you good luck," he said.

Conan nodded somberly. "Crom grant you the strength to fight through life," he replied—though it sounded odder in Stygian than Cimmerian. "And protect your kin, your woman and your children."

Ich'keomon grinned. "When you find Stygian man, kill him twice—once for you, once for me," he said. "Dung-lickers. Cheats!"

He turned and trotted away, nearly vanishing in the tall grass and brush that turned the clear areas into patches isolated amid taller growth. Conan watched him go, then shrugged to settle himself to the work of the day.

It was going to be tight, whether he overtook Nebset before the Stygian caught up to Valeria. The Cimmerian would kill him either way... but he'd much rather have a living, grateful, beautiful Valeria to thank him in a dozen different ways, instead of just fulfilling a comrade's obligation to avenge her blood.

Tracking at this level was partly a matter of the signs, and partly a matter of just calculating where anyone with sense would pick their way. Valeria wasn't overly woods-wise, but she had plenty of good sense... except in her choice of men, and he could help her with that. He'd have to keep his eyes mostly up, looking at the ground a distance away, or he'd have no chance of success.

Laughing, he led his horse onto the trail. Two overlapping sets of tracks were visible... here and there, where a shod hoof scored a stone, or stamped into a spot where some trick of the terrain protected it from the heavy downpours they'd experienced in recent days.

The hills ahead were much more visible now, only a few miles away. Hills, or in spots low mountains. That would help, if he could determine which hill-track they had taken. Steep country made following a bit easier, because there were usually far fewer ways to cross it.

There.

The horseshoe with the nick in it had left a clear print. He swung into the saddle and legged his mount up to a slow trot.

28

The trail led to a single winding pass. Once he was a few thousand feet up, Conan appreciated the relative coolness, but when it came time to camp for the night he found himself strangely reluctant to halt.

"That damned snake," he muttered to himself, scanning for a good spot. Even the landscape around him was strange. Parts of it reminded him of the rugged part of Cimmeria in which he'd grown up, and others were utterly unknown. The general steepness and rockiness were familiar, as was the deep cleft to his left with a river bawling over boulders, casting spray up a hundred feet toward him. The smells of wet rock were familiar, but there was no snow, no glaciers on the heights.

The vegetation had changed, some overtly, other times more subtly so. The overall scent was new to his senses, spicier somehow, and lacking the cool tang of pines.

Snakes, he thought. *This place has more poisonous snakes in the space of one crofter's farm than would cover all of Cimmeria.* Otherwise the animal life was relatively sparse, and what he saw was... different—like the large eagle that flew past, giving him the eye and then moving off with a tilt of its spread pinfeathers.

As he drew closer to his prey, urgency lent speed to his passage.

I'm not just out to save Valeria's *life*, he knew. *If I don't find Nebset and find a way to end the curse, what are my odds of making it out of this land alive?* Not everything was his enemy, and he wasn't under constant assault. If that happened, he'd be dead long since. So the curse couldn't be *that* powerful. But if every creature *might* seek his blood, day or night, it was only a matter of time…

"Death is always only a matter of time," he muttered to himself with a shrug. "Still, best to take precautions."

The light faded faster in a narrow canyon like this—that was the same everywhere—and as it did, he cast about for a suitable place to stop. He spotted a deep cleft in the rock, almost a cave though not quite. A dead tree grew from the rock not far away. From that he kindled a torch and investigated; solid stone on three sides, some sort of dense reddish granite, smoothed by water in the long-distant past.

In the cleft lay the detritus of years, including the skull of a large monkey of some sort. He kicked it out of the space, collected fodder for his horse, and combined it with a handful of hoarded grain. Then he used his hatchet to cut more wood, roasted the last of the rhino—it wasn't gone off, not quite—and ate, ignoring the slight rankness. He also munched down some of the roots and nuts the Sākhoen women had gathered for him.

They had provided generously. He spread his blanket of woven, soft-tanned leather strips with the fur still on, what they called a *kaross*. It was surprisingly comfortable even when laid on bare rock like this.

He built the fire up higher, too, right at the mouth of the cleft. It nearly filled it and would only be visible directly from across the valley. There was nothing there but sheer rock, so he was reasonably safe.

That left both the blaze and the horse between him and the night, so he laid himself down with his sword and a stout stick, and a pile of splinters and twigs next to the fire. There was no sign of rain, just high cloud now and then. Red light shone through his eyelids as he stolidly set himself to sleep.

A dream took him. He knew he was dreaming, but it was distant, abstract, like the waking world itself. Yet the dream felt intensely *real*. the Stygian priest he'd killed was there, dancing. Above his head he held… his head. Gripped it in his dead hands, and behind him was a man who danced as if he were the priest's shadow.

The head on the shadow's slim, graceful body was that of a cobra, and its yellow slit eyes were fixed on Conan. The steps of that dance were slow, sinuous, graceful… and utterly malevolent, soaked in a hatred of all that lived and possessed warm blood. Somehow those eyes looked through the glazed, dead glare of the slain priest to see the Cimmerian.

Music played through the dance, drums and something like a flute… but a flute that *hissed*. Then the cobra-headed man passed *through* the dead priest, their forms merging, or the priest was sucked into and subsumed by the snake-man. The cobra mouth gaped, fangs folding down to strike, a drop of venom glistening on each. Something else stirred in the dancing figure's loins, a phallus that was also a serpent—

Conan awoke with a start and a shout. His horse was neighing and bugling, rearing against the strong line and hobbles that held it. His own convulsive motion kicked the dry pile into the fire, and it flared up with a crackle and a wash of light, bright and red in the intense darkness of pre-dawn.

A snake had wiggled through the narrow gap between the hot embers of the campfire and the rock wall. It was coiling to strike as the Cimmerian came to his feet in a flexing jump that left him crouching before it. The serpent was big, more than six feet long, and had a flared hood like the figure in his dream. Yellow eyes with slits that were windows into an infinite darkness, rustling with movement like scales on dry bones.

He leapt as it struck, and the flat head went beneath the soles of his feet by a fraction of an inch. It coiled again as he landed, and it struck—

Quick as a snake, a remote part of his mind thought.

Conan leapt again, but his time backward, into the full depth of the cleft in the rock, his skin against the stone. The snake came at him in a blur, and he could never dodge it again, not pinned in like this.

But his arms could brace, and he could swing his legs up. That made it miss, and even as it flashed beneath him he was pounding a heel downward. His foot struck, hard enough to send a jarring flash of pain up from his heel through his groin and into the small of his back.

Even as his foot smashed down he threw himself forward,

doing a roll across his kaross and pivoting erect with his back to the fire, close enough for the glow to singe the little hairs on the backs of his muscled legs. Its back broken, the snake writhed. He checked to make sure it hadn't managed to fang him in that brief instant of contact.

Then he picked up the stick beside the kaross, the one he hadn't had time to snatch up when something—probably the horse, or perhaps his dreadful dream, or both—woke him. With considerable satisfaction, he slammed the bludgeon down on the snake's head, over and over. That left a wet spot on the rock, a combination of blood and brain-matter and venom.

Carefully avoiding that, he took his knife and cut the body just behind what was notionally its neck. Then he squatted by the fire and set to skinning and gutting it. The meat would make breakfast. Somehow, consuming the flesh of his opponent lent additional satisfaction.

An inner sense, and the feel of his surroundings, told him that it was about an hour before dawn. The time of sunrise and sunset changed much less here than in the land of his birth. The air had that particularly still, dead quality that this time of night usually evoked. That let the roar of a lion carry clearly across miles, a lonely sound. The sobbing laughter of a pack of hyenas followed it.

He continued with his task until he had a pound or two of meat, ready to grill on skewers taken from the little pile of firewood. Then he threw the rest of the body into the night, over the edge of the trail and down the near-vertical slope. That provoked another snort and roll of the eyes from his long-suffering horse.

The smashed remains of the snake's head followed after

that. He used two sticks to pick it up, and threw the sticks after it.

As he made his simple preparations for the beginnings of the day, smelling the good scent of grilling meat sizzling, he considered what lay ahead.

"Valeria cannot be under the same curse, else how is she still alive?" he murmured to the horse, who paid him little mind. "She must be alive, or that Stygian dog wouldn't have kept going southward."

Then he chuckled. "No, Nebset wants to kill her himself—not have a snake or a lion do it for him," he said to the first gray sign of dawn. "Stygians put great stock in blood vengeance. He will accept no less." Unless Conan could stop him.

He began to eat the grilled snake, then cracked a nut like an elongated triangle between thumb and forefinger before he popped the white nutmeat into his mouth.

"Probably wants to rape her before he kills her, too," he said, and laughed aloud. "Since his dung-munching brother never managed to get on top of her before she killed him."

If he tried that, even with an ambusher's surprise on his side, the Stygian would probably be dead before Conan got within sword's length of him. Though he might not be quite that stupid.

In any case Conan had his own score to settle, and killing Nebset would be likely to make Valeria look more kindly on his suit.

"I want to kill him for my own sake," he added, and the horse nodded. "I could probably have persuaded Valeria to try for the coast some other way, if the progeny of a dog and a goat hadn't led me on this chase."

Conan laughed again—were ifs and buts all candied nuts, everyone would be fat, as the Argossean saying went. He walked out to the edge of the trail, looking down at the river far below. There were probably a lot of snakes down there in the rocky slope, too. The thought prompted him to make water over it, after checking that the wind wouldn't blow it back at him.

Then he went back to tie on his loincloth, don his breeks and sword-belt and boots, and saddle the horse. He led it for the first few miles—he could have ridden, but there was no need to take chances on this narrow way, and the horse was worn. He passed the crest of this line of hills, and then the land in front of him flattened a little and the trail widened, kinking around the side of it.

Conan gave a long whistle.

The view southward unfolded. The hill stretched to his right and left and ended a short distance in front of him. Beyond that it was a sea of green as the jungle stretched as far as the eyes could see. The tops tossed in the morning breeze, which for a wonder wasn't uncomfortably warm. Huge flights of birds took wing, twisting skyward in skeins like twisting smoke, and troops of long-tailed monkeys went past like schools of fish in a true ocean, rising now and then into sight.

The odd taller tree pushed through the canopy, and their huge girths even at the top showed him just how big even the ordinary ones were. Down there with timber towering densely a hundred and fifty or two hundred feet, the air would be still and wet, but out of the baking sun at least.

"Today or tomorrow, Nebset," he shouted. "Today or tomorrow you die, and your dead cousin the priest with you!"

29

Conan blinked.

He'd been heading south on this track… only now, he was heading north, back toward the hills. He pulled the horse to a halt and ignored its resentful snort, shaking his head. Then he caught himself just before he heeled it into motion again.

"Sorcery," he whispered.

Even the word sounded too much like a snake.

It was one of the very few things he genuinely feared. The impulse was strong, to spur the horse and simply *leave* all this. Sweat dripped from his body and ran down his flanks, more than the wet heat of the jungle could cause. He cast himself out of the saddle, walked over to a smooth-barked forest giant with buttresses on the base of its trunk and slammed his fist into it, over and over until the pain brought himself back to himself.

He looked at the bloodied knuckles ruefully.

Well, I already had scars a-plenty there. Then he turned in the deep gloom and thought to himself, *South. I march south.*

Each step was like walking through water, then through amber honey. He paused to rest, exhausted. When he looked northward, Conan realized he'd only come two miles since the last pause. He rose, went a dozen paces—

—and saw that he was leading the horse northward.

His roar of frustration and rage sent fleeing in terror a chattering flock of black monkeys with white ruffs around their necks, up the big trees until they were dots that vanished into the sea of flower-starred green that was the lower edge of the canopy. Flights of white-and-gray parrots moved, too, through the almost solid dimness of the jungle.

Insects buzzed and whirred, including ones that bit.

Conan ignored them. He had to keep his mind on one thing, and one only. *Keep moving south.* Fortunately, there was only this trail—he thought it was cut by elephants. He no longer needed to do much tracking.

Occasionally he would stop and pay attention to the spoor. Nebset was down to one horse, like him... and Valeria. The contrast between the woman's tracks and the Stygian noble's had shrunk again. He thought she was about one day ahead, now.

As much as he found her alluring, wanted to take her to bed, Conan knew it was more than that. She was his comrade at arms, had stood at his back when it was needed. Infuriating at times, certainly, but there was a code they shared. It demanded that he continue.

South. South. South.

He stopped with a grunt. He was heading *north*. Fortunately, he'd only lost a hundred yards or so. The horse snorted resentfully when he turned it around yet again. Couldn't he make up his mind?

Perhaps I could just let it pick its way, he thought. Then, *No.* If he let his mind drift away like that, he'd turn the horse without noticing until miles had been eaten. So he plodded forward.

The beast let out a terrified squeal.

It reared and the reins burned painfully through his hand. Conan ignored that; there was a racking snarl. He drew his sword and pivoted in a blur. That required no thought, no maddening overriding of a portion of his mind. This he needn't *think* about. This was draw...

Draw and strike.

The heavy broadsword sang through the air, a song like a childhood lullaby to the Cimmerian as his left hand joined right on the long hilt. He'd been striking by instinct at the sound he'd heard behind him, but now he saw the target.

It was a leopard, black-spotted yellow grace, in a soaring leap that would have landed on his back. Forelegs spread and claws out to grip, and jaws gaping in the killing bite that *would* have struck at the back of his neck. The long hind legs were deadly, too, ready to scoop out a man's guts like a gralloched deer if they locked into your stomach.

Blade met body with the sweet certainty of a stroke going exactly where it should, with all the power of Conan's arms and shoulders behind it, and the weight of his blurring-fast turn. Even then the cat tried to dodge, twisting in mid-air, but it had no point of contact on the ground to use as leverage. Steel hammered into flesh and bone, an infinitely familiar sensation.

The leopard felt to be a hundred and twenty pounds, a middling-big male. Conan's sword caught it at the junction of neck and shoulder, and with all his frustrated rage behind the blow. Its head and one leg fell separately from the rest of the carcass. A gout of blood caught him in the face and flew into his open shouting mouth, salty rankness that had him spitting and wiping.

It landed where his horse had been. The corpse was kicking and blood still flowing with the pulse that meant the heart hadn't quite stopped yet, though it did as he watched, panting. The sound of hoofbeats faded away to the northward, the horse just disappearing around a long slow bend in the trail.

He took a couple of steps after it. The beast would probably stop to drink at that stream that crossed the trail about a mile back, and he could—

Conan turned his back to the sight of the vanishing beast and faced south again.

"I can take Nebset's horse and Nebset's gear," he growled, and it was a sound almost as bestial as what the leopard had made. "I will take his *life*."

That nearly killed me, Conan thought.

The attacks had come more frequently, and he felt as if sorcery surrounded him on every side, submerging him in its darkness. To calm his mind, he told himself that this meant he was getting close. That Nebset was feeling fear.

He managed to keep himself going south by main force of will.

Unfortunately, that nearly caused him to blunder into Nebset's camp in the night, ready to be hacked down like a child. He stopped short of that and restrained an impulse to beat his head on the ground. Instead he turned aside from the trail, going right into the mostly open space where the jungle giants shaded out most undergrowth. His feet squelched slightly in the damp muck beneath, and dangling vines and lianas brushed at his face as he moved.

He stopped again, going to one knee and panting with his left hand pressed to the leaf-mold. Putting his other hand to his sword-hilt he slowly drew the blue Aquilonian steel. The weight and rough wire-and-leather grip and the sheer solid *realness* of it helped clear his mind. The night was dark, and the double canopy of leaves high above served as well as thick overcast. He was used to the dimness, however, and the red flicker of Nebset's campfire was all the brighter in the middle distance. Judging from the height, the ground rose perhaps a hundred feet between here and there.

From the blurring, there was some thick brush between them, as well. As he came closer he went down on his belly and crawled, parting the growth ahead of him with slow gentle movements of the blade and eeling through. The Cimmerian had stalked dangerous beasts and still more dangerous men this way, many a time. He was still alive and for the most part they weren't.

The thought of what might be crawling through the night *with* him, unseen until it sank deadly fangs into his flesh, made that flesh crawl a little until he banished the thought with a harder grip on the sword.

One of Set's epithets was "he who is stealth in the night."

Conan reflected grimly that two could play at that game.

Breathe, move, tense stillness. Another short crawl, pause, crawl. It wasn't possible to move utterly silent in the darkness, especially in thick-grown country like this. It was possible to use the natural noises to disguise his, however, as long as he was patient enough. It was a pattern of human-style sounds that grabbed attention, and moving irregularly with frequent stops broke that pattern. His movement blended into the background.

Closer, closer, and a smell of roasting meat reminded Conan of how hungry he was. His stomach twisted. That was a familiar sensation, one he'd felt off and on from childhood, and he didn't let it distract him. Instead, he used it for focus.

The ground changed under him. It was drier, and occasional rocks jabbed at him. A low hill, and the top was clear—the soil too thin to support the giant trees, or even much brush. A six-foot shelf of rock, lit from underneath by the flames, and then the jungle resumed on the other side. In fact it towered higher than the hill all around.

There was one figure visible.

Nebset.

The camp was as any single traveler might make it. The fire beneath the rise of rock, the bedroll laid not far from that, a bow and a spear nearby and the sheathed kopesh-sword laid across the woven-hide blanket. Meat-gobbets sizzled on skewers held between two rocks, and the man's tethered horse nosed disconsolately at a pile of vegetation cut and heaped up before it.

The narrow hawk-face of the Stygian noble, so like his brother's—

And not unlike that priest's, Conan observed.

—was unmistakable. The linen headdress was thrown beside the sword on the kaross, and the stubble was plain on the man's long head. He'd managed to shave, as well, save for the chin-beard bound with gold bands.

Nebset knelt now, holding up something that glittered, his eyes locked on it. A little closer, and Conan saw that it was an amulet—a serpent icon, coiled to fit an arm and startlingly lifelike, with yellow topaz eyes that caught the firelight with a numbing flicker. The Stygian laid it down before him, kneeling, chanting softly with his arms spread wide, though it took Conan a moment to penetrate the archaic dialect.

> *"Under a nighted pyramid*
> *Great Set coils asleep;*
> *And in the shadows of the tombs*
> *His faithful people creep…*
> *From the nighted gulfs*
> *That never saw the sun*
> *Send me a servant for my hate*
> *Oh scaled and shining One!"*

For a moment, listening, Conan could have sworn he saw Valeria, riding her horse down a jungle trail.

Aha, that's how he's been tracking her so closely!

Moving even closer, the Cimmerian noticed little stakes that were set out in a shape like a horseshoe backed against the upthrust jut of rock. Placed along the perimeter, they surrounded the campsite. Wooden, but each was carved and painted in the likeness of a man's body, posed in the stiff Stygian style—hands clenched in fists beside the body and one foot advanced, with a stylized kilt and linen headdress. On each the head was not that of a man.

It was a cobra with its hood flared out.

Certain his prey could not see him, Conan reached toward one, and pain flared—not in the hand, but in his head, and then his entire body; a white agony that blanked out vision.

When it died away he was half a dozen paces back from where he had been. He waited with bared teeth until he could move again.

I could run forward, he thought. *Break through that barrier... but then Nebset could spear me like a fish before I recovered.*

Perhaps...

He smiled grimly. There was a game he'd played in the forests of his homeland, with a rope made of twisted vines. The vines here were much bigger and stronger.

Conan backed another hundred paces and looked upward at the silhouettes of the trees surrounding the little clearing. It was too dark to see clearly, but he could determine outlines. When he went to the one he selected, lianas dangled temptingly from the branches high above. He tested one, and then the one beside it. Sheathed his sword, bent his knees, and leapt.

The vine stayed firm when his hands clamped home.

He froze to see if he had been heard.

Nothing.

Grunting, he climbed upward—take the vine between the soles of his feet with his knees drawn up, clamp and push upward with his legs, grab on with both hands, repeat, repeat, repeat. Hard effort that left his sweat streaming in the hot moist night.

Three-quarters of the way to the branch he was aiming for, the vine began to sag beneath his weight. He reached over quickly, grabbing the other vine just as the first gave way, and fell rustling downward into the darkness at the base of the huge tree.

Again he froze, but down below, the figure didn't move.

The second vine held. Conan puffed out relief and began to climb again. The vine grew thicker. The branch he aimed for was wider than his own thighs. He hauled himself up to sit with a leg on either side. With difficulty he hugged the limb with both legs and locked one foot with the other ankle.

Taking a deep breath, he began hauling the vine up hand-over-hand, laying a loop over the branch every time he had another eight feet or so. As before he stopped and started, stopped and started, to avoid raising the alarm. The weight steadily decreased, which was fortunate, for the first few lengths required back-cracking effort, and his grip couldn't span the entire thickness of the bigger upper end.

At last it all lay before him, the smaller bottom end in his fists. He climbed upright, balancing easily on the branch, took a firmer grip and ran outward for twenty paces, then leapt. A long sickening swoop, and he didn't know if the vine would hold or leave him a broken bag of bones on the jungle floor.

Shock.

It hammered at his wrists, flexing his body like a whip and snapping his teeth together with a click. Then he was tracing an arc through the air, away from Nebset's campsite, up and up until he was nearly as high as the branch again.

He aimed at the red dot of firelight.

The return arc would take him right over the campsite.

If it doesn't, I'll feel like I'm an idiot.

More likely, he would feel dead.

There was a moment of pain as he flashed past the perimeter, and then he let the vine go and fell. Fell twelve feet, the impact hammering up through his feet and into his back, leaving him in a deep crouch with his heels touching his backside. The sword flew into his hand as he spat blood from a cut on the inside of his mouth, opened by his own teeth.

Nebset's back was to him, but suddenly it wasn't the amulet that rested before him. It was the priest of Set, the one from the ford... standing with his head held over the ragged stump of his neck. *Something* loomed behind him, shining and dark at the same time, and the dead lips moved.

"*My slayer comes.*" The voice was in Conan's head, more than his ears. "*The one who would deny us vengeance for your kinsman!*"

Nebset reacted with a swift sideways leap and roll that left him on his feet with the blade of the kopesh in his hand.

"You!" he hissed, eyes wide.

"Me," Conan snarled in agreement, taking the long hilt of the broadsword in both hands and stalking forward. He struck—

—and it wasn't Nebset before him. Instead a giant serpent lunged at him, and the amulet Gagooli had given him burned hot on his left wrist. The Cimmerian dodged with a yell, and it was the Stygian's sword coming at him. He dodged again.

An upward strike brought a clang of steel and Nebset staggered backward. Conan placed himself for a lunge—and then had to leap aside as a six-foot serpent struck at him from the side. His backhand strike flashed through the snake, but the creature wasn't there, and his sword buried itself in the dirt. He barely managed to get the blade up again in time to block a chop from the curved end of the kopesh. Another snake... and something prompted him to strike again, and this time it was a serpent of flesh, and its blood bathed him as he dodged the Stygian noble's next slash.

He did dodge, but only just.

The keen edge kissed the skin of his ribs. A shallow slash appeared.

Clang and clatter, and he was backing away.

Around and behind and beside Nebset other figures loomed: a giant serpent swaying in a way that *meant* things, things no man should know, a squid-headed monster with bat wings that crouched and gibbered words that twisted at the mind, more and more and more, blinding his sight to the deadly steel reaching for his life.

He backed a little more, and then twisted aside. As he neared the perimeter of carven stakes, a paw slashed at him out of the night, taking a patch of skin with it. Blood ran down his back, distracting him *nearly* enough for the kopesh to chop into the side of his neck. The missed stroke left Nebset over-extended, but a sudden swirl of biting insects swarmed about Conan's head and made him miss in his turn.

The amulet burned, and he was tempted to rip it off and throw it aside. He didn't, because he realized with a chill that it was indeed blocking most of the dead magician's power. Without it he'd already be dead.

The sweat seemed to turn cold on his torso.

Nebset struck and struck, clang and clatter and sparks in the darkness. Conan blocked, but that was a lifetime's training. The active part of his warrior's mind was elsewhere, feeling the impalpable menace of the slain magician's regard, ready to throw a deadly challenge at any instant— or an illusion he dared not disregard, because it *might* be all too real.

Around Nebset other figures loomed.

That distraction would kill him, too—the Stygian wasn't the warrior he was, but he was better than good. A moment's inattention and it would be death by blade, even if the slain priest's spell didn't kill him directly. Minutes of leap and duck and strike went by, like a fight in a dream. In a nightmare, one that led to only one conclusion.

The Abomean amulet clamped tighter, as if it was trying to tug him aside from the fight. Then he realized *where* it was trying to tug him.

Recklessly he turned his back on Nebset and leapt to where the snake amulet had lain. Nebset shouted in horror as he realized what Conan sought to do, and his sword took a sliver from the Cimmerian's heel as he cast himself forward recklessly.

Conan's blade flashed through the image of the dead-alive priest, finding no more resistance than air might make.

It struck the amulet with the clang of metal cleaving metal.

There was a flash of something that wasn't quite light. Behind him Nebset screamed in horror again—horror and an agony—and he felt a huge weight lifted from his shoulders. One he hadn't realized was there.

No, from my soul, he thought as he wheeled and met Nebset's slashing attack.

But it was no more than a sword, and the Stygian no more than a man—though still a skilled one. Blood ran from Nebset's nose and ears and eyes, some backlash of the magical bond the Aquilonian broadsword had severed. Conan cut, backhand, forehand, then again.

It ended with a jarring thump, and the kopesh spun into the night—taking the right hand and wrist of the wielder with it as it arced through the air and vanished, to land with a clatter.

Nebset screeched, and fell to his knees, left hand clutching at his spouting right wrist in a futile attempt to staunch the flow. Conan stepped forward and cut sideways with every ounce of force in him. A thud and crunch, and the nobleman's head followed his hand. The corpse fell at the Cimmerian's feet.

"It took too long, but it's done," he panted.

A moment more, and he gripped the body by one ankle. slinging it after the head. The severed amulet followed, and the ring of little wooden statues, though he used a stick of firewood for that rather than touching them with his bare skin. The Stygian's horse was snorting and backing, but its line held until it calmed, and Conan looked around.

"Well, I have a ride again," he said to himself, "and a better one than that Darfari nag." A sniff told him that the grilling meat was about ready, and a clay jug by the bedroll proved to have red Stygian wine.

"Everything I need," he mused to himself. "Except a woman."

His eyes turned southward as he blew on the skewer and took a bite.

"Tomorrow."

PART FOUR

XUCHOTL

"That's one tired horse," Conan murmured to himself.

Speaking his thoughts aloud was one of the habits he'd acquired as a wandering man, when he spent much time alone or among people who didn't know his language. He'd have to put it back in its bag for now.

He swung down from his own mount, with the jungle towering around him, knelt, and examined a track in the gray mud of the jungle path. The distinctly worn shoe on the right fore-hoof of the beast he was tracking still showed that distinctive nick, though it had worn down until it took a good eye to see it. That had been his easiest confirmation since the beginning.

Here Valeria had paused to dismount and water the bushes, which in various ways proved it was her on the horse, and he could see how the beast had stood with its legs braced wide, its head drooping enough to leave a thread of gold tassel-work from the red-leather bridle he remembered.

It had silver stirrups, and the saddle was gilt-worked, too, something she'd bought as soon as they got back from the expedition to the Wedi Shebelli gold mine, and she'd accumulated enough loot for some luxuries. Not that he objected; he liked to swank with his gear when he could, too. Most wandering fighters did, and with pirates it was virtually compulsory.

Valeria had a healthy vanity about her accoutrements.

Like me, she's down to one horse, he thought. *But it's still the one she started with, while I'm on my third or fourth. She learned how to handle a beast before she took to the sea.*

Conan frowned a little, looking around as he kept his mount to a mix of a quick walk and a slow trot, dismounting every half-hour or so to lead it at a jog for a short time. She rode much lighter than he did, but his horse was in better condition, so he ought to catch up sometime today.

"Between noon and sunset, with luck."

What bothered him was how *quiet* the jungle was. He peered about, eyes flicking from one place to another. Yes, the same sort of trees—many towering two hundred feet or better high, closing in a rustling sea of green far overhead like a ceiling of multiple arches. Smaller trees made a secondary canopy, a patchier one, a hundred feet up. The boles of the giants were straight, mostly thicker through than his body, clear of branches except for the massive tufts at the top, but laced together with vines sometimes as thick as his calf.

There was little or no underbrush, except where a forest titan had fallen and let in bright sunlight, creating a riot of it, and it blazed with flowers. Drifts of butterflies as big as his palm went by in storms of color.

It was warm, but not as hot as it had been on the open savannah. It smelled of slow vegetable rot and the enormous flowers, including orchids, that starred the background with hanging tendrils of royal purple and bursts of crimson and white.

Just this last hour or so, though, the sounds had ceased.

Rustle and creak of vegetation, yes. The buzz and click and chirrup of insects, yes—and he'd just seen a column of driver ants paralleling the trail, a mile long and so numerous that the horde of thumb-sized little black-and-red killers was wearing a perceptible trench as deep as his ankle in the jungle's duff-covered floor. He avoided them carefully, because the things could swarm even a buffalo and strip it to the bone if it couldn't get away fast enough.

No flocks of parrots and parakeets, however, swarming and screeching like giant versions of the butterflies. No hooting, yodeling monkeys as big as a small child sporting among the branches. No grunting wild pig, no striped forest antelope, no forest buffalo with their sparse reddish hair, smaller and more solitary than their savannah cousins but just as savage in temper.

Not a trace of the forest elephants either, except for their distinctive trails through the jungle and the broken stripped branches that were evidence of their foraging. Judging from the dung they'd been gone for days.

Nor the scream of a hunting leopard, not since just after dawn.

Something's scared them off, since I crossed that river this morning. Black and wide and slow-moving, but no crocodiles, thanks be to Lir and Manannán Mac Lir, and perhaps to Gagooli... though I think I shed the curse with my sword's edge.

Whatever had frightened the jungle's bigger denizens into silence or flight, he really didn't want to meet it. He shrugged like a man shaking off an irritation, deciding he would meet whatever his fate decreed, neither more nor less.

Another hour's quiet was broken only by the dull *thock* of hooves in the damp earth, or the softer fall of his own footsteps, and he saw a small pool ahead, of relatively clear water. Beside it a horse, tied to the fork of a sapling. It was adorned with a red-leather bridle with gold tassels, and a saddle with silver stirrups—looped up now—and elaborate tooling. And—

Valeria! All woman, for all her breeks and blade, and that she's as tall as most men and stronger than many.

She wasn't there, though. He pictured her dismounting and loosening the bridle so the exhausted horse could crop at the ferns and other greenery, which it was doing—while rolling a suspicious eye at him. It flared its nostrils at the unfamiliar scent of his mount. Against the background of somber, primitive forest his mental vision of her seemed bizarre and out of place... but then, she'd been out of place in Sukhmet, too, even more than most of Zarallo's Free Companions.

A ship, that's where she belongs. Clouds towering over a sunset ocean, painted crimson and gold, painted masts and wheeling gulls. *And her eyes... the color of the sea in her wide eyes. Valeria of the Red Brotherhood, and soon mine!*

Conan dismounted, loosened the girths, looped up the stirrups, slipped the bit out of his mount's mouth, and tethered it on a long rein. As it snorted suspiciously at Valeria's mare, he looked up at the canopy; not much light, but what there was showed that the sun was heading west.

We will be too, soon, he thought. *A long trek, but I have friends along the way. And then the ocean, and a ship! Back to the rover's life. Then let fat Argossean merchantmen know fear, gold-laden Shemites curse, and Zingaran slavers rue the day they left their home ports, when they hear that Conan and Valeria are abroad and a-loose.*

The Cimmerian cast around for the distinctive prints of the woman's sea boots. There they were… two wide-spread, and he grinned again to imagine her standing with her fists on her hips, feet braced as if on a heaving deck as she peered about. Then they led off toward the east; he could tell she was glancing back toward the pool from time to time, in order to fix her route in her mind, and now and then breaking off a twig or making an inconspicuous scuffmark.

Even through his eagerness, the silence of the jungle prickled at his wilderness-bred senses. Still no birds sang or squawked in the lofty boughs, nor did any rustling in the bushes indicate the presence of any small animals. He was not used to the sound of his own passage being the only thing to be heard.

He plucked a sweet-sour pod of monkey-fruit nuts, slitting the green rinds with his thumb and popping them into his mouth. From the spat-out seeds and bits of peel Valeria had been doing that, too, and taking advantage of the mangosteens that seemed to be abundant. He grunted thoughtfully as he took a few himself, ripping off the purple-black rinds and eating the sweet segments within.

Mangosteen grew in hot wet places, but they were always thickest near settlements, current or abandoned. So there might be natives near here. There were guavas, too, the type with a soft sweet rind and a taste like a mixture of strawberry and lemon.

The fruit's good in these southlands, he thought. *Mind you, it's no substitute for a haunch of beef, or venison or a roast pig.*

Cimmerians had a belief that eating too much vegetable food was likely to make you soft and cowardly. Conan wasn't sure about that; he'd seen plenty of places that seemed to prove it wasn't so… but his youth had settled a lot of his tastes, if not always the beliefs that went with them.

Valeria hadn't tried to hide her passage. On the contrary, she was leaving a clear trail by which she could backtrack, which was clever of her given that she didn't have anything like his experience. He made himself go cautiously, as well— she was perfectly capable of an ambush, using that blinding-fast lunge-thrust he'd seen her use, only from behind a bush or tree instead of a brawl in tavern or alley.

Conan sensed the ground rising before he could see that it was, a subtle thing that was as much the way your feet and calves and thighs felt as anything. Then the forest changed. Trees shorter, and more undergrowth. Here and there he could see where Valeria had slashed at it to clear a passage.

He didn't, simply bending and dipping as he went.

Then an upthrust ridge of rock, dark and flint-like, glimpsed through a gap in the canopy. He grunted thoughtfully. That was a good idea. It looked to be taller than the trees, and might offer a clearer view of what lay ahead. The jungle was harder travel than the savannah, less game, and poor fodder for horses, but just backtracking…

His skin crawled at the thought.

The track he was following ended where a narrow ridge formed a natural ramp that led up the steep face of the crag. Fifty feet up would put him above the level of the jungle's top, and he slowed to proceed carefully. He held his sword-scabbard up in his left hand so that it wouldn't clank against stone. The trees didn't come close to the rock, but their tops were broad enough that the ends of their lower branches extended around it, veiling it with their foliage.

Where the leafy maze met the rock, he halted for a few moments to let his eyes adjust. Peering through them, he could see that the crag flattened out into a broad shelf which was about even with the tree-tops, and from there it rose a spire-like jut that was the ultimate peak of the crag.

His smile grew broader.

Valeria was there on the peak, carefully scanning north, east, west, and south. Something interesting was to the southward, from the way she started and then moved her lips in a ripe sea-oath.

On the bench below was the skeleton of a man—he could see where she'd kicked the duff aside, but the bones looked otherwise little disturbed, and there were none of the cuts and splintering that indicated violent death. Someone could have just stabbed him in the belly, of course.

Valeria turned to come back down to the ledge. Conan pushed forward, not trying to hide his passage, throat a little tight with eagerness.

At last!

She wheeled cat-like at the sound, snatched at her sword, and then froze motionless, staring wide-eyed at him.

"Conan, the Cimmerian!" she said. "What are you doing on my trail?"

"Don't you know?" he laughed. "Haven't I made my admiration for you plain ever since I first saw you?"

She made an unflattering reference to his resemblance to a male horse, or part thereof. The conversation went downhill from there, the frustration of the long peril-filled journey filling him as she sneered. It ended with her drawing her blade—which he knew no man could try to take from her bare-handed, and live to tell the tale.

"Blast your soul, you hussy!" he exclaimed. "I'm going to take off your—"

Back in the forest below, an appalling medley of screams arose, the screams of horses in terror and agony. Mingled with their screams there came the snap of splintering bone.

"Lions are slaying the horses!" Valeria cried.

"Lions, nothing!" Conan snorted, his eyes blazing. "Did you hear a lion roar?" No one could spend time in these lands without becoming all too familiar with that sound.

She paused in thought.

"Neither did I," he said. "Listen to those bones snap—not even a lion could make that much noise killing a horse."

Side by side, blades in hand, they hurried back down the natural ramp.

RED
NAILS

ROBERT E. HOWARD

I

THE SKULL
ON THE CRAG

The woman on the horse reined in her weary steed. It stood with its legs widebraced, its head drooping, as if it found even the weight of the gold-tassled, red leather bridle too heavy. The woman drew a booted foot out of the silver stirrup and swung down from the gilt-worked saddle. She made the reins fast to the fork of a sapling, and turned about, hands on her hips, to survey her surroundings.

They were not inviting. Giant trees hemmed in the small pool where her horse had just drunk. Clumps of undergrowth limited the vision that quested under the somber twilight of the lofty arches formed by intertwining branches. The woman shivered with a twitch of her magnificent shoulders, and then cursed.

She was tall, full-bosomed and large-limbed, with compact shoulders. Her whole figure reflected an unusual strength, without detracting from the femininity of her appearance. She was all woman, in spite of her bearing and her garments. The latter were incongruous, in view of her present environs. Instead of a skirt she wore short, wide legged silk breeches, which ceased a hand's breadth short of her knees, and were upheld by a wide silken sash worn as a girdle. Flaring-topped boots of soft leather came almost to her knees, and a low-necked, wide-collared, wide-sleeved silk shirt completed her costume. On one shapely hip she wore a straight double-edged sword, and on the other a long dirk. Her unruly golden hair, cut square at her shoulders, was confined by a band of crimson satin.

Against the background of somber, primitive forest she posed with an unconscious picturesqueness, bizarre and out of place. She should have been posed against a background of sea-clouds, painted masts and wheeling gulls. There was the color of the sea in her wide eyes. And that was as it should have been, because this was Valeria of the Red Brotherhood, whose deeds are celebrated in song and ballad wherever seafarers gather.

She strove to pierce the sullen green roof of the arched branches and see the sky which presumably lay about it, but presently gave it up with a muttered oath.

Leaving her horse tied she strode off toward the east, glancing back toward the pool from time to time in order to fix her route in her mind. The silence of the forest depressed her. No birds sang in the lofty boughs, nor did any rustling in the bushes indicate the presence of any small animals. For leagues she had traveled in a realm of brooding stillness, broken only by the sounds of her own flight.

She had slaked her thirst at the pool, but she felt the gnawings of hunger and began looking about for some of the fruit on which she had sustained herself since exhausting the food she had brought in her saddle-bags.

Ahead of her, presently, she saw an outcropping of dark, flint-like rock that sloped upward into what looked like a rugged crag rising among the trees. Its summit was lost to view amidst a cloud of encircling leaves. Perhaps its peak rose above the tree-tops, and from it she could see what lay beyond—if, indeed, anything lay beyond but more of this apparently illimitable forest through which she had ridden for so many days.

A narrow ridge formed a natural ramp that led up the steep face of the crag. After she had ascended some fifty feet she came to the belt of leaves that surrounded the rock. The trunks of the trees did not crowd close to the crag, but the ends of their lower branches extended about it, veiling it with their foliage. She groped on in leafy obscurity, not able to see either above or below her; but presently she glimpsed blue sky, and a moment later came out in the clear, hot sunlight and saw the forest roof stretching away under her feet.

She was standing on a broad shelf which was about even with the tree-tops, and from it rose a spire-like jut that was the ultimate peak of the crag she had climbed. But something else caught her attention at the moment. Her foot had struck something in the litter of blown dead leaves which carpeted the shelf. She kicked them aside and looked down on the skeleton of a man. She ran an experienced eye over the bleached frame, but saw no broken bones nor any sign of violence. The man must have died a natural death; though why he should have climbed a tall crag to die she could not imagine.

She scrambled up to the summit of the spire and looked toward the horizons. The forest roof—which looked like a floor from her vantage-point—was just as impenetrable as from below. She could not even see the pool by which she had left her horse. She glanced northward, in the direction from which she had come. She saw only the rolling green ocean stretching away and away, with only a vague blue line in the distance to hint of the hill-range she had crossed days before, to plunge into this leafy waste.

West and east the view was the same; though the blue hill-line was lacking in those directions. But when she turned her eyes southward she stiffened and caught her breath. A mile away in that direction the forest thinned out and ceased abruptly, giving way to a cactus-dotted plain. And in the midst of that plain rose the walls and towers of a city. Valeria swore in amazement. This passed belief. She would not have been surprised to sight human habitations of another sort—the beehive-shaped huts of the black people, or the cliff-dwellings of the mysterious brown race which legends declared inhabited some country of this unexplored region. But it was a startling experience to come upon a walled city here so many long weeks' march from the nearest outposts of any sort of civilization.

Her hands tiring from clinging to the spire-like pinnacle, she let herself down on the shelf, frowning in indecision. She had come far—from the camp of the mercenaries by the border town of Sukhmet amidst the level grasslands, where desperate adventurers of many races guard the Stygian frontier against the raids that come up like a red wave from Darfar. Her flight had been blind, into a country of which she was wholly ignorant. And now she wavered between an urge to ride directly to that city in the plain, and the instinct of caution which prompted her to skirt it widely and continue her solitary flight.

Her thoughts were scattered by the rustling of the leaves below her. She wheeled cat-like, snatched at her sword; and then she froze motionless, staring wide-eyed at the man before her.

He was almost a giant in stature, muscles rippling smoothly under his skin which the sun had burned brown. His garb was similar to hers, except that he wore a broad leather belt instead of a girdle. Broadsword and poniard hung from this belt.

"Conan, the Cimmerian!" ejaculated the woman. "What are you doing on my trail?"

He grinned hardly, and his fierce blue eyes burned with a light any woman could understand as they ran over her magnificent figure, lingering on the swell of her splendid breasts beneath the light shirt, and the clear white flesh displayed between breeches and boot-tops.

"Don't you know?" he laughed. "Haven't I made my admiration for you plain ever since I first saw you?"

"A stallion could have made it no plainer," she answered disdainfully. "But I never expected to encounter you so far from the ale-barrels and meat-pots of Sukhmet. Did you really follow me from Zarallo's camp, or were you whipped forth for a rogue?"

He laughed at her insolence and flexed his mighty biceps.

"You know Zarallo didn't have enough knaves to whip me out of camp," he grinned. "Of course I followed you. Lucky thing for you, too, wench! When you knifed that Stygian officer, you forfeited Zarallo's favor and protection, and you outlawed yourself with the Stygians."

"I know it," she replied sullenly. "But what else could I do? You know what my provocation was."

"Sure," he agreed. "If I'd been there, I'd have knifed him

myself. But if a woman must live in the war-camps of men, she can expect such things."

Valeria stamped her booted foot and swore.

"Why won't men let me live a man's life?"

"That's obvious!" Again his eager eyes devoured her. "But you were wise to run away. The Stygians would have had you skinned. That officer's brother followed you; faster than you thought, I don't doubt. He wasn't far behind you when I caught up with him. His horse was better than yours. He'd have caught you and cut your throat within a few more miles."

"Well?" she demanded.

"Well what?" He seemed puzzled.

"What of the Stygian?"

"Why, what do you suppose?" he returned impatiently. "I killed him, of course, and left his carcass for the vultures. That delayed me, though, and I almost lost your trail when you crossed the rocky spurs of the hills. Otherwise I'd have caught up with you long ago."

"And now you think you'll drag me back to Zarallo's camp?" she sneered.

"Don't talk like a fool," he grunted. "Come, girl, don't be such a spitfire. I'm not like that Stygian you knifed, and you know it."

"A penniless vagabond," she taunted.

He laughed at her.

"What do you call yourself? You haven't enough money to buy a new seat for your breeches. Your disdain doesn't deceive me. You know I've commanded bigger ships and more men than you ever did in your life. As for being penniless—what rover isn't, most of the time? I've squandered enough gold in the sea-ports of the world to fill a galleon. You know that, too."

"Where are the fine ships and the bold lads you commanded, now?" she sneered.

"At the bottom of the sea, mostly," he replied cheerfully. "The Zingarans sank my last ship off the Shemite shore—that's why I joined Zarallo's Free Companions. But I saw I'd been stung when we marched to the Darfar border. The pay was poor and the wine was sour, and I don't like black women. And that's the only kind that came to our camp at Sukhmet—rings in their noses and their teeth filed—bah! Why did you join Zarallo? Sukhmet's a long way from salt water."

"Red Ortho wanted to make me his mistress," she answered sullenly. "I jumped overboard one night and swam ashore when we were anchored off the Kushite coast. Off Zabhela, it was. There a Shemite trader told me that Zarallo had brought his Free Companies south to guard the Darfar border. No better employment offered. I joined an east-bound caravan and eventually came to Sukhmet."

"It was madness to plunge southward as you did," commented Conan, "but it was wise, too, for Zarallo's patrols never thought to look for you in this direction. Only the brother of the man you killed happened to strike your trail."

"And now what do you intend doing?" she demanded.

"Turn west," he answered. "I've been this far south, but not this far east. Many days' traveling to the west will bring us to the open savannahs, where the black tribes graze their cattle. I have friends among them. We'll get to the coast and find a ship. I'm sick of the jungle."

"Then be on your way," she advised. "I have other plans."

"Don't be a fool!" He showed irritation for the first time. "You can't keep on wandering through this forest."

"I can if I choose."

"But what do you intend doing?"

"That's none of your affair," she snapped.

"Yes, it is," he answered calmly. "Do you think I've followed you this far, to turn around and ride off empty-handed? Be sensible, wench. I'm not going to harm you."

He stepped toward her, and she sprang back, whipping out her sword.

"Keep back, you barbarian dog! I'll spit you like a roast pig!"

He halted, reluctantly, and demanded: "Do you want me to take that toy away from you and spank you with it?"

"Words! Nothing but words!" she mocked, lights like the gleam of the sun on blue water dancing in her reckless eyes.

He knew it was the truth. No living man could disarm Valeria of the Brotherhood with his bare hands. He scowled, his sensations a tangle of conflicting emotions. He was angry, yet he was amused and filled with admiration for her spirit. He burned with eagerness to seize that splendid figure and crush it in his iron arms, yet he greatly desired not to hurt the girl. He was torn between a desire to shake her soundly, and a desire to caress her. He knew if he came any nearer her sword would be sheathed in his heart. He had seen Valeria kill too many men in border forays and tavern brawls to have any illusions about her. He knew she was as quick and ferocious as a tigress. He could draw his broadsword and disarm her, beat the blade out of her hand, but the thought of drawing a sword on a woman, even without intent of injury, was extremely repugnant to him.

"Blast your soul, you hussy!" he exclaimed in exasperation. "I'm going to take off your—"

He started toward her, his angry passion making him reckless, and she poised herself for a deadly thrust. Then came a startling interruption to a scene at once ludicrous and perilous.

"What's that?"

It was Valeria who exclaimed, but they both started violently, and Conan wheeled like a cat, his great sword flashing into his hand. Back in the forest had burst forth an appalling medley of screams—the screams of horses in terror and agony. Mingled with their screams there came the snap of splintering bones.

"Lions are slaying the horses!" cried Valeria.

"Lions, nothing!" snorted Conan, his eyes blazing. "Did you hear a lion roar? Neither did I! Listen at those bones snap—not even a lion could make that much noise killing a horse."

He hurried down the natural ramp and she followed, their personal feud forgotten in the adventurers' instinct to unite against common peril. The screams had ceased when they worked their way downward through the green veil of leaves that brushed the rock.

"I found your horse tied by the pool back there," he muttered, treading so noiselessly that she no longer wondered how he had surprised her on the crag. "I tied mine beside it and followed the tracks of your boots. Watch, now!"

They had emerged from the belt of leaves, and stared down into the lower reaches of the forest. Above them the green roof spread its dusky canopy. Below them the sunlight filtered in just enough to make a jade-tinted twilight. The giant trunks of trees less than a hundred yards away looked dim and ghostly.

"The horses should be beyond that thicket, over there," whispered Conan, and his voice might have been a breeze moving through the branches. "Listen!"

Valeria had already heard, and a chill crept through her veins; so she unconsciously laid her white hand on her companion's muscular brown arm. From beyond the thicket came the noisy crunching of bones and the loud rending of flesh, together with the grinding, slobbering sounds of a horrible feast.

"Lions wouldn't make that noise," whispered Conan. "Something's eating our horses, but it's not a lion—Crom!"

The noise stopped suddenly, and Conan swore softly. A suddenly risen breeze was blowing from them directly toward the spot where the unseen slayer was hidden.

"Here it comes!" muttered Conan, half lifting his sword.

The thicket was violently agitated, and Valeria clutched Conan's arm hard. Ignorant of jungle-lore, she yet knew that no animal she had ever seen could have shaken the tall brush like that.

"It must be as big as an elephant," muttered Conan, echoing her thought. "What the devil—" His voice trailed away in stunned silence.

Through the thicket was thrust a head of nightmare and lunacy. Grinning jaws bared rows of dripping yellow tusks;

above the yawning mouth wrinkled a saurian-like snout. Huge eyes, like those of a python a thousand times magnified, stared unwinkingly at the petrified humans clinging to the rock above it. Blood smeared the scaly, flabby lips and dripped from the huge mouth.

The head, bigger than that of a crocodile, was further extended on a long scaled neck on which stood up rows of serrated spikes, and after it, crushing down the briars and saplings, waddled the body of a titan, a gigantic, barrel-bellied torso on absurdly short legs. The whitish belly almost raked the ground, while the serrated back-bone rose higher than Conan could have reached on tiptoe. A long spiked tail, like that of a gargantuan scorpion, trailed out behind.

"Back up the crag, quick!" snapped Conan, thrusting the girl behind him. "I don't think he can climb, but he can stand on his hind-legs and reach us—"

With a snapping and rending of bushes and saplings the monster came hurtling through the thickets, and they fled up the rock before him like leaves blown before a wind. As Valeria plunged into the leafy screen a backward glance showed her the titan rearing up fearsomely on his massive hinder legs, even as Conan had predicted. The sight sent panic racing through her. As he reared, the beast seemed more gigantic than ever; his snouted head towered among the trees. Then Conan's iron hand closed on her wrist and she was jerked headlong into the blinding welter of the leaves, and out again into the hot sunshine above, just as the monster fell forward with his front feet on the crag with an impact that made the rock vibrate.

Behind the fugitives the huge head crashed through the twigs, and they looked down for a horrifying instant at the nightmare visage framed among the green leaves, eyes flaming, jaws gaping. Then the giant tusks clashed together futilely, and after that the head was withdrawn, vanishing from their sight as if it had sunk in a pool.

Peering down through broken branches that scraped the rock, they saw it squatting on its haunches at the foot of the crag, staring unblinkingly up at them.

Valeria shuddered.

"How long do you suppose he'll crouch there?"

Conan kicked the skull on the leaf-strewn shelf.

"That fellow must have climbed up here to escape him, or one like him. He must have died of starvation. There are no bones broken. That thing must be a dragon, such as the black people speak of in their legends. If so, it won't leave here until we're both dead."

Valeria looked at him blankly, her resentment forgotten. She fought down a surging of panic. She had proved her reckless courage a thousand times in wild battles on sea and land, on the blood-slippery decks of burning war-ships, in the storming of walled cities, and on the trampled sandy beaches where the desperate men of the Red Brotherhood bathed their knives in one another's blood in their fights for leadership. But the prospect now confronting her congealed her blood. A cutlass stroke in the heat of battle was nothing; but to sit idle and helpless on a bare rock until she perished of starvation, besieged by a monstrous survival of an elder age—the thought sent panic throbbing through her brain.

"He must leave to eat and drink," she said helplessly.

"He won't have to go far to do either," Conan pointed out. "He's just gorged on horse meat, and like a real snake, he can go for a long time without eating or drinking again. But he doesn't sleep after eating, like a real snake, it seems. Anyway, he can't climb this crag."

Conan spoke imperturbably. He was a barbarian, and the terrible patience of the wilderness and its children was as much a part of him as his lusts and rages. He could endure a situation like this with a coolness impossible to a civilized person.

"Can't we get into the trees and get away, traveling like apes through the branches?" she asked desperately.

He shook his head. "I thought of that. The branches that touch the crag down there are too light. They'd break with our weight. Besides, I have an idea that devil could tear up any tree around here by its roots."

"Well, are we going to sit here on our rumps until we starve, like that?" she cried furiously, kicking the skull clattering across the ledge. "I won't do it! I'll go down there and cut his damned head off—"

Conan had seated himself on a rocky projection at the foot of the spire. He looked up with a glint of admiration at her blazing eyes and tense, quivering figure, but, realizing that she was in just the mood for any madness, he let none of his admiration sound in his voice.

"Sit down," he grunted, catching her by her wrist and pulling her down on his knee. She was too surprised to resist as he took her sword from her hand and shoved it back in its sheath. "Sit still and calm down. You'd only break your steel on his scales. He'd gobble you up at one gulp, or smash you like an egg with that spiked tail of his. We'll get out of this jam some way, but we shan't do it by getting chewed up and swallowed."

She made no reply, nor did she seek to repulse his arm from about her waist. She was frightened, and the sensation was new to Valeria of the Red Brotherhood. So she sat on her companion's—or captor's—knee with a docility that would have amazed Zarallo, who had anathematized her as a she-devil out of hell's seraglio.

Conan played idly with her curly yellow locks, seemingly intent only upon his conquest. Neither the skeleton at his feet nor the monster crouching below disturbed his mind or dulled the edge of his interest.

The girl's restless eyes, roving the leaves below them, discovered splashes of color among the green. It was fruit, large, darkly crimson globes suspended from the boughs of a tree whose broad leaves were a peculiarly rich and vivid green. She became aware of both thirst and hunger, though thirst had not assailed her until she knew she could not descend from the crag to find food and water.

"We need not starve," she said. "There is fruit we can reach."

Conan glanced where she pointed.

"If we ate that we wouldn't need the bite of a dragon," he grunted. "That's what the black people of Kush call the Apples of Derketa. Derketa is the Queen of the Dead. Drink a little of the juice, or spill it on your flesh, and you'd be dead before you could tumble to the foot of this crag."

"Oh!"

She lapsed into dismayed silence. There seemed no way out of their predicament, she reflected gloomily. She saw no way of escape, and Conan seemed to be concerned only with her supple waist and curly tresses. If he was trying to formulate a plan of escape he did not show it.

"If you'll take your hands off me long enough to climb up on that peak," she said presently, "you'll see something that will surprise you."

He cast her a questioning glance, then obeyed with a shrug of his massive shoulders. Clinging to the spire-like pinnacle, he stared out over the forest roof.

He stood a long moment in silence, posed like a bronze statue on the rock.

"It's a walled city, right enough," he muttered presently. "Was that where you were going, when you tried to send me off alone to the coast?"

"I saw it before you came. I knew nothing of it when I left Sukhmet."

"Who'd have thought to find a city here? I don't believe the Stygians ever penetrated this far. Could black people build a city like that? I see no herds on the plain, no signs of cultivation, or people moving about."

"How could you hope to see all that, at this distance?" she demanded.

He shrugged his shoulders and dropped down on the shelf.

"Well, the folk of the city can't help us just now. And they might not, if they could. The people of the Black Countries are generally hostile to strangers. Probably stick us full of spears—"

He stopped short and stood silent, as if he had forgotten

what he was saying, frowning down at the crimson spheres gleaming among the leaves.

"Spears!" he muttered. "What a blasted fool I am not to have thought of that before! That shows what a pretty woman does to a man's mind."

"What are you talking about?" she inquired.

Without answering her question, he descended to the belt of leaves and looked down through them. The great brute squatted below, watching the crag with the frightful patience of the reptile folk. So might one of his breed have glared up at their troglodyte ancestors, treed on a high-flung rock, in the dim dawn ages. Conan cursed him without heat, and began cutting branches, reaching out and severing them as far from the end as he could reach. The agitation of the leaves made the monster restless. He rose from his haunches and lashed his hideous tail, snapping off saplings as if they had been toothpicks. Conan watched him warily from the corner of his eye, and just as Valeria believed the dragon was about to hurl himself up the crag again, the Cimmerian drew back and climbed up to the ledge with the branches he had cut. There were three of these, slender shafts about seven feet long, but not larger than his thumb. He had also cut several strands of tough, thin vine.

"Branches too light for spear-hafts, and creepers no thicker than cords," he remarked, indicating the foliage about the crag. "It won't hold our weight—but there's strength in union. That's what the Aquilonian renegades used to tell us Cimmerians when they came into the hills to raise an army to invade their own country. But we always fight by clans and tribes."

"What the devil has that got to do with those sticks?" she demanded.

"You wait and see."

Gathering the sticks in a compact bundle, he wedged his poniard hilt between them at one end. Then with the vines he bound them together, and when he had completed his task, he had a spear of no small strength, with a sturdy shaft seven feet in length.

"What good will that do?" she demanded. "You told me that a blade couldn't pierce his scales—"

"He hasn't got scales all over him," answered Conan. "There's more than one way of skinning a panther."

Moving down to the edge of the leaves, he reached the spear up and carefully thrust the blade through one of the Apples of Derketa, drawing aside to avoid the darkly purple drops that dripped from the pierced fruit. Presently he withdrew the blade and showed her the blue steel stained a dull purplish crimson.

"I don't know whether it will do the job or not," quoth he. "There's enough poison there to kill an elephant, but—well, we'll see."

Valeria was close behind him as he let himself down among the leaves. Cautiously holding the poisoned pike away from him, he thrust his head through the branches and addressed the monster.

"What are you waiting down there for, you misbegotten offspring of questionable parents?" was one of his more printable queries. "Stick your ugly head up here again, you long-necked brute—or do you want me to come down there and kick you loose from your illegitimate spine?"

There was more of it—some of it couched in eloquence that made Valeria stare, in spite of her profane education among the seafarers. And it had its effect on the monster. Just as the incessant yapping of a dog worries and enrages more constitutionally silent animals, so the clamorous voice of a man rouses fear in some bestial bosoms and insane rage in others. Suddenly and with appalling quickness, the mastodonic brute reared up on its mighty hind legs and elongated its neck and body in a furious effort to reach this vociferous pigmy whose clamor was disturbing the primeval silence of its ancient realm.

But Conan had judged his distance with precision. Some five feet below him the mighty head crashed terribly but futilely through the leaves. And as the monstrous mouth gaped like that of a great snake, Conan drove his spear into the red angle of the jaw-bone hinge. He struck downward with all the strength of both arms, driving the long poniard blade to the hilt in flesh, sinew and bone.

Instantly the jaws clashed convulsively together, severing the triple-pieced shaft and almost precipitating Conan from his perch. He would have fallen but for the girl behind him, who caught his sword-belt in a desperate grasp. He clutched at a rocky projection, and grinned his thanks back at her.

Down on the ground the monster was wallowing like a dog with pepper in its eyes. He shook his head from side to side, pawed at it, and opened his mouth repeatedly to its widest extent. Presently he got a huge front foot on the stump of the shaft and managed to tear the blade out. Then he threw up his head, jaws wide and spouting blood, and glared up at the crag with such concentrated and intelligent fury that Valeria trembled and drew her sword. The scales along his back and flanks turned from rusty brown to a dull lurid red. Most horribly the monster's silence was broken. The sounds that issued from his blood-streaming jaws did not sound like anything that could have been produced by an earthly creation.

With harsh, grating roars, the dragon hurled himself at the crag that was the citadel of his enemies. Again and again his mighty head crashed upward through the branches, snapping vainly on empty air. He hurled his full ponderous weight against the rock until it vibrated from base to crest. And rearing upright he gripped it with his front legs like a man and tried to tear it up by the roots, as if it had been a tree.

This exhibition of primordial fury chilled the blood in Valeria's veins, but Conan was too close to the primitive himself to feel anything but a comprehending interest. To the barbarian, no such gulf existed between himself and other men, and the animals, as existed in the conception of Valeria. The monster below them, to Conan, was merely a form of life differing from himself mainly in physical shape. He attributed to it characteristics similar to his own, and saw in its wrath a counterpart of his rages, in its roars and bellowings merely reptilian equivalents to the curses he had bestowed upon it. Feeling a kinship with all wild things, even dragons, it was impossible for him to experience the sick horror which assailed Valeria at the sight of the brute's ferocity.

He sat watching it tranquilly, and pointed out the various changes that were taking place in its voice and actions.

"The poison's taking hold," he said with conviction.

"I don't believe it." To Valeria it seemed preposterous to suppose that anything, however lethal, could have any effect on that mountain of muscle and fury.

"There's pain in his voice," declared Conan. "First he was merely angry because of the stinging in his jaw. Now he feels the bite of the poison. Look! He's staggering. He'll be blind in a few more minutes. What did I tell you?"

For suddenly the dragon had lurched about and went crashing off through the bushes.

"Is he running away?" inquired Valeria uneasily.

"He's making for the pool!" Conan sprang up, galvanized into swift activity. "The poison makes him thirsty. Come on! He'll be blind in a few moments, but he can smell his way back to the foot of the crag, and if our scent's here still, he'll sit there until he dies. And others of his kind may come at his cries. Let's go!"

"Down there?" Valeria was aghast.

"Sure! We'll make for the city! They may cut our heads off there, but it's our only chance. We may run into a thousand more dragons on the way, but it's sure death to stay here. If we wait until he dies, we may have a dozen more to deal with. After me, in a hurry!"

He went down the ramp as swiftly as an ape, pausing only to aid his less agile companion, who, until she saw the Cimmerian climb, had fancied herself the equal of any man in the rigging of a ship or on the sheer face of a cliff.

They descended into the gloom below the branches and slid to the ground silently, though Valeria felt as if the pounding of her heart must surely be heard from far away. A noisy gurgling and lapping beyond the dense thicket indicated that the dragon was drinking at the pool.

"As soon as his belly is full he'll be back," muttered Conan. "It may take hours for the poison to kill him—if it does at all."

Somewhere beyond the forest the sun was sinking to the horizon. The forest was a misty twilight place of black shadows and dim vistas. Conan gripped Valeria's wrist and glided away from the foot of the crag. He made less noise than a breeze blowing among the tree-trunks, but Valeria felt as if her soft boots were betraying their flight to all the forest.

"I don't think he can follow a trail," muttered Conan. "But if a wind blew our body-scent to him, he could smell us out."

"Mitra grant that the wind blow not!" Valeria breathed.

Her face was a pallid oval in the gloom. She gripped her sword in her free hand, but the feel of the shagreen-bound hilt inspired only a feeling of helplessness in her.

They were still some distance from the edge of the forest when they heard a snapping and crashing behind them. Valeria bit her lip to check a cry.

"He's on our trail!" she whispered fiercely.

Conan shook his head.

"He didn't smell us at the rock, and he's blundering about through the forest trying to pick up our scent. Come on! It's the city or nothing now! He could tear down any tree we'd climb. If only the wind stays down—"

They stole on until the trees began to thin out ahead of them. Behind them the forest was a black impenetrable ocean of shadows. The ominous crackling still sounded behind them, as the dragon blundered in his erratic course.

"There's the plain ahead," breathed Valeria. "A little more and we'll—"

"Crom!" swore Conan.

"Mitra!" whispered Valeria.

Out of the south a wind had sprung up.

It blew over them directly into the black forest behind them. Instantly a horrible roar shook the woods. The aimless snapping and crackling of the bushes changed to a sustained crashing as the dragon came like a hurricane straight toward the spot from which the scent of his enemies was wafted.

"Run!" snarled Conan, his eyes blazing like those of a trapped wolf. "It's all we can do!"

Sailors' boots are not made for sprinting, and the life of a pirate does not train one for a runner. Within a hundred yards Valeria was panting and reeling in her gait, and behind them the crashing gave way to a rolling thunder as the monster broke out of the thickets and into the more open ground.

Conan's iron arm about the woman's waist half lifted her; her feet scarcely touched the earth as she was borne along at a speed she could never have attained herself. If he could keep out of the beast's way for a bit, perhaps that betraying wind would shift—but the wind held, and a quick glance over his shoulder showed Conan that the monster was almost upon them, coming like a war-galley in front of a hurricane. He thrust Valeria from him with a force that sent her reeling a dozen feet to fall in a crumpled heap at the foot of the nearest tree, and the Cimmerian wheeled in the path of the thundering titan.

Convinced that his death was upon him, the Cimmerian acted according to his instinct, and hurled himself full at the awful face that was bearing down on him. He leaped, slashing like a wildcat, felt his sword cut deep into the scales that sheathed the mighty snout—and then a terrific impact knocked him rolling and tumbling for fifty feet with all the wind and half the life battered out of him.

How the stunned Cimmerian regained his feet, not even he could have ever told. But the only thought that filled his brain was of the woman lying dazed and helpless almost in the path of the hurtling fiend, and before the breath came whistling back into his gullet he was standing over her with his sword in his hand.

She lay where he had thrown her, but she was struggling to a sitting posture. Neither tearing tusks nor trampling feet had touched her. It had been a shoulder or front leg that struck Conan, and the blind monster rushed on, forgetting the victims whose scent it had been following, in the sudden agony of its death throes. Headlong on its course it thundered until its low-hung head crashed into a gigantic tree in its path. The impact tore the tree up by the roots and must have dashed the brains from the misshapen skull. Tree and monster fell together, and the dazed humans saw the branches and leaves shaken by the convulsions of the creature they covered—and then grow quiet.

Conan lifted Valeria to her feet and together they started away at a reeling run. A few moments later they emerged into the still twilight of the treeless plain.

Conan paused an instant and glanced back at the ebon fastness behind them. Not a leaf stirred, nor a bird chirped. It stood as silent as it must have stood before Man was created.

"Come on," muttered Conan, taking his companion's hand. "It's touch and go now. If more dragons come out of the woods after us—"

He did not have to finish the sentence.

The city looked very far away across the plain, farther than it had looked from the crag. Valeria's heart hammered until she felt as if it would strangle her. At every step she expected to hear the crashing of the bushes and see another colossal nightmare bearing down upon them. But nothing disturbed the silence of the thickets.

With the first mile between them and the woods, Valeria breathed more easily. Her buoyant self-confidence began to thaw out again. The sun had set and darkness was gathering over the plain, lightened a little by the stars that made stunted ghosts out of the cactus growths.

"No cattle, no plowed fields," muttered Conan. "How do these people live?"

"Perhaps the cattle are in pens for the night," suggested Valeria, "and the fields and grazing-pastures are on the other side of the city."

"Maybe," he grunted. "I didn't see any from the crag, though."

The moon came up behind the city, etching walls and towers blackly in the yellow glow. Valeria shivered. Black against the moon the strange city had a somber, sinister look.

Perhaps something of the same feeling occurred to Conan, for he stopped, glanced about him, and grunted: "We stop here. No use coming to their gates in the night.

They probably wouldn't let us in. Besides, we need rest, and we don't know how they'll receive us. A few hours' sleep will put us in better shape to fight or run."

He led the way to a bed of cactus which grew in a circle—a phenomenon common to the southern desert. With his sword he chopped an opening, and motioned Valeria to enter.

"We'll be safe from snakes here, anyhow."

She glanced fearfully back toward the black line that indicated the forest some six miles away.

"Suppose a dragon comes out of the woods?"

"We'll keep watch," he answered, though he made no suggestion as to what they would do in such an event. He was staring at the city, a few miles away. Not a light shone from spire or tower. A great black mass of mystery, it reared cryptically against the moonlit sky.

"Lie down and sleep. I'll keep the first watch."

She hesitated, glancing at him uncertainly, but he sat down cross-legged in the opening, facing toward the plain, his sword across his knees, his back to her. Without further comment she lay down on the sand inside the spiky circle.

"Wake me when the moon is at its zenith," she directed.

He did not reply nor look toward her. Her last impression, as she sank into slumber, was of his muscular figure, immobile as a statue hewn out of bronze, outlined against the low-hanging stars.

II

BY THE BLAZE OF THE FIRE JEWELS

Valeria awoke with a start, to the realization that a gray dawn was stealing over the plain.

She sat up, rubbing her eyes. Conan squatted beside the cactus, cutting off the thick pears and dexterously twitching out the spikes.

"You didn't awake me," she accused. "You let me sleep all night!"

"You were tired," he answered. "Your posterior must have been sore, too, after that long ride. You pirates aren't used to horseback."

"What about yourself ?" she retorted.

"I was a kozak before I was a pirate," he answered. "They live in the saddle. I snatch naps like a panther watching beside the trail for a deer to come by. My ears keep watch while my eyes sleep."

And indeed the giant barbarian seemed as much refreshed as if he had slept the whole night on a golden bed. Having removed the thorns, and peeled off the tough skin, he handed the girl a thick, juicy cactus leaf.

"Skin your teeth in that pear. It's food and drink to a

desert man. I was a chief of the Zuagirs once—desert men who live by plundering the caravans."

"Is there anything you haven't been?" inquired the girl, half in derision and half in fascination.

"I've never been king of an Hyborian kingdom," he grinned, taking an enormous mouthful of cactus. "But I've dreamed of being even that. I may be too, some day. Why shouldn't I?"

She shook her head in wonder at his calm audacity, and fell to devouring her pear. She found it not unpleasing to the palate, and full of cool and thirst-satisfying juice. Finishing his meal, Conan wiped his hands in the sand, rose, ran his fingers through his thick black mane, hitched at his sword-belt and said:

"Well, let's go. If the people in that city are going to cut our throats they may as well do it now, before the heat of the day begins."

His grim humor was unconscious, but Valeria reflected that it might be prophetic. She too hitched her sword-belt as she rose. Her terrors of the night were past. The roaring dragons of the distant forest were like a dim dream. There was a swagger in her stride as she moved off beside the Cimmerian. Whatever perils lay ahead of them, their foes would be men. And Valeria of the Red Brotherhood had never seen the face of the man she feared.

Conan glanced down at her as she strode along beside him with her swinging stride that matched his own.

"You walk more like a hillman than a sailor," he said. "You must be an Aquilonian. The suns of Darfar never burnt your white skin brown. Many a princess would envy you."

"I am from Aquilonia," she replied. His compliments no longer irritated her. His evident admiration pleased her. For another man to have kept her watch while she slept would have angered her; she had always fiercely resented any man's attempting to shield or protect her because of her sex. But she found a secret pleasure in the fact that this man had done so. And he had not taken advantage of her fright and the weakness resulting from it. After all, she reflected, her companion was no common man.

The sun rose behind the city, turning the towers to a sinister crimson.

"Black last night against the moon," grunted Conan, his eyes clouding with the abysmal superstition of the barbarian. "Blood-red as a threat of blood against the sun this dawn. I do not like this city."

But they went on, and as they went Conan pointed out the fact that no road ran to the city from the north.

"No cattle have trampled the plain on this side of the city," said he. "No plowshare has touched the earth for years, maybe centuries. But look: once this plain was cultivated."

Valeria saw the ancient irrigation ditches he indicated, half filled in places, and overgrown with cactus. She frowned with perplexity as her eyes swept over the plain that stretched on all sides of the city to the forest edge, which marched in a vast, dim ring. Vision did not extend beyond that ring.

She looked uneasily at the city. No helmets or spear-heads gleamed on battlements, no trumpets sounded, no challenge rang from the towers. A silence as absolute as that of the forest brooded over the walls and minarets.

The sun was high above the eastern horizon when they stood before the great gate in the northern wall, in the shadow of the lofty rampart. Rust flecked the iron bracings of the mighty bronze portal. Spiderwebs glistened thickly on hinge and sill and bolted panel.

"It hasn't been opened for years!" exclaimed Valeria.

"A dead city," grunted Conan. "That's why the ditches were broken and the plain untouched."

"But who built it? Who dwelt here? Where did they go? Why did they abandon it?"

"Who can say? Maybe an exiled clan of Stygians built it. Maybe not. It doesn't look like Stygian architecture. Maybe the people were wiped out by enemies, or a plague exterminated them."

"In that case their treasures may still be gathering dust and cobwebs in there," suggested Valeria, the acquisitive instincts of her profession waking in her; prodded, too, by feminine curiosity. "Can we open the gate? Let's go in and explore a bit."

Conan eyed the heavy portal dubiously, but placed his massive shoulder against it and thrust with all the power of his muscular calves and thighs. With a rasping screech of rusty hinges the gate moved ponderously inward, and Conan straightened and drew his sword. Valeria stared over his shoulder, and made a sound indicative of surprise.

They were not looking into an open street or court as one would have expected. The opened gate, or door, gave directly into a long, broad hall which ran away and away until its vista grew indistinct in the distance. It was of heroic proportions, and the floor of a curious red stone, cut in square tiles, that seemed to smolder as if with the reflection of flames. The walls were of a shiny green material.

"Jade, or I'm a Shemite!" swore Conan.

"Not in such quantity!" protested Valeria.

"I've looted enough from the Khitan caravans to know what I'm talking about," he asserted. "That's jade!"

The vaulted ceiling was of lapis lazuli, adorned with clusters of great green stones that gleamed with a poisonous radiance.

"Green fire-stones," growled Conan. "That's what the people of Punt call them. They're supposed to be the petrified eyes of those prehistoric snakes the ancients called Golden Serpents. They glow like a cat's eyes in the dark. At night this hall would be lighted by them, but it would be a hellishly weird illumination. Let's look around. We might find a cache of jewels."

"Shut the door," advised Valeria. "I'd hate to have to outrun a dragon down this hall." Conan grinned, and replied: "I don't believe the dragons ever leave the forest."

But he complied, and pointed out the broken bolt on the inner side.

"I thought I heard something snap when I shoved against it. That bolt's freshly broken. Rust has eaten nearly through it. If the people ran away, why should it have been bolted on the inside?"

"They undoubtedly left by another door," suggested Valeria.

She wondered how many centuries had passed since the light of outer day had filtered into that great hall through the open door. Sunlight was finding its way somehow into the hall, and they quickly saw the source. High up in the vaulted ceiling skylights were set in slot-like openings— translucent sheets of some crystalline substance. In the splotches of shadow between them, the green jewels winked like the eyes of angry cats. Beneath their feet the dully lurid floor smoldered with changing hues and colors of flame. It was like treading the floors of hell with evil stars blinking overhead.

Three balustraded galleries ran along on each side of the hall, one above the other.

"A four-storied house," grunted Conan, "and this hall extends to the roof. It's long as a street. I seem to see a door at the other end."

Valeria shrugged her white shoulders.

"Your eyes are better than mine, then, though I'm accounted sharp-eyed among the sea-rovers."

They turned into an open door at random, and traversed a series of empty chambers, floored like the hall, and with walls of the same green jade, or of marble or ivory or chalcedony, adorned with friezes of bronze, gold or silver. In the ceilings the green fire-gems were set, and their light was as ghostly and illusive as Conan had predicted. Under the witch-fire glow the intruders moved like specters.

Some of the chambers lacked this illumination, and their doorways showed black as the mouth of the Pit. These Conan and Valeria avoided, keeping always to the lighted chambers.

Cobwebs hung in the corners, but there was no perceptible

accumulation of dust on the floor, or on the tables and seats of marble, jade or carnelian which occupied the chambers. Here and there were rugs of that silk known as Khitan which is practically indestructible. Nowhere did they find any windows, or doors opening into streets or courts. Each door merely opened into another chamber or hall.

"Why don't we come to a street?" grumbled Valeria. "This place or whatever we're in must be as big as the king of Turan's seraglio."

"They must not have perished of plague," said Conan, meditating upon the mystery of the empty city. "Otherwise we'd find skeletons. Maybe it became haunted, and everybody got up and left. Maybe—"

"Maybe, hell!" broke in Valeria rudely. "We'll never know. Look at these friezes. They portray men. What race do they belong to?"

Conan scanned them and shook his head.

"I never saw people exactly like them. But there's the smack of the East about them—Vendhya, maybe, or Kosala."

"Were you a king in Kosala?" she asked, masking her keen curiosity with derision.

"No. But I was a war-chief of the Afghulis who live in the Himelian mountains above the borders of Vendhya. These people favor the Kosalans. But why should Kosalans be building a city this far to west?"

The figures portrayed were those of slender, olive-skinned men and women, with finely chiseled, exotic features. They wore filmy robes and many delicate jeweled ornaments, and were depicted mostly in attitudes of feasting, dancing or love-making.

"Easterners, all right," grunted Conan, "but from where

I don't know. They must have lived a disgustingly peaceful life, though, or they'd have scenes of wars and fights. Let's go up that stair."

It was an ivory spiral that wound up from the chamber in which they were standing. They mounted three flights and came into a broad chamber on the fourth floor, which seemed to be the highest tier in the building. Skylights in the ceiling illuminated the room, in which light the fire-gems winked pallidly. Glancing through the doors they saw, except on one side, a series of similarly lighted chambers. This other door opened upon a balustraded gallery that overhung a hall much smaller than the one they had recently explored on the lower floor.

"Hell!" Valeria sat down disgustedly on a jade bench. "The people who deserted this city must have taken all their treasures with them. I'm tired of wandering through these bare rooms at random."

"All these upper chambers seem to be lighted," said Conan. "I wish we could find a window that overlooked the city. Let's have a look through that door over there."

"You have a look," advised Valeria. "I'm going to sit here and rest my feet."

Conan disappeared through the door opposite that one opening upon the gallery, and Valeria leaned back with her hands clasped behind her head, and thrust her booted legs out in front of her. These silent rooms and halls with their gleaming green clusters of ornaments and burning crimson floors were beginning to depress her. She wished they could find their way out of the maze into which they had wandered and emerge into a street. She wondered idly what furtive, dark feet had glided over those flaming floors in past centuries, how many deeds of cruelty and mystery those winking ceiling-gems had blazed down upon.

It was a faint noise that brought her out of her reflections. She was on her feet with her sword in her hand before she realized what had disturbed her. Conan had not returned, and she knew it was not he that she had heard.

The sound had come from somewhere beyond the door that opened on to the gallery. Soundlessly in her soft leather boots she glided through it, crept across the balcony and peered down between the heavy balustrades.

A man was stealing along the hall.

The sight of a human being in this supposedly deserted city was a startling shock. Crouching down behind the stone balusters, with every nerve tingling, Valeria glared down at the stealthy figure.

The man in no way resembled the figures depicted on the friezes. He was slightly above middle height, very dark, though not negroid. He was naked but for a scanty silk clout that only partly covered his muscular hips, and a leather girdle, a hand's breadth broad, about his lean waist. His long black hair hung in lank strands about his shoulders, giving him a wild appearance. He was gaunt, but knots and cords of muscles stood out on his arms and legs, without that fleshy padding that presents a pleasing symmetry of contour. He was built with an economy that was almost repellent.

Yet it was not so much his physical appearance as his attitude that impressed the woman who watched him. He slunk along, stooped in a semi-crouch, his head turning from side to side. He grasped a wide-tipped blade in his right hand, and she saw it shake with the intensity of the emotion that gripped him. He was afraid, trembling in the grip of some dire terror. When he turned his head she caught the blaze of wild eyes among the lank strands of black hair.

He did not see her. On tiptoe he glided across the hall and vanished through an open door. A moment later she heard a choking cry, and then silence fell again.

Consumed with curiosity, Valeria glided along the gallery until she came to a door above the one through which the man had passed. It opened into another, smaller gallery that encircled a large chamber.

This chamber was on the third floor, and its ceiling was not so high as that of the hall. It was lighted only by the fire-stones, and their weird green glow left the spaces under the balcony in shadows.

Valeria's eyes widened. The man she had seen was still in the chamber.

He lay face down on a dark crimson carpet in the middle of the room. His body was limp, his arms spread wide. His curved sword lay near him.

She wondered why he should lie there so motionless. Then her eyes narrowed as she stared down at the rug on which he lay. Beneath and about him the fabric showed a slightly different color, a deeper, brighter crimson.

Shivering slightly, she crouched down closer behind the balustrade, intently scanning the shadows under the overhanging gallery. They gave up no secret.

Suddenly another figure entered the grim drama. He was a man similar to the first, and he came in by a door opposite that which gave upon the hall.

His eyes glared at the sight of the man on the floor, and he spoke something in a staccato voice that sounded like "Chicmec!" The other did not move.

The man stepped quickly across the floor, bent, gripped the fallen man's shoulder and turned him over. A choking cry escaped him as the head fell back limply, disclosing a throat that had been severed from ear to ear.

The man let the corpse fall back upon the blood-stained carpet, and sprang to his feet shaking like a wind-blown leaf. His face was an ashy mask of fear. But with one knee flexed for flight, he froze suddenly, became as immobile as an image, staring across the chamber with dilated eyes.

In the shadows beneath the balcony a ghostly light began to glow and grow, a light that was not part of the fire-stone gleam. Valeria felt her hair stir as she watched it; for, dimly visible in the throbbing radiance, there floated a human skull, and it was from this skull—human yet appallingly misshapen—that the spectral light seemed to emanate. It hung there like a disembodied head, conjured out of night and the shadows, growing more and more distinct; human, and yet not human as she knew humanity.

The man stood motionless, an embodiment of paralyzed horror, staring fixedly at the apparition. The thing moved out from the wall and a grotesque shadow moved with it. Slowly the shadow became visible as a man-like figure whose naked torso and limbs shone whitely, with the hue of bleached bones. The bare skull on its shoulders grinned eyelessly, in the midst of its unholy nimbus, and the man confronting it seemed unable to take his eyes from it. He stood still, his sword dangling from nerveless fingers, on his face the expression of a man bound by the spells of a mesmerist.

Valeria realized that it was not fear alone that paralyzed him. Some hellish quality of that throbbing glow had robbed him of his power to think and act. She herself, safely above the scene, felt the subtle impact of a nameless emanation that was a threat to sanity.

The horror swept toward its victim and he moved at last, but only to drop his sword and sink to his knees, covering his eyes with his hands. Dumbly he awaited the stroke of the blade that now gleamed in the apparition's hand as it reared above him like Death triumphant over mankind.

Valeria acted according to the first impulse of her wayward nature. With one tigerish movement she was over the balustrade and dropping to the floor behind the awful shape. It wheeled at the thud of her soft boots on the floor, but even as it turned, her keen blade lashed down, and a fierce exultation swept her as she felt the edge cleave solid flesh and mortal bone.

The apparition cried out gurglingly and went down, severed through shoulder, breast bone and spine, and as it fell the burning skull rolled clear, revealing a lank mop of black hair and a dark face twisted in the convulsions of death. Beneath the horrific masquerade there was a human being, a man similar to the one kneeling supinely on the floor.

The latter looked up at the sound of the blow and the cry, and now he glared in wild-eyed amazement at the white-skinned woman who stood over the corpse with a dripping sword in her hand.

He staggered up, yammering as if the sight had almost

unseated his reason. She was amazed to realize that she understood him. He was gibbering in the Stygian tongue, though in a dialect unfamiliar to her.

"Who are you? Whence come you? What do you in Xuchotl?" Then rushing on, without waiting for her to reply: "But you are a friend—goddess or devil, it makes no difference! You have slain the Burning Skull! It was but a man beneath it, after all! We deemed it a demon they conjured up out of the catacombs! *Listen!*"

He stopped short in his ravings and stiffened, straining his ears with painful intensity. The girl heard nothing.

"We must hasten!" he whispered. "*They* are west of the Great Hall! They may be all around us here! They may be creeping upon us even now!"

He seized her wrist in a convulsive grasp she found hard to break.

"Whom do you mean by 'they'?" she demanded.

He stared at her uncomprehendingly for an instant, as if he found her ignorance hard to understand.

"They?" he stammered vaguely. "Why—why, the people of Xotalanc! The clan of the man you slew. They who dwell by the eastern gate."

"You mean to say this city is inhabited?" she exclaimed.

"Aye! Aye!" He was writhing in the impatience of apprehension. "Come away! Come quick! We must return to Tecuhltli!"

"Where is that?" she demanded.

"The quarter by the western gate!" He had her wrist again and was pulling her toward the door through which he had first come. Great beads of perspiration dripped from his dark forehead, and his eyes blazed with terror.

"Wait a minute!" she growled, flinging off his hand. "Keep your hands off me, or I'll split your skull. What's all this about? Who are you? Where would you take me?"

He took a firm grip on himself, casting glances to all sides, and began speaking so fast his words tripped over each other.

"My name is Techotl. I am of Tecuhltli. I and this man who lies with his throat cut came into the Halls of Silence to try and ambush some of the Xotalancas. But we became separated and I returned here to find him with his gullet slit. The Burning Skull did it, I know, just as he would have slain me had you not killed him. But perhaps he was not alone. Others may be stealing from Xotalanc! The gods themselves blench at the fate of those they take alive!"

At the thought he shook as with an ague and his dark skin grew ashy. Valeria frowned puzzledly at him. She sensed intelligence behind this rigmarole, but it was meaningless to her.

She turned toward the skull, which still glowed and pulsed on the floor, and was reaching a booted toe tentatively toward it, when the man who called himself Techotl sprang forward with a cry.

"Do not touch it! Do not even look at it! Madness and death lurk in it. The wizards of Xotalanc understand its secret—they found it in the catacombs, where lie the bones of terrible kings who ruled in Xuchotl in the black centuries of the past. To gaze upon it freezes the blood and withers the brain of a man who understands not its mystery. To touch it causes madness and destruction."

She scowled at him uncertainly. He was not a reassuring figure, with his lean, muscle-knotted frame, and snaky locks. In his eyes, behind the glow of terror, lurked a weird light she had never seen in the eyes of a man wholly sane. Yet he seemed sincere in his protestations.

"Come!" he begged, reaching for her hand, and then recoiling as he remembered her warning. "You are a stranger. How you came here I do not know, but if you were a goddess or a demon, come to aid Tecuhltli, you would know all the things you have asked me. You must be from beyond the great forest, whence our ancestors came. But you are our friend, or you would not have slain my enemy. Come quickly, before the Xotalancas find us and slay us!"

From his repellent, impassioned face she glanced to the sinister skull, smoldering and glowing on the floor near the dead man. It was like a skull seen in a dream, undeniably human, yet with disturbing distortions and malformations of contour and outline. In life the wearer of that skull must have presented an alien and monstrous aspect. Life? It seemed to possess some sort of life of its own. Its jaws yawned at her and snapped together. Its radiance grew brighter, more vivid, yet the impression of nightmare grew too; it was a dream; all life was a dream—it was Techotl's urgent voice which snapped Valeria back from the dim gulfs whither she was drifting.

"Do not look at the skull! Do not look at the skull!" It was a far cry from across unreckoned voids.

Valeria shook herself like a lion shaking his mane. Her vision cleared. Techotl was chattering: "In life it housed the awful brain of a king of magicians! It holds still the life and fire of magic drawn from outer spaces!"

With a curse Valeria leaped, lithe as a panther, and the
skull crashed to flaming bits under her swinging sword.
Somewhere in the room, or in the void, or in the dim
reaches of her consciousness, an inhuman voice cried out in
pain and rage.

Techotl's hand was plucking at her arm and he was
gibbering: "You have broken it! You have destroyed it! Not
all the black arts of Xotalanc can rebuild it! Come away!
Come away quickly, now!"

"But I can't go," she protested. "I have a friend somewhere
near by—"

The flare of his eyes cut her short as he stared past her
with an expression grown ghastly. She wheeled just as four
men rushed through as many doors, converging on the pair
in the center of the chamber.

They were like the others she had seen, the same knotted
muscles bulging on otherwise gaunt limbs, the same lank
blue-black hair, the same mad glare in their wide eyes. They
were armed and clad like Techotl, but on the breast of each
was painted a white skull.

There were no challenges or war-cries. Like blood-mad
tigers the men of Xotalanc sprang at the throats of their
enemies. Techotl met them with the fury of desperation,
ducked the swipe of a wide-headed blade, and grappled with
the wielder, and bore him to the floor where they rolled and
wrestled in murderous silence.

The other three swarmed on Valeria, their weird eyes red
as the eyes of mad dogs.

She killed the first who came within reach before he could strike a blow, her long straight blade splitting his skull even as his own sword lifted for a stroke. She sidestepped a thrust, even as she parried a slash. Her eyes danced and her lips smiled without mercy. Again she was Valeria of the Red Brotherhood, and the hum of her steel was like a bridal song in her ears.

Her sword darted past a blade that sought to parry, and sheathed six inches of its point in a leather-guarded midriff. The man gasped agonizedly and went to his knees, but his tall mate lunged in, in ferocious silence, raining blow on blow so furiously that Valeria had no opportunity to counter. She stepped back coolly, parrying the strokes and watching for her chance to thrust home. He could not long keep up that flailing whirlwind. His arm would tire, his wind would fail; he would weaken, falter, and then her blade would slide smoothly into his heart. A sidelong glance showed her Techotl kneeling on the breast of his antagonist and striving to break the other's hold on his wrist and to drive home a dagger.

Sweat beaded the forehead of the man facing her, and his eyes were like burning coals. Smite as he would, he could not break past nor beat down her guard. His breath came in gusty gulps, his blows began to fall erratically. She stepped back to draw him out—and felt her thighs locked in an iron grip. She had forgotten the wounded man on the floor.

Crouching on his knees, he held her with both arms locked about her legs, and his mate croaked in triumph and began working his way around to come at her from the left side. Valeria wrenched and tore savagely, but in vain. She could free herself of this clinging menace with a downward flick of her sword, but in that instant the curved blade of the tall warrior would crash through her skull. The wounded man began to worry at her bare thigh with his teeth like a wild beast.

She reached down with her left hand and gripped his long hair, forcing his head back so that his white teeth and rolling eyes gleamed up at her. The tall Xotalanc cried out fiercely and leaped in, smiting with all the fury of his arm. Awkwardly she parried the stroke, and it beat the flat of her blade down on her head so that she saw sparks flash before her eyes, and staggered. Up went the sword again, with a low, beast-like cry of triumph—and then a giant form loomed behind the Xotalanc and steel flashed like a jet of blue lightning. The cry of the warrior broke short and he went down like an ox beneath the pole-ax, his brains gushing from his skull that had been split to the throat.

"Conan!" gasped Valeria. In a gust of passion she turned on the Xotalanc whose long hair she still gripped in her left hand. "Dog of hell!" Her blade swished as it cut the air in an upswinging arc with a blur in the middle, and the headless body slumped down, spurting blood. She hurled the severed head across the room.

"What the devil's going on here?" Conan bestrode the corpse of the man he had killed, broadsword in hand, glaring about him in amazement.

Techotl was rising from the twitching figure of the last Xotalanc, shaking red drops from his dagger. He was bleeding from the stab deep in the thigh. He stared at Conan with dilated eyes.

"What is all this?" Conan demanded again, not yet recovered from the stunning surprise of finding Valeria engaged in a savage battle with these fantastic figures in a city he had thought empty and uninhabited. Returning from an aimless exploration of the upper chambers to find Valeria missing from the room where he had left her, he had followed the sounds of strife that burst on his dumfounded ears.

"Five dead dogs!" exclaimed Techotl, his flaming eyes reflecting a ghastly exultation. "Five slain! Five crimson nails for the black pillar! The gods of blood be thanked!"

He lifted quivering hands on high, and then, with the face of a fiend, he spat on the corpses and stamped on their faces, dancing in his ghoulish glee. His recent allies eyed him in amazement, and Conan asked, in the Aquilonian tongue: "Who is this madman?"

Valeria shrugged her shoulders.

"He says his name's Techotl. From his babblings I gather that his people live at one end of this crazy city, and these others at the other end. Maybe we'd better go with him. He seems friendly, and it's easy to see that the other clan isn't."

Techotl had ceased his dancing and was listening again, his head tilted sidewise, dog like, triumph struggling with fear in his repellent countenance.

"Come away, now!" he whispered. "We have done enough! Five dead dogs! My people will welcome you! They will honor you! But come! It is far to Tecuhltli. At any moment the Xotalancas may come on us in numbers too great even for your swords.

"Lead the way," grunted Conan.

Techotl instantly mounted a stair leading up to the gallery, beckoning them to follow him, which they did, moving rapidly to keep on his heels. Having reached the gallery, he plunged into a door that opened toward the west, and hurried through chamber after chamber, each lighted by skylights or green fire-jewels.

"What sort of a place can this be?" muttered Valeria under her breath.

"Crom knows!" answered Conan. "I've seen his kind before, though. They live on the shores of Lake Zuad, near the border of Kush. They're a sort of mongrel Stygians, mixed with another race that wandered into Stygia from the east some centuries ago and were absorbed by them. They're called Tlazitlans. I'm willing to bet it wasn't they who built this city, though."

Techotl's fear did not seem to diminish as they drew away from the chamber where the dead men lay. He kept twisting his head on his shoulder to listen for sounds of pursuit, and stared with burning intensity into every doorway they passed.

Valeria shivered in spite of herself. She feared no man. But the weird floor beneath her feet, the uncanny jewels over her head, dividing the lurking shadows among them, the stealth and terror of their guide, impressed her with a nameless apprehension, a sensation of lurking, inhuman peril.

"They may be between us and Tecuhltli!" he whispered once. "We must beware lest they be lying in wait!"

"Why don't we get out of this infernal palace, and take to the streets?" demanded Valeria.

"There are no streets in Xuchotl," he answered. "No squares nor open courts. The whole city is built like one giant palace under one great roof. The nearest approach to a street is the Great Hall which traverses the city from the north gate to the south gate. The only doors opening into the outer world are the city gates, through which no living man has passed for fifty years."

"How long have you dwelt here?" asked Conan.

"I was born in the castle of Tecuhltli thirty-five years ago. I have never set foot outside the city. For the love of the gods, let us go silently! These halls may be full of lurking devils. Olmec shall tell you all when we reach Tecuhltli."

So in silence they glided on with the green fire-stones blinking overhead and the flaming floors smoldering under their feet, and it seemed to Valeria as if they fled through hell, guided by a dark-faced, lank-haired goblin.

Yet it was Conan who halted them as they were crossing an unusually wide chamber. His wilderness-bred ears were keener even than the ears of Techotl, whetted though these were by a lifetime of warfare in those silent corridors.

"You think some of your enemies may be ahead of us, lying in ambush?"

"They prowl through these rooms at all hours," answered Techotl, "as do we. The halls and chambers between Tecuhltli and Xotalanc are a disputed region, owned by no man. We call it the Halls of Silence. Why do you ask?"

"Because men are in the chambers ahead of us," answered Conan. "I heard steel clink against stone."

Again a shaking seized Techotl, and he clenched his teeth to keep them from chattering.

"Perhaps they are your friends," suggested Valeria.

"We dare not chance it," he panted, and moved with frenzied activity. He turned aside and glided through a doorway on the left which led into a chamber from which an ivory staircase wound down into darkness.

"This leads to an unlighted corridor below us!" he hissed, great beads of perspiration standing out on his brow. "They may be lurking there, too. It may all be a trick to draw us into it. But we must take the chance that they have laid their ambush in the rooms above. Come swiftly, now!"

Softly as phantoms they descended the stair and came to the mouth of a corridor black as night. They crouched there for a moment, listening, and then melted into it. As they moved along, Valeria's flesh crawled between her shoulders in momentary expectation of a sword-thrust in the dark. But for Conan's iron fingers gripping her arm she had no physical cognizance of her companions. Neither made as much noise as a cat would have made. The darkness was absolute. One hand, outstretched, touched a wall, and occasionally she felt a door under her fingers. The hallway seemed interminable.

Suddenly they were galvanized by a sound behind them. Valeria's flesh crawled anew, for she recognized it as the soft opening of a door. Men had come into the corridor behind them. Even with the thought she stumbled over something that felt like a human skull. It rolled across the floor with an appalling clatter.

"Run!" yelped Techotl, a note of hysteria in his voice, and was away down the corridor like a flying ghost.

Again Valeria felt Conan's hand bearing her up and sweeping her along as they raced after their guide. Conan could see in the dark no better than she, but he possessed a sort of instinct that made his course unerring. Without his support and guidance she would have fallen or stumbled against the wall. Down the corridor they sped, while the swift patter of flying feet drew closer and closer, and then suddenly Techotl panted: "Here is the stair! After me, quick! Oh, quick!"

His hand came out of the dark and caught Valeria's wrist as she stumbled blindly on the steps. She felt herself half dragged, half lifted up the winding stair, while Conan released her and turned on the steps, his ears and instincts telling him their foes were hard at their backs. *And the sounds were not all those of human feet.*

Something came writhing up the steps, something that slithered and rustled and brought a chill in the air with it. Conan lashed down with his great sword and felt the blade shear through something that might have been flesh and bone, and cut deep into the stair beneath. Something touched his foot that chilled like the touch of frost, and then the darkness beneath him was disturbed by a frightful thrashing and lashing, and a man cried out in agony.

The next moment Conan was racing up the winding staircase, and through a door that stood open at the head.

Valeria and Techotl were already through, and Techotl slammed the door and shot a bolt across it—the first Conan had seen since they left the outer gate.

Then he turned and ran across the well-lighted chamber into which they had come, and as they passed through the farther door, Conan glanced back and saw the door groaning and straining under heavy pressure violently applied from the other side.

Though Techotl did not abate either his speed or his caution, he seemed more confident now. He had the air

of a man who has come into familiar territory, within call
of friends.

But Conan renewed his terror by asking: "What was that
thing that I fought on the stair?"

"The men of Xotalanc," answered Techotl, without
looking back. "I told you the halls were full of them."

"This wasn't a man," grunted Conan. "It was something
that crawled, and it was as cold as ice to the touch. I think
I cut it asunder. It fell back on the men who were following
us, and must have killed one of them in its death throes."

Techotl's head jerked back, his face ashy again. Convulsively
he quickened his pace.

"It was the Crawler! A monster they have brought out
of the catacombs to aid them! What it is, we do not know,
but we have found our people hideously slain by it. In Set's
name, hasten! If they put it on our trail, it will follow us to
the very doors of Tecuhltli!"

"I doubt it," grunted Conan. "That was a shrewd cut I
dealt it on the stair."

"Hasten! Hasten!" groaned Techotl.

They ran through a series of green-lit chambers, traversed
a broad hall, and halted before a giant bronze door.

Techotl said: "This is Tecuhltli!"

III

THE PEOPLE
OF THE FEUD

Techotl smote on the bronze door with his clenched hand, and then turned sidewise, so that he could watch back along the hall.

"Men have been smitten down before this door, when they thought they were safe," he said.

"Why don't they open the door?" asked Conan.

"They are looking at us through the Eye," answered Techotl. "They are puzzled at the sight of you." He lifted his voice and called: "Open the door, Xecelan! It is I, Techotl, with friends from the great world beyond the forest!—They will open," he assured his allies.

"They'd better do it in a hurry, then," said Conan grimly. "I hear something crawling along the floor beyond the hall."

Techotl went ashy again and attacked the door with his fists, screaming: "Open, you fools, open! The Crawler is at our heels!"

Even as he beat and shouted, the great bronze door swung noiselessly back, revealing a heavy chain across the entrance, over which spearheads bristled and fierce countenances regarded them intently for an instant. Then the chain was dropped and Techotl grasped the arms of his friends in a nervous frenzy and fairly dragged them over the threshold. A glance over his shoulder just as the door was closing showed Conan the long dim vista of the hall, and dimly framed at the other end an ophidian shape that writhed slowly and painfully into view, flowing in a dull-hued length from a chamber door, its hideous blood-stained head wagging drunkenly. Then the closing door shut off the view.

Inside the square chamber into which they had come heavy bolts were drawn across the door, and the chain locked into place. The door was made to stand the battering of a siege. Four men stood on guard, of the same lank-haired, dark-skinned breed as Techotl, with spears in their hands and swords at their hips. In the wall near the door there was a complicated contrivance of mirrors which Conan guessed was the Eye Techotl had mentioned, so arranged that a narrow, crystal-paned slot in the wall could be looked through from within without being discernible from without. The four guardsmen stared at the strangers with wonder, but asked no question, nor did Techotl vouchsafe any information. He moved with easy confidence now, as if he had shed his cloak of indecision and fear the instant he crossed the threshold.

"Come!" he urged his new-found friends, but Conan glanced toward the door.

"What about those fellows who were following us? Won't they try to storm that door?"

Techotl shook his head.

"They know they cannot break down the Door of the

Eagle. They will flee back to Xotalanc, with their crawling
fiend. Come! I will take you to the rulers of Tecuhltli."

One of the four guards opened the door opposite the one
by which they had entered, and they passed through into
a hallway which, like most of the rooms on that level, was
lighted by both the slot-like skylights and the clusters of
winking fire-gems. But unlike the other rooms they had
traversed, this hall showed evidences of occupation. Velvet
tapestries adorned the glossy jade walls, rich rugs were on
the crimson floors, and the ivory seats, benches and divans
were littered with satin cushions.

The hall ended in an ornate door, before which stood no
guard. Without ceremony Techotl thrust the door open and
ushered his friends into a broad chamber, where some thirty
dark-skinned men and women lounging on satin-covered
couches sprang up with exclamations of amazement.

The men, all except one, were of the same type as Techotl,
and the women were equally dark and strange-eyed, though
not unbeautiful in a weird dark way. They wore sandals,
golden breast-plates, and scanty silk skirts supported by
gem-crusted girdles, and their black manes, cut square at their
naked shoulders, were bound with silver circlets.

On a wide ivory seat on a jade dais sat a man and a woman
who differed subtly from the others. He was a giant, with
an enormous sweep of breast and the shoulders of a bull.
Unlike the others, he was bearded, with a thick, blue-black
beard which fell almost to his broad girdle. He wore a robe
of purple silk which reflected changing sheens of color with

his every movement, and one wide sleeve, drawn back to his elbow, revealed a forearm massive with corded muscles. The band which confined his blue-black locks was set with glittering jewels.

The woman beside him sprang to her feet with a startled exclamation as the strangers entered, and her eyes, passing over Conan, fixed themselves with burning intensity on Valeria. She was tall and lithe, by far the most beautiful woman in the room. She was clad more scantily even than the others; for instead of a skirt she wore merely a broad strip of gilt-worked purple cloth fastened to the middle of her girdle which fell below her knees. Another strip at the back of her girdle completed that part of her costume, which she wore with a cynical indifference. Her breast-plates and the circlet about her temples were adorned with gems. In her eyes alone of all the dark-skinned people there lurked no brooding gleam of madness. She spoke no word after her first exclamation; she stood tensely, her hands clenched, staring at Valeria.

The man on the ivory seat had not risen.

"Prince Olmec," spoke Techotl, bowing low, with arms outspread and the palms of his hands turned upward, "I bring allies from the world beyond the forest. In the Chamber of Tezcoti the Burning Skull slew Chicmec, my companion—"

"The Burning Skull!" It was a shuddering whisper of fear from the people of Tecuhltli.

"Aye! Then came I, and found Chicmec lying with his throat cut. Before I could flee, the Burning Skull came upon me, and when I looked upon it my blood became as ice and the marrow of my bones melted. I could neither fight nor run. I could only await the stroke. Then came this white-skinned woman and struck him down with her sword; and lo, it was only a dog of Xotalanc with white paint upon his skin and the living skull of an ancient wizard upon his head! Now that skull lies in many pieces, and the dog who wore it is a dead man!"

An indescribably fierce exultation edged the last sentence, and was echoed in the low, savage exclamations from the crowding listeners.

"But wait!" exclaimed Techotl. "There is more! While I talked with the woman, four Xotalancas came upon us! One I slew—there is the stab in my thigh to prove how desperate was the fight. Two the woman killed. But we were hard pressed when this man came into the fray and split the skull of the fourth! Aye! Five crimson nails there are to be driven into the pillar of vengeance!"

He pointed at a black column of ebony which stood behind the dais. Hundreds of red dots scarred its polished surface—the bright scarlet heads of heavy copper nails driven into the black wood.

"Five red nails for five Xotalanca lives!" exulted Techotl, and the horrible exultation in the faces of the listeners made them inhuman.

"Who are these people?" asked Olmec, and his voice was like the low, deep rumble of a distant bull. None of the people of Xuchotl spoke loudly. It was as if they had absorbed into their souls the silence of the empty halls and deserted chambers.

"I am Conan, a Cimmerian," answered the barbarian briefly. "This woman is Valeria of the Red Brotherhood, an Aquilonian pirate. We are deserters from an army on the Darfar border, far to the north, and are trying to reach the coast."

The woman on the dais spoke loudly, her words tripping in her haste.

"You can never reach the coast! There is no escape from Xuchotl! You will spend the rest of your lives in this city!"

"What do you mean?" growled Conan, clapping his hand to his hilt and stepping about so as to face both the dais and the rest of the room. "Are you telling us we're prisoners?"

"She did not mean that," interposed Olmec. "We are your friends. We would not restrain you against your will. But I fear other circumstances will make it impossible for you to leave Xuchotl."

His eyes flickered to Valeria, and he lowered them quickly.

"This woman is Tascela," he said. "She is a princess of Tecuhltli. But let food and drink be brought our guests. Doubtless they are hungry, and weary from their long travels."

He indicated an ivory table, and after an exchange of glances, the adventurers seated themselves. The Cimmerian was suspicious. His fierce blue eyes roved about the chamber, and he kept his sword close to his hand. But an invitation to eat and drink never found him backward. His eyes kept wandering to Tascela, but the princess had eyes only for his white-skinned companion.

Techotl, who had bound a strip of silk about his wounded thigh, placed himself at the table to attend to the wants of his friends, seeming to consider it a privilege and honor to see after their needs. He inspected the food and drink the others brought in gold vessels and dishes, and tasted each before he placed it before his guests. While they ate, Olmec sat in silence on his ivory seat, watching them from under his broad black brows. Tascela sat beside him, chin cupped in her hands and her elbows resting on her knees. Her dark, enigmatic eyes, burning with a mysterious light, never left Valeria's supple figure. Behind her seat a sullen handsome girl waved an ostrich-plume fan with a slow rhythm.

The food was fruit of an exotic kind unfamiliar to the wanderers, but very palatable, and the drink was a light crimson wine that carried a heady tang.

"You have come from afar," said Olmec at last. "I have read the books of our fathers. Aquilonia lies beyond the lands of the Stygians and the Shemites, beyond Argos and Zingara; and Cimmeria lies beyond Aquilonia."

"We have each a roving foot," answered Conan carelessly.

"How you won through the forest is a wonder to me," quoth Olmec. "In by-gone days a thousand fighting-men scarcely were able to carve a road through its perils."

"We encountered a bench-legged monstrosity about the size of a mastodon," said Conan casually, holding out his wine goblet which Techotl filled with evident pleasure. "But when we'd killed it we had no further trouble."

The wine vessel slipped from Techotl's hand to crash on the floor. His dusky skin went ashy. Olmec started to his feet, an image of stunned amazement, and a low gasp of awe or terror breathed up from the others. Some slipped to their knees as if their legs would not support them. Only Tascela seemed not to have heard. Conan glared about him bewilderedly.

"What's the matter? What are you gaping about?"

"You—you slew the dragon-god?"

"God? I killed a dragon. Why not? It was trying to gobble us up."

"But dragons are immortal!" exclaimed Olmec. "They slay each other, but no man ever killed a dragon! The thousand fighting-men of our ancestors who fought their way to Xuchotl could not prevail against them! Their swords broke like twigs against their scales!"

"If your ancestors had thought to dip their spears in the poisonous juice of Derketa's Apples," quoth Conan, with his mouth full, "and jab them in the eyes or mouth or somewhere like that, they'd have seen that dragons are not more immortal than any other chunk of beef. The carcass lies at the edge of the trees, just within the forest. If you don't believe me, go and look for yourself."

Olmec shook his head, not in disbelief but in wonder.

"It was because of the dragons that our ancestors took refuge in Xuchotl," said he. "They dared not pass through the plain and plunge into the forest beyond. Scores of them were seized and devoured by the monsters before they could reach the city."

"Then your ancestors didn't build Xuchotl?" asked Valeria.

"It was ancient when they first came into the land. How long it had stood here, not even its degenerate inhabitants knew."

"Your people came from Lake Zuad?" questioned Conan.

"Aye. More than half a century ago a tribe of the Tlazitlans rebelled against the Stygian king, and, being defeated in battle, fled southward. For many weeks they wandered over grasslands, desert and hills, and at last they came into the great forest, a thousand fighting-men with their women and children.

"It was in the forest that the dragons fell upon them, and tore many to pieces; so the people fled in a frenzy of fear before them, and at last came into the plain and saw the city of Xuchotl in the midst of it.

"They camped before the city, not daring to leave the plain, for the night was made hideous with the noise of the battling monsters throughout the forest. They made war incessantly upon one another. Yet they came not into the plain.

"The people of the city shut their gates and shot arrows at our people from the walls. The Tlazitlans were imprisoned on the plain, as if the ring of the forest had been a great wall; for to venture into the woods would have been madness.

"That night there came secretly to their camp a slave from the city, one of their own blood, who with a band of exploring soldiers had wandered into the forest long before, when he was a young man. The dragons had devoured all his companions, but he had been taken into the city to dwell in servitude. His name was Tolkemec." A flame lighted the dark eyes at mention of the name, and some of the people muttered obscenely and spat. "He promised to open the gates to the warriors. He asked only that all captives taken be delivered into his hands.

"At dawn he opened the gates. The warriors swarmed in and the halls of Xuchotl ran red. Only a few hundred folk dwelt there, decaying remnants of a once great race. Tolkemec said they came from the east, long ago, from Old Kosala, when the ancestors of those who now dwell in Kosala came up from the south and drove forth the original inhabitants of the land. They wandered far westward and finally found this forest-girdled plain, inhabited then by a tribe of black people.

"These they enslaved and set to building a city. From the hills to the east they brought jade and marble and lapis lazuli, and gold, silver and copper. Herds of elephants provided them with ivory. When their city was completed, they slew all the black slaves. And their magicians made a terrible magic to guard the city; for by their necromantic arts they recreated the dragons which had once dwelt in this lost land, and whose monstrous bones they found in the forest. Those bones they clothed in flesh and life, and the living beasts walked the earth as they walked it when Time was young. But the wizards wove a spell that kept them in the forest and they came not into the plain.

"So for many centuries the people of Xuchotl dwelt in their city, cultivating the fertile plain, until their wise men learned how to grow fruit within the city—fruit which is not planted in soil, but obtains its nourishment out of the air—and then they let the irrigation ditches run dry, and dwelt more and more in luxurious sloth, until decay seized them. They were a dying race when our ancestors broke through the forest and came into the plain. Their wizards had died, and the people had forgot their ancient necromancy. They could fight neither by sorcery nor the sword.

"Well, our fathers slew the people of Xuchotl, all except a hundred which were give living into the hands of Tolkemec, who had been their slave; and for many days and nights the halls re-echoed to their screams under the agony of his tortures.

"So the Tlazitlans dwelt here, for a while in peace, ruled by the brothers Tecuhltli and Xotalanc, and by Tolkemec. Tolkemec took a girl of the tribe to wife, and because he had opened the gates, and because he knew many of the arts of the Xuchotlans, he shared the rule of the tribe with the brothers who had led the rebellion and the flight.

"For a few years, then, they dwelt at peace within the city, doing little but eating, drinking and making love, and raising children. There was no necessity to till the plain, for Tolkemec taught them how to cultivate the air-devouring fruits. Besides, the slaying of the Xuchotlans broke the spell that held the dragons in the forest, and they came nightly and bellowed about the gates of the city. The plain ran red with the blood of their eternal warfare, and it was then that—" He bit his tongue in the midst of the sentence, then presently continued, but Valeria and Conan felt that he had checked an admission he had considered unwise.

"Five years they dwelt in peace. Then"—Olmec's eyes rested briefly on the silent woman at his side—"Xotalanc took a woman to wife, a woman whom both Tecuhltli and old Tolkemec desired. In his madness, Tecuhltli stole her from her husband. Aye, she went willingly enough. Tolkemec, to spite Xotalanc, aided Tecuhltli. Xotalanc demanded that she be given back to him, and the council of the tribe decided that the matter should be left to the woman. She chose to remain with Tecuhltli. In wrath Xotalanc sought to take her back by force, and the retainers of the brothers came to blows in the Great Hall.

"There was much bitterness. Blood was shed on both

sides. The quarrel became a feud, the feud an open war. From the welter three factions emerged—Tecuhltli, Xotalanc, and Tolkemec. Already, in the days of peace, they had divided the city between them. Tecuhltli dwelt in the western quarter of the city, Xotalanc in the eastern, and Tolkemec with his family by the southern gate.

"Anger and resentment and jealousy blossomed into bloodshed and rape and murder. Once the sword was drawn there was no turning back; for blood called for blood, and vengeance followed swift on the heels of atrocity. Tecuhltli fought with Xotalanc, and Tolkemec aided first one and then the other, betraying each faction as it fitted his purposes. Tecuhltli and his people withdrew into the quarter of the western gate, where we now sit. Xuchotl is built in the shape of an oval. Tecuhltli, which took its name from its prince, occupies the western end of the oval. The people blocked up all doors connecting the quarter with the rest of the city, except one on each floor, which could be defended easily. They went into the pits below the city and built a wall cutting off the western end of the catacombs, where lie the bodies of the ancient Xuchotlans, and of those Tlazitlans slain in the feud. They dwelt as in a besieged castle, making sorties and forays on their enemies.

"The people of Xotalanc likewise fortified the eastern quarter of the city, and Tolkemec did likewise with the quarter by the southern gate. The central part of the city was left bare and uninhabited. Those empty halls and chambers became a battle-ground, and a region of brooding terror.

"Tolkemec warred on both clans. He was a fiend in the form of a human, worse than Xotalanc. He knew many secrets of the city he never told the others. From the crypts of the catacombs he plundered the dead of their grisly secrets—secrets of ancient kings and wizards, long forgotten by the degenerate Xuchotlans our ancestors slew. But all his magic did not aid him the night we of Tecuhltli stormed his castle and butchered all his people. Tolkemec we tortured for many days."

His voice sank to a caressing slur, and a far-away look grew in his eyes, as if he looked back over the years to a scene which caused him intense pleasure.

"Aye, we kept the life in him until he screamed for death as for a bride. At last we took him living from the torture chamber and cast him into a dungeon for the rats to gnaw as he died. From that dungeon, somehow, he managed to escape, and dragged himself into the catacombs. There without doubt he died, for the only way out of the catacombs beneath Tecuhltli is through Tecuhltli, and he never emerged by that way. His bones were never found, and the superstitious among our people swear that his ghost haunts the crypts to this day, wailing among the bones of the dead. Twelve years ago we butchered the people of Tolkemec, but the feud raged on between Tecuhltli and Xotalanc, as it will rage until the last man, the last woman is dead.

"It was fifty years ago that Tecuhltli stole the wife of Xotalanc. Half a century the feud has endured. I was born in it. All in this chamber, except Tascela, were born in it. We expect to die in it.

"We are a dying race, even as those Xuchotlans our ancestors slew. When the feud began there were hundreds in each faction. Now we of Tecuhltli number only these you see before you, and the men who guard the four doors: forty in all. How many Xotalancas there are we do not know, but I doubt if they are much more numerous than we. For fifteen years no children have been born to us, and we have seen none among the Xotalancas.

"We are dying, but before we die we will slay as many of the men of Xotalanc as the gods permit."

And with his weird eyes blazing, Olmec spoke long of that grisly feud, fought out in silent chambers and dim halls under the blaze of the green fire-jewels, on floors smoldering with the flames of hell and splashed with deeper crimson from severed veins. In that long butchery a whole generation had perished. Xotalanc was dead, long ago, slain in a grim battle on an ivory stair. Tecuhltli was dead, flayed alive by the maddened Xotalancas who had captured him.

Without emotion Olmec told of hideous battles fought in black corridors, of ambushes on twisting stairs, and red butcheries. With a redder, more abysmal gleam in his deep dark eyes he told of men and women flayed alive, mutilated and dismembered, of captives howling under tortures so ghastly that even the barbarous Cimmerian grunted. No wonder Techotl had trembled with the terror of capture. Yet he had gone forth to slay if he could, driven by hate that was stronger than his fear. Olmec spoke further, of dark and mysterious matters, of black magic and wizardry conjured out of the black night of the catacombs, of weird creatures invoked out of darkness for horrible allies. In these things the Xotalancas had the advantage, for it was in the eastern catacombs where lay the bones of the greatest wizards of the ancient Xuchotlans, with their immemorial secrets.

Valeria listened with morbid fascination. The feud had become a terrible elemental power driving the people of Xuchotl inexorably on to doom and extinction. It filled their whole lives. They were born in it, and they expected to die in it. They never left their barricaded castle except to steal forth into the Halls of Silence that lay between the opposing fortresses, to slay and be slain. Sometimes the raiders returned with frantic captives, or with grim tokens of victory in fight. Sometimes they did not return at all, or returned only as severed limbs cast down before the bolted bronze doors. It was a ghastly, unreal nightmare existence these people lived, shut off from the rest of the world, caught together like rabid rats in the same trap, butchering one another through the years, crouching and creeping through the sunless corridors to maim and torture and murder.

While Olmec talked, Valeria felt the blazing eyes of Tascela fixed upon her. The princess seemed not to hear what Olmec was saying. Her expression, as he narrated victories or defeats, did not mirror the wild rage or fiendish exultation that alternated on the faces of the other Tecuhltli. The feud that was an obsession to her clansmen seemed meaningless to her. Valeria found her indifferent callousness more repugnant than Olmec's naked ferocity.

"And we can never leave the city," said Olmec. "For fifty years no one has left it except those—" Again he checked himself.

"Even without the peril of the dragons," he continued, "we who were born and raised in the city would not dare leave it. We have never set foot outside the walls. We are not accustomed to the open sky and the naked sun. No; we were born in Xuchotl, and in Xuchotl we shall die."

"Well," said Conan, "with your leave we'll take our chances with the dragons. This feud is none of our business. If you'll show us to the west gate we'll be on our way."

Tascela's hands clenched, and she started to speak, but Olmec interrupted her: "It is nearly nightfall. If you wander forth into the plain by night, you will certainly fall prey to the dragons."

"We crossed it last night, and slept in the open without seeing any," returned Conan.

Tascela smiled mirthlessly. "You dare not leave Xuchotl!"

Conan glared at her with instinctive antagonism; she was not looking at him, but at the woman opposite him.

"I think they dare," retorted Olmec. "But look you, Conan and Valeria, the gods must have sent you to us, to cast victory into the laps of the Tecuhltli! You are professional fighters—why not fight for us? We have wealth in abundance—precious jewels are as common in Xuchotl as cobblestones are in the cities of the world. Some the Xuchotlans brought with them from Kosala. Some, like the fire-stones, they found in the hills to the east. Aid us to wipe out the Xotalancas, and we will give you all the jewels you can carry."

"And will you help us destroy the dragons?" asked Valeria. "With bows and poisoned arrows thirty men could slay all the dragons in the forest."

"Aye!" replied Olmec promptly. "We have forgotten the use of the bow, in years of hand-to-hand fighting, but we can learn again."

"What do you say?" Valeria inquired of Conan.

"We're both penniless vagabonds," he grinned hardily. "I'd as soon kill Xotalancas as anybody."

"Then you agree?" exclaimed Olmec, while Techotl fairly hugged himself with delight.

"Aye. And now suppose you show us chambers where we can sleep, so we can be fresh tomorrow for the beginning of the slaying."

Olmec nodded, and waved a hand, and Techotl and a woman led the adventurers into a corridor which led through a door off to the left of the jade dais. A glance back showed Valeria Olmec sitting on his throne, chin on knotted fist, staring after them. His eyes burned with a weird flame. Tascela leaned back in her seat, whispering to the sullen-faced maid, Yasala, who leaned over her shoulder, her ear to the princess' moving lips.

The hallway was not so broad as most they had traversed, but it was long. Presently the woman halted, opened a door, and drew aside for Valeria to enter.

"Wait a minute," growled Conan. "Where do I sleep?"

Techotl pointed to a chamber across the hallway, but one door farther down. Conan hesitated, and seemed inclined to raise an objection, but Valeria smiled spitefully at him and shut the door in his face. He muttered something uncomplimentary about women in general, and strode off down the corridor after Techotl.

In the ornate chamber where he was to sleep, he glanced up at the slot-like skylights. Some were wide enough to admit the body of a slender man, supposing the glass were broken.

"Why don't the Xotalancas come over the roofs and shatter those skylights?" he asked.

"They cannot be broken," answered Techotl. "Besides, the roofs would be hard to clamber over. They are mostly spires and domes and steep ridges."

He volunteered more information about the "castle" of Tecuhltli. Like the rest of the city it contained four stories, or tiers of chambers, with towers jutting up from the roof. Each tier was named; indeed, the people of Xuchotl had a name for each chamber, hall and stair in the city, as people of more normal cities designate streets and quarters. In Tecuhltli the floors were named The Eagle's Tier, The Ape's Tier, The Tiger's Tier and The Serpent's Tier, in the order as enumerated, The Eagle's Tier being the highest, or fourth, floor.

"Who is Tascela?" asked Conan. "Olmec's wife?"

Techotl shuddered and glanced furtively about him before answering.

"No. She is—Tascela! She was the wife of Xotalanc—the woman Tecuhltli stole, to start the feud."

"What are you talking about?" demanded Conan. "That woman is beautiful and young. Are you trying to tell me that she was a wife fifty years ago?"

"Aye! I swear it! She was a full-grown woman when the Tlazitlans journeyed from Lake Zuad. It was because the king of Stygia desired her for a concubine that Xotalanc and his brother rebelled and fled into the wilderness. She is a witch, who possesses the secret of perpetual youth."

"What's that?" asked Conan.

Techotl shuddered again.

"Ask me not! I dare not speak. It is too grisly, even for Xuchotl!"

And touching his finger to his lips, he glided from the chamber.

IV

SCENT OF
BLACK LOTUS

Valeria unbuckled her sword-belt and laid it with the sheathed weapon on the couch where she meant to sleep. She noted that the doors were supplied with bolts, and asked where they led.

"Those lead into adjoining chambers," answered the woman, indicating the doors on right and left. "That one"—pointing to a copper-bound door opposite that which opened into the corridor—"leads to a corridor which runs to a stair that descends into the catacombs. Do not fear; naught can harm you here."

"Who spoke of fear?" snapped Valeria. "I just like to know what sort of harbor I'm dropping anchor in. No, I don't want you to sleep at the foot of my couch. I'm not accustomed to being waited on—not by women, anyway. You have my leave to go."

Alone in the room, the pirate shot the bolts on all the doors, kicked off her boots and stretched luxuriously out on the couch. She imagined Conan similarly situated across the corridor, but her feminine vanity prompted her to visualize him as scowling and muttering with chagrin as he cast himself on his solitary couch, and she grinned with gleeful malice as she prepared herself for slumber.

Outside, night had fallen. In the halls of Xuchotl the green fire-jewels blazed like the eyes of prehistoric cats. Somewhere among the dark towers a night wind moaned like a restless spirit. Through the dim passages stealthy figures began stealing, like disembodied shadows.

Valeria awoke suddenly on her couch. In the dusky emerald glow of the fire-gems she saw a shadowy figure bending over her. For a bemused instant the apparition seemed part of the dream she had been dreaming. She had seemed to lie on the couch in the chamber as she was actually lying, while over her pulsed and throbbed a gigantic black blossom so enormous that it hid the ceiling. Its exotic perfume pervaded her being, inducing a delicious, sensuous languor that was something more and less than sleep. She was sinking into scented billows of insensible bliss, when something touched her face. So supersensitive were her drugged senses, that the light touch was like a dislocating impact, jolting her rudely into full wakefulness. Then it was that she saw, not a gargantuan blossom, but a dark-skinned woman standing above her.

With the realization came anger and instant action. The woman turned lithely, but before she could run Valeria was on her feet and had caught her arm. She fought like a wildcat for an instant, and then subsided as she felt herself crushed by the superior strength of her captor. The pirate wrenched the woman around to face her, caught her chin with her free hand and forced her captive to meet her gaze. It was the sullen Yasala, Tascela's maid.

"What the devil were you doing bending over me? What's that in your hand?"

The woman made no reply, but sought to cast away the object. Valeria twisted her arm around in front of her, and the thing fell to the floor—a great black exotic blossom on a jade-green stem, large as a woman's head, to be sure, but tiny beside the exaggerated vision she had seen.

"The black lotus!" said Valeria between her teeth. "The blossom whose scent brings deep sleep. You were trying to drug me! If you hadn't accidentally touched my face with the petals, you'd have—why did you do it? What's your game?"

Yasala maintained a sulky silence, and with an oath Valeria whirled her around, forced her to her knees and twisted her arm up behind her back.

"Tell me, or I'll tear your arm out of its socket!"

Yasala squirmed in anguish as her arm was forced excruciatingly up between her shoulder-blades, but a violent shaking of her head was the only answer she made.

"Slut!" Valeria cast her from her to sprawl on the floor. The pirate glared at the prostrate figure with blazing eyes. Fear and the memory of Tascela's burning eyes stirred in her, rousing all her tigerish instincts of self-preservation. These people were decadent; any sort of perversity might be expected to be encountered among them. But Valeria sensed here something that moved behind the scenes, some secret terror fouler than common degeneracy. Fear and revulsion of this weird city swept her. These people were neither sane nor normal; she began to doubt if they were even human. Madness smoldered in the eyes of them all—all except the cruel, cryptic eyes of Tascela, which held secrets and mysteries more abysmal than madness.

She lifted her head and listened intently. The halls of Xuchotl were as silent as if it were in reality a dead city. The green jewels bathed the chamber in a nightmare glow, in which the eyes of the woman on the floor glittered eerily up at her. A thrill of panic throbbed through Valeria, driving the last vestige of mercy from her fierce soul.

"Why did you try to drug me?" she muttered, grasping the woman's black hair, and forcing her head back to glare into her sullen, long-lashed eyes. "Did Tascela send you?"

No answer. Valeria cursed venomously and slapped the woman first on one cheek and then the other. The blows resounded through the room, but Yasala made no outcry.

"Why don't you scream?" demanded Valeria savagely. "Do you fear someone will hear you? Whom do you fear? Tascela? Olmec? Conan?"

Yasala made no reply. She crouched, watching her captor with eyes baleful as those of a basilisk. Stubborn silence always fans anger. Valeria turned and tore a handful of cords from a nearby hanging.

"You sulky slut!" she said between her teeth. "I'm going to strip you stark naked and tie you across that couch and whip you until you tell me what you were doing here, and who sent you!"

Yasala made no verbal protest, nor did she offer any resistance, as Valeria carried out the first part of her threat with a fury that her captive's obstinacy only sharpened. Then for a space there was no sound in the chamber except the whistle and crackle of hard-woven silken cords on naked flesh. Yasala could not move her fast-bound hands or feet. Her body writhed and quivered under the chastisement, her head swayed from side to side in rhythm with the blows. Her teeth were sunk into her lower lip and a trickle of blood began as the punishment continued. But she did not cry out.

The pliant cords made no great sound as they encountered the quivering body of the captive; only a sharp crackling snap, but each cord left a red streak across Yasala's dark flesh. Valeria inflicted the punishment with all the strength of her war-hardened arm, with all the mercilessness acquired during a life where pain and torment were daily happenings, and with all the cynical ingenuity which only a woman displays toward a woman. Yasala suffered more, physically and mentally, than she would have suffered under a lash wielded by a man, however strong.

It was the application of this feminine cynicism which at last tamed Yasala.

A low whimper escaped from her lips, and Valeria paused, arm lifted, and raked back a damp yellow lock. "Well, are you going to talk?" she demanded. "I can keep this up all night, if necessary!"

"Mercy!" whispered the woman. "I will tell."

Valeria cut the cords from her wrists and ankles, and pulled her to her feet. Yasala sank down on the couch, half reclining on one bare hip, supporting herself on her arm, and writhing at the contact of her smarting flesh with the couch. She was trembling in every limb.

"Wine!" she begged, dry-lipped, indicating with a quivering hand a gold vessel on an ivory table. "Let me drink. I am weak with pain. Then I will tell you all."

Valeria picked up the vessel, and Yasala rose unsteadily to receive it. She took it, raised it toward her lips—then dashed the contents full into the Aquilonian's face. Valeria reeled backward, shaking and clawing the stinging liquid out of her eyes. Through a smarting mist she saw Yasala dart across the room, fling back a bolt, throw open the copper-bound door and run down the hall. The pirate was after her instantly, sword out and murder in her heart.

But Yasala had the start, and she ran with the nervous agility of a woman who has just been whipped to the point of hysterical frenzy. She rounded a corner in the corridor, yards ahead of Valeria, and when the pirate turned it, she saw only an empty hall, and at the other end a door that gaped blackly. A damp moldy scent reeked up from it, and Valeria shivered. That must be the door that led to the catacombs. Yasala had taken refuge among the dead.

Valeria advanced to the door and looked down a flight of stone steps that vanished quickly into utter blackness. Evidently it was a shaft that led straight to the pits below the city, without opening upon any of the lower floors. She shivered slightly at the thought of the thousands of corpses lying in their stone crypts down there, wrapped in their moldering cloths. She had no intention of groping her way down those stone steps. Yasala doubtless knew every turn and twist of the subterranean tunnels.

She was turning back, baffled and furious, when a sobbing cry welled up from the blackness. It seemed to come from a great depth, but human words were faintly distinguishable, and the voice was that of a woman. "Oh, help! Help, in Set's name! Ahhh!" It trailed away, and Valeria thought she caught the echo of a ghostly tittering.

A long-drawn scream of agony rang through the halls.

Valeria felt her skin crawl. What had happened to Yasala down there in the thick blackness? There was no doubt that it had been she who had cried out. But what peril could have befallen her? Was a Xotalanca lurking down there? Olmec had assured them that the catacombs below Tecuhltli were walled off from the rest, too securely for their enemies to break through. Besides, that tittering had not sounded like a human being at all.

Valeria hurried back down the corridor, not stopping to close the door that opened on the stair. Regaining her chamber, she closed the door and shot the bolt behind her. She pulled on her boots and buckled her sword-belt about her. She was determined to make her way to Conan's room and urge him, if he still lived, to join her in an attempt to fight their way out of that city of devils.

But even as she reached the door that opened into the corridor, a long-drawn scream of agony rang through the halls, followed by the stamp of running feet and the loud clangor of swords.

V

TWENTY RED
NAILS

Two warriors lounged in the guardroom on the floor known as the Tier of the Eagle. Their attitude was casual, though habitually alert. An attack on the great bronze door from without was always a possibility, but for many years no such assault had been attempted on either side.

"The strangers are strong allies," said one. "Olmec will move against the enemy tomorrow, I believe."

He spoke as a soldier in a war might have spoken. In the miniature world of Xuchotl each handful of feudists was an army, and the empty halls between the castles was the country over which they campaigned.

The other meditated for a space.

"Suppose with their aid we destroy Xotalanc," he said. "What then, Xatmec?"

"Why," returned Xatmec, "we will drive red nails for them all. The captives we will burn and flay and quarter."

"But afterward?" pursued the other. "After we have slain them all? Will it not seem strange, to have no foes to fight? All my life I have fought and hated the Xotalancas. With the feud ended, what is left?"

Xatmec shrugged his shoulders. His thoughts had never gone beyond the destruction of their foes. They could not go beyond that.

Suddenly both men stiffened at a noise outside the door.

"To the door, Xatmec!" hissed the last speaker. "I shall look through the Eye—"

Xatmec, sword in hand, leaned against the bronze door, straining his ear to hear through the metal. His mate looked into the mirror. He started convulsively. Men were clustered thickly outside the door; grim, dark-faced men with swords gripped in their teeth—and their fingers thrust into their ears. One who wore a feathered head-dress had a set of pipes which he set to his lips, and even as the Tecuhltli started to shout a warning, the pipes began to skirl.

The cry died in the guard's throat as the thin, weird piping penetrated the metal door and smote on his ears. Xatmec leaned frozen against the door, as if paralyzed in that position. His face was that of a wooden image, his expression one of horrified listening. The other guard, farther removed from the source of the sound, yet sensed the horror of what was taking place, the grisly threat that lay in that demoniac fifing. He felt the weird strains plucking like unseen fingers at the tissues of his brain, filling him with alien emotions and impulses of madness. But with a soul-tearing effort he broke the spell, and shrieked a warning in a voice he did not recognize as his own.

But even as he cried out, the music changed to an unbearable shrilling that was like a knife in the ear-drums. Xatmec screamed in sudden agony, and all the sanity went out of his face like a flame blown out in a wind. Like a madman he ripped loose the chain, tore open the door and rushed out into the hall, sword lifted before his mate could stop him. A dozen blades struck him down, and over his mangled body the Xotalancas surged into the guardroom, with a long-drawn, blood-mad yell that sent the unwonted echoes reverberating.

His brain reeling from the shock of it all, the remaining guard leaped to meet them with goring spear. The horror of the sorcery he had just witnessed was submerged in the stunning realization that the enemy were in Tecuhltli. And as his spearhead ripped through a dark-skinned belly he knew no more, for a swinging sword crushed his skull, even as wild-eyed warriors came pouring in from the chambers behind the guardroom.

It was the yelling of men and the clanging of steel that brought Conan bounding from his couch, wide awake and broadsword in hand. In an instant he had reached the door and flung it open, and was glaring out into the corridor just as Techotl rushed up it, eyes blazing madly.

"The Xotalancas!" he screamed, in a voice hardly human. "*They are within the door!*"

Conan ran down the corridor, even as Valeria emerged from her chamber.

"What the devil is it?" she called.

"Techotl says the Xotalancas are in," he answered hurriedly. "That racket sounds like it."

With the Tecuhltli on their heels they burst into the throneroom and were confronted by a scene beyond the most frantic dream of blood and fury. Twenty men and women, their black hair streaming, and the white skulls gleaming on their breasts, were locked in combat with the people of Tecuhltli. The women on both sides fought as madly as the men, and already the room and the hall beyond were strewn with corpses.

Olmec, naked but for a breech-clout, was fighting before his throne, and as the adventurers entered, Tascela ran from an inner chamber with a sword in her hand.

Xatmec and his mate were dead, so there was none to tell the Tecuhltli how their foes had found their way into their citadel. Nor was there any to say what had prompted that mad attempt. But the losses of the Xotalancas had been greater, their position more desperate, than the Tecuhltli had known. The maiming of their scaly ally, the destruction of the Burning Skull, and the news, gasped by a dying man, that mysterious white-skin allies had joined their enemies, had driven them to the frenzy of desperation and the wild determination to die dealing death to their ancient foes.

The Tecuhltli, recovering from the first stunning shock of the surprize that had swept them back into the throneroom and littered the floor with their corpses, fought back with an equally desperate fury, while the door-guards from the lower floors came racing to hurl themselves into the fray. It was the death-fight of rabid wolves, blind, panting, merciless. Back and forth it surged, from door to dais, blades whickering and striking into flesh, blood spurting, feet stamping the crimson floor where redder pools were forming. Ivory tables crashed over, seats were splintered, velvet hangings torn down were stained red. It was the bloody climax of a bloody half-century, and every man there sensed it.

But the conclusion was inevitable. The Tecuhltli

outnumbered the invaders almost two to one, and they were heartened by that fact and by the entrance into the mêlée of their light-skinned allies.

These crashed into the fray with the devastating effect of a hurricane plowing through a grove of saplings. In sheer strength no three Tlazitlans were a match for Conan, and in spite of his weight he was quicker on his feet than any of them. He moved through the whirling, eddying mass with the surety and destructiveness of a gray wolf amidst a pack of alley curs, and he strode over a wake of crumpled figures.

Valeria fought beside him, her lips smiling and her eyes blazing. She was stronger than the average man, and far quicker and more ferocious. Her sword was like a living thing in her hand. Where Conan beat down opposition by the sheer weight and power of his blows, breaking spears, splitting skulls and cleaving bosoms to the breastbone, Valeria brought into action a finesse of sword-play that dazzled and bewildered her antagonists before it slew them. Again and again a warrior, heaving high his heavy blade, found her point in his jugular before he could strike. Conan, towering above the field, strode through the welter smiting right and left, but Valeria moved like an illusive phantom, constantly shifting, and thrusting and slashing as she shifted. Swords missed her again and again as the wielders flailed the empty air and died with her point in their hearts or throats, and her mocking laughter in their ears.

Neither sex nor condition was considered by the maddened combatants. The five women of the Xotalancas were down with their throats cut before Conan and Valeria entered the fray, and when a man or woman went down under the stamping feet, there was always a knife ready for the helpless throat, or a sandaled foot eager to crush the prostrate skull.

From wall to wall, from door to door rolled the waves of combat, spilling over into adjoining chambers. And presently only Tecuhltli and their white-skinned allies stood upright in the great throne-room. The survivors stared bleakly and blankly at each other, like survivors after Judgment Day or the destruction of the world. On legs wide-braced, hands gripping notched and dripping swords, blood trickling down their arms, they stared at one another across the mangled corpses of friends and foes. They had no breath left to shout, but a bestial mad howling rose from their lips. It was not a human cry of triumph. It was the howling of a rabid wolf-pack stalking among the bodies of its victims.

Conan caught Valeria's arm and turned her about.

"You've got a stab in the calf of your leg," he growled.

She glanced down, for the first time aware of a stinging in the muscles of her leg. Some dying man on the floor had fleshed his dagger with his last effort.

"You look like a butcher yourself," she laughed.

He shook a red shower from his hands.

"Not mine. Oh, a scratch here and there. Nothing to bother about. But that calf ought to be bandaged."

Olmec came through the litter, looking like a ghoul with his naked massive shoulders splashed with blood, and his black beard dabbled in crimson. His eyes were red, like the reflection of flame on black water.

"We have won!" he croaked dazedly. "The feud is ended! The dogs of Xotalanc lie dead! Oh, for a captive to flay alive! Yet it is good to look upon their dead faces. Twenty dead dogs! Twenty red nails for the black column!"

"You'd best see to your wounded," grunted Conan, turning away from him. "Here, girl, let me see that leg."

"Wait a minute!" she shook him off impatiently. The fire of fighting still burned brightly in her soul. "How do we know these are all of them? These might have come on a raid of their own."

"They would not split the clan on a foray like this," said Olmec, shaking his head, and regaining some of his ordinary intelligence. Without his purple robe the man seemed less like a prince than some repellent beast of prey. "I will stake my head upon it that we have slain them all. There were less of them than I dreamed, and they must have been desperate. But how came they in Tecuhltli?"

Tascela came forward, wiping her sword on her naked thigh, and holding in her other hand an object she had taken from the body of the feathered leader of the Xotalancas.

"The pipes of madness," she said. "A warrior tells me that Xatmec opened the door to the Xotalancas and was cut down as they stormed into the guardroom. This warrior came to the guardroom from the inner hall just in time to see it happen and to hear the last of a weird strain of music which froze his very soul. Tolkemec used to talk of these pipes, which the Xuchotlans swore were hidden somewhere in the catacombs with the bones of the ancient wizard who used them in his lifetime. Somehow the dogs of Xotalanc found them and learned their secret."

"Somebody ought to go to Xotalanc and see if any remain alive," said Conan. "I'll go if somebody will guide me."

Olmec glanced at the remnants of his people. There were

only twenty left alive, and of these several lay groaning on the floor. Tascela was the only one of the Tecuhltli who had escaped without a wound. The princess was untouched, though she had fought as savagely as any.

"Who will go with Conan to Xotalanc?" asked Olmec.

Techotl limped forward. The wound in his thigh had started bleeding afresh, and he had another gash across his ribs.

"I will go!"

"No, you won't," vetoed Conan. "And you're not going either, Valeria. In a little while that leg will be getting stiff."

"I will go," volunteered a warrior, who was knotting a bandage about a slashed forearm.

"Very well, Yanath. Go with the Cimmerian. And you, too, Topal." Olmec indicated another man whose injuries were slight. "But first aid us to lift the badly wounded on these couches where we may bandage their hurts."

This was done quickly. As they stooped to pick up a woman who had been stunned by a war-club, Olmec's beard brushed Topal's ear. Conan thought the prince muttered something to the warrior, but he could not be sure. A few moments later he was leading his companions down the hall.

Conan glanced back as he went out the door, at that shambles where the dead lay on the smoldering floor, blood-stained dark limbs knotted in attitudes of fierce muscular effort, dark faces frozen in masks of hate, glassy eyes glaring up at the green fire-jewels which bathed the ghastly scene in a dusky emerald witch-light. Among the dead the living moved aimlessly, like people moving in a trance. Conan heard Olmec call a woman and direct her to bandage Valeria's leg.

The pirate followed the woman into an adjoining chamber, already beginning to limp slightly.

Warily the two Tecuhltli led Conan along the hall beyond the bronze door, and through chamber after chamber shimmering in the green fire. They saw no one, heard no sound. After they crossed the Great Hall which bisected the city from north to south, their caution was increased by the realization of their nearness to enemy territory. But chambers and halls lay empty to their wary gaze, and they came at last along a broad dim hallway and halted before a bronze door similar to the Eagle Door of Tecuhltli. Gingerly they tried it, and it opened silently under their fingers. Awed, they stared into the green-lit chambers beyond. For fifty years no Tecuhltli had entered those halls save as a prisoner going to a hideous doom. To go to Xotalanc had been the ultimate horror that could befall a man of the western castle. The terror of it had stalked through their dreams since earliest childhood. To Yanath and Topal that bronze door was like the portal of hell.

They cringed back, unreasoning horror in their eyes, and Conan pushed past them and strode into Xotalanc.

Timidly they followed him. As each man set foot over the threshold he stared and glared wildly about him. But only their quick, hurried breathing disturbed the silence.

They had come into a square guardroom, like that behind the Eagle Door of Tecuhltli, and, similarly, a hall ran away from it to a broad chamber that was a counterpart of Olmec's throneroom.

Conan glanced down the hall with its rugs and divans and hangings, and stood listening intently. He heard no noise, and the rooms had an empty feel. He did not believe there were any Xotalancas left alive in Xuchotl.

"Come on," he muttered, and started down the hall.

He had not gone far when he was aware that only Yanath was following him. He wheeled back to see Topal standing in an attitude of horror, one arm out as if to fend off some threatening peril, his distended eyes fixed with hypnotic intensity on something protruding from behind a divan.

"What the devil?" Then Conan saw what Topal was staring at, and he felt a faint twitching of the skin between his giant shoulders. A monstrous head protruded from behind the divan, a reptilian head, broad as the head of a crocodile, with down-curving fangs that projected over the lower jaw. But there was an unnatural limpness about the thing, and the hideous eyes were glazed.

Conan peered behind the couch. It was a great serpent which lay there limp in death, but such a serpent as he had never seen in his wanderings. The reek and chill of the deep black earth were about it, and its color was an indeterminable hue which changed with each new angle from which he surveyed it. A great wound in the neck showed what had caused its death.

"It is the Crawler!" whispered Yanath.

"It's the thing I slashed on the stair," grunted Conan. "After it trailed us to the Eagle Door, it dragged itself here to die. How could the Xotalancas control such a brute?"

The Tecuhltli shivered and shook their heads.

"They brought it up from the black tunnels below the catacombs. They discovered secrets unknown to Tecuhltli."

"Well, it's dead, and if they'd had any more of them, they'd have brought them along when they came to Tecuhltli. Come on."

They crowded close at his heels as he strode down the hall and thrust on the silver-worked door at the other end.

"If we don't find anybody on this floor," he said, "we'll descend into the lower floors. We'll explore Xotalanc from the roof to the catacombs. If Xotalanc is like Tecuhltli, all the rooms and halls in this tier will be lighted—what the devil!"

They had come into the broad throne-chamber, so similar to that one in Tecuhltli. There were the same jade dais and ivory seat, the same divans, rugs and hangings on the walls. No black, red-scarred column stood behind the throne-dais, but evidences of the grim feud were not lacking.

Ranged along the wall behind the dais were rows of glass-covered shelves. And on those shelves hundreds of human heads, perfectly preserved, stared at the startled watchers with emotionless eyes, as they had stared for only the gods knew how many months and years.

Topal muttered a curse, but Yanath stood silent, the mad light growing in his wide eyes. Conan frowned, knowing that Tlazitlan sanity was hung on a hair-trigger.

Suddenly Yanath pointed to the ghastly relics with a twitching finger.

"There is my brother's head!" he murmured. "And there is my father's younger brother! And there beyond them is my sister's eldest son!"

Suddenly he began to weep, dry-eyed, with harsh, loud sobs that shook his frame. He did not take his eyes from the heads. His sobs grew shriller, changed to frightful, high-pitched laughter, and that in turn became an unbearable screaming. Yanath was stark mad.

Conan laid a hand on his shoulder, and as if the touch had released all the frenzy in his soul, Yanath screamed and whirled, striking at the Cimmerian with his sword. Conan parried the blow, and Topal tried to catch Yanath's arm. But the madman avoided him and with froth flying from his lips, he drove his sword deep into Topal's body. Topal sank down with a groan, and Yanath whirled for an instant like a crazy dervish; then he ran at the shelves and began hacking at the glass with his sword, screeching blasphemously.

Conan sprang at him from behind, trying to catch him unaware and disarm him, but the madman wheeled and lunged at him, screaming like a lost soul. Realizing that the warrior was hopelessly insane, the Cimmerian side-stepped, and as the maniac went past, he swung a cut that severed the shoulder-bone and breast, and dropped the man dead beside his dying victim.

Conan bent over Topal, seeing that the man was at his last gasp. It was useless to seek to stanch the blood gushing from the horrible wound.

"You're done for, Topal," grunted Conan. "Any word you want to send to your people?"

"Bend closer," gasped Topal, and Conan complied—and an instant later caught the man's wrist as Topal struck at his breast with a dagger.

"Crom!" swore Conan. "Are you mad, too?"

"Olmec ordered it!" gasped the dying man. "I know

not why. As we lifted the wounded upon the couches he whispered to me, bidding me to slay you as we returned to Tecuhltli—" And with the name of his clan on his lips, Topal died.

Conan scowled down at him in puzzlement. This whole affair had an aspect of lunacy. Was Olmec mad, too? Were all the Tecuhltli madder than he had realized? With a shrug of his shoulders he strode down the hall and out of the bronze door, leaving the dead Tecuhltli lying before the staring dead eyes of their kinsmen's heads.

Conan needed no guide back through the labyrinth they had traversed. His primitive instinct of direction led him unerringly along the route they had come. He traversed it as warily as he had before, his sword in his hand, and his eyes fiercely searching each shadowed nook and corner; for it was his former allies he feared now, not the ghosts of the slain Xotalancas.

He had crossed the Great Hall and entered the chambers beyond when he heard something moving ahead of him—something which gasped and panted, and moved with a strange, floundering, scrambling noise. A moment later Conan saw a man crawling over the flaming floor toward him—a man whose progress left a broad bloody smear on the smoldering surface. It was Techotl and his eyes were already glazing; from a deep gash in his breast blood gushed steadily between the fingers of his clutching hand. With the other he clawed and hitched himself along.

"Conan," he cried chokingly, "Conan! Olmec has taken the yellow-haired woman!"

"So that's why he told Topal to kill me!" murmured Conan, dropping to his knee beside the man, who his experienced eye told him was dying. "Olmec isn't so mad as I thought."

Techotl's groping fingers plucked at Conan's arm. In the cold, loveless and altogether hideous life of the Tecuhltli his admiration and affection for the invaders from the outer world formed a warm, human oasis, constituted a tie that connected him with a more natural humanity that was totally lacking in his fellows, whose only emotions were hate, lust and the urge of sadistic cruelty.

"I sought to oppose him," gurgled Techotl, blood bubbling frothily to his lips. "But he struck me down. He thought he had slain me, but I crawled away. Ah, Set, how far I have crawled in my own blood! Beware, Conan! Olmec may have set an ambush for your return! Slay Olmec! He is a beast. Take Valeria and flee! Fear not to traverse the forest. Olmec and Tascela lied about the dragons. They slew each other years ago, all save the strongest. For a dozen years there has been only one dragon. If you have slain him, there is naught in the forest to harm you. He was the god Olmec worshipped; and Olmec fed human sacrifices to him, the very old and the very young, bound and hurled from the wall. Hasten! Olmec has taken Valeria to the Chamber of the—"

His head slumped down and he was dead before it came to rest on the floor.

Conan sprang up, his eyes like live coals. So that was Olmec's game, having first used the strangers to destroy his foes! He should have known that something of the sort would be going on in that black-bearded degenerate's mind.

The Cimmerian started toward Tecuhltli with reckless speed. Rapidly he reckoned the numbers of his former allies. Only twenty-one, counting Olmec, had survived that fiendish battle in the throne room. Three had died since, which left seventeen enemies with which to reckon. In his rage Conan felt capable of accounting for the whole clan single-handed.

But the innate craft of the wilderness rose to guide his berserk rage. He remembered Techotl's warning of an ambush. It was quite probable that the prince would make such provisions, on the chance that Topal might have failed to carry out his order. Olmec would be expecting him to return by the same route he had followed in going to Xotalanc.

Conan glanced up at a skylight under which he was passing and caught the blurred glimmer of stars. They had not yet begun to pale for dawn. The events of the night had been crowded into a comparatively short space of time.

He turned aside from his direct course and descended a winding staircase to the floor below. He did not know where the door was to be found that let into the castle on that level, but he knew he could find it. How he was to force the locks he did not know; he believed that the doors of Tecuhltli would all be locked and bolted, if for no other reason than the habits of half a century. But there was nothing else but to attempt it.

Sword in hand, he hurried noiselessly on through a maze of green-lit or shadowy rooms and halls. He knew he must be near Tecuhltli, when a sound brought him up short. He recognized it for what it was—a human being trying to cry out through a stifling gag. It came from somewhere ahead of him, and to the left. In those deathly-still chambers a small sound carried a long way.

Conan turned aside and went seeking after the sound, which continued to be repeated. Presently he was glaring through a doorway upon a weird scene. In the room into which he was looking a low rack-like frame of iron lay on the floor, and a giant figure was bound prostrate upon it. His head rested on a bed of iron spikes, which were already crimson-pointed with blood where they had pierced his scalp. A peculiar harness-like contrivance was fastened about his head, though in such a manner that the leather band did not protect his scalp from the spikes. This harness was connected by a slender chain to the mechanism that upheld a huge iron ball which was suspended above the captive's hairy breast. As long as the man could force himself to remain motionless the iron ball hung in its place. But when the pain of the iron points caused him to lift his head, the ball lurched downward a few inches. Presently his aching neck muscles would no longer support his head in its unnatural position and it would fall back on the spikes again. It was obvious that eventually the ball would crush him to a pulp, slowly and inexorably. The victim was gagged, and above the gag his great black ox-eyes rolled wildly toward the man in the doorway, who stood in silent amazement. The man on the rack was Olmec, prince of Tecuhltli.

VI

THE EYES
OF TASCELA

"Why did you bring me into this chamber to bandage my legs?" demanded Valeria. "Couldn't you have done it just as well in the throneroom?"

She sat on a couch with her wounded leg extended upon it, and the Tecuhltli woman had just bound it with silk bandages. Valeria's red-stained sword lay on the couch beside her.

She frowned as she spoke. The woman had done her task silently and efficiently, but Valeria liked neither the lingering, caressing touch of her slim fingers nor the expression in her eyes.

"They have taken the rest of the wounded into the other chambers," answered the woman in the soft speech of the Tecuhltli women, which somehow did not suggest either softness or gentleness in the speakers. A little while before, Valeria had seen this same woman stab a Xotalanca woman through the breast and stamp the eyeballs out of a wounded Xotalanca man.

"They will be carrying the corpses of the dead down into the catacombs," she added, "lest the ghosts escape into the chambers and dwell there."

"Do you believe in ghosts?" asked Valeria.

"I know the ghost of Tolkemec dwells in the catacombs," she answered with a shiver. "Once I saw it, as I crouched in a crypt among the bones of a dead queen. It passed by in the form of an ancient man with flowing white beard and locks, and luminous eyes that blazed in the darkness. It was Tolkemec; I saw him living when I was a child and he was being tortured."

Her voice sank to a fearful whisper: "Olmec laughs, but I know Tolkemec's ghost dwells in the catacombs! They say it is rats which gnaw the flesh from the bones of the newly dead—but ghosts eat flesh. Who knows but that—"

She glanced up quickly as a shadow fell across the couch. Valeria looked up to see Olmec gazing down at her. The prince had cleansed his hands, torso and beard of the blood that had splashed them; but he had not donned his robe, and his great dark-skinned hairless body and limbs renewed the impression of strength bestial in its nature. His deep black eyes burned with a more elemental light, and there was the suggestion of a twitching in the fingers that tugged at his thick blue-black beard.

He stared fixedly at the woman, and she rose and glided from the chamber. As she passed through the door she cast a look over her shoulder at Valeria, a glance full of cynical derision and obscene mockery.

"She has done a clumsy job," criticized the prince, coming to the divan and bending over the bandage. "Let me see—"

With a quickness amazing in one of his bulk he snatched her sword and threw it across the chamber. His next move was to catch her in his giant arms.

Quick and unexpected as the move was, she almost

matched it; for even as he grabbed her, her dirk was in her hand and she stabbed murderously at his throat. More by luck than skill he caught her wrist, and then began a savage wrestling match. She fought him with fists, feet, knees, teeth and nails, with all the strength of her magnificent body and all the knowledge of hand-to-hand fighting she had acquired in her years of roving and fighting on sea and land. It availed her nothing against his brute strength. She lost her dirk in the first moment of contact, and thereafter found herself powerless to inflict any appreciable pain on her giant attacker.

The blaze in his weird black eyes did not alter, and their expression filled her with fury, fanned by the sardonic smile that seemed carved upon his bearded lips. Those eyes and that smile contained all the cruel cynicism that seethes below the surface of a sophisticated and degenerate race, and for the first time in her life Valeria experienced fear of a man. It was like struggling against some huge elemental force; his iron arms thwarted her efforts with an ease that sent panic racing through her limbs. He seemed impervious to any pain she could inflict. Only once, when she sank her white teeth savagely into his wrist so that the blood started, did he react. And that was to buffet her brutally upon the side of the head with his open hand, so that stars flashed before her eyes and her head rolled on her shoulders.

Her shirt had been torn open in the struggle, and with cynical cruelty he rasped his thick beard across her bare breasts, bringing the blood to suffuse the fair skin, and fetching a cry of pain and outraged fury from her. Her convulsive resistance was useless; she was crushed down on a couch, disarmed and panting, her eyes blazing up at him like the eyes of a trapped tigress.

A moment later he was hurrying from the chamber, carrying her in his arms. She made no resistance, but the smoldering of her eyes showed that she was unconquered in spirit, at least. She had not cried out. She knew that Conan was not within call, and it did not occur to her that any in Tecuhltli would oppose their prince. But she noticed that Olmec went stealthily, with his head on one side as if listening for sounds of pursuit, and he did not return to the throne chamber. He carried her through a door that stood opposite that through which he had entered, crossed another room and began stealing down a hall. As she became convinced that he feared some opposition to the abduction, she threw back her head and screamed at the top of her lusty voice.

She was rewarded by a slap that half stunned her, and Olmec quickened his pace to a shambling run.

But her cry had been echoed, and twisting her head about, Valeria, through the tears and stars that partly blinded her, saw Techotl limping after them.

Olmec turned with a snarl, shifting the woman to an uncomfortable and certainly undignified position under one huge arm, where he held her writhing and kicking vainly, like a child.

"Olmec!" protested Techotl. "You cannot be such a dog as to do this thing! She is Conan's woman! She helped us slay the Xotalancas, and—"

Without a word Olmec balled his free hand into a huge fist and stretched the wounded warrior senseless at his feet. Stooping, and hindered not at all by the struggles and imprecations of his captive, he drew Techotl's sword from its sheath and stabbed the warrior in the breast. Then casting aside the weapon he fled on along the corridor. He did not see a woman's dark face peer cautiously after him from behind a hanging. It vanished, and presently Techotl groaned and stirred, rose dazedly and staggered drunkenly away, calling Conan's name.

Olmec hurried on down the corridor, and descended a winding ivory staircase. He crossed several corridors and halted at last in a broad chamber whose doors were veiled with heavy tapestries, with one exception—a heavy bronze door similar to the Door of the Eagle on the upper floor.

He was moved to rumble, pointing to it: "That is one of the outer doors of Tecuhltli. For the first time in fifty years it is unguarded. We need not guard it now, for Xotalanc is no more."

"Thanks to Conan and me, you bloody rogue!" sneered Valeria, trembling with fury and the shame of physical coercion. "You treacherous dog! Conan will cut your throat for this!"

Olmec did not bother to voice his belief that Conan's own gullet had already been severed according to his whispered command. He was too utterly cynical to be at all interested in her thoughts or opinions. His flame-lit eyes devoured her, dwelling burningly on the generous expanses of clear white flesh exposed where her shirt and breeches had been torn in the struggle.

"Forget Conan," he said thickly. "Olmec is lord of Xuchotl. Xotalanc is no more. There will be no more fighting. We shall spend our lives in drinking and lovemaking. First let us drink!"

He seated himself on an ivory table and pulled her down on his knees, like a dark-skinned satyr with a white nymph in his arms. Ignoring her un-nymphlike profanity, he held her helpless with one great arm about her waist while the other reached across the table and secured a vessel of wine.

"Drink!" he commanded, forcing it to her lips, as she writhed her head away.

The liquor slopped over, stinging her lips, splashing down on her naked breasts.

"Your guest does not like your wine, Olmec," spoke a cool, sardonic voice.

Olmec stiffened; fear grew in his flaming eyes. Slowly he swung his great head about and stared at Tascela who posed negligently in the curtained doorway, one hand on her smooth hip. Valeria twisted herself about in his iron grip, and when she met the burning eyes of Tascela, a chill tingled along her supple spine. New experiences were flooding Valeria's proud soul that night. Recently she had learned to fear a man; now she knew what it was to fear a woman.

Olmec sat motionless, a gray pallor growing under his swarthy skin. Tascela brought her other hand from behind her and displayed a small gold vessel.

"I feared she would not like your wine, Olmec," purred the princess, "so I brought some of mine, some I brought with me long ago from the shores of Lake Zuad—do you understand, Olmec?"

Beads of sweat stood out suddenly on Olmec's brow. His muscles relaxed, and Valeria broke away and put the table between them. But though reason told her to dart from the room, some fascination she could not understand held her rigid, watching the scene.

Tascela came toward the seated prince with a swaying, undulating walk that was mockery in itself. Her voice was soft, slurringly caressing, but her eyes gleamed. Her slim fingers stroked his beard lightly.

"You are selfish, Olmec," she crooned, smiling. "You would keep our handsome guest to yourself, though you knew I wished to entertain her. You are much at fault, Olmec!"

The mask dropped for an instant; her eyes flashed, her face was contorted and with an appalling show of strength her hand locked convulsively in his beard and tore out a great handful. This evidence of unnatural strength was no more terrifying than the momentary baring of the hellish fury that raged under her bland exterior.

Olmec lurched up with a roar, and stood swaying like a bear, his mighty hands clenching and unclenching.

"Slut!" His booming voice filled the room. "Witch! She-devil! Tecuhltli should have slain you fifty years ago! Begone! I have endured too much from you! This white-skinned wench is mine! Get hence before I slay you!"

The princess laughed and dashed the blood-stained strands into his face. Her laughter was less merciful than the ring of flint on steel.

"Once you spoke otherwise, Olmec," she taunted. "Once, in your youth, you spoke words of love. Aye, you were my lover once, years ago, and because you loved me, you slept in my arms beneath the enchanted lotus—and thereby put into my hands the chains that enslaved you. You know you cannot withstand me. You know I have but to gaze into your eyes, with the mystic power a priest of Stygia taught me, long ago, and you are powerless. You remember the night beneath the black lotus that waved above us, stirred by no worldly breeze; you scent again the unearthly perfumes that stole and rose like a cloud about you to enslave you. You cannot fight against me. You are my slave as you were that night—as you shall be so long as you shall live, Olmec of Xuchotl!"

Her voice had sunk to a murmur like the rippling of a stream running through starlit darkness. She leaned close to the prince and spread her long tapering fingers upon his giant breast. His eyes glazed, his great hands fell limply to his sides.

With a smile of cruel malice, Tascela lifted the vessel and placed it to his lips.

"Drink!"

Mechanically the prince obeyed. And instantly the glaze passed from his eyes and they were flooded with fury, comprehension and an awful fear. His mouth gaped, but no sound issued. For an instant he reeled on buckling knees, and then fell in a sodden heap on the floor.

His fall jolted Valeria out of her paralysis. She turned and sprang toward the door, but with a movement that would have shamed a leaping panther, Tascela was before her. Valeria struck at her with her clenched fist, and all the power of her supple body behind the blow. It would have stretched a man senseless on the floor. But with a lithe twist of her torso, Tascela avoided the blow and caught the pirate's wrist. The next instant Valeria's left hand was imprisoned, and holding her wrists together with one hand, Tascela calmly bound them with a cord she drew from her girdle. Valeria thought she had tasted the ultimate in humiliation already that night, but her shame at being manhandled by Olmec was nothing to the sensations that now shook her supple frame. Valeria had always been inclined to despise the other members of her sex; and it was overwhelming to encounter another woman who could handle her like a child. She scarcely resisted at all when Tascela forced her into a chair and drawing her bound wrists down between her knees, fastened them to the chair.

Casually stepping over Olmec, Tascela walked to the bronze door and shot the bolt and threw it open, revealing a hallway without.

"Opening upon this hall," she remarked, speaking to her feminine captive for the first time, "there is a chamber which in old times was used as a torture room. When we retired into Tecuhltli, we brought most of the apparatus with us, but there was one piece too heavy to move. It is still in working order. I think it will be quite convenient now."

An understanding flame of terror rose in Olmec's eyes. Tascela strode back to him, bent and gripped him by the hair.

"He is only paralyzed temporarily," she remarked conversationally. "He can hear, think, and feel—aye, he can feel very well indeed!"

With which sinister observation she started toward the door, dragging the giant bulk with an ease that made the pirate's eyes dilate. She passed into the hall and moved down it without hesitation, presently disappearing with her captive into a chamber that opened into it, and whence shortly thereafter issued the clank of iron.

Valeria swore softly and tugged vainly, with her legs braced against the chair. The cords that confined her were apparently unbreakable.

Tascela presently returned alone; behind her a muffled groaning issued from the chamber. She closed the door but did not bolt it. Tascela was beyond the grip of habit, as she was beyond the touch of other human instincts and emotions.

Valeria sat dumbly, watching the woman in whose slim hands, the pirate realized, her destiny now rested.

Tascela grasped her yellow locks and forced back her head, looking impersonally down into her face. But the glitter in her dark eyes was not impersonal.

"I have chosen you for a great honor," she said. "You shall restore the youth of Tascela. Oh, you stare at that! My appearance is that of youth, but through my veins creeps the sluggish chill of approaching age, as I have felt it a thousand times before. I am old, so old I do not remember my childhood. But I was a girl once, and a priest of Stygia loved me, and gave me the secret of immortality and youth everlasting. He died, then—some said by poison. But I dwelt in my palace by the shores of Lake Zuad and the passing years touched me not. So at last a king of Stygia desired me, and my people rebelled and brought me to this land. Olmec called me a princess. I am not of royal blood. I am greater than a princess. I am Tascela, whose youth your own glorious youth shall restore."

Valeria's tongue clove to the roof of her mouth. She sensed here a mystery darker than the degeneracy she had anticipated.

The taller woman unbound the Aquilonian's wrists and pulled her to her feet. It was not fear of the dominant strength that lurked in the princess' limbs that made Valeria a helpless, quivering captive in her hands. It was the burning, hypnotic, terrible eyes of Tascela.

VII

HE COMES FROM
THE DARK

"Well, I'm a Kushite!"

Conan glared down at the man on the iron rack.

"What the devil are you doing on that thing?"

Incoherent sounds issued from behind the gag and Conan bent and tore it away, evoking a bellow of fear from the captive; for his action caused the iron ball to lurch down until it nearly touched the broad breast.

"Be careful, for Set's sake!" begged Olmec.

"What for?" demanded Conan. "Do you think I care what happens to you? I only wish I had time to stay here and watch that chunk of iron grind your guts out. But I'm in a hurry. Where's Valeria?"

"Loose me!" urged Olmec. "I will tell you all!"

"Tell me first."

"Never!" The prince's heavy jaws set stubbornly.

"All right." Conan seated himself on a near-by bench. "I'll find her myself, after you've been reduced to a jelly. I believe I can speed up that process by twisting my sword-point around in your ear," he added, extending the weapon experimentally.

"Wait!" Words came in a rush from the captive's ashy lips. "Tascela took her from me. I've never been anything but a puppet in Tascela's hands."

"Tascela?" snorted Conan, and spat. "Why, the filthy—"

"No, no!" panted Olmec. "It's worse than you think. Tascela is old—centuries old. She renews her life and her youth by the sacrifice of beautiful young women. That's one thing that has reduced the clan to its present state. She will draw the essence of Valeria's life into her own body, and bloom with fresh vigor and beauty."

"Are the doors locked?" asked Conan, thumbing his sword edge.

"Aye! But I know a way to get into Tecuhltli. Only Tascela and I know, and she thinks me helpless and you slain. Free me and I swear I will help you rescue Valeria. Without my help you cannot win into Tecuhltli; for even if you tortured me into revealing the secret, you couldn't work it. Let me go, and we will steal on Tascela and kill her before she can work magic—before she can fix her eyes on us. A knife thrown from behind will do the work. I should have killed her thus long ago, but I feared that without her to aid us the Xotalancas would overcome us. She needed my help, too; that's the only reason she let me live this long. Now neither needs the other, and one must die. I swear that when we have slain the witch, you and Valeria shall go free without harm. My people will obey me when Tascela is dead."

Conan stooped and cut the ropes that held the prince, and Olmec slid cautiously from under the great ball and rose, shaking his head like a bull and muttering imprecations as he fingered his lacerated scalp. Standing shoulder to shoulder the two men presented a formidable picture of primitive power. Olmec was as tall as Conan, and heavier; but there was something repellent about the Tlazitlan, something abysmal and monstrous that contrasted unfavorably with the clean-cut, compact hardness of the Cimmerian. Conan had discarded the remnants of his tattered, blood-soaked shirt, and stood with his remarkable muscular development impressively revealed. His great shoulders were as broad as those of Olmec, and more cleanly outlined, and his huge breast arched with a more impressive sweep to a hard waist that lacked the paunchy thickness of Olmec's midsection. He might have been an image of primal strength cut out of bronze. Olmec was darker, but not from the burning of the sun. If Conan was a figure out of the dawn of Time, Olmec was a shambling, somber shape from the darkness of Time's pre-dawn.

"Lead on," demanded Conan. "And keep ahead of me. I don't trust you any farther than I can throw a bull by the tail."

Olmec turned and stalked on ahead of him, one hand twitching slightly as it plucked at his matted beard.

Olmec did not lead Conan back to the bronze door, which the prince naturally supposed Tascela had locked, but to a certain chamber on the border of Tecuhltli.

"This secret has been guarded for half a century," he said. "Not even our own clan knew of it, and the Xotalancas never learned. Tecuhltli himself built this secret entrance, afterward slaying the slaves who did the work; for he feared that he might find himself locked out of his own kingdom some day because of the spite of Tascela, whose passion for him soon changed to hate. But she discovered the secret, and barred the hidden door against him one day as he fled back from an unsuccessful raid, and the Xotalancas took him and flayed him. But once, spying upon her, I saw her enter Tecuhltli by this route, and so learned the secret."

He pressed upon a gold ornament in the wall, and a panel swung inward, disclosing an ivory stair leading upward.

"This stair is built within the wall," said Olmec. "It leads up to a tower upon the roof, and thence other stairs wind down to the various chambers. Hasten!"

"After you, comrade!" retorted Conan satirically, swaying his broadsword as he spoke, and Olmec shrugged his shoulders and stepped onto the staircase. Conan instantly followed him, and the door shut behind them. Far above a cluster of fire-jewels made the staircase a well of dusky dragon-light.

They mounted until Conan estimated that they were above the level of the fourth floor, and then came out into a cylindrical tower, in the domed roof of which was set the bunch of fire-jewels that lighted the stair. Through gold-barred windows, set with unbreakable crystal panes, the first windows he had seen in Xuchotl, Conan got a glimpse of high ridges, domes and more towers, looming darkly against the stars. He was looking across the roofs of Xuchotl.

Olmec did not look through the windows. He hurried down one of the several stairs that wound down from the tower, and when they had descended a few feet, this stair changed into a narrow corridor that wound tortuously on for some distance. It ceased at a steep flight of steps leading downward. There Olmec paused.

Up from below, muffled, but unmistakable, welled a woman's scream, edged with fright, fury and shame. And Conan recognized Valeria's voice.

In the swift rage roused by that cry, and the amazement of wondering what peril could wring such a shriek from Valeria's reckless lips, Conan forgot Olmec. He pushed past the prince and started down the stair. Awakening instinct brought him about again, just as Olmec struck with his great mallet-like fist. The blow, fierce and silent, was aimed at the base of Conan's brain. But the Cimmerian wheeled in time to receive the buffet on the side of his neck instead. The impact would have snapped the vertebræ of a lesser man. As it was, Conan swayed backward, but even as he reeled he dropped his sword, useless at such close quarters, and grasped Olmec's extended arm, dragging the prince with him as he fell. Headlong they went down the steps together, in a revolving whirl of limbs and heads and bodies. And as they went Conan's iron fingers found and locked in Olmec's bull-throat.

The barbarian's neck and shoulder felt numb from the sledge-like impact of Olmec's huge fist, which had carried all the strength of the massive forearm, thick triceps and great shoulder. But this did not affect his ferocity to any appreciable extent. Like a bulldog he hung on grimly, shaken and battered and beaten against the steps as they rolled, until at last they struck an ivory panel-door at the bottom with such an impact that they splintered it its full length and crashed through its ruins. But Olmec was already dead, for those iron fingers had crushed out his life and broken his neck as they fell.

Conan rose, shaking the splinters from his great shoulder, blinking blood and dust out of his eyes.

He was in the great throneroom. There were fifteen people in that room besides himself. The first person he saw was Valeria. A curious black altar stood before the throne-dais. Ranged about it, seven black candles in golden candle-sticks sent up oozing spirals of thick green smoke, disturbingly scented. These spirals united in a cloud near the ceiling, forming a smoky arch above the altar. On that altar lay Valeria, stark naked, her white flesh gleaming in shocking contrast to the glistening ebon stone. She was not bound. She lay at full length, her arms stretched out above her head to their fullest extent. At the head of the altar knelt a young man, holding her wrists firmly. A young woman knelt at the other end of the altar, grasping her ankles. Between them she could neither rise nor move.

Eleven men and women of Tecuhltli knelt dumbly in a semicircle, watching the scene with hot, lustful eyes.

On the ivory throne-seat Tascela lolled. Bronze bowls of incense rolled their spirals about her; the wisps of smoke curled about her naked limbs like caressing fingers. She could not sit still; she squirmed and shifted about with sensuous abandon, as if finding pleasure in the contact of the smooth ivory with her sleek flesh.

The crash of the door as it broke beneath the impact of the hurtling bodies caused no change in the scene. The kneeling men and women merely glanced incuriously at the corpse of their prince and at the man who rose from the ruins of the door, then swung their eyes greedily back to the writhing white shape on the black altar. Tascela looked insolently at him, and sprawled back on her seat, laughing mockingly.

"Slut!" Conan saw red. His hands clenched into iron hammers as he started for her. With his first step something clanged loudly and steel bit savagely into his leg. He stumbled and almost fell, checked in his headlong stride. The jaws of an iron trap had closed on his leg, with teeth that sank deep and held. Only the ridged muscles of his calf saved the bone from being splintered. The accursed thing had sprung out of the smoldering floor without warning. He saw the slots now, in the floor where the jaws had lain, perfectly camouflaged.

"Fool!" laughed Tascela. "Did you think I would not guard against your possible return? Every door in this chamber is guarded by such traps. Stand there and watch now, while I fulfill the destiny of your handsome friend! Then I will decide your own."

Conan's hand instinctively sought his belt, only to encounter an empty scabbard. His sword was on the stair behind him. His poniard was lying back in the forest, where the dragon had torn it from his jaw. The steel teeth in his leg were like burning coals, but the pain was not as savage as the fury that seethed in his soul. He was trapped, like a wolf. If he had had his sword he would have hewn off his leg and crawled across the floor to slay Tascela. Valeria's eyes rolled toward him with mute appeal, and his own helplessness sent red waves of madness surging through his brain.

Dropping on the knee of his free leg, he strove to get his fingers between the jaws of the trap, to tear them apart by sheer strength. Blood started from beneath his finger nails, but the jaws fitted close about his leg in a circle whose segments jointed perfectly, contracted until there was no space between his mangled flesh and the fanged iron. The sight of Valeria's naked body added flame to the fire of his rage.

Tascela ignored him. Rising languidly from her seat she swept the ranks of her subjects with a searching glance, and asked: "Where are Xamec, Zlanath and Tachic?"

"They did not return from the catacombs, princess," answered a man. "Like the rest of us, they bore the bodies of the slain into the crypts, but they have not returned. Perhaps the ghost of Tolkemec took them."

"Be silent, fool!" she ordered harshly. "The ghost is a myth."

She came down from her dais, playing with a thin gold-hilted dagger. Her eyes burned like nothing on the hither side of hell. She paused beside the altar and spoke in the tense stillness.

"Your life shall make me young, white woman!" she said. "I shall lean upon your bosom and place my lips over yours, and slowly—ah, slowly!—sink this blade through your heart, so that your life, fleeing your stiffening body, shall enter mine, making me bloom again with youth and with life everlasting!"

Slowly, like a serpent arching toward its victim, she bent down through the writhing smoke, closer and closer over the now motionless woman who stared up into her glowing dark eyes—eyes that grew larger and deeper, blazing like black moons in the swirling smoke.

The kneeling people gripped their hands and held their breath, tense for the bloody climax, and the only sound was Conan's fierce panting as he strove to tear his leg from the trap.

All eyes were glued on the altar and the white figure there; the crash of a thunderbolt could hardly have broken the spell, yet it was only a low cry that shattered the fixity of the scene and brought all whirling about—a low cry, yet one to make the hair stand up stiffly on the scalp. They looked, and they saw.

Framed in the door to the left of the dais stood a nightmare figure. It was a man, with a tangle of white hair and a matted white beard that fell over his breast. Rags only partly covered his gaunt frame, revealing half-naked limbs strangely unnatural in appearance. The skin was not like that of a normal human. There was a suggestion of scaliness about it, as if the owner had dwelt long under conditions almost antithetical to those conditions under which human life ordinarily thrives. And there was nothing at all human about the eyes that blazed from the tangle of white hair. They were great gleaming disks that stared unwinkingly, luminous, whitish, and without a hint of normal emotion or sanity. The mouth gaped, but no coherent words issued— only a high-pitched tittering.

"Tolkemec!" whispered Tascela, livid, while the others crouched in speechless horror. "No myth, then, no ghost! Set! You have dwelt for twelve years in darkness! Twelve years among the bones of the dead! What grisly food did you find? What mad travesty of life did you live, in the stark blackness of that eternal night? I see now why Xamec and Zlanath and Tachic did not return from the catacombs—and never will return. But why have you waited so long to strike? Were you seeking something, in the pits? Some secret weapon you knew was hidden there? And have you found it at last?"

That hideous tittering was Tolkemec's only reply, as he bounded into the room with a long leap that carried him over the secret trap before the door—by chance, or by some faint recollection of the ways of Xuchotl. He was not mad, as a man is mad. He had dwelt apart from humanity so long that he was no longer human. Only an unbroken thread of memory embodied in hate and the urge for vengeance had connected him with the humanity from which he had been cut off, and held him lurking near the people he hated. Only that thin string had kept him from racing and prancing off for ever into the black corridors and realms of the subterranean world he had discovered, long ago.

"You sought something hidden!" whispered Tascela, cringing back. "And you have found it! You remember the feud! After all these years of blackness, you remember!"

For in the lean hand of Tolkemec now waved a curious jade-hued wand, on the end of which glowed a knob of crimson shaped like a pomegranate. She sprang aside as he thrust it out like a spear, and a beam of crimson fire lanced from the pomegranate. It missed Tascela, but the woman holding Valeria's ankles was in the way. It smote between her shoulders. There was a sharp crackling sound and the ray of fire flashed from her bosom and struck the black altar, with a snapping of blue sparks. The woman toppled sidewise, shriveling and withering like a mummy even as she fell.

Valeria rolled from the altar on the other side, and started for the opposite wall on all fours. For hell had burst loose in the throneroom of dead Olmec.

The man who had held Valeria's hands was the next to die. He turned to run, but before he had taken half a dozen steps, Tolkemec, with an agility appalling in such a frame, bounded around to a position that placed the man between him and the altar. Again the red fire-beam flashed and the Tecuhltli rolled lifeless to the floor, as the beam completed its course with a burst of blue sparks against the altar.

Then began slaughter. Screaming insanely the people rushed about the chamber, caroming from one another, stumbling and falling. And among them Tolkemec capered and pranced, dealing death. They could not escape by the doors; for apparently the metal of the portals served like the metal-veined stone altar to complete the circuit for whatever hellish power flashed like thunderbolts from the witch-wand the ancient waved in his hand. When he caught a man or a woman between him and a door or the altar, that one died instantly. He chose no special victim. He took them as they came, with his rags flapping about his wildly gyrating limbs, and the gusty echoes of his tittering sweeping the room above the screams. And bodies fell like falling leaves about the altar and at the doors. One warrior in desperation rushed at him, lifting a dagger, only to fall before he could strike. But the rest were like crazed cattle, with no thought for resistance, and no chance of escape.

The last Tecuhltli except Tascela had fallen when the princess reached the Cimmerian and the girl who had taken refuge beside him. Tascela bent and touched the floor, pressing a design upon it. Instantly the iron jaws released the bleeding limb and sank back into the floor.

"Slay him if you can!" she panted, and pressed a heavy knife into his hand. "I have no magic to withstand him!"

With a grunt he sprang before the women, not heeding his lacerated leg in the heat of the fighting-lust. Tolkemec was coming toward him, his weird eyes ablaze, but he hesitated at the gleam of the knife in Conan's hand. Then began a grim game, as Tolkemec sought to circle about Conan and get the barbarian between him and the altar or a metal door, while Conan sought to avoid this and drive home his knife. The women watched tensely, holding their breath.

There was no sound except the rustle and scrape of quick-shifting feet. Tolkemec pranced and capered no more. He realized that grimmer game confronted him than the people who had died screaming and fleeing. In the elemental blaze of the barbarian's eyes he read an intent deadly as his own. Back and forth they weaved, and when one moved the other moved as if invisible threads bound them together. But all the time Conan was getting closer and closer to his enemy. Already the coiled muscles of his thighs were beginning to flex for a spring, when Valeria cried out. For a fleeting instant a bronze door was in line with Conan's moving body. The red line leaped, searing Conan's flank as he twisted aside, and even as he shifted he hurled the knife. Old Tolkemec went down, truly slain at last, the hilt vibrating on his breast.

Tascela sprang—not toward Conan, but toward the wand where it shimmered like a live thing on the floor. But as she leaped, so did Valeria, with a dagger snatched from a dead man, and the blade, driven with all the power of the pirate's muscles, impaled the princess of Tecuhltli so that the point stood out between her breasts. Tascela screamed once and fell dead, and Valeria spurned the body with her heel as it fell.

"I had to do that much, for my own self-respect!" panted Valeria, facing Conan across the limp corpse.

"Well, this cleans up the feud," he grunted. "It's been a hell of a night! Where did these people keep their food? I'm hungry."

"You need a bandage on that leg." Valeria ripped a length of silk from a hanging and knotted it about her waist, then tore off some smaller strips which she bound efficiently about the barbarian's lacerated limb.

"I can walk on it," he assured her. "Let's begone. It's dawn, outside this infernal city. I've had enough of Xuchotl. It's well the breed exterminated itself. I don't want any of their accursed jewels. They might be haunted."

"There is enough clean loot in the world for you and me," she said, straightening to stand tall and splendid before him.

The old blaze came back in his eyes, and this time she did not resist as he caught her fiercely in his arms.

"It's a long way to the coast," she said presently, withdrawing her lips from his.

"What matter?" he laughed. "There's nothing we can't conquer. We'll have our feet on a ship's deck before the Stygians open their ports for the trading season. And then we'll show the world what plundering means!"

AFTERWORD

The book in your hands includes the original story "Red Nails" by Robert E. Howard, creator of Conan. This is the story that inspired author S. M. Stirling to write *Blood of the Serpent*, a prequel to Howard's work, thus revealing the events that led Conan to first meet Valeria of the Red Brotherhood.

"Red Nails" is pure Howard, restored from his original manuscript. Raw and powerful, it's also very much of its time—written almost a century ago, when our culture could be less socially aware and genre fiction in particular often exhibited rough edges some of today's readers may find jarring.

Yet this is seminal fantasy by a writer whose work Stephen King has called "so highly charged that it nearly gives off sparks." Rather than alter it in any way, we've chosen to offer it in its original form for the reader to experience.

ACKNOWLEDGMENTS

Thanks to Steve Saffel, editor, for suggesting this gig to me and very considerable help with the writing.

To the folks at Titan Books, for deciding to do a new series hewing more closely to R. E. Howard's vision: Nick Landau, Vivian Cheung, Laura Price, Davi Lancett, Paul Simpson, and Julia Lloyd. And at Conan Properties: Fredrik Malmberg, Jay Zetterberg, Matt Murray, and Steve Booth.

And to Robert E. Howard, for coming up with Conan and the whole wild, glorious mishmash of the Hyborian Age, where I wandered as a lad and to which the genre will be eternally indebted. My first attempt at a novel, when I was thirteen, was a truly terrible Howardian pastiche. I hope decades of experience have finally made me worthy to be allowed into the master's playpen.

To Joe's Diner (http://joesdining.com/), Ecco Gelato & Expresso (http://www.eccogelato.com/), and Tribe's Coffee House, (https://www.tribescoffeehouse.net/) here in Santa Fe, for putting up with my interminable presence and my habit of making faces and muttering dialogue as I write. May they survive the apocalypse and flourish once more, and aid my creativity with coffee and pastries.

ABOUT THE AUTHOR

S. M. STIRLING was born in France in 1953, to Canadian parents—although his mother was born in England and grew up in Peru. After that he lived in Europe, Canada, Africa, and the US and visited several other continents. He graduated from Osgoode Hall law school in Canada but had his dorsal fin surgically removed, and published his first novel (*Snowbrother*) in 1984, going full-time as a writer in 1988, the year of his marriage to Janet Moore of Milford, Massachusetts, who he met, wooed and proposed to at successive World Fantasy Conventions. In 1995 he suddenly realized that they could live anywhere and they decamped from Toronto, that large, cold, gray city on Lake Ontario, and moved to Santa Fe, New Mexico. He became an American citizen in 2004. His latest books are *The Sky-Blue Wolves* (2018), *Black Chamber* (2018), *Theater Of Spies* (2019), *Shadows Of Annihilation* (2020), and *Daggers In Darkness* (2021).

For more fantastic fiction, author events,
exclusive excerpts, competitions, limited editions and more

VISIT OUR WEBSITE
titanbooks.com

LIKE US ON FACEBOOK
facebook.com/titanbooks

FOLLOW US ON TWITTER AND INSTAGRAM
@TitanBooks

EMAIL US
readerfeedback@titanemail.com